The City of Palaces

Terrace Books, a trade imprint of the University of Wisconsin Press, takes its name from the Memorial Union Terrace, located at the University of Wisconsin–Madison. Since its inception in 1907, the Wisconsin Union has provided a venue for students, faculty, staff, and alumni to debate art, music, politics, and the issues of the day. It is a place where theater, music, drama, literature, dance, outdoor activities, and major speakers are made available to the campus and the community. To learn more about the Union, visit www.union.wisc.edu.

The City
 of
Palaces

a novel

Michael Nava

Terrace Books
A trade imprint of the University of Wisconsin Press

Terrace Books
A trade imprint of the University of Wisconsin Press
1930 Monroe Street, 3rd Floor
Madison, Wisconsin 53711-2059
uwpress.wisc.edu

3 Henrietta Street
London WC2E 8LU, England
eurospanbookstore.com

Printed in the United States of America

Library of Congress Cataloging-in-Publication Data

Nava, Michael, author.
The city of palaces: a novel / Michael Nava.
pages   cm
ISBN 978-0-299-29910-1 (cloth: alk. paper)
ISBN 978-0-299-29913-2 (e-book)
1. Mexico—History—1867–1910—Fiction.
2. Mexico—History—Revolution, 1910–1920—Fiction.
3. Mexico City (Mexico)—Fiction.   I. Title.
PS3564.A8746C58   2014
813'.54—dc23
2013033799

This is a work of fiction. All incidents, dialogue, and characters, with the exception of historical
figures, are products of the author's imagination. Where historical figures appear, the situations,
incidents, and dialogue concerning them are entirely fictional and are not intended to depict actual
events. Any historical event depicted in the work is also the product of the author's imagination
and is not intended to be an accurate historical representation of such event. In all other respects,
any resemblance to persons living or dead is entirely coincidental.

Para mis abuelos

Ángelina Trujillo Acuña
(1902–74)

Ramón Herrera Acuña
(1905–80)

We Mexicans are the sons of two countries and two races. We were born of the conquest; our roots are in the land where the aborigines lived and in the soil of Spain. This fact rules our whole history; to it we owe our soul.

Justo Sierra

Those who serve the revolution plough the sea.

Simón Bolívar

Book 1

The Palace of the Gaviláns

1897–1899

1

The first time Sarmiento saw the woman who would become his wife, he thought she was a nun. She rushed toward him across one of the fetid courtyards of Belem prison, where he had gone to find his father. She was clad in a long, dark dress he assumed was a nun's habit and her face, also like a nun's, was veiled. She called out to him urgently, "Señor, Señor, are you a doctor?" He raised his medical bag in assent as she reached him, breathless. It was then he realized her costume was not that of a religious order because, although drab, the material was rich. The dress was a shimmering silk of midnight blue, and the veil in the same shade dropped like a curtain from her bonnet and was a finely woven lace mesh that revealed only the shadowy contours of her face. Her appearance in the courtyard had attracted the attention of the inmates— dirty, barefoot men in tattered clothes, dark faces shaded by the broad brims of their high-peaked sombreros. They left off their fighting and dice to shout crude epithets at her.

"Señora," Sarmiento said. "This is not a safe place for a lady."

"A woman inmate is dying in childbirth," she said. "The midwife is late. Please, come quickly."

There was a quality in her voice that, notwithstanding her distress, was singularly soothing and the voice itself was soft, husky, musical. Through the heavy veil he detected the liquid emerald of her eyes. She must be beautiful, he thought, and that as much as the urgency of her errand persuaded him to take a detour from his search for his father.

"Take me to her," he said.

He followed her through a series of squalid courtyards. Open privies spilled their reek and a few mangy dogs lapped brackish water from fountains where nuns had dipped their pails when Belem had been a wealthy convent in the seventeenth century. Ciudad de México was then the crown jewel of New Spain. So regal were the edifices the Spanish had built on the ruins of the Aztec capital, Tenochtitlán, that a visitor had christened it the City of Palaces. Now, as the nineteenth century drew to a close, the ancient palaces had been abandoned, converted to mercantile uses or, like Belem, were in near ruins. In their place were the garish new public works of the government of the dictator, Porfirio Díaz, all shiny brass and Carrara marble.

They came to a small courtyard less filthy than the others. On either side were the tiny cells that had housed the convent's servants. The veiled woman led Sarmiento into one of them where, on a straw mat, a naked woman screamed in agony while two other women held her down. The smell of blood and ordure drove him back a step, but the veiled woman plunged forward into the dimly lit room and said to him, "Please, Doctor, come."

Sarmiento had amputated limbs and cut holes into the throats of diphtheria patients so they could breathe, but, out of preference, he had rarely delivered children. Even the sight of pregnant women stirred painful memories of the girl he had killed and now, as he entered the room, raw images of Paquita's death agonies made his fingers tremble and his heart race. He hesitated and looked wildly around the room as if for an escape hatch.

The veiled woman extended a gloved hand to him and said, in her calm, soothing voice, "Doctor, two lives hang in the balance."

"*Claro*," he said, shaking himself out of his paralysis.

He knelt at the feet of the screaming woman and saw a tiny, red foot emerging from her womb. He knew immediately what he must do. He opened his bag, found the bottle of antiseptic, and had the veiled woman pour it on his hands. Then he carefully pushed the tiny leg back into the womb and reached into the woman to turn the child. The woman shrieked and jerked back.

"Calm her down," he said tightly to the veiled woman.

The veiled woman knelt beside the woman and murmured a stream of comforting words. In a moment, the woman's body relaxed a little and Sarmiento continued to probe her. With exquisite care, he moved the child so that its head faced downward.

"Now get her to push," he said. "Yes, like that. Push! Push!"

Slowly, the child—a boy—emerged, gray-faced and silent. Sarmiento extracted him, severed the umbilical cord, and slapped his back. The child made a choking sound and then a thin wail issued from the tiny body.

"Something to wrap him in," he commanded.

The veiled woman gave him a bundle of fine linen, incongruous in these dank surroundings. He wrapped the child and handed him to her. He gazed sadly at the infant in her arms and then examined the ashen-faced mother. She knelt beside the mother and gently placed the bundled child beside her. "See, my dear. A son."

Sarmiento beckoned her to the doorway and in a low voice asked, "What will become of the infant? Clearly, he cannot remain here."

"For a day or two," the woman replied, "and then I will take him to Lorena's sister and husband, who have agreed to watch over him until she is released."

"What is . . . Lorena doing in this pit?"

The woman answered quietly, "She killed the father of the child in a quarrel because he had abandoned her for another and left her begging on the streets. Will she recover?"

"Yes, she should be fine," he said to the veiled woman. "My father is here; I must see to him. Will you be able to care for her now?"

"Yes. Thank you. God bless you. What is your name, Doctor?"

"Miguel Sarmiento," he said. "And you, Señora, who are you?"

"Alicia Gavilán," she replied.

At that moment a stout woman appeared at the doorway, out of breath and murmuring apologies. The midwife. She bustled into the room, shoving Sarmiento aside.

"Go to your father now, doctor," Alicia Gavilán said. "We will be fine, here."

Sarmiento grabbed his bag and left.

He found his father in a spacious room in the wing of the prison reserved for opposition politicians and journalists who criticized the government. Here they were kept for a few days or a few weeks in relative comfort until the dictator remembered them and ordered their release.

There was no official censorship in México, and the Constitution of 1857, which his father had helped write, guaranteed freedom of speech. The government tolerated the minimum of dissent required to satisfy the need of foreign observers for the illusion of a democratic México. Sometimes, though, a journalist or a politician took the promise of free speech too seriously and found himself picked up by *la seguridad*, Díaz's secret police, and deposited in one of these cells, like an impertinent child sent to his room.

Sarmiento's father was sitting at a table covered with sheets of paper, scribbling fiercely with ink-stained fingers. His black suit was shiny with age, he was unshaven, and his white hair was disheveled from his habit of twisting strands of it between his fingers when he was thinking. Rodrigo Sarmiento was, like his son, a physician. He had long ago given up medicine in favor of writing manifestos against the government, printed at his own expense, that he posted all over the city. Sarmiento sometimes stopped and read one of his father's broadsheets but he rarely got to the end. While they began rationally, even eloquently, they quickly degenerated into paranoid rants against Don Porfirio and his government.

His father's fury at the despot who had governed México for almost thirty years was as much a personal vendetta as the product of an abstract allegiance to democratic principles because his father and Don Porfirio had once been comrades-in-arms. When the French had invaded México in 1862, forcing the elected president, Don Benito Juárez, from the capital, his father had accompanied him as his personal physician and close advisor. Díaz had been one of Don Benito's generals, and his string of victories against the vastly superior French army had helped finally drive them out of México. After the execution of the puppet emperor, Maximiliano, and the restoration of the Republic, Sarmiento's father had promoted Díaz as the logical successor to the presidency upon Don Benito's retirement. But Díaz had little patience and, after Juárez was reelected in 1871, unsuccessfully attempted to overthrow him. To Sarmiento's father, the failed coup was a betrayal of the democratic principles that he had believed he and Don Porfirio shared. That was to be only the beginning of his disillusionment with Díaz. In 1876, after a second revolt against the government, Díaz installed himself in the presidency to which he was later repeatedly reelected, with increasingly improbable majorities. Díaz, who continued to call his political organization the Liberal Party, paid lip service to the principles of free speech, effective suffrage, and separation of church and state while suppressing the former and ignoring the latter. Rodrigo Sarmiento had tried to reason with, cajole, and shame his old comrade, privately at first and then in opposition newspapers until these were closed, one by one, and his only recourse was through his broadsheets.

The attitude of the dictator toward Sarmiento's father was one of amused contempt. It was an attitude mirrored in the government's newspapers, where his father became an object of ridicule: deranged Doctor Rodrigo. One newspaper cartoonist caricatured him as a latter-day Martin Luther nailing a scroll to the door—of an outhouse. The caption explained that the paper on which he wrote his screeds could serve a useful purpose for those entering the facility. Yet even the most disrespectful account of his father's antics reminded its readers that he was a hero of the resistance to the French invasion. Only his heroic past kept Rodrigo Sarmiento out of even danker prisons than Belem, the nightmare facilities where the dictator's real enemies were sent to their deaths. It had also been intimated to Sarmiento by his father's remaining friends that his father was permitted to post his rants because it was useful to the regime that its most vocal opponent could be dismissed as a lunatic. He suspected that the mockery drove his father—a man of rigid integrity and a committed democrat—ever deeper into irrationality. It grieved Sarmiento that he was helpless to draw his father out of his mental darkness and he feared that it would one day overwhelm him completely.

"Father," he said loudly, stepping into the room.

The old man looked up. "Eh, what are you doing here?"

"Your brother told me you had been arrested," he said. "I've come to take you home."

"My brother!" he spat. "That fathead. Bootlicker."

Sarmiento let the statement pass. His Uncle Cayetano, unlike his father, had remained in Díaz's good graces and had been rewarded with a seat in the Senate.

His father, however, was just warming to the subject. "My brother followed me here from Spain forty years ago after I had made a place for myself and he is still riding my coattails." He glared at his son. "I made

Sarmiento an illustrious name in this country, and now my brother defiles it by collaborating with the dictator."

At moments like this, Sarmiento had learned to detach himself and regard his father as if he were simply a particularly choleric patient. He observed that the old man's hands were trembling and his face was drawn.

"When did you last eat?" Sarmiento asked.

"When I was last fed," his father replied sharply.

"Gather your things, Father, and I will take you home."

"No," he said, with more petulance than anger. "I am a prisoner of conscience and here I will remain until I am charged, tried, and vindicated."

"Father," Sarmiento replied patiently. "There will be no charges and no trial. You were arrested because you insist on posting your broadsheets on the doors of the National Palace. Your brother has secured your release."

"You understand nothing," his father said. He gestured at the paper-strewn table. "Go away, Miguel. I have work to do." He sank back into his chair and began to write and mumble. "I must rouse México against the tyrant. This tyrant . . ." He stopped, looked at his hands as if he were seeing them for the first time, and then gazed at his son with the same expression. In a calm, concerned voice, he said, "I worry about you, Miguel."

Sarmiento had become accustomed to these abrupt shifts in his father's moods, when the cloud of mental confusion dissipated for a moment and he was his old self. Looking into his father's eyes he saw not the crazy old man he had become but the parent he had once been — stern, demanding, even frightening, but always gruffly loving.

"Why is that, Father?"

"I can smell the alcohol on your breath and it's what? Ten o'clock in the morning? Your drinking accelerates and we both know why. To wash away . . . the memory. But that's all it is, Miguel, a memory. What cannot be changed is best forgotten."

"How can I forget, Father? I killed that girl, that child. My child. You said so yourself. You called me a murderer."

"I was angry," he said regretfully. "I thought you had thrown your life away."

"Didn't I? I spent a decade in exile. That changes a man."

"You are still young and now that you have come home, you can start again."

"Home?" he said. "This place does not feel like home to me. I am a stranger here, Father, as I am a stranger everywhere." He shrugged. "I only returned to México for you, but even you refuse my help."

"I am not in need of help. I know I am mocked, but I am mocked for a reason. A man must live his life in service of something, Miguel. Without a cause, existence is pointless. Whatever the stupid Christians may believe, the real hell is a life without purpose or meaning. You must find yours."

"I am a criminal who evaded justice," Sarmiento said. "A life without purpose or meaning is my punishment."

"You could find redemption in service to a cause greater than your private sentiments."

"Redemption is a Christian concept and, like you, Father, I am a nonbeliever." Taking advantage of his father's lucidity, he said, "Let me take you home."

The old man shook his head. "No, Son. I think I will stay here for a bit longer. It's quiet here. I can rest." He put his head in his hands. "There is so much noise sometimes, Miguel, so much noise. Go. I will be fine."

"Yes, Father," he said reluctantly. He kissed the top of the old man's head, leaving him there to quarrel with voices only he could hear.

As Sarmiento trudged through the prison courtyards, he thought he heard female voices, but when he looked he saw they belonged to men, made up and dressed like women, hanging coquettishly on the arms of their grizzled *novios*. He thought of the veiled woman—Alicia Gavilán—of her lovely voice and the green flicker of her eyes. Since his return to México a year earlier, he had developed a practice among the society women living in the newly built baronial mansions off the Paseo de la Reforma. It suited them to have the handsome young doctor with his European medical degrees come around to their houses, where they lived lives of luxurious boredom, and listen to their imaginary ailments. Now and then, one of them would present a marriageable daughter for his inspection or, more discreetly, offer herself. Sarmiento fended off their advances as tactfully as he could. The daughters, far too young, were either facetious or coy, and the mothers lived in romantic fantasies of salvation through passion fueled by too many French novels.

His part in Paquita's gruesome death had dispelled any notions of his own romantic capacity. He quelled his physical needs with brief, clinical visits to one of the city's better whorehouses. It had been years since he had allowed himself to be curious about a woman, but as the day wore on he could not put Alicia Gavilán out of his mind. She was clearly a woman of breeding and quality; courageous, too, to have set foot into the squalid swamp of Belem without a male escort. Who was she? Why was she there? What husband would have allowed it? He assumed she had worn the heavy veil to avoid attracting the crude attentions of male prisoners. He found himself imagining what she must look like—a lovely face framed by abundant, dark hair, green eyes flickering, lips soft and full. He caught himself remembering the husky musicality of her voice. He wanted to hear that voice again, to know her story. If she had any status in society, there was one person who would know her, because he knew everyone: his cousin Jorge Luis.

An old but elegant rockaway, drawn by two fine horses with braided manes, carried Doña Alicia Gavilán through the narrow streets behind the Zócalo—the city's immense central square—east to the ancient *plazuela* of San Andrés. In the curtained carriage, she removed her hat and veil and inspected her dress. Its dark folds were stained with blood and afterbirth, for which she would hear a lecture from the laundress, Alfonsina. She would have to return to Belem in a day or two to take Lorena's son from her and give him to his aunt for safekeeping until such time, if ever, that Lorena was released. The thought of removing a child from his mother sent a singular pang of sadness through her as she remembered her own child. At least, she reflected, Lorena would be able to see her son, if only when he was brought to visit her in the prison. Her own child she would never see again, not in this existence.

She parted the curtain slightly and gazed out the window, finding solace in the familiar scenes of her beloved city. Beneath tattered muslin awnings, Indian women sold peanuts by the piece and slices of sweet potato grilled in small, ceramic wood-fire ovens. *Aguadores* pushed their way through the crowded streets, bearing the enormous clay jars filled with water that they carried from the city's central fountains to sell in the makeshift tenements filling in the edges of the city. A *cargador* carried a steamer trunk on his back from the train station to a downtown hotel. The barefoot, smudged-faced children hawking lottery tickets paused in their cries to watch her sleek coach pass.

The distinctive face of the church of San Andrés, where she had been baptized, confirmed, and expected to be buried, came into view. Deep green walls—unusual in a city of reds, tans, and ochers—enclosed the carved facade that still earned the church a place in the tourist guides. Above the portal was an immense panel composed of *tezontle*, the light volcanic stone that had been the building blocks of the colonial city. Most of the carvings were the typical and dizzying churrigueresque ornamentations—fruits and cherubs, saints and lions, prophets and penitents, figures and forms piled one atop the other like a mad sermon in stone. But in the center of the panel was an immense cross carved with a profusion of flowers: daisies, roses, lilies, and other blossoms that had evidently existed only in the imagination of the mason. There was nothing else like this cross in the entire Ciudad de México. Her ancestor who had commissioned the facade two hundred years earlier was ordered by the archbishop to remove it. To the archbishop, the absence of the figure of the crucified Christ on so public a symbol of the Catholic faith rendered the cross suspect, if not heretical. The proud Marqués de Guadalupe Gavilán, rather than admit he was ignorant as to the meaning of the cross, refused. The archbishop—who was, after all, a cousin— eventually withdrew his writ after the *marqués* agreed to increase his contribution to the building of the cathedral. And so the Church of the Flowering Cross—La Iglesia de la Cruz Florecimiento—remained one of the city's mysteries.

The rockaway came to a stop before the great doors of the palace of Gaviláns. Carved in stone above the portal was the family's coat of arms and its motto, God Alone Commands Us. A niche above the crest held a statue of the family's patron saint, the warrior archangel, Michael. Other decorations carved into the facade and set atop the finials continued the theme of arrogance and belligerence adopted by the first *marqués*. But three centuries of rain and wind had beat against the walls, cracking ornaments, chipping tiles, and covering the walls with dust and silt; floods had eaten into the wood of the great doors and earth-quakes had brought down half the parapets; the king of Spain who had conferred upon the Gaviláns their lands and title when México was his property was dust in the tombs of the Escorial; the lands were long gone, sold off, abandoned, or expropriated. All that was left to the family were its titles and its residence. The palace had become the mausoleum of an antiquated kind of privilege honored solely for its ornamental value.

The porter hurried from his cell to hold open the carriage door. Alicia settled her hat on her head, drawing down the veil, and descended. The porter let her into the palace while the carriage was driven around to the stables. As soon as the doors closed behind her, Alicia again re-moved her hat and handed it to a servant girl who was waiting for her in the first of two large courtyards.

"Thank you, my dear," she murmured as she stood and allowed her treasured residence to welcome her return.

Each of the two courtyards was enclosed by two floors of archways. The many rooms of the palace were set back from the courtyard by broad corridors of polished tile. Along the corridors of the bottom floor of the first courtyard were large planters in which the cooks grew herbs for the house and bamboo cages filled with songbirds. The rooms on this floor housed the kitchens, laundry, and workshops. On the second floor were the quarters where the servants lived. In the middle of the courtyard was a three-tiered cantera stone fountain reached by path-ways that cut through flower beds thick with geraniums, lilies, and musk roses. The exterior walls were painted a deep pink-red and each archway was outlined in limestone. The paint was faded and the stone was pitted with age. The fountain, too, gave the appearance of great age and even the flowers seemed to issue a perfume from a distant time.

A towering wrought-iron gate separated the second courtyard from the first. Through the gate was visible a similar layout of arched corridors surrounding a garden with a fountain. The second courtyard, however, was larger than the first by half. The flower beds in its garden were more luxuriant; the fountain was taller and more ornate and it fed a pond adorned with clusters of blue-flowered papyrus and water lilies. The limestone facings around the archways were carved with acanthus leaves and on the keystone of each arch was the family crest. This was the family's residence. The first floor held public rooms—salons, a formal dining room, the library, the chapel—while on the second floor were the private apartments of the family. Beyond the second courtyard was another gate from which could be glimpsed an enclosed garden.

At its height, the palace had vibrated like a self-contained village with the comings and goings of the servants and the lords and ladies of the house. But now, most of the rooms were unused and many were bare except for mice and cobwebs. The remaining servants performed their negligible duties in a hushed atmosphere of an infirmary.

Alicia followed the scents of spices and bread into the vast kitchen. Inside were the familiar iron wall racks holding generations of ladles, spoons, and whisks; pine cabinets filled with mortars, molds, and presses; mahogany and rosewood cabinets where the family plate was kept under lock and key; long plank tables covered with baskets holding fruits and vegetables, herbs, breads, and tortillas; and shelves of spices and preserves. The cooks and kitchen maids were busy at the *brasero* and the *horno*, where they were cooking the main meal of the day, the *comida corrida* for the ten servants of the house and the only remaining family members— Alicia and her mother.

Chepa, the head cook, seeing Alicia enter the room exclaimed, "Doña Alicia, I heard the carriage. Sit, let me bring you some coffee, a crust of something sweet."

"No, my dear," she replied. "I only stopped to ask if my mother is awake."

"She called for her chocolate a few minutes ago. I was about to send the girl up with it."

"Give me the tray," Alicia said. "I will take it to her."

Chepa looked dubious. "You carry food? *Pues, no es costumbre!* Let the girl carry the tray and you can accompany her."

"You are correct, of course," she said. Addressing a young maid, she continued, "Come, Dolores, let us go up and sweeten my mother's disposition."

From behind the door of her mother's bedroom came a muffled, mechanical whine that, when the door was opened by Manuelita, her mother's maid, was the voice of a woman singing. The song was an aria from Rossini's *La Cenerentola*, played on her mother's gramophone, a cylindrical device mounted on a rosewood box to which was attached a great brass horn. It had a place of honor on a marble pedestal at the foot of a capacious bed. A chambermaid stood beside the machine; her sole function was to change the tinfoil recording cylinders and turn the crank. There was a scattering of books on the great lady's bed, the French and English romances she read far into the night. On the walls of her rooms were paintings of Venice, Paris, London, Rome—cities she had never visited except in art, music, and literature.

From a pile of luxurious linens emerged a tiny figure, Alicia's mother, María de Jesús. Her mother's many titles—acquired through the intermarriage of aristocratic families—were the stuff of society legend. In her own household, however, the Marquesa de Guadalupe Gavilán had always been known simply as La Niña, the girl. Propped up on a cloud of silk-sheathed pillows, in a voluminous white nightgown, tufts of white hair visible beneath a lace cap, La Niña could have been mistaken for a wizened, pink-faced child until one saw her hands, age-spotted and thick-veined, and the reptilian cast of her eyes in which childhood innocence had long ago been extinguished.

"Good morning, Mother," Alicia said, as the kitchen maid laid her tray on the bedside table. She removed the embroidered towel to reveal a demitasse of chocolate and a slice of warm bread with butter and honey.

The old woman glanced at her daughter, picked up the cup, and sipped. "Where were you this morning? The orphanage, the hospital, or the prison?" She sniffed the air. "That smell! The prison. And what are those stains on your dress? Really, Alicia, do you care nothing at all for your family's standing in this city?"

Alicia declined to be drawn into their old quarrel about the propriety of her charitable activities and asked, instead, "What is this music? I don't recognize it."

"Adelina Patti," she said. "Your brother-in-law obtained it for me. The banker, not the baker or the candlestick maker. Of course, listening to the diva on this machine is like imagining the sound of the ocean by holding a shell to one's ear, but still." She closed her eyes for a moment. "When she performed at the Nacional in 1877, the president of the

Republic placed a gold crown on her head. We went mad! We were still applauding the empty stage an hour after the last notes of 'Sempre libera' had faded."

Alicia lifted from the pile of books on her mother's bedside table a well-worn copy of George Sand's novel *Consuelo*. "You live in dreams, Mother."

"Perhaps," she replied. "But certainly for women of our family better that than to haunt the poorhouses and orphanages like La Llorona searching for her children."

"Only you know how truly unkind that statement is."

The old woman raised her pale eyebrows. "Sometimes I think that your great display of virtue is simply a very cunning form of revenge you take on me for what I did with you and that boy."

"I have long since forgiven you," she replied.

"Phew! There is nothing to forgive. My actions were entirely proper."

Alicia went to her rooms, where she changed her dress and then sat at her vanity and loosened her hair. She studied her reflection in the mirror. To the city, she was Doña Alicia Gavilán, the *solterona* of her noble family whose old maid eccentricity took the form of practicing to a fault the Works of Mercy required of all Christians: feeding the hungry, clothing the naked, sheltering the homeless, visiting the sick and the imprisoned. Her ministrations, while admirable in principle, required a level of familiarity with the destitute that her aristocratic peers found repulsive in practice. She was nothing like the fabled noble lady who, upon being accosted by a beggar as she was leaving a lavish charity ball, dismissed him without a centavo, exclaiming, "But I have already danced my feet to the bone for you!" But then, of course, it was whispered, given what had happened to her, what other path was open to Alicia Gavilán?

Alicia ran her fingers along her pitted cheek. She had once met an American girl, red-haired with fair skin, whose face was covered with freckles. Alicia had never seen freckles before and had at first imagined they were scars, like hers. But the American's freckles were on the surface of her skin, a distinctive and charming feature of her lovely face, like her straight nose and brilliantly white teeth: something a man would remember fondly. Alicia's scars were nearly as extensive as the American girl's freckles, but not superficial. It was as if her face had been soft wax and the pox a seal that stamped itself deeply into her flesh over and over, obliterating all traces of the pretty child she had been.

She chided herself for indulging in self-pity. The smallpox had taken her looks, but had spared her life, unlike the infant who had died in her arms before Alicia had even had a chance to name her. For the second time that day, a tremor passed through her heart. The old sadness came so rarely now that she could almost welcome it like a long-absent friend with whom she had shared the most intense moments of pain and love that had ever wracked her soul; it was an instant when God seemed simultaneously infinitely remote and unbearably present. The God who had been deaf to her pleas to save her child had nonetheless released a torrent of love in her for that child, a love so deep, so fierce, so all-consuming that the experience had changed her forever.

Convalescing at the palace after her daughter's death, she had felt the change but did not understand its meaning. She knew only that where she might have experienced emptiness, grief, anger, shame, there was instead peace, stillness, expectancy. She had never demonstrated more than the conventional interest in her faith, but now she asked for a Bible. She read the New Testament with a surging sense of identification that culminated when she reached the words of Saint John: "Beloved, let us love one another, for love is from God and whoever loves has been born of God and knows God. Anyone who does not love does not know God, because God is love." It was as if the letters were being written in flames on her heart.

"God is love" was the answer to the question that her life had become after her illness and her child's death. "God is love" was her instruction, her vocation, her purpose, and had been so from that moment she had stumbled across those words when she was fourteen years old. She lifted her eyes to her ruined face in the mirror and thought, "What is there to regret?" Her deformity had humbled her, closed the doors to a conventional life of marriage and children, and led her to a life devoted to what her mother scornfully called her "good works."

She knew other women in her circle, including her own sisters, wondered why she had not simply become a nun. But she had had no desire to lock herself away in a palatial cloister with the old maid daughters of other affluent families to dwell in aimless comfort. She felt called to a life of service, not contemplation. Over the years, she had created for herself a circuit that took her among the poorest of the city where she gave whatever material and spiritual assistance she could.

When she had first set out, shyly, uncertainly, she had had no idea what to expect of herself or of those whom she wished to help. Her deformity relaxed the suspicion of the poor toward people of her class because in their eyes her scars rendered her as poor, in her way, as they were in theirs. There was never any question of her being one of them— she wasn't and would never be—but in time they trusted her enough to be who they were in her presence, a wounded and vibrant people, the truest Mexicans of México. She loved them in all their imperfections. She loved the life force that sustained them even as the world—her world—ground them into the dust. She loved that they forgave her for coming from that world and accepted her as she was. She felt most alive among them and closest to the faith that had broken her open when John's letters of light had entered her heart.

And yet no matter how intensely alive she felt among these friends, how grateful she was for the love she felt for and from them, she remained a solitary woman. This sense of her solitude had grown upon her as the time slipped away when, had life been different, she would have been a wife and mother. She often felt her thoughts returning to that unlived life and sometimes, as this morning, when she had helped to deliver Lorena's child, the thoughts could not be banished with prayers for strength and acceptance.

Recalling the events of the morning, she found herself thinking with some guilt about Miguel Sarmiento. She recognized his name as soon as he said it—society women friends of her sisters were among his patients and her sisters had repeated the gossip about him. They said he was the only child of crazy Doctor Rodrigo, and he had departed México abruptly a decade earlier under a cloud. The particulars of the scandal were unknown but the subject of endless, tittering speculation, all of it involving love gone awry. He had returned a year earlier, a full-fledged physician, handsome and unmarried and as mysteriously aloof as a Heathcliff or a Mr. Darcy. The association with a character from an English romantic novel was heightened by his fair skin, pale green eyes, and chestnut-colored hair: "Pure Spanish stock," her sisters said approvingly. "Not a drop of Indian in him."

Gossip bored Alicia and she had only half-listened to her sisters' breathless accounts of Miguel Sarmiento. Even so, a mental picture of him had formed in the creases of her mind: a cold, proud macho; a rooster. She knew she was being unkind, but as she had no expectation of ever meeting the man except perhaps in passing, her unkindness seemed a venial sin at best. But now that she had met him, the injustice of her judgment shamed her.

When she had rushed through the courtyards of Belem to see if the midwife had arrived, all she had consciously noticed about him was that he was carrying a doctor's black leather satchel. Only later, after he had left, had she sifted through her other impressions. He was as handsome as advertised, but disheveled in a way that suggested to her an absence of vanity. His black suit was dusty, his collar had seen better days, his hair was somewhat greasy, and there were patches of stubble on his face indicating that his morning ablutions had been performed in haste or indifference. She had detected the stale smell of alcohol on his breath and his eyes were red-rimmed and weary. She also remembered the look that had flickered across his face as he stood in the doorway of Lorena's cell; it was akin to shock, as if the scene recalled some private horror. Nonetheless, once he began to attend to her, it was without hesitation or doubt. He knew what he had to do and he did it. He had saved Lorena's life and her child's life. Afterward, when he looked at the baby in Alicia's arms, another surprising expression passed across his face—sadness. Why, she wondered, would the birth of a child he had saved from death be the cause of grief?

She understood now why he inspired the gossips; there was something paradoxical about Miguel Sarmiento. He *should* have been the rooster she had imagined him to be—handsome, accomplished, arrogant—but instead he seemed like a man who was lost in the corridors of a private sorrow. She had felt her heart open spontaneously toward him, her compassion flow. She resisted. Miguel Sarmiento was not one of the poor to whom she could bring practical assistance—food, clothing, consolation. It was absurd to think she could help him and yet she could not help but hope to see him again.

2

Sarmiento sat at a window table at the Café Royale watching a barefoot *pelado* herd a flock of turkeys down the center of Calle de los Plateros. The Indian, cinnamon-skinned and malnourished with a mop of inky hair, was, like most Indians to Sarmiento's eyes, of indeterminate age— perhaps twenty, perhaps sixty. He wore a tattered, long-tailed shirt, and in apparent ignorance of a recently passed city ordinance commanding the wearing of undergarments, a soiled breech cloth tied around his waist and loosely looped around his genitals. The bobble of his penis was disgracefully visible to passersby as he made his way down the narrow road. Expertly, he kept the squawking turkeys in a straight line with a long stick to rein them in when they began to wander. The birds were small and stringy, but their plumage was as darkly iridescent as a ball gown. Sarmiento assumed the turkeys were on their way to one of the city's markets and that day's end would find them defeathered, cut up, and boiled beneath a layer of *mole poblano*.

In Europe, where Sarmiento had lived for the past decade, the incursion of the country into the city would have been deemed picturesque. But in Ciudad de México, the reflection of a peasant in the plate glass windows of shops that sold French wines and English frock coats reproached the pretensions of the nouveau riche who shopped there and they were not amused. Even now, a police officer—whose blue uniform aped the Parisian gendarmerie right down to the short cape— bestirred himself from his corner post. A moment later, the Indian and his birds had been harshly directed to a side street and away from Sarmiento's view.

Across the capital the church bells tolled ten. The shops would not open for another hour. The city would not fully awaken until the sifted gold light that now filled its streets achieved the transparency that made a stroll through them a walk into a dream. During his exile, Sarmiento had often tried to explain México's quality of light, but words, in whichever of the four languages he spoke, always failed him. The light's lucidity was partly a matter of altitude—at eight thousand feet the air was so thin that visitors gasped for breath upon first arriving. Then too, the city lay at the lowest point in a valley ringed by volcanoes creating a canopy of the sky. Whatever the cause, the light poured down with a purity that made every object it touched seem both immediately present and illusory, like something simultaneously seen and remembered.

This effect was heightened by the phantasmagorical nature of the city itself. The ancient stones of the Spanish colonial city sat upon the even more ancient stones of the Aztec city, Tenochtitlán. The Spanish had razed the Aztecs' island capital and dumped its palaces and temples into the vast lake that had ringed it. The great native cypresses—*ahuehuetes*—still grew in the park at Chapultepec, where they had shaded the summer palace of the last Aztec emperor. When the light poured through their leaves, it was as if ten thousand green, translucent eyes looked with unimaginable grief upon the slain city of Tenochtitlán, which the Aztecs had called the navel of the earth.

This is what Sarmiento had been unable to explain to the Romans he befriended on his travels. In their city, the imperial ruins were like the abandoned rooms in the family palazzo, places where their ancestors had lived lives different only in degree, not kind. But in México, the stones beneath the hulking churches and palaces of the Spanish were the gravestones of an alien race whose men had been murdered and its women raped. The conquest had also robbed that race of its vitality. Each generation following the conquest was more servile and lethargic than the last until the Aztecs had devolved from plumed emperors to turkey herders in soiled loincloths. When Sarmiento told his Roman friends that his country was the product of rape, they had laughed gaily and replied, "But all nations are." Perhaps so, he thought, but in México the memory was burned into the stones and the air.

"Primo, why the brown study?"

Sarmiento smiled up at his cousin, Jorge Luis. "Primo, I didn't really expect you'd awaken to meet me at such an early hour."

The younger man sat in a quick, tight motion. It could not have been otherwise—his French-cut suit fit him like a straitjacket, constraining his movements, emphasizing his slenderness. Above the stiff collar and black-and-red silk cravat loomed his large head. His eyes were like molten chocolate flecked with cinnamon and his lips were thick and soft. His black, curling hair was only partly subdued by the liberal use of lavender-scented pomade. There was an ever-present flush beneath his dark skin; he was as lovely as a girl. Perhaps aware of this, he compensated for his prettiness with a cynical attitude, an unkind wit, and a tone of voice that implied the knowledge of scandal. Officially he held the position of secretary to his father, Sarmiento's senator uncle, Cayetano, but spent his days writing verse and his nights in what passed for debauchery in the capital—drinking, gambling at the Jockey Club, patronizing the better brothels—with a cohort of other young men whose only purpose in life was the pursuit of pleasure. Ennui was part of Jorge Luis's affectation, but sometimes Sarmiento imagined that his cousin's boredom with this pointless circuit of cheap sensations and easy amusements was real and that, beneath his cultivated image of frivolity, a man of substance was struggling to emerge.

Jorge Luis arranged himself, as best he could, in a languid posture. He withdrew an English cigarette from a silver cigarette case and lit it. "Awaken? I have not yet been to bed. Coffee!" he shouted to no one in particular. "And you? Why did you insist on meeting at this uncivilized hour?"

"I always wake early," Sarmiento said. "A habit from my student days in Germany. Nothing clears one's head of last night's wine more quickly than cutting into a cadaver in a freezing room at seven in the morning while an elderly professor screams instructions in German."

Jorge Luis shuddered. "I don't know what is more appalling about that story, the cadavers or the Germans. My grand tour of the continent will begin and end in Paris."

The waitress appeared with Jorge Luis's coffee. She was a plump, pretty Indian girl who moved uncomfortably in her starched, striped shirtwaist and dark skirt; her braids were piled atop her head and her broad feet were shoved into narrow boots. She caught Sarmiento's eye and he smiled encouragingly at her. She carefully set down the cup and saucer, napkins, spoon, pot of heated milk, and a bowl of sugar cubes. When she finished, she nervously wiped her hands on her apron and murmured, "Anything else, sir?"

Jorge Luis flicked his fingers at her dismissively.

"My God," he said to Sarmiento, "did you see her fingernails? Filthy. I don't know why you come here. The Café de l'Opera employs French waiters, not the local 'niggers.'"

The American word dropped from his cousin's lips with a harsh contempt that amazed Sarmiento since Jorge Luis was nearly the same shade of brown as the waitress. Like most Mexicans, Jorge Luis was a mestizo, in whose veins ran a mixture of American Indian and Spanish blood. His mother, Sarmiento's aunt by marriage, had been a full-blooded Indian, a country girl whom his uncle had married during the war against the French. She died giving birth to Jorge Luis, who had, therefore, no memories of her. But Sarmiento, seven years older than his cousin, recalled her with affection. It surprised him that his quick-witted cousin seemed oblivious of the irony of his contempt for the Indian poor of the city, but, Sarmiento had observed, it was an oblivi-ousness shared by most of the city's mestizo upper class who also dis-dained the *pelados*. Sarmiento imagined that Jorge Luis had imbibed this attitude with the absinthe he drank in the Frenchified bars and cafés with the other young men of his set who were desperate to be mistaken for Europeans.

"There you go again, Miguel, disappearing on me," Jorge Luis complained. "You're the host here, remember?"

"I'm sorry, Primito," Sarmiento replied. "Listen, I want to ask you about a woman."

Jorge Luis widened his eyes in mock surprise. "A woman! Are you thinking of leaving the priesthood, Miguel?"

Sarmiento shook his head. "You exaggerate."

"Do I? In all the time we have spoken since you returned, you have never before asked about a woman. Who is this paragon who tempts you from your vow of chastity?"

"Her name is Alicia Gavilán."

This time Jorge Luis's surprise was genuine. "You're joking."

"I am not."

His cousin burst into laughter. "No, really, this is a joke."

Impatiently, Sarmiento said, "If you don't know the lady, fine, but I am completely serious."

Jorge Luis exclaimed, "But Miguel, the Gorgon!"

His face flushed with anger. "Really, Primo, you go too far."

Jorge Luis gathered himself. "You *are* serious," he said with wonder. "All right. I know the lady, by reputation only, for one seldom sees her out in society. Alicia Gavilán, Condesa de San Juan de Aguayo. The youngest of the four daughters of Don Alphonso, Marqués de Guadalupe Gavilán."

Sarmiento managed a shocked gasp. "A countess? Are you sure?"

"Oh, yes. The family's titles go back to colonial times. Of course, I suppose she and her family should properly be called ex-nobles since we are a proper republic now," he said, placing a mocking hand over his heart. "After the French invasion their titles and an old palace were all they had left. The old *marqués*—that traitor—sided with the French and their puppet emperor, Maximiliano. He was lucky he wasn't shot. Instead, his properties were confiscated and he was ruined. I heard for a while they were so hard up they were eating beans off of gold plates. But the old man was able to marry off his eldest daughters to various rich friends of our beloved president," he continued. "Nothing makes new money respectable more swiftly than a wife with a title and an old name. Sadly, he could not find any takers for the Condesa de San Juan."

"Why was that?"

"Did you see her face?"

"She was wearing a veil."

"I have never seen her without one," he said. "She had smallpox as a child. Evidently she is hideously scarred."

Sarmiento was stunned into silence.

"She devotes herself to charity," Jorge Luis continued. "A most worthy lady, but . . ." He shrugged. "I'm sorry to be the bearer of bad news, Miguel."

"You yourself have never seen her face," Sarmiento said. "So you are only repeating gossip."

His cousin raised an eyebrow. "Miguel, the lady is nearly thirty, has never married, rarely goes into society, and never without covering her face. The smallpox story is universally known and accepted. If it were untrue, there would be other explanations for her unusual behavior." He yawned. "My God, I am exhausted. Forgive me, Primo, I must go home and get some sleep. I have a full night ahead of me at the gaming tables at the Jockey Club."

"You're incorrigible," Sarmiento said.

With more melancholy than he had perhaps intended, his cousin replied, "Sadly, you are correct."

His cousin's tale about Alicia Gavilán and her family only whetted Sarmiento's curiosity about the lady. The smallpox story was a plausible explanation for her mysterious appearance, but Sarmiento reasoned that a vaccine would have been available to a woman of her age when she was a child. He casually inquired of a few of his well-bred women patients about whether they had been vaccinated against the pox and was appalled to discover that, to a woman, they had not.

"But why?" he asked a flirtatious chatelaine in her pink-and-gold salon. "Didn't your doctor insist?"

"Dear old Don Octavio?" she replied with amusement. "*Mais non!* He was a traditional doctor. He never laid a hand on me except to take my pulse and even then my mother and a maid had to be present. That he should penetrate me with a needle was unthinkable." Her eyes flashed naughtily. "Of course, if you wished to do so, I would willingly submit."

"You are past the age when smallpox is a threat to your health," he replied.

"No penetration, then? *Quel dommage!*" she said, smiling. "Now, dearest Doctor Miguelito, I am still suffering from the most excruciating headaches. Won't you give me a little more laudanum for my pain? Just a few more pills?"

As discreetly as he knew how, he asked a few of his patients about Alicia directly. They repeated the same story his cousin had told him: a catastrophic childhood encounter with smallpox had ruined her face and her prospects, so she had thrown herself into charitable works. The tone of the telling varied—some of the ladies spoke pityingly, others admiringly—but all implicitly agreed that Alicia Gavilán's fate was a sad one. He wondered about that because Alicia Gavilán's misfortune had evidently given her a license to move about in the world that none of his grand ladies enjoyed. His patients could not leave their homes except on the arm of their husbands, unless it was to attend Mass or to shop. Even then, more than one woman complained, she could not enter unescorted any of the new department stores that had sprung up in the city. Propriety demanded that she remain in her closed carriage while female clerks brought items for her inspection. It was unimaginable that he would have encountered one of his ladies roaming through the courtyards of the prison at Belem. Did Alicia Gavilán appreciate her mobility, he wondered, or did she regard the necessity of performing her good works at places like Belem yet another mark of her misfortune? That seemed unlikely. In contrast to his unhappily self-absorbed patients languishing in the lap of luxury, Alicia Gavilán had not appeared to him in their brief encounter to be unduly concerned with herself. She had completely given herself over to the messy task at hand, staining her costly gown with blood and afterbirth. The more he thought about her, the greater his desire to meet the lady again, but he could not imagine the circumstances that would permit an unmarried woman and an unmarried man to renew their accidental acquaintance without causing a scandal.

A bemused Sarmiento stood in a corner of the anteroom in the Church of the Flowering Cross that sheltered the baptismal fount. The smells of incense, oiled wood, candle smoke, and human musk sent him back in memory to Sunday Mass with his mother, who had died when he was five. His father, a militant atheist, mocked her churchgoing and Sarmiento had eventually adopted his father's view of religion, albeit without his belligerence; faith seemed to the rational Sarmiento simply unintelligent. Still, those hours at Mass with his mother, his hand wrapped in hers, were among the warmest memories of his childhood. This was the first time since her funeral that he had been in a church for a religious service. He was aware of a faint luminosity in the scented air that, had he been religious and believed such things, he would have said was his mother's spirit hovering beside him.

He had come at the invitation of Alicia Gavilán to witness the baptism of the infant whom he had delivered at Belem prison. Her note had reminded him the child was being cared for by the mother's sister and her husband, but, she had written, the mother had chosen the boy's name to honor the man who had saved both their lives: Miguel. Doña Alicia thought Sarmiento might wish to be present at his namesake's christening. Rationally, he knew that she could have had no idea of the emotions her invitation had stirred in him, reminding him, as it did, of his own lost son. Yet he could not help but imagine that the purpose of her invitation was to assuage some part of the secret grief for his son he had carried around with him for over a decade. As he stood in the church, watching the ritual proceed, remembering his mother and his son, the sadness that clouded his heart was softened by nostalgia.

The infant's young aunt, her braided hair covered by her rebozo, held him in her arms while a bespectacled priest in an elaborate lace vestment poured water over the child's head and intoned, "Miguel Ángel, I baptize you in the name of the Father, and of the Son, and of the Holy Spirit."

In a white gown and a broad-brimmed hat with a heavy white veil, Alicia stood behind the parents, acting as the boy's godmother. At the moment the water splashed the child's forehead, he howled, his cries dispersing like wisps of incense as they rose to the vaulted ceiling. His tiny dark face darkened to purple as he wailed. The priest glanced with displeasure at the child's uncle, a homely boy uncomfortable in his Sunday best. He tried to shush the child, to no avail.

Alicia said, "Father, he is frightened, let me calm him."

"Daughter, the time," the priest said pointedly. Sarmiento guessed the priest was thinking of his lunch and his glass of amontillado.

But Alicia had taken the wriggling infant from the aunt and carried him beneath a fresco depicting the baptism of Jesus. She began to sing to the child, but not in Spanish. Sarmiento recognized a few words of Nahuatl, the language of the *pelados*. Where, he thought wonderingly, had this aristocratic lady learned the language of the slums? After a moment, the child's cries ceased and Alicia returned the child to his aunt.

"We can continue now, Father."

The priest completed the rite by which Miguel Ángel Trujillo was received into the one holy catholic and apostolic Church. Alicia slipped the priest a small brocade purse that he received with satisfaction. No paper currency for a Gavilán, Sarmiento thought. The old families still dealt in gold coin.

She turned to Miguel. "Señor Doctor, come and be properly introduced to your namesake."

He stepped forward toward the family, who greeted him with downcast eyes and shy smiles.

"This is the doctor who brought your nephew into the world," Alicia said. "Let him hold the boy, Remedios."

The girl surrendered the now-passive infant to Sarmiento, who took him reluctantly, fearing that he would see his dead son's face and be unable to contain himself. But when he took the child and looked at him he saw only a baby with big shining eyes, stray tufts of hair, and the bland expression of an animal on a face in which human consciousness had not yet fully dawned. After a moment, Sarmiento handed the child to his aunt.

"I think I will wait outside," he said to Alicia, "and then, if I may, I will see you to your home."

"Yes," she said. "I will only be a minute."

He left her in conversation with the child's aunt and he saw her slip the girl a purse that was fuller than the one she had given the priest.

He stood on the steps of the church, which faced the *plazuela* of San Andrés. San Andrés was typical of the old colonial neighborhoods that lay northeast of the Zócalo, the great plaza anchored by the cathedral and the National Palace that was the heart of the city and the nation. In the center of the *plazuela* was an old fountain that had been the neighborhood's water source for centuries; women still came to dip their clay pots into its brackish stream. Around the fountain was an open-air market where the Indian vendors had set up their blankets and hawked their wares. Street peddlers lumbered by, their goods attached to their bodies with poles and straps—one of them carried a dozen bamboo cages filled with songbirds—singing the merits of their wares: "Such excellent sweets! The saints themselves desire them!" "Who can resist my roasted corn? Not you, not you, not you!" The *plazeula* was bounded on the south by an old mercantile arcade. Beneath its arches, men in shabby frock coats sat at rough tables that held fountain pens, jugs of ink, and sheaves of colored paper. They were the *evangelistas*, scriveners who for a few pesos composed letters for the illiterate poor of the city. To the south of the little plaza was the bulk of a massive colonial palace that Sarmiento now knew was the ancestral residence of the Gaviláns.

It was a scene that deepened the nostalgia he had felt in the church because this was the city he remembered from his childhood and the city he had carried in his heart during the years of his exile. Yet now that he was back, he felt like a tourist, a stranger, as if his long sojourn in Europe had irreparably broken the cord that had tethered him to home. He drifted through old neighborhoods like this one and the flashy new neighborhoods of Don Porfirio's modern city feeling like a ghost.

He sensed her presence before he heard her speak. "Thank you for coming, Doctor," she said, pausing beside him. "I do not think you are a regular churchgoer."

"No, I'm not a believer, Doña Alicia," he said. He glanced upward at the massive, flower-covered cross. "I must say, though, I have seen many churches but never one with this particular decoration."

"The flowering cross? It is unique, in the city at least," she replied. "One of my ancestors commissioned it, and even he did not understand its meaning."

"Do you?"

"Yes," she said. "I will tell you as you walk me to my residence."

He extended his arm, and she slipped hers through it. He was aware of the scent of rose water. The white veil was more translucent than the dark veil she had worn at the prison and he could more clearly make out the contours of her face, which seemed covered by a thick layer of powder. He turned his eyes away, not wishing to stare.

Alicia was aware that he was making an effort not to stare at her. Perhaps, she thought, she should simply raise the veil and let him look, but then all he would see was the white mask she had fashioned from creams and powders. She felt a pang of sadness but then composed herself and told him the story of the flowering cross that she had first heard as a child in the kitchens of the palace.

She could not remember a time when she had not sought out the dark, fragrant warmth of the kitchens and the company of the women and girls who labored there at the tiled stoves and ovens and the big tables where chickens were plucked, corn was ground, and fruit and vegetables chopped. When she had first begun to appear in the kitchen as a child in pigtails, the cooks tried to bribe her to leave with sweets, and when that failed, she was scolded, ignored, and reported to her mother. "*No es la costumbre*," her mother told her—it is not customary—in what would become a refrain of her childhood. She did not argue or defend herself, but simply returned to the kitchen again and again until, by sheer, silent persistence, she overcame all objections. Her post was a tall, three-legged stool near where the head cook, Chepa, commanded her realm. Although she was not allowed to do any of the work—that was far beyond the pale for a daughter of the house—she learned by watching. One morning, the *molendera* failed to appear, causing consternation as she was the only one who knew the exact formula of the morning chocolate for the lady of the house. Alicia took up the mortar and pestle, ground the cocoa herself, and added the proper amounts of cinnamon and sugar. The maid returning with the empty cup also brought a coin from the mistress to the *molendera*. Alicia gave the coin to the maid. After that, although her rank was never forgotten, it no longer created an inviolable distance between her and the other women. They no longer talked around her, but with her, and to her, and they shared their stories, which were as old and complex as the stories of her own family.

The flowering cross, for example. Graciela the baker, with hands like leather from decades of reaching into stoves, told Alicia that the stonemason who carved the cross had been from a wild tribe in the far north called the Yaquis. "Nahautl, like us," she explained, "but when the rest of us came to Tenochtitlán, the Yaquis stayed behind in a river valley that was like the Garden of Eden. They worshipped the deer who gave up his life to give them meat to eat and hides for clothes. When the priests came and told them about Jesus, well, to the Yaquis, Jesus and the deer were the same and they converted.

"Flowers are sacred to the Yaquis," Alicia told Sarmiento, repeating the words Graciela had told her. "They call heaven the flower world. They say that when Jesus was on the cross, flowers sprang up where his drops of blood touched the earth. That's why the artist carved flowers on the cross. For him they are the blood and resurrection of Jesus."

"The Yaquis?" Sarmiento said. "The same tribe the government is fighting up in the north?"

"I was not aware we were at war with them," she said. "What caused the conflict?"

"Settlers have moved into land the Yaquis claim as their own."

"I'm sure it is my ignorance," she said, as they reached the immense doors of the palace, "but could the land not be apportioned in a way that would satisfy both groups?"

"A good question, Doña," he replied. "Not one I imagine the combatants bothered to ask themselves before they took up arms. Men never do."

From a small room attached to the palace at the side of the door, a porter emerged, and, with a suspicious glance at Sarmiento, asked, "Doña Alicia, is everything all right?"

With a smile in her voice, she said, "Yes, Pablito. I will enter in a moment." To Sarmiento she asked, "What do you mean when you say men never do?"

"Only that men are thoughtless creatures," he replied. "Their first impulse is always to take action, however rash or misguided. Or fatal."

After a long, considering silence, she said, "Do you speak from experience, Señor Doctor?"

The kindness in her lovely, low voice was as palpable as a warm hand laid on his. The sadness and nostalgia he had felt since entering the church clutched at his heart and squeezed tears from him. He hastily wiped his sleeve across his face and said, "Well, one has made many mistakes in life, of course."

He was afraid she would comment on his tears, but she said, "Yes, that is true of all of us. But one need not become imprisoned by one's errors."

"How does one avoid that?" he asked.

"For a believer, there is confession," she said.

"A few Hail Marys and it all goes away?" he replied.

She retreated into silence and he thought he had offended her, but then she said, "The value of confession for me is not in the penance but in saying aloud the things I would keep secret in my guilt and then having my confessor put them in their proper place for me. To give them—what is the word artists use? Perspective. For in my guilt, my sins loom large and I can see little else. Another person, disinterested but sympathetic, can look and see things as they are, not as I imagine them to be."

Again, he felt her kindness like a physical balm and it was all he could do not to spill his secret then and there about Paquita and his son.

"But, as I said, Doña Alicia, I am a nonbeliever. Who would hear my confession?"

"I would," she said simply. "Won't you come in and have a cup of something warm, a bit of something to eat?"

Longing and fear fought in his heart: a longing to confess his faults to her and a fear that, once she heard them, she would turn away from him in revulsion. Fear won out.

"Thank you, Doña, but I must take my leave. I have my rounds, patients to see." Yet he found himself reluctant to go. "Perhaps," he added, "I could call on you another time?"

"Of course," she replied graciously. "You need only send me a message and I would be happy to receive you." She touched his hand. "Good-bye, Doctor Sarmiento. God go with you."

"Doña," he said with a little bow and rushed away before she could see that the tears had reappeared in the corners of his eyes.

As the rest of the household slumbered, Alicia made her way into the garden, an overgrown wilderness of orange and lemon trees, heavy swags of climbing roses that spilled over the garden walls, clumps of calla and trumpet lilies, heliotrope, rose geraniums, and jasmine. A rosace-shaped pond in the center of the garden was anchored by a fountain carved with the symbols of the evangelists—a lion, an eagle, an ox, and a man. The fountain, too, was in disrepair and only a brackish trickle now reached the pond. At the far end of the garden was a mirador made of marble. The family crest and the date 1702 were carved over the entrance of the small pavilion.

She sat on the bench in the pavilion and removed her veil so that she might better inhale the heavy fragrance of the flowers in the still, autumn air. She thought of Miguel Sarmiento, and the sadness with which he had looked at the infant when she had given him the baby to hold; it was the same sadness she had seen in the birth room. She recognized it as the sadness of loss, a loss to which he remained unreconciled. That pain she saw in his eyes was not unknown to her. She closed her eyes. Mingled with the scent of flowers were the smells of the stables on the other side of the garden wall. Now and then she heard the muffled whinny of a horse or the voice of a groom or stable boy.

"Anselmo."

Her eyelids fluttered open and she looked around the garden to see who had spoken that name. There was no one else in the garden but a little black cat hunting lizards.

"Anselmo."

That voice, that name, again. And then, with a small gasp, she realized that it was she who had spoken. Her voice was speaking the name she had not openly uttered in many years.

She spoke his name again, consciously, deliberately. "Anselmo."

The cat looked up, distracted from its hunt by the weeping woman.

She had been tolerated in the kitchen because it was the domain of women performing women's work, but when Alicia began to wander into the stables, she was brought before her father, a rare and frightening event. The *marqués* received her as if she were an errant servant. With scarcely a glance at her, he said, "Henceforth, you will stay out of the stables."

"I only wanted to see how they braid the horses' manes."

He looked at her sharply. "Were you asked to speak?"

Trembling, she replied, "No, Señor Marqués."

"Go."

She had run into the garden, weeping.

"Why are you crying?"

She looked around for the questioner. A boy's head appeared above the wall that was common to the garden and the stables. It was Anselmo, one of the grooms. He had been her guide on her excursion to the stables, telling her about the horses and how he took care of them. Now he jumped the wall and came into the garden.

"Did your *papá* hit you?" he asked.

He was two or three years older than she—fifteen or sixteen—a slender, cinnamon-colored boy with golden eyes. He smelled soothingly of straw and liniment.

"No," she said. "He has forbidden me from visiting the stables. Now I will never see how you braid the manes."

He sat beside her on the bench and took a strand of her long hair. "I could braid your hair. Do you want me to?"

His fingers in her hair, the whispered question, the lustrous sun, and the sweet smells of the garden produced in her a thrill that raised goose bumps on her then flawless skin and, without understanding why, but knowing she must, she pressed her lips to his. His mouth opened—her shock was quickly followed by the delicious sensation of his warm, wet tongue and the heat of his body radiating from beneath his thin shirt. As they pressed their bodies tightly together, she did not know whether it was his heart or hers that beat like a bird flapping its wings against its cage.

On the warm autumn nights, he laid his *zarape* in the clearing among the roses to dispel the chill from the earth. Then, too, their naked bodies generated a heat so intense that curlicues of steam rose from them. She learned he was from Coahuila and had come with his family to the city looking for work when their small farm was taken from them by a friend of the governor. He was vague on details, saying only, "The sheriff came with some papers. My *papá* said we had to leave." She related her own uneventful history—she had lived her entire life within the walls of the palace, except for the hours she was at school or at church. He had four brothers and three sisters and they lived with his parents in two rooms in the *colonia* of La Merced, but he lived in the stables, visiting home only on Sunday. She told him about her three sisters, all much older than she, the two eldest married, the third engaged. He told her he missed his family, and his descriptions of his loneliness gave her a name for her own feelings of solitude.

He could not read or write. One night she brought pencil and paper. Guiding his hand, she showed him how to write his name and then he insisted that she teach him how to write hers as well. After that, he practiced by writing their names with his fingertips on her flesh. She loved his touch. His tongue rasped her small nipples and he told her she tasted like apple. The skin of his scrotum was as plush as velvet in her hands and the two stones it sheathed were fascinating to her, hard yet spongy; more than once he yelped when she pressed too firmly. Each time he penetrated her, her first feeling was of separation—his body clearly divisible from hers—but then as he continued his thrusts were like pebbles tossed into a pond. The ripples spread and deepened across and inside her body, and as they both sank into the same swamp of sensation, she could no longer tell her flesh from his. He was the first to say, "*te amo*," but said it only sparingly after that, as if the phrase were a jewel, the only one he would ever be able to give her. She was freer with "I love you" because it resounded in her mind all day, and to prevent herself from saying it aloud when he was not present, she had to give it voice when he was. They undressed and dressed by moonlight. "Our moon," he told her. One night he brought her a pearl, a single pearl that he said he had bought at the Monte de Piedad, the city's pawnshop. It was yellowing with age, like the autumn moon.

Alicia was neither as alone nor as insignificant in her family as she imagined. La Niña noticed the change—the combination of swooping and inexplicable happiness alternating with expressions of gnawing melancholy as she mumbled to herself. She instructed her personal maid to spy on her daughter. Manuelita followed her into the garden and watched, from a distance, as the two children made love. They were beautiful together and Manuelita pitied them for what was to come. She reported to her mistress. Anselmo was gone by nightfall. Within a month, Alicia began to show signs of pregnancy. Her mother immured her within her rooms and, borrowing from her favorite novel, *La dame aux camélias*, let word go out that Alicia suffered from consumption. When she was about to deliver, Alicia was secretly transported to the foundling home, where she gave birth to a daughter in the Departamento de Partos Ocultos—the Department of Hidden Births. It was there, as she was recovering, that she was infected with the smallpox virus, as was the child she was nursing. Her daughter died.

Fifteen years had passed but the garden was much the same as it had been the last night she and Anselmo had parted. She dried her tears. She remembered that during the confrontation with her mother she had cried out, "But Mamá we are no different than *Romeo y Julieta*!" Her mother, narrowing her eyes, had replied, "Romeo was a nobleman, not an Indian from the slums, and at any rate, that was a fairy tale." "But I love him, Mamá." "I assure you, you will forget," her mother said. "As Julieta would have forgotten Romeo, had she lived. Time defaces every memory. You will see."

Now, reflecting upon that encounter, she thought that her mother's choice of "defaces" was deliberate. Her mother had not expected that Alicia would forget Anselmo, but rather that as she reached maturity, she would appreciate the absurdity of the romance between the princess and the stable boy. It would devolve from a tragedy into a farce, and passion would be replaced by embarrassment. Her mother was wrong.

The love she had felt for Anselmo had been the portal through which Alicia had discovered her capacity for love, and love had become her vocation. The loss of her own daughter—the only child she knew she would ever bear—had made her the mother to all children she encountered. Her mother could cruelly jest that Alicia was like La Llorona—the woman of legend who had drowned her children and, after her death, was condemned for eternity to search for them along the waterways of México, weeping and shrieking—but there was perhaps a grain of truth in her words. For in each child she encountered, Alicia saw traces of her own child, and she loved them as she would have loved her own.

Then abruptly, Alicia understood something about Miguel Sarmiento's expression of sorrow as he had held the baby Miguel in his arms and about the tears he had wiped away so she would not see them. Doctor Sarmiento had also lost a child! And if he had lost a child and was unmarried, then there had also been a woman. He had come very close to telling her the story as they stood before the gates of the palace. Would he tell her if they met again? Plainly, whatever the details, his tale had left him with a heavy burden of guilt. Too heavy for a man whose essential goodness was clear to her. Miguel Sarmiento might not believe in God, but God—her God, the God who was love—hovered around the man waiting to be invited in but prevented by his guilt and shame. Was it vain and foolish of her to believe that she might be the instrument through which God would relieve the doctor's burden and release him to do the good work he was undoubtedly intended for? *No*, she thought, *not me!* But a voice that was not hers whispered its reply. *Yes, Daughter. You.*

3

A servant led Sarmiento through the palace of the Gaviláns in stiff-shouldered, disapproving silence. In Europe, he had met members of the nobility and they had received him at their residences, which were older and more elaborate than the colonial mansions of México, but in Europe he was a tourist collecting experiences as if they were postcards. México was home and its streets and buildings were resonant for him in a way the castles and museums of Europe had never been. The colonial palaces had awed him when he was a boy, an awe that was not lessened by his republican father's fulminations against the aristocrats who inhabited them. They might well be "parasites," but to a small boy they were also marvelous as they swanned about the city in their beautiful carriages and led mysterious lives behind immense carved doors.

Now he was inside one of the great houses. In contrast to the baroque palaces of Italy and France, the interior was rather plain, a reminder that it had been intended to be as much a military fortress as a residence. The decorative work—the acanthus carvings on the archways, the delicate Ionic columns that ran the length of the second floor—was exquisite, but the true luxury was simply the space itself. Amid the bustling city, whose natives jostled in forced intimacy on the streets, sidewalks, and markets, and where most of the population lived in tenements and shanties, was this stone leviathan. The noise of the city did not penetrate its thick walls, and its inhabitants breathed not the city's miasmatic air but the perfumed scents of its gardens. Here there was light in plentitude and a contemplative stillness in which fountains murmured and doves cooed. It was their possession of privacy that was the real wealth of the rich.

He was led into a great salon. As was the custom in Mexican houses, the furniture was pushed against the walls, leaving large, empty spaces.

The accretion of three hundred years of possessions—rosewood and mahogany furnishings from the Philippines, blue-and-white Chinese porcelains, an enormous carpet woven in Persia, Spanish cabinets inlaid with ivory and mother-of-pearl—seemed insufficient to fill its vastness. Life-sized portraits of a ruff-collared aristocrat and his wife hung on the wall behind a long couch upholstered in pink damask.

"Wait here," the servant commanded before turning on his heel and marching out.

He prowled the room nervously. At his last meeting with Alicia Gavilán he had felt she had looked into him and seen his secret. Unable to bear the scrutiny, he had run. Later, however, recalling the kindness in her low, musical voice he had been filled with a longing to see her again and to unburden himself. Impulsively, he had sent her a note asking to meet. He had been encouraged by the invitation she had extended to him when they had stood at the doors of the palace, for it had been offered without conditions and out of her kindness. But, perhaps, he thought as he penned the note, her kind impulse would cool when confronted by his actual request. For he was as aware as she must be that unless he was offering himself as her suitor or as her physician, there was no social precedent for the private meeting of an unmarried man and an unmarried woman. Nonetheless, he was heartened by her prompt reply. Yet now, as he stood in this great room, surrounded by the bric-a-brac of her aristocratic lineage and uncertain of the propriety of their meeting, he could not help but feel out of place and intimidated. He paced the room, trying to allay his urge to flee.

"Señor Doctor."

He turned to greet her. She was unveiled and her face was bare of powders and cream. He was grateful for his medical training because it allowed him to suppress his shock at the extent of her scarring. Her face was a mask of lesions and pustules in which the lovely emerald eyes flickered like the eyes of one imprisoned.

"I'm sorry I wasn't here to greet you when you arrived," she said. "Shall we sit? I've asked for tea and coffee to be brought."

She arranged herself on a settee and with an elegant wave of her hand invited him to sit beside her.

"Thank you for receiving me," he said. "Your residence is quite beautiful."

"Ah," she said. "It is drafty and inconvenient. My ancestors stored their clothes in chests, so there are no closets, and they feared the night air, so there are few windows. And of course the only lighting is candles and oil lamps. In my sisters' homes, you touch a button on the wall and the entire room is brilliantly illuminated."

He recognized the deprecation for what it was, an aristocrat's mild reproach for his comment about the beauty of her house. He had encountered this attitude among his noble acquaintances in Europe, where to compliment such things implied surprise that they should be other than of the highest caliber. It reminded him that, for all her kindness, she was a member of an ancient nobility, which, even if superannuated in modern México, remained fully intact within itself.

Two servants appeared, weighted down with silver trays that held urns, cups, saucers, pitchers, and plates of pastries. They set them down on a low table before Doña Alicia. As the servants arranged the repast, Sarmiento stole a glance at his hostess. The first shock had passed and he studied her with the dispassion that was not only the fruit of his medical training but in his nature as well. The scarring had not obliterated the structure of her face and he saw that she would have been beautiful. She was like a princess in a fairy tale consumed by a dragon. Her hair, piled in braids atop her head, was heavy, dark, and scented with attar of roses. Her neck was long, lovely, and to his surprise unscarred. He glanced at her hands and they, too, bore no scars. Only her face appeared to have been affected: a medical anomaly that, under different circumstances, would have excited his professional interest. But he could not imagine asking her to submit to an examination or to the intrusive questions of a clinician.

"I hope you are not too repulsed by my appearance," she said quietly when the servants had left.

"Doña Alicia, I am trained as a doctor to see past physical afflictions to the person who bears them."

There was sadness in her eyes when she glanced at him, but she only said, "Will you take coffee or tea?"

"Coffee, thank you," he said.

She poured him a cup of coffee and added milk and sugar. Their fingers touched as she handed him the cup. "I rarely have visitors here," she said. "Because I would feel I must spare them the shock of my appearance with veils or cosmetics, but in my own home I wish to be free of those disguises and to be myself."

"I am honored that you have received me," he said.

"All of us need a place where we are free of our burdens," she continued. "A refuge where we are accepted as we are. This is my place. And yours, doctor? Where is the place where you lay down your cross?"

The words of confession formed in his mind, but he could still not bring himself to say them, so he temporized. "What weight do you think I carry on my back?"

"I think you carry the weight of a child," she said. "And a woman."

He was shocked. Only his father knew Sarmiento's secret. How could she have guessed? He shot her a look. She raised her cup to her lips calmly and sipped her tea, waiting for him to reply, but he could not. Not yet.

"Who lives here with you?" he asked abruptly.

"Only my mother," she replied, concealing with perfect manners any surprise at his clumsy deflection of the conversation.

"Where is the *marquesa*?"

"On Tuesday afternoons she goes to Chapultepec Castle to attend a luncheon of the Daughters of Jerusalem, a charitable group founded by the president's wife."

"You do not attend?"

"Not today," she said. "I thought on this occasion you might wish to speak to me alone." When he failed to reply, she said, "Doctor, I see I have been too forward. My sincerest apology."

"No," he replied hesitantly. "You need not apologize. You have offered me the opportunity to confide in you and for that I am most grateful, but if I did, Doña Alicia, you would regret your generosity. You see, there's a difference between your burden and mine. Yours was visited on you through no fault of your own. Mine is of my own making."

She glanced at him. He grasped the cup in his hands so tightly she worried it would shatter. Her hand began to move impulsively toward his, but she stopped herself. Whatever troubled him would not be soothed by a friendly hand on his or a few kind words, no matter how sincerely meant. She sensed that his wounds were as deep, pervasive, and complex as the scars that disfigured her face. She chided herself for her clumsy approach because it had cornered him and left him no graceful way to retreat from the conversation. She must give him a way out.

"I understand from my friends who are your patients that you only recently returned to México," she said. "Where were you?"

His fingers relaxed their grip on the cup. "I spent the last decade in Europe, studying at the medical faculties in Paris and Heidelberg."

"You did not study at our own school of medicine?" she prompted.

"I began my studies here," he replied, "and I would have continued, but . . ." He paused uncomfortably. "My father felt it would be beneficial for me to study in France and Germany, which are the modern centers of so much important medical research."

"Like Louis Pasteur?" Alicia offered.

"Yes," he said, evidently grateful to be at last on safe conversational ground. "Pasteur in France, Koch in Germany."

"Did you ever meet him? Monsieur Pasteur?"

"I had the pleasure of attending a dinner at which he spoke two years before his untimely death," the doctor replied reverently. "I shall never forget his remarks. He said, 'Science knows no country, because knowledge belongs to humanity, and is the torch that illuminates the world.'"

"Is that also your creed, Doctor Sarmiento?"

"It must be the creed of every real scientist," he said. His face was animated and even more striking than when in repose. "The principle of all existence is cause and effect. Scientific knowledge illuminates causes so that men are not condemned to go on living ignorantly in effects. In my own field of medicine, one disease after another has yielded the secrets of its causes, thus diminishing human suffering."

"That is a noble objective," she said.

His face lapsed into melancholy. "Yes, it is, but I'm afraid I do very little toward its accomplishment by spending my days prescribing laudanum to unhappy women."

"Are there no venues for you to do the kind of work you would find more fulfilling?" she asked.

"Notwithstanding Don Porfirio's superficial improvements to the city, México lags behind Europe in achieving true modernity. Electric streetlamps along the Paseo de la Reforma are one thing, but a real center for medical and scientific research is another and we do not have that, nor does it seem the government is very interested in creating one."

"Oh, I see," she said. "Still, if you have an interest in improving the health of the people, I may be able to help you with that, at least."

He leaned back and looked at her. "How, Doña? Are you in need of a physician?"

Her smile—heartbreaking, incandescent—exposed the latent beauty beneath the monstrous flesh.

"I have only been ill once in my life," she said. "God evidently thought once was enough. No, not for me, but for the people I try to help. Many of them suffer from the diseases of the poor and I am useless to them. But you, Señor Doctor, you could heal them and perhaps in that small way diminish the human suffering you speak of."

His first thought was that if he accepted her proposal he would be able to spend more time in her company. This alone would have been reason enough to accept, even without the prospect of being able to practice actual medicine, as opposed to administering panaceas and placebos to the bored rich women of Ciudad de México.

"I would be honored," he said.

She remained in the salon after he left as Dolores cleared the table. The maid loaded the tray and asked, "Is there anything else you would like, Doña Alicia?"

"No, my dear," she replied. "Thank you."

"He is very handsome," the girl said, lifting the tray. "*Su novio.*"

"Yes, only he is not my suitor, but my friend," she said. "You must be careful not to start any gossip about our meeting."

"Yes, Doña," she said somewhat skeptically and left Alicia to her own thoughts.

What she had told him was true. She did go unveiled at home, but only when family alone was present. As she had sat at her vanity before he arrived with her jars and pots of creams and powders, preparing to make her face into a mask to receive him, a thought had stayed her hand: *Let him see me as I am.* She had learned to distinguish between her personal thoughts and those thoughts that came to her like messages from a deeper source than her own personality. These deeper messages were sometimes consoling, but more often they had a challenging and unsettling quality. Her first impulse was always to resist them as she had when it had occurred to her she might help relieve his burden of sadness. Yet as always happened, the thought simply repeated itself until she was forced to examine her reasons for rejecting it. She looked into the mirror and searched herself.

The reason, she discovered, was simple. She wanted him to fall in love with her and that fantasy required her to conceal her face from him. It was a fantasy not merely because she could not hide her face from his gaze forever. It was also a fantasy because her life excluded the possibility of such things. Alicia had long accepted that the usual path of happiness open to women—marriage and children—was closed to her. In its place she had cultivated a different path, a life of service that repaid her in love for her modest efforts to ameliorate the sufferings of others. This was her happiness. She must accept that, embrace it, and abandon the dreams of what was not possible, for in those dreams that could not be fulfilled she would find only unhappiness and ingratitude. She sealed the jars of cream and powders, rose from her vanity, and went down to meet him with her naked face.

As he steered his buggy through the narrow streets of San Andrés, Sarmiento's habitually lucid mind was jumbled. All that was clear to him was that no woman had ever made as powerful an impression on him as Alicia Gavilán. What confused him was whether the impression was due to her magnetism or her tragedy, if they could even be separated. Would she have been the same woman had the misfortune of a preventable disease not ruined her appearance? Was the kindness at the core of her personality so profound it would have guided her life even if she had grown into the beautiful woman he glimpsed beneath the mask of sores, scars, and lesions? Or would she have become another unhappy rich lady pacing her mansion on the Paseo de la Reforma, waiting for a handsome doctor to relieve her boredom? And why did it matter to him? Because—the thought formed hesitantly, reluctantly—he felt for her the stirrings of personal affection. But what kind of affection, that of a friend for a friend, or of a man for a woman? In Europe, where such things were permitted in society, he had had purely platonic friendships with women, but what Alicia Gavilán provoked in him was deeper than those cordial feelings. But the other, a man's passion for a woman? With her? With her . . . her face as it was? He could not imagine . . .

A beggar boy ran in front of his buggy, forcing him to rein in his horse and allowing him for a moment to set aside his mental agitation.

At precisely ten o'clock, Alicia Gavilán's landau came to a halt in front of his apartment building, where he was waiting with his bag. It was a fine old coach, the black body polished to a high gloss, the family crest emblazoned on the door in red and gold. The curtains were drawn. The driver cast a wary look at him as he turned the silver handle and pulled open the door. The interior was filled with food, clothing, and children's toys; Alicia sat in a corner with a bit of embroidery in her lap. As she had when he had first seen her, she wore a silk gown of midnight blue and a lace hat decorated with feathers. A veil was fixed to the brim, but was up, revealing her face. He wedged himself in and sat beside her.

"Good morning, Doña," he said.

"Good morning, Señor Doctor," she replied. "Thank you for joining me today."

"Where, precisely, are we going?"

"To visit my godchildren," she said. She pulled a gold cord that ran above the door. A bell chimed and the carriage began to move.

Her godchildren were scattered in the poorest neighborhoods of the city, places he knew by name but into which he had never ventured: San Sebastián, Tepito, San Lázaro. They were shanty towns that had grown up around crumbling colonial churches, which had once been the center of tiny Indian villages swallowed up by the city. Now they housed the tens of thousands of poor who had flocked to the city looking for work after Don Porfirio's land reforms had squeezed country people off their ancestral lands to create the massive ranches of his favored friends. The more fortunate lived in tiny adobe houses that faced narrow dirt roads where naked children played in the dust and packs of rabid-looking dogs scavenged piles of debris. The less fortunate lived in *vecindades*, which were tenements carved out of old colonial mansions, where a single windowless room might house a family of six or more.

The least fortunate lived, as far as Sarmiento could tell, on the streets. The air reeked of raw sewage and sour pulque, the milky liquor of the agave that kept half the *pelados* in a state of pleasureless semi-inebriation. The poor had existed only on the periphery of his vision as servants, laborers, or beggars, indistinguishable one from another, with their muddy skin and inky hair, torn clothes, averted eyes, soft voices. This was the city of the dregs—the city of the *pelados*, the *léperos*—concealed within the city of the palaces, which was, he realized, the city where he lived.

Alicia Gavilán, even more than he, belonged to the wealthy city superimposed on the city of misery through which the Gavilán carriage made its way, stopping before a whitewashed adobe hut or perhaps a former monastery now carved into a warren of hovels. These were places he would have hesitated entering, but Doña Alicia crossed the thresholds cheerfully, familiarly, calling out the names of her godchildren. He followed, doubtfully, and behind him came the coachman loaded with food and clothes, candy and toys. Wherever they went, Doña Alicia was received with joy and guided to the single chair in the tiny rooms, where babies and children piled into her lap. After the gifts were distributed she would talk to the father or, more often, the mother of the family, picking up the threads of what it seemed to him were long-standing conversations. For he observed that she came not as an aristocratic benefactress distributing alms, but as a beloved friend, guide, and confidant. She was treated with respect but not servility. Her godchildren addressed her not with the formal *usted* but with the familial *tú*. They joked with her, poured out their hearts to her, complained about drunken husbands and short-changing shopkeepers, worried with her about their children, and begged her to remember them in her prayers. Meanwhile, she sat with a child in her lap, listening, encouraging, admonishing, praising. Her face was unveiled, her disfigurement freely exposed and evidently unremarkable.

But then, he thought, if there was anywhere in the city where she might have passed almost unnoticed, it would have been in the city of the poor. The filthy streets of its *colonias* teemed with men and women who, without access to the most basic medical services, labored beneath disfigurements and deformities: a man missing both legs pushing himself along with his hands on a makeshift cart, a woman with an enormous goiter on her neck, a blind child begging on a corner, men and women whose faces bloomed with violent skin diseases or bore the scars of smallpox like Doña Alicia.

When she introduced him to her godchildren, they received him courteously, more for her sake than his, he quickly surmised, and politely declined his offers of medical assistance. Even Doña Alicia's gentle cajolery could not persuade a shy mother to part with her sick child, and in the end, Sarmiento was simply an observer, greeted and then ignored.

"How is it you acquired so many godchildren?" he asked her as they bumped along a dirt road in a nameless neighborhood at the northern edge of the city.

"Most of them were foundlings at the Casa de Niños Expósitos who were in need of a godmother so they could be baptized," she replied. "A priest at the cathedral where the orphans are taken knows he can always call on me to perform that function."

"But some of these people we've seen are adults now," he said. "Have you continued your bond with them all these years?"

"One is a godmother for life," she said. "It is my responsibility to bear witness to my faith through my words and my actions as long as I live and they live."

"You do more than that," he pointed out. "You assist materially."

She smiled. "A very wise priest I know, Padre Cáceres, once told me that the word of God is best heard on a full stomach." After a moment she asked tentatively, "Do you truly have no faith?"

"I do not wish to be disrespectful of your beliefs, but in my view religion is no more than superstition, a way to explain natural phenomena for which there are now rational and scientific explanations. Those superstitions may have served their purpose once, but their time has passed. The longer they persist, the more pernicious they become."

"What do you mean, natural phenomena?"

"Disease, for example. It is not caused by demons nor is it divine punishment. Nor was the world created in seven days and seven nights, nor man from dust or woman from his rib. The creation of the world, the emergence of humans, those were geological and biological processes that took millennia. There is no heaven in the sky, there is no hell beneath the earth's crust. I apologize if I offend you, Doña Alicia, but you asked and I should like to be direct with you in all matters."

"I envy your education," she said. She smiled again. "Mine ended with embroidery and piano lessons. There is so much more I would like to have studied but as my mother would say, that is not our custom. So I cannot contest your opinions of religion with equal erudition. I can only tell you there is more to my faith than superstition."

"What is that, Doña?" he asked.

She gazed out of the carriage for a long time collecting her thoughts. "You see what my life is," she said finally. "Bounded by custom on one hand, by my disfigurement on the other. My space is very small, Señor Doctor. Like a cell in the prison at Belem. I do not imagine that this sense of imprisonment is special to me. We are all bounded in one way or another and my cell is comfortable, unlike those unfortunates who starve in the streets. We are all birds in cages, but some of us find reason to sing. My faith is my reason to sing. I sing and my song is answered."

"By whom?"

"By others singing from their cages and by the birds of the air, the spirits of those who have been released from their cages, and by the one who came to free us all from our cages by bursting his own, my Lord Jesus Christ."

"You ascribe to your faith what are your own inherent virtues," he said. "I don't know whether I think you are being foolish or humble. But it doesn't matter what I think. The world is a better place because you are in it."

"You, too, Miguel," she said, using his given name for the first time.

He shook his head. "All I have done today is frighten children with my stethoscope and quarrel with an old woman about herbal remedies."

She shook her head, still gazing out the window at the streets of the poor. "There is a place for you in this world. I feel it."

A place with you. The thought came unbidden but once it had formed in his mind, it seemed both improbable and true.

A<small>h</small>, here you are at last!" his cousin said with a mock bow. He had risen from his seat at a marble-topped table beneath the stained glass dome of maidens gathering lilies that had given the café its name, Los Lirios. The dome, like the mahogany bar that curved between Corinthian columns, had been imported from France.

Sarmiento sat down. "I'm sorry to be late. I was delayed."

A white-jacketed waiter in a red fez approached to take their orders. When he had departed, Jorge Luis said suspiciously, "There is something different about you, Miguel."

Sarmiento shrugged and answered, "No, I don't think so."

"You seem unusually hale," Jorge Luis continued. "Not the pale ghost I have become accustomed to." He made a show of inspecting Sarmiento's face. "Your eyes are clear. Have you stopped drinking?"

"You just heard me order a whiskey," he replied with a smile.

"By this time of the afternoon you would already have had several whiskies, but not today. There are only two causes for sobriety, Primo, God or a woman, and since you are an atheist, I must assume there is a woman."

Jorge Luis paused to allow the waiter to set their drinks on the table. He lifted his glass of absinthe, touched it to Sarmiento's, and said, "Who is this paragon, Miguel? Presumably not the little French girl at Silvestre's place I recommended last time we met. She's lovely, but falling for a whore requires more imagination than you have ever demonstrated."

"Do you never tire of being clever?"

"Don't change the subject," he said, lifting the glass of green liquor to his lips. He paused, stared at Sarmiento, and blurted out, "No! It can't be. Not Alicia Gavilán!" Sarmiento felt his face flush. "It is! My God, Miguel . . ."

He grabbed Jorge Luis's wrist and said, in an angry whisper, "Will you keep your voice down!"

"Then rumors are true," he marveled. "Beauty and the beast, the gossips call you, the roles inverted of course. You the beauty and—"

"Do not dare complete that sentence," Sarmiento said, his voice tight with fury.

Jorge Luis fell back in his chair as if he had been struck. He swallowed his drink and laid the empty glass on the table. "But this is unbelievable, Miguel," he said in a quiet, serious voice. "What does the lady say?"

Sarmiento's hand fluttered helplessly.

"You haven't shared your sentiments with her?" his cousin asked.

"How can I, when I am uncertain of their meaning or their cause?"

"Surely, their cause is the lady and as for their meaning . . ."

Sarmiento swallowed some whiskey. "I have seen her without her veil. I cannot feel toward her the ordinary physical attraction one feels for women and yet, Primo, when I am with her, her very presence gives me a feeling of peace and well-being as if every sordid and wasteful thing I have ever done has been forgiven. Is that love? Is it gratitude? Do I want her to be my wife or my mother? Is my feeling of being forgiven an illusion that would shatter once she knew—" He stopped and raised his glass to the waiter.

"Once she knew what, Miguel?" his cousin asked when the waiter had come and gone.

"I have lived less than an exemplary life," he said. "Let's leave it at that."

Their drinks came and they finished them and the next round in silence.

When the fourth round came, Jorge Luis said, "Listen, Miguel, let's not be glum. You want to know whether or not you are in love with the lady? Perhaps I can help you answer that question."

"How so?"

"The president's wife is throwing a charity ball on Saturday evening. Come with me and we will see how strong your sentiment is for the Condesa Alicia when you are surrounded by all the available beauties of the city."

"A charity ball? Which charity?"

Jorge Luis smirked. "I offer you a garden of earthly delights and you worry about which charity is being feted? Really, Miguel, first things first. In any event, the charity is entirely respectable. It's the foundling home. First Lady Carmen's pet project. You know she is as barren as the Sahara herself so she likes to go and coo at the babies that have been abandoned there by their slattern mothers. You must come."

Sarmiento shrugged. "I do not wish to meet other women."

"Then come because your Doña Alicia may be there."

"How do you know that?"

"She also is a patron of the orphanage."

"Yes," Sarmiento acknowledged, thinking of Alicia's many god-children. "That's true. She is."

"I will be at your apartment Saturday night at nine on the point. Be dressed and ready." He gulped his drink and stood up. "*Hasta sábado*, Primo."

"Until then," Sarmiento said.

Alicia and her three sisters took tea with their mother in her yellow salon every afternoon. Alicia always arrived first, followed by her sisters, and then her mother. So when she entered the room today, she was surprised to find La Niña already present. Under her mother's gimlet-eyed gaze, the servants nervously set out the tea service and hastily retreated. Her mother glanced up at her and said, "Who is this man in whose company you have been seen by half the city?"

Alicia sat down on a gilded chair from the reign of Louis XV. "You are referring, no doubt, to my friend Doctor Miguel Sarmiento."

Her mother looked at her with hooded eyes, like an ancient bird of prey. "Your friend? An unmarried reprobate? Do not imagine, my good daughter, that your unfortunate condition puts you beyond the reach of scandal."

"I assure you, Mother, Miguel Sarmiento is no reprobate," she replied hotly. "He is a sensitive, honorable man who assists me in my charity."

"He is a lunatic's son who was forced to leave México a decade ago under a cloud."

"He went to study medicine in Germany and France."

"That isn't what the gossips say," her mother observed.

"Since when do you listen to the gossips?"

Her mother frowned. "When they are gossiping about my daughter." She raised a hand to prevent Alicia from replying. "Listen to me, Daughter. I have permitted you unusual freedom to do your good works, but there is a limit to my liberality."

"Will you lock me up in my room?" Alicia asked coolly.

"Don't be a fool!" her mother snapped. "You have become the laughingstock of the city, throwing yourself like a lovelorn girl at a man who has no interest in you. I am merely attempting to save you and this family from further embarrassment."

Alicia's face burned with shame. "Is that what the gossips say? That I am throwing myself at him?"

"Like a hideous witch pursing a handsome prince," her mother replied. "That is what they say." La Niña sighed. "I am sorry to repeat it, but I want you to hear what is whispered behind your back."

"But it is not true, Mother. I am not pursing him. He is my friend," she said, sounding pitiable even to herself, like a little girl begging to be allowed to keep a stray kitten.

"Yet you have seen fit not to introduce me to this friend of yours," her mother replied.

Alicia, remembering how carefully she had arranged Miguel's visit to the palace when her mother would be out, had no satisfactory response.

Her mother, noting her discomfiture, continued. "I do not blame you for wanting the attentions of a man. You are normal, after all, notwithstanding your misfortune. But what you are doing with this doctor is not permitted, Alicia. It is also unnecessary. Even as you are, there are men who would gladly have you as their wife in exchange for the social prestige you would bring to them."

"Even as I am," Alicia said bitterly. "What you are describing is not marriage but barter."

"My dear," she said. "Except in the novels of the Brontës, marriage is a barter. You make the best bargain you can before I die. A woman alone has no place in the world. Your brothers-in-law will undoubtedly wrest control of your inheritance, paltry as it will be, and appropriate it to their own uses. You will end up living on their sufferance."

"My sisters would not allow that."

"They are entirely dependent on their husbands for everything but the air they breathe. I would not look to them for help."

"Then Christ will be my help," Alicia said.

"Oh, him," La Niña replied. "A man like other men. What was Jesus's mother to him but nine months' food and lodging? Seriously, Daughter, think of what I have said."

"You know, as no one else does, where I am truly scarred," Alicia replied. "What man knowing that would have me—even as I am?"

"He need never know."

"On our wedding night he would know."

The old woman raised her eyebrows. "There are plausible explanations. It is time you grew up, Alicia, and accepted the world as it is, not as you wish it to be. You need a husband and we shall procure one for you. You will accompany me to the first lady's ball wearing my finest jewels."

"Why not simply hang a for-sale sign around my neck?"

"Don't be vulgar. You are a daughter of this ancient house, a *condesa*. Let society pay attention to that. I want you noticed, not pitied. In the meantime there will be no further assignations with this Sarmiento. Do you understand?"

Alicia bowed her head in resignation and assent.

4

On the evening of the first lady's ball, the wind blew across the surface of dead Lake Texcoco, the city's ancient sewer, creating a cloud of putrescence that descended into every nook and cranny of the city. Sarmiento and his cousin, in white tie and tails, smoking cigars to mask the excremental odor, made their way along the northern edge of the Zócalo to the Casino Español. The street lights burned in the still night and in the middle of every intersection were the red lanterns of the police, the officers themselves concealed in the shadows or slaking their thirst at a *pulquería*.

"Do you know what I love about our city?" Jorge Luis asked. "Wherever one goes, at whatever time of day or night, stone eyes watch over us."

"What are you talking about, Primo?"

Jorge Luis stopped and gestured with the red tip of his cigar to a niche carved above an eighteenth-century doorway that held the figure of John the Baptist.

"Saints above the doors, waterspouts carved in the shapes of dragons, the capitals of columns decorated with angels and lions," he said. "In every wall, on every roof, there is a creature in stone—man, animal, angel, saint—gazing at the passersby. I think of them as the eyes of our ancestors."

"Our guardians?" Sarmiento said.

"Not at all," Jorge Luis replied. "The angels, yes, of necessity, and I suppose that is also true of the saints and all the Virgins of Guadalupe that surround us. But there are other figures carved into the walls. Effigies of the dead who must watch us with envy because we are alive and they are not. Demons who would loosen the stones into which they are carved and send them crashing down on our heads. Snakes who would poison us. Lions who would consume us. The stone inhabitants of the city are no more benign than the breathing ones. Still, it greatly comforts me to know that I am never alone. Not you, Primo?"

"I am not afraid of being alone, Jorge Luis."

His cousin shot him a pitying look and said, "That is all too evident, Miguel."

They stood before the Casino Español on the Calle Espiritu Santo. Although it was as massive as the colonial edifices that surrounded it, the Casino was new. Nonetheless, the Spanish millionaires who had commissioned the building chose an architect whose design combined elements of Spain's chief architectural legacies to its former colony, the Gothic church and the baroque palace. Between twin towers, the limestone facade featured Corinthian tipped columns, a quattrocento balustrade, and escutcheons carved with Spain's coat of arms. The dignity of the Casino was somewhat compromised by the cigar shop, the cafe, and the stationary store that occupied its ground floor. The shops were closed but the windows of the upper floors were suffused with honey-colored light. Beautifully dressed women leaned against the balustrade on the second-story balcony and fanned themselves. A door opened somewhere and a Juventino Rosas waltz spilled into the night. Sarmiento felt, almost despite himself, anticipation, excitement.

"Come, Prince Charming," Jorge Luis said. "I hope the glass slipper is secure in your pocket. La Cenicienta is waiting for you inside."

They passed through a passageway in the style of a nave and entered an enormous two-story atrium. They paused to admire the stained glass ceiling emblazoned with the Spanish royal crest in yellow, black, and red, and followed the music up a sweeping staircase. The ball was being held in the Salón de los Reyes, a barrel-vaulted space in which gilded columns and the terrazzo floor caught and reflected back the shimmering light of enormous crystal chandeliers creating a golden haze. On either side of the dance floor were linen-covered tables and delicate chairs painted gold. At the front of the room, on a dais, sat the president of the Republic and the first lady. Don Porfirio was flanked by a line of soldiers in dark blue dress uniforms adorned with gold braid and epaulets while

Doña Carmen was attended by a group of women in pale pastel silken gowns that complemented her gown—a cloud-like pink confection of lace, pearls, and rosettes.

When Sarmiento was a child, Díaz had sometimes come to visit his father, but he had not seen Don Porfirio in the flesh for many years. He found it hard to believe that the wiry man who had sat him on his knee and told him stories of his exploits against the French and who smelled pleasantly of horses and tobacco was the same person as the waxen, white-haired, stolid figure at the far end of the room. The most striking change of all was to the man's complexion.

"Primo," he said in a low voice to Jorge Luis. "Don Porfirio seems . . . rather paler than I remember him."

Jorge Luis flashed him a smile. "You know the saying, Miguel. Power whitens and absolute power whitens absolutely."

"Should we pay our respects?"

"Us? No, we are insects to *el presidente*." The orchestra struck up a schottische. "Come on, Miguel, let's pick among these many feminine flowers ones that will not wilt on the dance floor."

"I want to look for Doña Alicia," Sarmiento said.

His cousin took his arm. "There will be time for that later, Primo. Now, we dance!"

After an hour, Sarmiento excused himself from his cousin's company, intent on finding Alicia Gavilán. The marriageable girls, who were his only suitable dance partners, were years younger than he, some as young as seventeen. Although they were lovely and skillful dancers, their convent-school conversation was inane. He wandered the corridor above the atrium, taking in the Gothic arches and somber stained glass windows. They reminded him of the gloomy castles and dank monasteries of his ancestral homeland. The Spanish, he decided, had a singular gift for investing any space with the charm of a mortuary. Out of the corner of his eye, he saw a door that opened to a room filled with books. He stepped inside. The library was a narrow rectangle, paneled in dark wood with floor-to-ceiling bookshelves of the same material. A long table surrounded by leather-upholstered chairs occupied the center of the room. The backs of the chairs were stamped with the coats of arms of Spanish cities. On the table were electric lamps in the shapes of bronze figures from Greek mythology holding globes illuminating fine old atlases. Arrangements of club chairs and small tables in the corners suggested old men napping with books in their laps and glasses of Jerez at their elbows.

He was not alone. A woman in a three-tiered gown of iridescent plum, the tiers bordered with black ribbon, stood with her back to him. She was gazing at a medallion carved in wood in the molding along the ceiling. He noticed her fine shoulders and lovely neck. Something glittered in her right hand. He recognized her.

"Doña Alicia?" he said.

She turned. He nearly gasped at the sight of her face. Buried under layers of creams and powders, lips and cheeks rouged, it was like the face the undertaker paints on the corpse for the final viewing.

"Miguel," she said. "I did not expect to see you here."

"My cousin insisted," he replied, "but I came only because he told me you would be here. You have not asked me to join you in your charitable work for several days now. I was afraid my uselessness had become all too apparent to you."

"I meant to send you a note," she said apologetically.

"A note?"

She sighed. "I'm afraid that I can no longer ask you to accompany me."

He frowned. "Why? Have I offended you in some way?"

"Never," she said. "But you have been away from our city for a long time and perhaps you have forgotten, as I sometimes do, its rules of propriety. An unmarried woman is not permitted to be in the company of any man who is not a relative." She paused, twisting the diamond necklace she was holding in her hand. "I'm afraid there was been talk about us. Not very pleasant talk."

"I care nothing for the rules of propriety!" he protested.

Something like a smile attempted to break through the heavy makeup. "That is the male prerogative," she said. "I must observe those rules, if not for myself, then for my family's sake. I am terribly sorry, but at least we part as friends."

He knew what he should say and what, in his heart, he wished to say—that the rules of propriety would allow him to see her as her suitor—but the words caught in his throat and before he could force them out, an old, deep voice spoke from the doorway: "Alicia, you are wanted in the salon."

Sarmiento looked and saw a tiny, ancient woman in a funereal ball gown of deepest black with a glittering tiara on her sparse hair.

He bowed slightly. "Señora Marquesa."

She strode into the room. "Who are you, young man?"

"I am Miguel Sarmiento, Señora Marquesa."

"Ah," she said. "The son of Catarina Soto de la Barrera."

"You knew my mother?"

"Your grandfather wanted to marry her off to my younger brother, Juan, but we still had our property then and a match with a merchant's daughter could be refused."

"Mother," Alicia said reproachfully.

La Niña waved dismissively. "This is ancient history and both parties are dead. The first lady is about to make her little speech and requires you at her side when she does. Where are my diamonds?"

Alicia held out the necklace. "I removed it. It has the power of making its wearer invisible."

"Not invisible," the old woman said. "But it does provide another object for the eye to rest upon."

Sarmiento bit back a reproach.

"You can't carry my diamonds around as if they were a handful of alms," the *marquesa* continued. "Put them on. Here, let me help with the clasp."

Alicia arranged the necklace around her neck and her mother fixed the clasp. The diamonds blazed against her dark gown, calling the eye to them and away from Alicia's motionless mask of a face.

"Please excuse me, Doctor. Carmen—the first lady—is a generous friend in her support of the Casa de Niños and if she wants me, I must go."

He bowed, deeply this time. "A pleasure, as always, to see you, Doña." When she had left, he turned to the *marquesa*. "Your daughter—"

"Is a woman of unquestionable probity, young man," she said. "And so she shall remain."

He understood at once she was the instigator of Alicia's decision to cut ties with him. "It was never my intention to call into question her probity."

"Certainly," the *marquesa* said, "a gentleman would have understood how to conduct himself with an unmarried woman."

The implied accusation hung in the air.

"I apologize for any offense I have given," he said. "Your daughter is a remarkable woman. I only wished to continue our friendship."

"That is not possible," the *marquesa* replied and swept out of the room with a curt "Good evening."

Sarmiento remained in the library for a few more minutes, ruminating over the turn of events. He could not get out of his mind the death-mask quality of Alicia's painted face, which was more shocking to him than his first encounter with her scars. Her scarred face was authentically her; the mask was unnatural, the face she was required to wear to appease the conventions of her privileged class. He remembered the cruel exchange between Alicia and her mother about the diamond necklace. The *marquesa* wished to empty Alicia of her personality and create a simulacrum, an image of an aristocratic woman as vacuous as the other aristocratic women who filled the ballroom. He reflected that she had seemed more at home in the hovels of the poor than in the lavishly decorated rooms of the Casino Español. Alicia had told him how narrow were the confines of her life, but until tonight he had not understood how forcefully they impinged upon her, preventing her from even choosing her own friends. From choosing him. And if she could not be his friend, he would never see her again except, perhaps, in stilted social circumstances like this ball. The thought of losing her friendship was unbearable to him. The affection he felt for her had deepened with each meeting and in her presence he had felt like the man he had hoped to become, unburdened by guilt and regret. He could not lose her.

But to keep her meant he too must bow to the conventions of their world and seek her out not as a friend but as a suitor. That meant he must be prepared to marry her. His first, shameful response to this thought was distaste. It was one thing to contemplate her ruined face as a clinician, but quite another to contemplate it as a prospective husband. He was honest enough to admit he could not enter a celibate marriage, and he could not imagine such a marriage would satisfy her, either, if only because it would be a constant reminder of her disfigurement. He did not know what to do. Perhaps, he thought, his worldly cousin could help him see his way out of the dilemma.

His cousin was nowhere to be seen in the golden ballroom. Sarmiento went out to the balcony to smoke. As he lit his cigarette he saw Jorge Luis standing in the shadows with another man. His cousin's back was to him. Sarmiento took a step forward, then stopped. Jorge Luis was in deep conversation with the man, whose face was hidden by darkness. They stood, not in the closeness of friends, but the closeness of intimacy, where the breath of the speaker grazes the cheek of the listener. The other man's hand emerged from shadow and slowly stroked the back of Jorge Luis's hand. Sarmiento turned and hurried into the salon.

Sarmiento's father lived in a dusty pink house on the Calle de los Parados in the old *colonia* that had seen better days. Sarmiento caught a tram to the Zócalo and got off at the gingerbread kiosk across from the cathedral. A few blocks' walk from the brightly lit streets surrounding the Zócalo brought him into the darkness of the eighteenth century. The *colonia* had then been home to merchants, artisans, and a few old, rich families. Even in his boyhood, there had been traces of its former prosperity. Dry goods shops had lined the arcade of the *plazuela* and there was brisk traffic on its rutted roads. Now, however, the streets were empty and grass sprouted in the cracks between the paving stones. The fine shops were shuttered or else had been converted to cheap restaurants or *pulquerías*, where the men of the neighborhood drank away their paltry earnings.

He pushed open the carved doors of his father's house and entered the little courtyard where pitch pine lamps burned on the exterior walls illuminating an overgrown garden. The soft gurgle of water issued from the fountain in the center of the patio. The air smelled of vegetable decay. He crossed the patio and entered the house, a dozen rooms set behind a tiled corridor covered by a beamed ceiling arranged in a rectangle around the courtyard. When he was a boy, the rooms were filled with the teak and rosewood furniture his mother had brought from her wealthy merchant family, along with paintings, tapestries, silver, and fine plates from China. His father had brought to the marriage his fair skin, blond hair and green eyes, his medical degree, Spanish provenance, and a remote but verifiable connection to Castilian nobility. Despite his impecuniosity, those credentials had been enough for his mother's family, themselves of Spanish descent and anxious to keep from their bloodlines any taint of Indian blood.

Now the rooms were stripped bare. When he had first returned to México, he had asked his father about the family possessions. His father's curt reply: "Your education." In this way, Sarmiento learned that his years in Europe had been financed by the sale of almost every object of value in his father's house. Had his mother been alive, she would have been heartbroken, but she had died when he was five and his father attached as little value to her possessions as he did to her memory.

He came to the room that had been the library. It was still filled with books—these his father had not sold—but it was now also his father's dwelling place, dining room, and, to judge by the smell of ordure emanating from an unseen chamber pot, his toilet. The library was illuminated by a single kerosene lamp burning on a table beside the narrow bed where his father slept. The old man lay there, his back turned to Sarmiento, motionless but for the soft shudder of his breathing. The bed was piled with books and papers.

Sarmiento laid his hand on his father's shoulder. "Father?"

His father rolled onto his back, sending a cascade of books to the floor. His eyes were bleary, his gray hair disheveled, and his face unshaven: an old man in soiled clothes in a filthy house.

"Father? Are you all right?"

The old man sat up. "Perfectly. Move, will you, so I can get up."

Sarmiento stepped aside. His father stood up, spilling more books and papers, and moved around the room, lighting candles and another lamp. The room took shape in all its squalor: clothes scattered everywhere; plates of half-finished meals; the long table used as a desk, every inch of its surface covered by moldering documents, books, and sheaves of paper bestrewn with his father's tiny script.

"How does your book progress?" Sarmiento asked.

After his release from Belem, his father had announced he was turning his broadsides into a single volume that would conclusively demonstrate the illegitimacy of Don Porfirio's government.

"As if you cared," his father replied scornfully. "No, you are like all the other young people basking in the warmth of Díaz's *pax romana.*

Does it matter to you that he keeps himself in power through sham elections and with secret police? Does it matter to you that he has betrayed the very ideas of the liberal party that he pretends to promote? No, no one cares about all this . . . ancient history except to those of us who fought for democracy and equality. Juárez, Alvarez, Comonfort. All dead or bought off, except me. I know that a man's honor means nothing to your generation, but it is all that a man possesses in this life."

Sarmiento, as always, had no response to his father's rants, so he changed the subject. "Let me take you out for a meal."

"I am perfectly capable of providing hospitality," he said, then shouted, "Emilia!"

The word echoed through the empty rooms. After a moment, footsteps shuffled softly across the floor, a door squeaked open, and a fat, pig-eyed Indian woman entered the room.

"Yes, Señor Doctor?" she murmured.

"Bring us some food."

"Yes, Señor Doctor. Immediately."

Sarmiento knew from past experience that Emilia's "immediately" could mean in ten minutes or never, depending on how she gauged the level of his father's irascibility. She had come into his father's life a few months earlier, when she had simply appeared and been introduced to him by his father as "my servant." To judge by the continuing level of squalor in which his father lived, she did very little service. She seemed to live somewhere in the house with other members of her family, whose silent shadows he sometimes saw flickering among the archways. The odds and ends of value that had remained in the house began to disappear. He had warned his father about her designs and offered to move back into the house himself to care for the old man. His concerns and offers had been rejected.

On this occasion, she chose to perform her allotted role and brought a simple meal to the table, where the two men sat and ate. In his familiar surroundings, the old man seemed more lucid than he had at Belem when Sarmiento had last seen him, so he raised the subject that had brought him here.

"I have come to ask your counsel, Father, about a woman."

His father dipped his bread into the garlicky chicken stew they were eating and, without looking up, said, "You are almost thirty. Surely by now you have worked out the basic biology of sexual attraction."

He reached out and stayed his father's hand. "I'm serious, father."

His father stopped eating and looked at him. "All right, speak."

Commanded to speak, Sarmiento's words dried up; how could he explain Alicia Gavilán? Sensing his father's impatience, he blurted out, "I believe I am in love."

His father frowned. "You are being sentimental. What men call love is a pathological state induced by lust and fantasy. It explains nothing, so if you want my advice, you must present your problem to me rationally."

This was the father Sarmiento remembered from his childhood who had met Sarmiento's boyhood crises with cerebral coolness and detachment.

"I have met a woman for whom I feel great affection," he said, "but she is physically . . . deformed. I wish to continue to see her, but her family has made it clear that I can only do so as her suitor." He paused to collect his thoughts. "If I did so, there would the expectation of marriage, but I am not sure I could fulfill my conjugal duties were we to marry. You understand, Father?"

"Of course," the old man snapped. "You don't think you could have sexual relations with the woman because of her deformity. Is that it, Miguel?"

"Yes," he murmured. "But in every other way, we are compatible."

His father shrugged. "Marry her and seek sexual release elsewhere."

"And hers?"

"Women are not men," his father replied. "They endure sexual contact; they do not enjoy it. This lady would probably be grateful if you left her unmolested."

"Or she would feel humiliated," Sarmiento replied. "Believing that I find her repulsive."

His father gulped wine, wiped his mouth, and said, "Well, don't you?"

Sarmiento closed his eyes and let the question sink into his mind. Love, his father said, was lust and fantasy, and if that was true, he did not love Alicia Gavilán because she was neither the object of physical desire nor a symbol of some unmet need of his. She was real, perhaps the most real human he had ever encountered: kind, humble, generous, humorous, uncertain, vulnerable. There was nothing repulsive in her. To the contrary, she was magnetic. She had drawn him to her not, as other women had, through pretense but by being fully and completely herself.

"No," he said. "I do not find her repulsive. She is, in fact, beautiful, Father. Perhaps the most beautiful woman I have ever met."

His father, who had resumed eating, looked up and said, "A moment ago you said she was deformed and now you say she is beautiful. You're talking nonsense, Miguel. Perhaps you *are* in love. Marry her and be done with it."

Sarmiento entered the grand salon of the palace of the Gaviláns expecting to find only Alicia and her mother. Instead, four women sat on the long couch pushed up against the wall, beneath the portraits of the ruff-collared aristocrat and his wife he had noticed the first time he had come. In the center of the couch was La Niña, her small, sharp face and old hands emerging from the flood of black silk. To her right were three women, who, from the similarities of their features, he surmised were Alicia's sisters. They were dressed in the extravagant style of fashionable ladies, their gowns appearing not so much sewn as confected. Across from the couch were two chairs and between couch and chairs was a low table that held a silver tea service. La Niña issued a curt invitation to sit.

"My daughter will be along presently," she said. "These are her sisters: Nilda, Leticia, and Eulalia. Daughters, this is Doctor Miguel Sarmiento." Before he could utter a greeting, the old woman clapped and a maid appeared. "Manuelita, the tea."

While the maid poured tea into nearly translucent cups, Alicia's three sisters conversed among themselves as if he were not present, while La Niña gazed at him with her small, sharp eyes.

One of the sisters said, "Your father is the crazy old man who plasters the city with denunciations of our dear President Díaz, no?"

"My father is a distinguished scientist who was once the personal physician to Don Benito Juárez," he answered stiffly.

"Yes," the sister—Eulalia—replied gaily. "That's the man. I hope you are no subversive, Doctor."

"I have no interest in politics," he replied.

"How old are you?" the second sister, Leticia, asked politely.

"Twenty-nine, Doña," he replied.

She lifted her teacup to her lips, paused, and said dubiously, "Twenty-nine. An age when most men are married and well settled into family life."

"My father also married late," he said. "It is, perhaps, a family trait. In any event, I've been abroad for most of the last decade, immersed in my medical studies."

The last sister, Nilda, stared at him with frank hostility.

"Is that the only reason you left México? To immerse yourself in your medical studies?" she asked caustically.

"Yes, Doña," he replied.

"One hears differently," she said.

He was spared from further conversation with the acerbic sister by Alicia's arrival. He stood up.

"Doña Alicia," he said, extending his hand.

She simultaneously smiled and touched her fingertips to his. "Doctor Sarmiento, how kind of you to visit."

She greeted her sisters. Nilda kissed the air on either side of her face; Leticia grasped her shoulders and kissed her lips; Eulalia gave her a light, affectionate kiss on the forehead.

"Sit beside the doctor," her mother said. "Manuelita, tea for my daughter."

"I'm sorry I wasn't here when you arrived," Alicia said to Sarmiento, but offered no excuse. Her face was bare and unveiled.

"I am very happy you are here now," he said. "I had the great pleasure of being introduced to your sisters."

"Good," she said. "And your family? Your father is well, I hope."

"Yes, quite well. Thank you."

Each saw in the other's eyes questions that neither could ask in this room so they grasped at conversational straws. The conversation moved awkwardly from topic to topic until, at length, La Niña said, "Thank you for coming, Doctor. Alicia, will you see our guest out?"

He rose, bowed to the three sisters, and said, "Enchanted."

The three women appeared surprised that he was still there.

"Señora Marquesa," he said, bowing to La Niña. "I am indebted to you for your gracious hospitality."

She nodded slightly and said formulaically, "My house is your house. Good afternoon."

They did not speak until the porter was opening the door for Sarmiento to leave.

"Why did you come?" she asked, her voice sad.

"To see you," he replied. "I hope my company was not unwelcome."

She shook her head. "This is a charade, Miguel. You cannot keep coming here and pretending—"

"I am not pretending," he said. "I met a woman of great strength and character and kindness. I came to see that woman." He smiled. "I will play the bear for you, if that is necessary, and parade beneath your window proclaiming my affection for you for the benefit of your neighbors."

She did not return his smile but said, "Why would a man like you, handsome and in the prime of his life, court a woman who has nothing to offer but character and kindness? Those are not the qualities in a woman most men want in their bed."

"You are very frank," he said, abashed.

"I apologize if my frankness is offensive, but I think we should understand each other."

He nodded. "You are perfectly correct, so let me be frank in return. I have had enough experience with women to know that the important qualities are not those one takes to bed, but those to which one awakens. Those are your qualities, Doña Alicia."

For a long moment, the audacity of their conversation rendered them speechless.

"So you think," she said with a smile, "that I would not enjoy watching you pace beneath my window like a lovelorn boy?'

"Point out your window and I will be there tonight."

"No need," she replied. "But you may come back for tea, and I promise my sisters will not be here, although I'm afraid we cannot avoid my mother's company. Good evening, Miguel."

"Until we meet again," he said, and pressed his lips to her fingertips.

As she approached the salon, she heard Nilda, her eldest sister, complain, "What possessed her to appear that way? Did she want to scare him off?"

Leticia, who always defended her, replied, "He had to see her sometime."

Eulalia said gaily, "My dear, that's what the wedding veil is for, to make sure he didn't see what he was getting until the deal was struck."

"You are a flock of vicious hens," her mother hissed.

"Oh, come, Mother," Eulalia said. "You think there's something wrong with him, don't you?"

"Twenty-nine, never married, all those years abroad," La Niña said. "Yes, there is definitely a story there and it cannot be as innocent as he pretends."

"Still," Leticia said, "he is very handsome."

"Handsome is as handsome does," La Niña replied. "I'm not going to marry off your sister to a man who might be hiding a dangerous secret."

Nilda laughed harshly. "Had you applied that standard to us, none of us would ever have married. What is so special about our sister?"

"Marriage is cruel," La Niña said. "Alicia has suffered enough."

Alicia, pausing outside the room, listened to their conversation. *Marriage is cruel.* Was that true of all marriage? Certainly, none of her sisters spoke well of their husbands. Nilda's man was a cold, acquisitive miser; Leticia was married to a philanderer; Eulalia's husband, while more amiable toward her than her sisters' husbands were to them, nonetheless lived so separate a life she rarely knew where he was or with whom. Alicia knew, as her mother only suspected, that Miguel had secrets, but unlike La Niña, she did not believe they were dangerous secrets. Rather, they were secrets that weighed him down with the melancholy that clung to him like a faint miasma comprised of guilt and sorrow. She wanted to believe what he had told her—that he came as her suitor for the good qualities he saw in her—but she could not help wondering whether paying court to her was a kind of expiation for whatever it was he had done that had so wounded him. If this was true, she thought, then surely he would one day awaken from his guilt and sorrow and stare in horror at her and that, she thought, would break her heart. She should end this now, before that happened, and yet, seeing him again had suffused her with happiness, a happiness that belonged to her alone, a happiness she had not felt since the long ago moment when Anselmo had touched her. God have mercy on her. She realized she was being selfish, but she could not bear to give up that happiness. Not yet.

As the weeks passed, Sarmiento returned often to the palace of the Gaviláns and sat with Alicia in the great salon while La Niña pretended to busy herself with an elaborate piece of embroidery. Each visit deepened the certainty of his affection for her. Alicia was the opposite of all the other women whom he had known. Their pleasing appearances had hidden whatever degree of moral disfigurement they suffered while Alicia's physical disfigurement concealed a luminous heart. Still, the disfigurement of her face was an unavoidable fact and he continued to struggle with the aversion he could not help but feel. The question of whether he could be a husband to her in every sense gnawed at him each time he saw a beautiful woman. He could condemn his superficiality, but he could not deny it—like all men, he was moved by female beauty and driven to possess it. He could dismiss this drive as simple biology, but it was as basic as breathing. He could not set it aside for her, but could he redirect it toward her? That was the question. Was the answer contained in Virgil's phrase—*omnia vincit amor*? Could love conquer all? He knew his father would likely dismiss his quandary as mere sentimentality, but he could think of no one else to whom he could present it.

The door to his father's house was open, and as soon as he stepped into the dark courtyard, he knew something was amiss.

"Papá," he called, as he stumbled across the patio to the library. "Papá, are you here?"

He smelled the decomposition before he opened the door, and when he entered the library the stink drove him back out. He retched and caught his breath before entering again, lighting matches as he searched for a lamp. When he found one, he lit the wick and followed the smell to the figure on the bed. His father's face had been gnawed on by rats, and beneath the blanket that covered him, his body was liquefying. He lifted the lamp and saw the room was empty—the books taken along with the pathetic sticks of furniture that his father had salvaged for himself. Furious, he blundered through the house shouting Emilia's name. His cries echoed in the emptiness. After a few moments, he returned to the library, fell to his knees, and sobbed like a child.

5

Alicia parted the curtain and looked out at the Alameda, filled at twilight with children and lovers strolling beneath the poplar trees that gave the park its name. She and Miguel had been to the park only two weeks earlier. Now that he was her suitor, the gossips could no longer insinuate scandal when they were together although their pairing continued to be mocked. The appellations they had been given were all variations of beauty and the beast; one of them, Perseus and the Gorgon, had reduced her to tears when her sister Nilda had repeated it to her. He *was* handsome and she was, she sighed, hideous. There were moments when her faith in their bond faltered and she would have ended it with him and returned to her old ways. Except, as the days and weeks had passed and she became accustomed to his presence in her life, she found it more and more difficult to imagine a life without him.

On that Sunday afternoon, he escorted Alicia on the pathways beneath the leafy trees. A band played waltzes in the distance and the park benches were filled with young men dressed in their best suits watching the girls in pastel-colored dresses pass by like a parade of flowers accompanied, always, by a dourly dressed chaperone. Little boys sped recklessly among the pedestrians on roller skates, and out of nowhere, a swarm of men in bowler hats rolled solemnly by on bicycles. Alicia wore a cream-colored lace dress and an enormous hat with a white veil.

"May we sit for a moment, Miguel?" she asked.

"Of course," he said. He led her to a marble bench and wiped it with his handkerchief. He pointed out that the bench was a gift of the undertaker Eusebio Gayosso.

"Ah," she said. "I always wondered about the philanthropist who donated the benches to the park. Now I will never be able to look at them again without thinking of tombstones."

"They were not here when I was a boy," he said. "Nor the wrought iron gazebos and fences. The park was not so grand then."

"Did you come here very often?" she asked, hoping to engage him in a rare discussion of his boyhood.

"When I was a school boy I spent many indolent afternoons here with my friends eating bags of sweets we bought at the Dulcería de Celaya," he replied, his eyes softening with remembrance. "We would sit here and flirt with the girls." He smiled, patting her hand. "By that I mean we would steal glances at them as they passed and hope against hope that one of them would look back."

"I'm sure they did, for you."

He was silent for a moment. "Back then, my schoolmates called me *güerito* for my green eyes and fair skin, or sometimes *el gachupín*. I didn't mind the first, but the second was a fighting word."

She nodded. The word was the insult term for a Spaniard. "That was cruel."

"Cruelty is like breath to boys," he observed. "But being called that made me feel different, unpleasantly so. I not only looked unlike my friends, I didn't even sound like them. No doubt you have noticed."

"Yes, your accent is that of a Spaniard."

"I acquired it first from my father. He considers himself *puro mexicano*, but even after decades of living here in México he sounds as if he's just stepped off the boat from Cadiz. And, of course," he went on, "living in Europe I was more likely to encounter Spaniards than Mexicans. Speaking to them only hardened my own accent. Even as a boy it was pronounced enough to be a source of amusement to my friends, who teased me about it."

"I think your accent is charming," she said.

"Thank you," he said. "Most people find it grating. In any event, I felt like an outsider, but then I noticed that my appearance and accent also had their advantages when I was with my friends in the park. They could sometimes slow the step of the girls in the Alameda as they passed us and earn me a smile." He took her hand and smiled. "Silly now to think of how I proud I was when that happened, but it was the first power I had ever known in a life lived in the shadow of my father's fame."

"Did you tell him?"

"Yes," he said, his smile fading. "He said, 'You amuse yourself on the site of where the Inquisition burned the innocent for no other reason than that they refused to partake of the venality and ignorance of the church.' After that, my accomplishment in getting a girl to look at me seemed quite petty."

"That seems rather unkind," she ventured.

"He did not intend unkindness," Miguel replied. "My father is a man who loves humanity but who has small use for actual human beings. That is simply his way. I think I may be the only person in the world he loves. Certainly, he is the only person in the world who knows me fully and, knowing me, accepts me."

The shadow of his sadness fell between them like a cloud crossing the sun. She had not pressed him again about the source of his melancholy and he had not been any more forthcoming.

"Come," he said. "This reminiscing has made me hungry for the sweets of my childhood. Let me take you to the Dulcería de Celaya for their *suspiros* and *camotes*."

When Miguel sent word his father had died, Alicia's first thought was, *Now he is alone with his secret.* She had immediately written a letter expressing her sympathy and asking if she might attend his father's funeral service. His return note thanked her and told her his father had requested no service. Ten days had passed. He had not called on her and her discreet inquiries revealed that he had not been to see his patients either. That morning she had written a second note, the one she held, expressing her concern for his well-being, but even as she wrote it she felt a growing sense of dread. She decided to deliver it herself.

La Niña was scandalized. "It is not customary for the woman to chase after her suitor because he fails to appear for tea."

"I worry that his father's death has unsettled him."

"Of course it has unsettled him, but if he is like most men, he grieves in the cantinas and the brothels and neither is any place for you. Leave it, Alicia. He will return."

"He is not like most men," Alicia replied.

"Your faith in his virtue is touching," her mother said dryly.

"It's not his virtue that concerns me," she said, "but his sorrow. His father was his only family. He must feel completely alone now. I only want to assure him that he is not."

"Really, Alicia, you sound like a lovelorn child," La Niña said. "Do you want to repel him? Let him be."

Her mother's words gnawed at her as the dirt roads gave way to the cobblestone streets of an old middle-class enclave in the impoverished *colonia*. Her inexperience with the ways of courtship often left her doubtful about the nature of their relations. His visits were relaxed and they spoke comfortably of his work and her charities, but the very amicability of their meetings seemed to imply friendship only. She asked her sisters whether she should behave differently toward him now that he was her suitor.

"Well, sister," Nilda told her, "your face is not really suited to the virgin's blushes is it? I suppose you could try some business with a fan, although at your age it might just look as if you were swatting at flies. I always told my own daughters to let the man do all the talking, but mother says you blabber away when he comes to visit, so it's too late for that. Next time he comes, put on your best jewels, dear, and try to talk less."

Leticia suggested she take him into the garden and strike poses among the rose bushes and the lavender. "Let him imagine you as a flower," she said. "You might want to start wearing a veil when he visits."

"You could play the piano for him. You do that beautifully," Eulalia suggested. "If that fails, low lights and stronger drink than tea might inspire him."

She dismissed these stratagems as absurd because each required her to pretend she was someone other than she was and, more relevantly, someone other than Miguel knew her to be. In the end, she applied perhaps slightly more perfume and sat away from the harshest light. She reminded herself that friendship was also a precious form of affection and took pleasure in looking at his strong body and handsome face.

The carriage came to a stop before a two-story building painted a faded rose. The driver, Alfredo, climbed down and helped her out. In the past, when she had come for Miguel to take him with her on her charitable rounds, he had awaited her outside. She, of course, had never entered his apartment, but Alfredo, who had delivered her first note of condolence to him, knew where he lived.

"His habitation is on the second floor," Alfredo said. "I will take you there."

She followed him through an iron door that led into a small whitewashed foyer and up a tiled staircase bordered with a wrought iron railing. On each step was a clay pot of red geraniums, which received light from an opening in the ceiling.

They came to a door just off the staircase. The driver banged his fist on it and called, "Señor Doctor, it is Alfredo from the house of the Gaviláns. I have come with Doña Alicia. She wishes to speak to you. Please, sir, out of courtesy to the gracious lady, open the door."

Decisive footsteps crossed the floor within and then Miguel stood before her in a collarless shirt and dark trousers. She smelled alcohol on his breath, but his green eyes were clear and alert. He was freshly shaved and his thick chestnut hair was perfectly groomed except for a stray lock that fell on his forehead. He had never looked so handsome, she thought. But he was also very pale and beneath his eyes were the dark circles of sleeplessness.

"Alicia," he said thickly. "What are you doing here?"

Her heart sank—her mother had been right. He had merely been grieving in the solitary way of men. She felt like a fool.

"I was concerned for you," she said. "I'm sorry to have disturbed you." She touched Alfredo's arm. "We will go now."

"No," Sarmiento said. "Please. Won't you come in?"

The driver tried to enter before her, but she placed her hand on his shoulder and said, "Wait in the carriage."

Alfredo, aghast, said, "Doña Alicia, you are an unmarried woman. You cannot be alone with this gentleman in his habitation."

"The gentleman is my friend," she answered, "and he has suffered the loss of his father. What we have to say to each other must be said privately."

"But La Niña, what will she say?"

"I will deal with my mother," Alicia replied.

"Sir?" the driver beseeched Sarmiento.

"I will leave the door partly open and you can wait here. If you hear anything that seems even slightly amiss, you have my permission to enter."

"Thank you, sir."

Miguel stepped aside. "Doña, my humble house is your house and I am at your service."

She entered. The apartment was a single room divided by an arch. In the front was a sofa and matching chair upholstered in horsehair; between the couch and chair was a lacquered black Chinese trunk inlaid with mother-of-pearl. Along one wall was a long table covered with carefully arranged stacks of books, journals, notebooks, medical apparatus, and a brass microscope. The walls were hung with anatomical charts of parts of the body. Through the arch she saw a narrow bed, a large plain pine armoire, and a stand with a brass basin and pitcher set. Everything in the apartment was immaculately clean and orderly. It was like looking into his mind, she thought, and then, on the Chinese trunk, she noticed a bottle of brandy, a glass, and a revolver.

"Would you like some tea?" he asked. "Or a glass of Jerez? There is a bottle somewhere."

"No, thank you," she said, removing her hat. "May I sit?"

"Of course," he said, leading her to the couch. He remained standing, looking uncertain. "I apologize for my dwelling. I live plainly, a habit from my student days."

"Your rooms are charming," she said. Indicating the brandy and the revolver, she added, "I feel that I have interrupted you."

He sat beside her and picked up the revolver. "This was my father's gun. He carried it with him when he accompanied Don Benito Juárez in the war against the French invaders. I found it beneath his pillow when I discovered his . . . his body. An old soldier's habit, I suppose, although he was no soldier, really. He was a scientist, a healer, a democrat." He paused to collect himself. "In every way, thoroughly admirable. I will never be even half the man he was." Without asking her permission, he poured brandy into the glass and drank it.

"You told me once he was the only person who knew you fully and that you were the only person he loved."

Miguel sighed. "Yes. It is strange to feel orphaned at my age, and yet I do. No one will ever know me as my father did."

"We are all known completely to the one who created us, Miguel," she said. "I am often comforted by the words of the psalm that say, 'Even the darkness is not dark to you; the night is as bright as day, for darkness is as light with you.'"

"I am an atheist, Alicia, as you know. My darkness is not illuminated by a supernatural light." He swallowed some brandy. "That is why I have decided." He faltered, then drew a deep breath. "I have decided I can never marry. I cannot bring my darkness into your life."

"Is that why you have not been to see me?" she asked softly. "Because you wish to break things off between us?"

"I do not wish it," he said. "I have no choice."

They sat for a moment and then she placed her hand on his. "I will accede to your decision, but not without knowing why. This darkness of yours, tell me its cause and let me understand so we can part as friends."

He finished the brandy. He sighed convulsively, as if he were about to sob, grasped her hand, and said, "When I finish, you will not wish even to be my friend. Nonetheless, I will tell you so that you will know you are blameless."

He stood up and paced the floor as he spoke. "My youth was not a credit to my family. I was heedless and self-indulgent, a disappointment to my father in my studies and in my deportment. I was expelled from the medical school for drinking and gambling, but even that disgrace was not enough to change my ways. I persisted in dishonoring my father's name." He paused for a moment and when he continued, his voice was filled with shame. "There was a girl, Paquita, employed as a maid in my father's house. I led her to believe that I was in love with her to lure her into my bed. After I had taken her virginity, I turned my back on her. A sordid story," he said, glancing at her, "but not an uncommon one for men of my class. In this case, however, she became pregnant with my child. When she told me, I panicked. I persuaded her it was best for both of us that the child not be born. I believed that my medical training would be sufficient to—" He stopped in his tracks. He looked at her. "I have never told this to anyone. Only my father knew."

Unsteadily, she said, "Please, continue."

"I promised her if she let me abort the child I would marry her. I took her to a room at a filthy inn to perform the procedure. But I had vastly overestimated my ability. She began . . . to bleed. She bled and bled. I could not stop the hemorrhaging."

"Oh, the poor child!"

"I ran through the streets covered with her blood to my father's house. I told him everything and begged him to come and save her life. He came, but too late. She and the child—I could see it would have been a boy—were dead."

He crumpled into a chair and picked up the brandy, drinking from the bottle. "My father sent me away that very night to Veracruz to await his instructions."

"That is why you left the country?"

He nodded. "My father told Paquita's parents the truth. He also told them he had sent me away and promised I would never return to México. He told me he would give me one final chance to make a man of myself before he cut me off completely. I went to Heidelberg, where I entered the medical school. After Heidelberg, I went to Paris to continue my studies. I lived like a monk, trying to atone for my crime. Trying to forget. But every morning I woke up in a foreign city, I remembered. I begged my father to let me return home, but as long as Paquita's parents were alive, he felt obliged to keep his promise to them. It was only after they were both gone that he wrote me and told me to come home." He glanced at her and then away. "I have discovered, however, there is no home for me. Like Cain, I am marked with guilt and I carry it everywhere I go, now and until the end of my life. As long as my father was alive, there was someone to shoulder part of my burden, but now that he is gone its weight crushes me." He looked at her. "I am a murderer, Alicia. I killed that girl and our child. There is no way to atone but with my own life."

A chill passed through her for, in that moment, she understood what she had interrupted. "You cannot atone for one murder by committing another."

"Not murder, execution."

"Your despair is selfish!" she exclaimed. "If you wish to atone, atone with your life, not your death. You have seen how this city overflows with the suffering of the poor, like the girl you betrayed. Sacrifice yourself to their need. Forget yourself by serving them."

"Like you, Alicia? Is that what you do?"

She breathed deeply, then exhaled. "I once sat before the mirror and pitied myself, lamenting the husband I would never have, the children I would never give birth to. I took to heart the cruel barbs that were directed at me and the expressions of disgust and let them hurt me. Doing so changed nothing, not my face, not my life. So I chose to step away from the mirror and to pretend not to hear or see the contempt. It brought me relief, but it was not until I lost myself in the work of aiding others that I felt peace. I am not the little plaster saint I am made out to be by the women in my circle who pity me for being a disfigured old maid. I am merely trying, like everyone else, to find some happiness in this world. The path that most women take was closed to me, so I had to find another. The first object of my charity has always been myself."

"I have never met anyone like you," he said. "No one so kind, so filled with love. You're right, Alicia, you're not a plaster saint. You're—"

"Stop, Miguel, please." She looked away. "We are speaking of you. What you did to Paquita was monstrous. Your guilt is justified. But you are not unforgiveable. God forgives you, forgives you even your disbelief. I forgive you, Miguel. It does not matter if we never see each other again. Know that in my heart you are and will always be cherished."

Overwhelmed by sentiment, she rushed from the room before he could reply. In the carriage, she pulled the curtains closed and wept, for the girl and the child Miguel had killed, for Miguel himself, and lastly for her own loss. She could not imagine, having told her his secret, he would want to see her again. She could only hope it was enough for his peace of mind that he had been able to tell her.

The following evening while she sat with her mother at tea, a maid entered with a calling card. It was Miguel's.

"The gentleman asks if he may enter," the maid said.

"Yes," Alicia said. "We are happy to receive him."

After Alicia left his rooms, Sarmiento had gone up to the roof of his building and stood there, revolver in his hand, smoking a cigarette. The sun set on the city's roofscape, the parapets, domes, bell towers, terraces and balconies, water tanks, clotheslines, and commercial signs, and the shadows of night seeped softly through the ancient streets. The last cries of the street vendors were silenced by the explosion of bells from the city's churches tolling the hour. He crushed the cigarette stub beneath his heel and made his decision. He emptied the revolver of its single round. Before Alicia had arrived, he had spun the loaded chamber twice, held it to his head and pulled the trigger. He had gone up to the roof uncertain of what he would do, but as he watched night coming on over his native city, he knew he had not come home, after so many years in exile, to kill himself. He considered what Alicia had told him. In her world of faith there was sin, forgiveness, and redemption overseen by a great, white-bearded monarch in the sky. In his world the sky was empty, the dead were without the power to forgive, and the living were lacerated by guilt for their offenses. He did not believe in atonement. But, he did believe, as his father had told him, that life needed purpose, not to store up treasures in heaven, but simply to justify the air he breathed. He would find his purpose. He would stay alive.

In the days that followed, Sarmiento considered his strengths, skills, and temperament and sought to match them to a project to which he could devote himself. One of the city's newspapers put on its front page a long story about the various public health plagues that beset the burgeoning city—an inadequate sewage system, the ever-present threat of flooding, contamination of food and water, the abject slums of the *pelados* that were incubators of disease, public drunkenness, malnutrition. The article reminded him of the suffering he had seen as he had accompanied Alicia on her visits to her godchildren. He kept in mind her words to him to sacrifice himself to the poor, to those, like Paquita, dwelling in misery, exploited, or forgotten. He could not save her life, but perhaps he could save the lives of others.

He knew he could not do this work as Alicia did, engaging the poor as a friend and confidant. His was not a warm and generous nature. Like his father, he was a scientist and a rationalist, detached, intellectually curious, and methodical. He must find a position that would allow him to apply those talents. Through the offices of his senator uncle, Jorge

Luis's father, he secured a letter of introduction to the director of the Board of Public Health from Don Porfirio himself.

The director's offices were located in the municipal palace on the west side of the Zócalo. Sarmiento entered a small anteroom where a male secretary took Díaz's letter and disappeared into an office behind a door engraved with the words "Doctor Eduardo Liceaga, Director of Public Health."

A few minutes later, the secretary came out and said, "The director wishes to know to what address your pay should be sent."

"I beg your pardon," Sarmiento said. "What about my duties?"

The secretary frowned, excused himself, and retreated to the director's office. When he returned, he said, "Doctor Liceaga wishes to speak to you. Please go in."

Liceaga's office was both spacious and cluttered. There were glass-faced cabinets filled with specimen jars, bookshelves crammed with books and journals, tables laden with official-looking documents bearing the board's insignia. Covering an entire wall were engineering drawings and photographs of the massive project currently under construction to drain the city of excess water and waste through a system of canals, dams, and tunnels. On another wall was a schemata of the city's sewer system and a map of the city divided into eight numbered sectors. On the wall behind the director's desk was a chromolithograph of Louis Pasteur and a framed copy of the first page of his 1876 address to the French Academy announcing his discovery of microbes as the source of contagious disease. A large window looked out upon the red-and-brown city and, rising serenely beyond it in the blue distance, Popocatépetl and Iztaccíhuatl—the tragic lovers who in Aztec myth had metamorphosed into volcanoes. Rows of mounted butterfly specimens hung on either side of the window, and there was a collection of butterfly nets in a corner.

At the desk sat a clean-shaven, sallow-skinned man of middle age; his dark hair was streaked with gray and he was wearing a white suit. He was scribbling in a journal with ink-stained fingers. Without looking up, he asked curtly, "Who are you? What do you want?"

"I am Doctor Miguel Sarmiento," he said. "I have come to offer my services in whatever manner may be useful to the promotion of public health."

Liceaga paused in his writing and looked up. Behind thick pince-nez spectacles, his dark eyes were skeptical. "I am on the faculty of the medical school and I have never seen you before in my life."

"My degrees are from the University of Heidelberg and the Sorbonne. I have only been back in México for a year. My father was also a doctor and, like you, a member of the faculty of the school of medicine. Doctor Rodrigo Sarmiento."

Liceaga touched a pensive finger to his lip, leaving a smear of ink. "Sarmiento? I knew him slightly, though he had left the faculty long before I arrived. He was your father? I am told he was a good doctor although his interests veered more toward the political than the scientific. I understand he died recently."

"Yes," Sarmiento said.

"My condolences. Sit down."

"I will, sir, if you will explain to me how I have offended you."

Liceaga handed him the unsealed letter from Díaz. Sarmiento read what the old man had written: "Put the bearer of this note on your payroll. Díaz."

"The payroll of every department in this building is padded with phantom workers," Liceaga said. "Naturally I assumed that you were another one of the president's friends in need of an income."

"No, Doctor, I assure you that I am a trained medical scientist."

"Tell me, Doctor," Liceaga said, leaning back in his swivel chair, "do you subscribe to the miasmatic theory of contagious disease?"

"Of course not. Pasteur and Koch have proven beyond a shadow of a doubt that disease is caused by microbes, and while some may be airborne, it is not the air itself, however much it stinks, that makes people sick. The miasmatic theory is simply a species of spontaneous generation, which," he said, indicating the framed page of Pasteur's speech, "that document incontrovertibly discredited."

Liceaga's smile erased all traces of severity and he beamed benignly at Sarmiento. "Exactly so, Doctor! And yet you would be surprised at how members of our profession here in the city cling to the belief that illness is caused by vapors in the air. Vapors! Or who still believe that health is a matter of keeping in balance the four humors. Some of the old physicians still bleed their patients! As if medical science had stopped with Galen."

"Rest assured, Doctor, I do not subscribe to the view that the basic constituents of the human body are black and yellow bile, phlegm, and blood."

"Excellent," he said. "I am sorry to have misjudged you, Doctor." He dropped his voice. "We try to do our work here unfettered by the demands of politics. That is not always possible."

"I have no interest in politics," Sarmiento said.

"I am glad to hear it. Let me tell you about our work." He gestured toward the window with its serene view of the volcanoes. "We live, sir, in one of the loveliest cities on the planet and one of the unhealthiest. One could not have designed a worse location for a metropolis than the Anáhuac Valley," he continued, almost gleefully. "Why, we are not even a true valley but a closed basin walled off by mountains and volcanoes. The city is a sinkhole at the lowest point of the basin surrounded by lakes and constructed on swampy landfill. Water, my boy! There is our curse. There is both too much and too little of it."

Sarmiento found himself smiling, both amused and engrossed by what was clearly a lecture-hall performance for Liceaga's medical students.

"The city sits on the corpse of the lake on which the aborigines built their capital. When the rains come the old lake churns beneath us like distended guts while our three nearest lakes—Texcoco, Chalco, and Xochimilco—pour their poisonous overflow into the canals and flood the city. Meanwhile, our ancient and inadequate sewage system backs up and contaminates our drinking water. The result is disease and death."

"Surely the new drainage system will alleviate some of these problems," Sarmiento offered.

"Yes, but without a modern network of sewers to flush wastes into that system the city will continue to stew in its own filth," Liceaga replied. "Part of my commission is to persuade the government to undertake that project. And of course, there is the human element."

"What is the human element, Doctor?"

"In the last thirty years, the city's population has increased by more than a third, largely through the arrival of country folk looking for work. Unfortunately, most of these immigrants belong to the ignorant, benighted, and stubborn race of Indians. They cling to their filthy habits and customs, living like animals in tenements that have never seen the disinfectant of sunlight or soap. They empty their bowels and bladders in the streets, fill rain gutters with their wastes, and anoint their sick children with holy oil instead of bathing them occasionally. They are the human equivalent of our sewers, and like our sewers, they must be flushed out and cleaned."

"The Indians cannot be rebuilt like the sewer system," Sarmiento ventured.

"No, unfortunately that is not an option." He opened a silver case on his desk and removed a cigarette, fixed it in an ivory holder, and lit it. "I and other public health advocates have long urged the government to encourage European immigration, like the North Americans and the Argentines. But we are not a port city like New York or Buenos Aires and so remain inaccessible to that better class of immigrant. Our immigration is entirely internal and from the dregs of our population. Cigarette?"

"No thank you," he said.

"We cannot rebuild our Indians," Liceaga said, "but we can try to transform them."

"How will you do that?"

Liceaga sprang from his desk and went to the map of the city on the wall. "As you can see from this map, the Board of Public Health has divided the city into eight sectors. In each sector there will be a head sanitation inspector, answerable to me alone. His job will be to investigate the sources and causes of diseases and to develop a plan to eradicate them. I have the government's full backing to use whatever means are necessary to put those plans into effect, including the judicious use of force."

"How can people be forced to be healthy?" Sarmiento wondered.

"They cannot, of course, but they can be quarantined and vaccinated if necessary to prevent the spread of contagious disease. Their houses can be fumigated and their diseased possessions destroyed. Of course, we would not resort to force without first attempting to educate them."

"I am glad to hear that," Sarmiento said.

Liceaga pursed his lips. "I realize some of these measures may sound extreme, Doctor, but we are in a war against disease and in that war, every weapon must be deployed."

"Of course."

"If you will join us in this battle, Doctor, I would like to appoint you to be the sanitation inspector for the second district. Here," he said, pointing to a spot on the map.

Sarmiento went to the wall and examined the map. The second sector was comprised of neighborhoods that stretched from the edge of the Zócalo south and east to the fetid shores of Lake Texcoco. "I am not familiar with these neighborhoods," he said.

"They are some of the city's worst because they border Texcoco," Liceaga explained. "They are subject to frequent epidemics of typhus, to flooding, and they have the highest rate of infant mortality in the entire valley. It will not be an easy commission, Doctor. But you seem young and vigorous and idealistic. The perfect candidate. Will you accept the post?"

Sarmiento did not hesitate. "I would be honored."

The March sun cast its placid warmth in the garden of the Gavláns, where the air smelled of rose geraniums. Beyond the walls came the muffled cries of street vendors singing out their wares: "*Mantequilla! Mantequilla!*" "*Carbón, señores, carbón!*" "*Gorditas de horna caliente!*" "*Caramelos de esperma! Bocadillos de coco!*" The vendors shrilled their wares as if the lard, coal, tortillas, or candies they were selling were the last of their kind. Their cries, as they blended together, were like bird calls, as if the city were a gigantic aviary. In the garden, actual birds sang from the fruit trees and hopped along the ground looking for grubs. Alicia and Sarmiento sat in the mirador transfixed by the warmth of the sun, the cascade of human and bird song, the geraniums' mingled fragrance of cinnamon and attar of rose.

"I am very glad you accepted the director's commission," Alicia said. "I know the parish of San Francisco Tlaloc in your district. The pastor—Padre Cáceres—is a kind man and devoted to his people."

"I do not think I will have reason to acquaint myself with the local clergy," he said. "Nor do I imagine they would welcome a man of science."

"Why do you say that, Miguel?"

"The church has been the enemy of science since the Vatican perse-cuted Galileo for pointing out the earth orbits the sun and not the other way around."

"There is more to the church than the Vatican," she replied. "There are the parish priests, like Padre Cáceres, who try, simply, to apply Christ's message of love in their everyday work. They would welcome your willingness to alleviate the suffering of the poor by whatever methods."

"If all Catholics were like you, my dear, the church would have a better reputation among the educated than it does."

"Oh, Miguel, life is too short, and there is too much to do, for me to concern myself with the church's reputation. I do what I can to be faithful to Christ's admonition to love God and to love my neighbor. Nothing else matters."

"To love God," he repeated. "How you can love a phantom?"

"Because he is not a phantom to me. I perceive him in the scent of the flowers and the sun's warmth on my face. Do you truly not feel at this moment a benign and loving presence?"

"Only yours," he said. "Alicia, I have something to ask you."

She drew a quick breath. "Miguel . . ."

He had gone to his knees and he clasped her hands in his. "Please, Alicia, would you do me the great honor of becoming my wife?"

"Before I can answer your proposal, there is something I must tell you about myself." She caressed his face. "Please, sit. Your knees will wear out before I finish."

He got up and sat beside her. "There is nothing you can say that will dissuade me."

She gave a brief, low laugh. "I hope not! But, that is for you to decide after you hear me." She sighed and began. "Many years ago, in this garden . . ."

When she finished telling him about Anselmo, the loss of her virgin-ity, and her child, Sarmiento sat quietly breathing in and out, staring ahead, and she thought, with a pang of grief, that he could be dissuaded after all.

"Your lost child, my lost child," he murmured, as if to himself. "Do you see the symmetry in our stories, Alicia? Each is half of the other's.

We need each other to complete them. To give each other a different and a happier ending. Will you marry me?"

He fell again to his knees, but this time he buried his head in her lap. He wept. She stroked his sun-warmed, thick hair and wondered, for whom did he weep? For his sin in taking the lives of the girl, Paquita, and their child? Or for the possibility of redemption? Yes, that was it, Alicia thought. He would marry her as an act of restitution. Not out of love. He had told her he admired her, respected her, felt humbled in her presence, but he had never said he loved her. Did she love him? Her hand hesitated and she threaded her fingers though his hair. Not as she had loved Anselmo, in whose body she had wished to be merged, one heart beating, forever and forever. No, what she felt toward Miguel was compassion and the desire to relieve his pain, as one would soothe a child who awakens in the night afraid of the dark.

He raised his head to her, his face streaked with tears. "Please, marry me."

She nodded. "Yes, Miguel," she said. "Gladly. I accept your proposal. I will be your wife."

6

At Sarmiento's final meeting with Liceaga before going out into the field, the director deployed his favorite metaphor: "Remember, Miguel, you are now a soldier in the war against disease! In this struggle you will battle against enemies seen and unseen. I await your victorious return!"

The barrio of San Francisco Tlalco did not resemble a battlefield so much as its aftermath—a dusty quadrant in the southeastern corner of the city strewn with detritus, human and otherwise, and reeking of decay. Sarmiento stood in the *plazuela* in the midday sun in his uniform, a white suit with gold stripes around the sleeves, the insignia of the Board of Public Health embroidered over his heart, and a pith helmet from which a fine mesh net fell over his face to protect him from inhaling toxins and microbes. He carried a white canvas bag filled with specimen jars, medical equipment, and a notebook for writing out citations for violations of the sanitation code. He had no idea of how or where to begin his work.

The *plazuela* was paved with ancient cobblestones, but the surrounding streets were packed earth without sidewalks or any evidence of illumination once the sun set. At the northern edge of the *plazuela* was a small colonial church. To the west, beneath tattered canopies, was a street market. To the east was a combination *pulquería* and pool hall called Templo de Amor; a garish version of Botticelli's *Birth of Venus* had been painted on its facade. Next to it was a grocery store whose shelves appeared to be bare. Beside the grocery store was a nameless *mesón*, one of the city's innumerable flophouses, where three women who were obviously prostitutes crowded the entry. On the south side were heaps of garbage being scavenged by fierce-looking, short-haired curs. Bordering the *plazuela* on the north was a ramshackle line of adobe huts that housed small manufacturers; in one hut he could see two men making chairs, in another, a group of women sitting around a table sewing, and in front of a third, a stack of unpainted pine coffins.

In the center of the *plazuela*, naked children clung to their mothers' dusty skirts as the women dipped clay pots into a stone fountain that seemed as old as the church. The fountain's carvings were covered with green slime or had been eaten away by time. The dusty, warm, foulsmelling air produced a lassitude that seemed to infect the people around him. They moved in a torpor, the men in tattered white trousers, shirts, and sombreros, the women in their dusty calico skirts and rebozos, nearly all of them barefoot. He could feel it himself, a weight that lowered his eyelids and slumped his shoulders. He roused himself from his lethargy and determined to begin his tasks. But where? he thought. He felt like Hercules at the Augean stables commissioned to clean out the accumulated filth of centuries. Unlike Hercules, he did not have a river to divert through the barrio to flush it out. Water, he thought, he could start with water. Squaring his shoulders, he walked briskly toward the fountain.

He pushed aside the women at the well to make room for himself, lowered his head, and sniffed. The water had a faint mineral odor.

"Do you know where this water comes from?" he asked the woman nearest him.

"No, sir," she replied nervously.

"What about the rest of you?" he demanded of the other women. Without meeting his eyes, they grabbed their children and their clay ollas and hurried away.

Frowning, he opened his canvas bag and removed a large spoon. He dipped the spoon into the water and tasted. The water was warm, musty, and, he thought, undoubtedly teeming with potential diseases. He spat it out and reached into his bag for a specimen jar that he filled to examine later in the department's laboratory. As he snapped shut his bag, he saw an Indian standing before the doors of the church watching him.

Sarmiento strode across the square to the street market and made his way among the vendors. Their goods were laid out on blankets in woven baskets, ollas, or in neat pyramidal piles. An old woman with cataracts sold beans and dried corn, another woman sold squash and onions, and a third woman sold *dulces* and *aguas frescas*. A butcher hung slabs of meat from wooden racks. There were stacks of huaraches and sombreros. The fresh fruits and vegetables were dimpled, wrinkled, spotted, and blotched and either underripe or overripe. The vendors' hands were in constant motion, flicking away swarms of fat black flies. The meat had begun to putrefy. Sarmiento took notes, inquired about the source of the food, threatened citations. The vendors responded to his presence with fear or sullen resignation, one or two of them offering him a bribe. When he had finished his inspection of the market, he turned his attention to the three prostitutes.

As he made his way across the square, a group of little boys trooped behind him from a slight distance, ready to scatter if need be. One of the three prostitutes was a baby-faced girl of no more than fifteen. She wore a green skirt over a purple petticoat and an embroidered blouse cut to reveal the tops of her unripened breasts. Her glossy black hair fell freely and she wore her rebozo not in the manner of decent women like a shawl but low on her back to display the roundness of her shoulders. Her clothes were stained and dusty and her bare feet were filthy. The other two women were much older with thin, hard faces and dirty hands. One wore a yellow skirt over a red petticoat, the other a blue skirt over an orange petticoat; both wore the same low-cut blouses. Their hair also fell loosely to bare shoulders, but it was streaked with gray.

Sarmiento's first words to them were "Let me see your *libretas*."

From within their voluminous skirts, the two older women produced their registration books. The woman in the yellow was Esmeralda Chávez, a third-class prostitute. The woman in blue was Carmen Flores, a fourth-class prostitute.

"And yours?" he asked the girl.

She jerked her chin toward the *mesón* and smiled. "Come inside, Señor, and I'll show it to you."

"Your registration, girl."

"Listen," she said. "I have the softest lips and the tightest hole in the city. I'll give you a taste if you'll forget about the book."

"She doesn't have a book," Carmen said. "We'll pay you to look the other way."

"Is she with you?" Sarmiento asked.

"She's my daughter, Reina," Carmen said. "We couldn't afford to register her."

"Then she can't be out here," Sarmiento replied. He grabbed the girl's arm. "Get off the street."

Reina began to scream, "Leave me alone, you motherfucker! I'm not doing anything to you! Virgen de Guadalupe, help me! Mother of God, help me!"

Two of the boys who had been watching the exchange ran into the *pulquería*, and when they emerged, they were followed by several men. Reina continued to scream at Sarmiento, alternating curses with pleas to Guadalupe.

"That's enough!" Sarmiento shouted. "Be quiet, girl, or I'll call the police to take you in."

"Hey, leave our girls alone," one of the men shouted.

Other voices chimed in, "Yeah, leave them alone!" "This is our neighborhood, go back where you belong." "You want a beating? Get out of here!"

Someone shoved him. He turned on his heel and faced the crowd. The men were drunk and angry, and now some of the vendors had joined them and were also screaming at him to get out of the neighborhood. Sarmiento ran through his options, none of them good. His back hit the wall, a fist struck his face, and then, abruptly, the crowd parted. The Indian whom he had seen watching him from the church was clearing a path. Behind him came a black-robed priest.

When they reached Sarmiento, the priest turned to the crowd and said, "*Hijos, Hijas*, what is all this commotion?"

"That guy was molesting Reina," someone shouted.

"Yeah, and he was threatening the vendors!"

The priest turned to Sarmiento. "Sir, I am Padre Pedro Cáceres. Who might you be?"

"I am Doctor Miguel Sarmiento, the district sanitation agent for the Board of Public Health."

The priest turned back to the crowd. "All right, children. I will talk to the gentleman. The rest of you go back to your business." He locked arms with Sarmiento. "Better come with me, Señor Doctor."

Sarmiento grabbed his canvas bag and allowed himself to be taken to the church as the crowd dispersed. When his heart stopped pounding, he thanked the priest, who smiled and said, "They would not have harmed you." The priest was a short man, fair-skinned, with a fringe of white hair around his tonsure and expressive eyes the color of almonds. He spoke, Sarmiento noticed, with the same Galician accent as Sarmiento's own father.

They did not enter the front door of the church but through a wooden gate in a side wall that led into a garden. A stone pathway forked through the flower beds heavy with sweet peas, lilies, geraniums, chrysanthemums, daisies, jasmine, dahlias, the red-leaved *nochebuena*, and golden poppies. In the center of the garden were rose bushes weighed down with the largest roses Sarmiento had ever seen, spilling their delicious fragrance into the air. The contrast between the dusty, impoverished streets and this oasis was so great it stopped Sarmiento in his tracks, and he exclaimed, "This is a paradise."

The priest replied, "Flowers were sacred to the Aztecs, who are the ancestors of my flock. They maintain this garden and I allow them to gather the flowers for their homes and celebrations. The gate is always open and often the people of the neighborhood come and sit to have a moment's rest from their cares and troubles. Come, Doctor, let me offer you some refreshment."

Sarmiento followed him into a small, whitewashed room. There, the silent Indian who had brought the priest to Sarmiento's rescue brought a pitcher of orange juice and two tumblers, poured the juice, and stepped back to stand against the wall. Sarmiento got his first good look at the man. He was short and wiry with the typical thatch of black hair and the black eyes of his race. His coloring was not the usual pinto-bean brown, however, but reddish, and his features were more angular than those of the Indians in the mob that had assaulted Sarmiento. Of particular interest to Sarmiento was the thick, ragged scar across the man's throat.

"Thank you, Ramoncito," the priest said. "You may go."

When he left, Sarmiento asked, "Who cut his throat?"

"Ramoncito is a Yaqui, from the north. He was captured by the soldiers and put into a cattle car with his tribesmen to be taken to the south where the Yaquis are sold into slavery. When the train arrived here, he attempted to escape. A soldier slashed his throat and, thinking he had killed him, pushed him out of the train. But he was still alive. Only his voice was gone."

"His larynx was cut? It's a miracle he survived."

"Yes, and it was a miracle that brought him here. He wandered the streets of the city, half-dead, and as he passed by the church, he smelled the flowers of the garden. Flowers are even more sacred to the Yaquis than to other Indians; their heaven they call the flower world. He followed the scent into the garden and collapsed. My people and I brought him back to health and he has been living here ever since." Cáceres sipped his juice. "But now, Doctor, we should talk about you."

"Yes, well, as I told you, I have been commissioned by the Board of Public Health as the sanitation agent for this district," Sarmiento replied, sounding unbearably officious even to himself.

"What are your duties, Doctor?"

"To report on the health and hygienic conditions of the neighborhoods, to identify potential sources of contagious disease, and to prevent its outbreak or its spread. This neighborhood is a particular concern since there was a typhus outbreak less than two years ago."

"I remember," the priest said. "I buried its victims. I have been here twenty years, Doctor, and there have been many waves of disease. It is a good thing that the city wishes to improve the people's health, but may I make a suggestion to avoid the kind of trouble you found yourself in today?"

Sarmiento bristled but said, "Certainly."

"I am supposing that you do not have many friends among the poor."

Sarmiento was taken aback by the remark, but, as he considered it, he realized the priest was correct. "Go on."

"Poor people are not simply a set of diseases or potential diseases, Señor Doctor. They are human souls. If you wish to change their habits, you must learn what those habits are and why they have acquired them. You must meet the people."

"I met them this morning." Sarmiento replied dryly. "It did not go well."

"You require a guide," the priest said, smiling. "Come back and I will take you around the parish and introduce you to my children."

"Why would you make that offer, I wonder?"

"Because," the priest replied, the smile gone, "you will be back at any rate, with your bag and the authority of the little badge on your breast. Perhaps, after today, you will return with police officers. I only wish to prevent any harm coming to my children."

"I accept your offer, but you must understand I will carry out my duties."

"Of course," Cáceres said. "Would it not be easier to carry them out with the cooperation of the people rather than their resistance?"

"Can you guarantee their cooperation?"

"No, but I can explain to them why it is to their benefit to cooperate with you and then, *ya veremos.*"

"All right," Sarmiento said. "Thank you. What shall I call you, sir? I'm not a believer."

"Not comfortable calling me 'Padre'?" the priest replied, smiling. "Then call me Pedro."

"Only if you call me Miguel," Sarmiento said. He rose. "Thank you for your help, Pedro. By the way, I believe you know my fiancée, Doña Alicia Guadalupe Gavilán?"

"Ah, yes, Doña Alicia," he said with pleasure. "She has graced our church with her presence and brought clothes, food, and toys at Christmas. Please send her my affectionate regards."

"I will. One last thing. You are Galician?"

"From Santiago de Campostela."

"My father was from A Coruña," Sarmiento said.

"Then we are countrymen, Miguel. A good sign for our future friendship."

As destitute as it was, San Francisco Tlalco was not the worst of the barrios in Sarmiento's district. At the edges of San Antonio Abad were massive garbage heaps scavenged by entire families who lived on-site in huts constructed of plywood and tin. In other neighborhoods, slop jars filled with human excrement were left on the roadways, where they were intermittently collected by the leaky night soil carts that rumbled through the dirt streets. One evening at dusk, he saw dozens of men, women, and children walk out of the city into the far distant fields, where, having nowhere else to sleep, they bedded down on the earth. He saw the decaying carcasses of burros, dogs, and cats left in streets where the city's garbage collectors refused to venture; fountains that gushed slime the people used for drinking, cooking, and cleaning; and malnourished infants at the breasts of skeletal mothers.

As he made these rounds, the priest's comment—that he had no friends among the poor—continued to reverberate within him. Liceaga's attitude was that the poor were a boil to be lanced in order to preserve the health of the body politic. The priest was convinced that it was the souls of the poor that made them worthy of respect. Sarmiento had never systematically examined his attitudes toward the poor, but he did so now. He observed, as if recording the results of an experiment, his disgust as well as his pity, his superficial identification with the poor as a matter of their common humanity, and his profounder feeling of superiority to them.

He did not deny the guilt he felt when he saw in the faces of young women Paquita's features, or when the grave eyes of an infant or toddler gazed at him with the eyes of his unborn son. He resurrected memories he had suppressed for years of his lover because Paquita was, after all, the poor person with whom he had been most intimate. He recalled the acrid smell of her armpits and the dirt beneath her fingernails, but also the silk of her skin and the fragrance of her hair, which was like concentrated sunlight. The memories made him sick with shame because he realized what he must have meant to her—a way out of poverty—and what he had brought her instead—her death. Ever the scientist, he tried to set aside his remorse and to use his knowledge of her to illuminate the character of the poor.

In the end, he felt anger. How, he wondered, could the poor persist in habits and customs that experience alone must have taught them were detrimental to their health and moral well-being? Why else, for example, would the men squander their pittances at filthy *pulquerías* while their women and children went ragged and hungry? But then rationality overcame emotion. Every human was born ignorant, he reasoned, and their habits and understanding were shaped by their environment. How could he reasonably expect those born into a cesspool from which there was no escape to acquire the habits of someone like him, born by comparison into a palace? He could not. Therefore, he concluded, his attitude toward the poor should be one of humility and understanding, not superiority or condemnation. He must meet the poor on their own ground. But then another question arose. Was it kind to reveal to those trapped in a cesspool that this was where they were condemned to live out their lives? Here the answer he came to surprised him. Yes, he owed the poor a duty to do whatever he could to improve their conditions because they were México. They were the soil on which the national edifice was constructed. They were *México profundo*—the bowels of the system, and if they were diseased then so, too, was the body of México. Strangely, when he thought of the poor from this perspective what he felt was a bothersome sentiment that, when he described it to Alicia, she told him was "love."

"Come now," he chided her. "My concern for these people is not a matter of personal affection. I don't even know them."

"Yet you wish to alleviate the suffering of these strangers," she replied. "That is love."

"No, it's simply good public policy," he said.

She touched his hand. "Call it what you want, Miguel. It makes me proud of you."

This sentiment toward the poor—whatever it was—was deepened by his encounters with their counterparts, the city's rich. Once his engagement to Alicia was announced, they dined at the houses of each of her three sisters, all of whom lived among the recently constructed mansions along the Paseo de la Reforma. The residences of Alicia's sisters were filled with furniture imported from the Continent gathering dust in immense rooms darkened by heavy velvet drapes and walls covered with dark brocades. Beneath crystal chandeliers, at long dining tables covered with silver bowls and platters, the same French meals were served, differing only in the number of courses, by his hostesses, who had never been out of México. The richness of the food could not disguise its mediocrity—Sarmiento had eaten far better meals in the student cafés of the Left Bank than those that graced the gleaming tables of his future sisters-in-law. The chasm between the rich and the poor increasingly troubled him. Eventually, he could not look upon a Sèvres vase without thinking that, for this fussy little bibelot, a child starved in the streets of San Antonio Abad.

His future brothers-in-law announced they were taking him out for what one of them called, using the English word, a "stag" dinner at the Concordia, yet another French restaurant where the fashionable were duped into eating low-quality food off of high-quality china. In a small, private dining room with red flocked wallpaper, bronze sconces, and starched white tablecloth and napkins, the three men greeted him as he came in from the laboratory of the Board of Public Health, where his analysis of milk sold by a vendor in his district revealed it had been thickened with cow brains obtained from a local slaughterhouse.

"Miguel! We have been waiting for you," exclaimed jovial Don Gonzalo, husband to Alicia's second sister, the melancholy Leticia.

He owned El Palacio de México, a large department store on Calle de los Plateros at which white-gloved doormen opened bronze doors to admit the carriage trade. He had a salesman's bonhomie and the jiggly jowls, ample belly, and roving eye of a libertine.

"Bring him champagne," said Don Saturino, the banker, to the white-coated waiter who had entered the room through the service door. Saturino was married to Alicia's eldest sister, Nilda, in a union that, to Sarmiento's eyes, seemed to be cemented by their mutual loathing. He was a scrawny man who looked as if he had been squeezed out of a tube and as officious as a bank teller confronting a client about an overdraft.

"Or would you rather have some of this fine English whiskey?" asked Don Damian, husband to gay Eulalia, Alicia's third sister.

Damian was not only the most charming of the three but he had made the sincerest attempt to befriend Sarmiento. He was a fair-skinned, exquisitely handsome little man, never a hair or thread of clothing out of place, with shockingly blue eyes. The first time they had met, Sarmiento had been unable to keep from staring. Damian, evidently used to having this effect, took him aside and explained, "My grandfather was Irish, a San Patricio. Do you know who they were?"

"Only vaguely. They fought against the Yankee invaders, didn't they?"

"Yes, exactly so," he said. "They were Irish immigrants impressed into the American army to fight against México when the Americans invaded in 1846. They were treated like animals by their Protestant officers. When they saw that the Mexicans went into battle behind the banner of the Virgin Mary, they decided they were fighting for the wrong God and switched sides. They called themselves the San Patricio Battalion. My blue-eyed grandfather was one of them."

"What happened to them?"

"The Yankees slaughtered them when they could find them. Those who survived, like my grandfather, became Mexican citizens. You see," he said, smiling, "we have something in common, Miguel. You are Spanish; I am Irish. Outsiders, no?" He winked and added, "By the way, I've done business with your uncle." Later, when Sarmiento asked his senator uncle about Damian, Cayetano told him, "Careful with that one. You never know if his schemes are going to pad your billfold or empty it."

"The whiskey, please," Sarmiento replied now.

The waiter went to a side table and poured a tumbler of scotch. Sarmiento tasted it—it was superb—and he tipped his glass in Damian's direction.

"We took the liberty of ordering the meal," Gonzalo said, "beginning with some excellent oysters."

"Oysters, brother," Damian said, with a laugh. "You must be planning a visit to that casita on Calle Trasquillo after dinner to see your little friend La Perla and do some pearl diving."

"Ah, well, brother, a man must maintain his strength for whatever eventuality," Gonzalo replied.

"Are you finished with these vulgarities?" Saturino asked. "Let's get down to business."

"What business is that, Don Saturino?" Sarmiento asked.

"Sit, sit," Damian said. "This is a pleasant meal between brothers, not a police interrogation."

They sat, wine was poured, and the oysters were presented on a bed of ice. Gonzalo's fat hand reached for one. He sniffed it and raised a wicked eyebrow in Damian's direction.

Damian burst out laughing. "You are incorrigible."

At the fish course, Sarmiento said, "Don Saturino, you mentioned business. What did you mean?"

The three men exchanged quick glances. Damian said, "Our wives are very protective of their sister. They asked us to explore your intentions."

"My intention is to marry Alicia," Sarmiento replied.

"Why?" Saturino demanded.

"What our brother means," Gonzalo said smoothly, "is that we cannot help wondering why a man like you, *un macho*, would make such a match?"

Sarmiento waited until their plates had been cleared and the waiter had departed before he replied. "Doña Alicia is the finest woman I have ever met. I am humbled that she would accept me as her husband."

"Your sentiments do you credit," Damian said, "but—"

"She is hideous," Saturino said coldly. "If you are marrying her because you believe she has money, I assure you she does not. It is we who support her and her mother and their ridiculously expensive residence."

"You think I am a 'fortune hunter'?" Sarmiento asked, using the English phrase.

"We like you very much, Miguel," Gonzalo replied quickly. "We would welcome you into the family, but we wanted to make clear to you your lady's financial position."

"Of course no one thinks you are a 'fortune hunter,'" Damian added soothingly. "But Miguel, with all due respect to my virtuous sister-in-law, you must admit it is an odd union."

"Gentlemen, that you cannot conceive of a marriage that is not mercenary is more a reflection of your character than mine. I can support my wife without your help." He stood up from the table. "Indeed, after our marriage you can keep your money and continue to spend it on oysters and whores."

Damian gripped his arm with a restraining hand. "Miguel, please, sit. As unpleasant as this conversation must be for you, you cannot imagine how much worse it would have been had we left it to our wives. I speak for all of us when I say that we apologize for any offense."

"Yes, Miguel, sit and finish your meal," Gonzalo said. "Let us put this behind us and have another glass of champagne. Right, Saturino?"

The banker shrugged. "You understand us. We understand you."

"That wasn't much of a toast," Damian said. He raised his glass. "To our brother Miguel, a long and happy marriage to our beloved sister."

The last plate was cleared. Saturino clamped his homburg on his head and left in a cloud of disapproval and Gonzalo went off to his bordello. Damian asked Sarmiento to stay behind with him for brandy and cigars.

"I hope you have forgiven us, Miguel," Damian said, waving away smoke.

"Did your wives really put you up to this, or was it the banker's idea?"

"The banker's wife," Damian replied. "Nilda is . . . forceful. She threatened a scene if we did not speak to you." He grinned. "And if she is not satisfied by Saturino's account, there may still be one." He inhaled, then slowly exhaled. "Delicious. Ironic, of course, that we should raise questions about your marriage given the states of our own. Nilda and Saturino hate each other and Gonzalo breaks Leticia's heart with his philandering. As for Eulalia and me . . ."

"What, Damian?"

"We see each other so rarely that she once passed me in the street without recognizing me. And yet, of the three of us, she and I have the most agreeable marriage. We accommodate each other."

"You don't love her?"

"You know the English poet Kipling? 'A woman is only a woman, but a good cigar is a smoke.'"

"Why did you marry her?"

He smiled. "Look at me, Miguel, a half-breed son of an army quartermaster with freakish eyes. I rose high enough on my brains, but to get through those gilded doors where the real money is made, I needed a wife like Eulalia from an old criollo family. Saturino and Gonzalo married for the same reason." He pointed at Sarmiento with his cigar. "But you? You are a virile man, the Spanish son of a famous father, a hero, though a little cracked. What do you need with a Gavilán girl, especially one who suffered Alicia's misfortune?"

"I believe I love her," Sarmiento said.

For a moment, the handsome little man looked abashed, but then he raised his glass and said, "Well, then, to love, in all its mysterious forms." When they had drunk he said, "So I hear you are working for Lalo Liceaga at Public Health."

"Yes, you know him?"

"It's my business to know everyone," Damian replied with a laugh. "And to know where they stand in the hierarchy of Don Porfirio's divine order. The butterfly catcher scarcely appears, Miguel. His department is a joke, something for foreign consumption, with no real authority or money. I could get you a real position of power in the government, or, if you want to stay at Public Health, you can have Lalo's job."

"Thank you, Damian, but I am happy where I am."

"My God," the other man exclaimed, "you and Alicia really are made for each other."

"What is your business exactly, Damian?" Sarmiento asked, feeling the effects of the drink.

"I buy and sell," he replied.

"What, like Gonzalo?"

Damian chuckled softly. "No, Miguel, not petticoats and pâtés. My dealings are in information, introductions, access."

"That's all very mysterious," Sarmiento said, pouring himself another brandy.

"Yes, in that way we are completely unalike," Damian said. "There is no mystery to you at all."

He spoke pleasantly enough, but Sarmiento felt the sting of judgment in his words.

On a Sunday afternoon, he escorted Alicia on the pathways beneath the leafy bowers of the Alameda. She wore a lavender lace dress and an enormous hat that shaded her powdered face. She smelled of rose and citron.

"May we sit for a moment, Miguel?" she asked. "I wish to discuss the wedding."

"Of course," he said. He led her to a bench, wiped it with his handkerchief, and they sat.

"Miguel, I do not require an elaborate wedding, but I must be married in the church."

He had anticipated this conversation. "As you know, the Ley Juárez made marriage a strictly civil contract. The church ceremony adds nothing."

"Without the sacrament, I would not consider myself married at all."

Sarmiento shared his father's atheism, but without his father's rancor. While his father had railed against the church, to Sarmiento, the Christian sky-king, the virgin impregnated by the air, and the man who came back from the dead were stories so manifestly absurd they did not merit much more than a raised eyebrow and a shrug at human credulity. Nonetheless, if Alicia required him to go through the religious ceremony, he was prepared to do so as a purely anthropological experience, like Doctor Livingston living among the Hottentots.

"Then, of course, my dear, we will marry in a church. There is just one thing I ask. Let me choose the priest."

She looked at him curiously. "I am surprised you number any priests among your friends."

"Only Pedro Cáceres at San Francisco Tlalco. He has been taking me around to the neighborhood and helping me in my work. I have come to admire him greatly. I would like him to marry us."

"In his church?"

"Yes, of course."

"Do you know how much it will annoy my sisters to have to come to that barrio? To venture south of the Zócalo for any reason?"

"I'm sorry, Alicia, but that is my condition for marrying in a church."

She laughed. "No, no, Miguel, you misunderstand me. I'm not upset. I'm delighted!"

"Delighted to be married at San Francisco Tlalco, or delighted that it will annoy your sisters?"

"Both!" she said.

She had never shown even the faintest malice toward anyone and he found it so unexpected and amusing that he spontaneously kissed her. It was their first kiss.

The priest was less understanding than Sarmiento had hoped. They had become friends and Sarmiento had learned from him a great deal about the Indians, not simply their habits, but their history and their beliefs. He had been surprised by much of what Cáceres had taught him, for in the official texts of his childhood, the history of México began with the conquest in 1519 and was a chronicle of Spanish kings and viceroys and the spread of Catholicism and European civilization. In that version of his country's history, the Indians were ancillary—primitives to be converted or subdued. The Aztecs, whose monuments still dotted the city, could not be ignored entirely. Instead, they were held up as the consummate example of Indian barbarism: human sacrificers, cannibals, demons.

Cáceres taught him there was a purpose behind even the seemingly inexplicable practice of human sacrifice. "The Mexica," he told Sarmiento, using the name Aztecs called themselves, "no less than we Christians believed that man was created in the image of God, but their gods made man of dust and their own blood. When they sacrificed humans, in their minds they were only returning to the gods the blood that belonged to them."

"Surely you're not saying you approve?"

The priest shook his head. "To understand is not to approve, Miguel. I am merely pointing out that what we condemn as evidence of the depravity of the Mexica had its reason and its purpose. It was part of a religious ritual as meaningful to them as the Eucharist is to us."

"To you, you mean," Sarmiento said. "But you're talking ancient history, Pedro. There is no more human sacrifice."

"God be praised for that," Cáceres said. "But it's not ancient history, Miguel. When our Spanish ancestors justified the conquest of the Mexica because of their so-called moral degeneracy, they were creating a justification for the abuse of the descendants of the Mexica that continues to this very day. Think of it, Miguel. Do you believe in your heart that the Indian you see walking down the street is your moral equal?"

After an uncomfortable pause, Sarmiento murmured, "Not if I am being completely truthful. No."

"And you are a good man with enough grace to be ashamed of his prejudices. Imagine the actions of those who are not."

He rattled around the room for a newspaper and spread it out on the table between them. On the front page was a drawing of a half-dozen Indians hanging from a gallows. Beneath it, the caption explained the men were Yaquis who had been caught raiding a hacienda in the northern state of Sonora.

"You see," Cáceres said. "We still exterminate the Indians."

"According to this story, these men were the aggressors," Sarmiento pointed out.

Cáceres shook his head. "We are the aggressors. The Yaquis are only attempting to defend their ancestral homeland against Don Porfirio's army. It is no different than when the Mexica resisted Cortés."

"Would you have had the Mexica prevail?" Sarmiento asked, genuinely curious.

"What's done is done," Cáceres replied. "My concern is not with the Indians who were killed three hundred and eighty years ago, but with those who are dying today."

But you are a nonbeliever," Cáceres sputtered when Sarmiento proposed that the priest marry Alicia and him.

"What does that matter? My wife believes."

They had been walking through the neighborhood to a tenement where a child was ill with symptoms that sounded ominously to Sarmiento like typhus.

"You can't just mumble the words of the sacrament as if they were lines from a play, Miguel. That would be an affront to the Lord."

"How could your God be affronted that I am doing something out of love for Alicia? God is love, isn't that what your Saint John says?"

"The devil quotes scripture," the priest grumbled. They walked in silence for a moment. "I will do it, on one condition."

"Name it."

"You must establish a clinic at the church for my children. For one year after your wedding, you will come regularly and tend to their medical needs."

"Agreed," Sarmiento said. They had arrived at the tenement. "Now, let's hope I won't be treating them for typhus."

From the shaded corridor where she embroidered a tiny smock for Reina's baby, Alicia half listened to the murmured conversation between her husband and a man with a large goiter on his neck. Reina, sitting beside her, clumsily attempted to imitate Alicia's needlework. She pricked herself and cried out, "Fuck!" She quickly added, "Forgive me, Doña. My fingers are so clumsy, not quick like yours."

Alicia took the cloth from the girl and examined it. "This is good work, Reina. When I first began to learn to chain stitch I stuck my fingers all the time. I can't tell you how much cloth I ruined by bleeding on it. It's simply a matter of practice and patience."

She returned the cloth to the girl, who said, "Sometimes I have patience and sometimes I want to jump out of my skin." She touched the little swell in her stomach. "Mamá says that's the baby."

"I'm sure your mother is right."

"You have no children, Doña?"

"No, my dear."

"But you are so old," the girl said. "I thought you would have many sons and daughters."

Alicia smiled. In the months that she had been coming to San Francisco Tlalco she had learned it was a sign of acceptance when the people of the neighborhood dispensed with extraneous gentility and spoke their minds. And to the girl, who was no more than fifteen, she realized she must seem ancient.

"I have just married," Alicia said. "My husband and I have not yet had time to have children."

The girl took up her sewing and said, "The doctor is much nicer now that he is married to you."

Alicia lifted her head from her own sewing and looked down the corridor into the room Miguel used as his clinic. His patient stood motionlessly as Miguel felt his neck. Palpitation, she thought, using the term he had taught her. "Diagnosis is an art, Alicia," he had explained, "and the doctor has four tools: inspection, palpitation, percussion, and auscultation. That is, we look, feel, thump, and listen." He had shaken his head in disbelief when she told him that her own childhood doctor, Don Ignacio, had never laid a finger on her except to briefly take her pulse.

"Then how did he diagnose and treat you?"

"My mother told him where my pain was and he gave her medicine for me. If I was truly ill, he bled me."

He shook his head. "That's not medicine. It's witchcraft."

He was distressed to discover that the inhabitants of San Francisco Tlalco shared Don Ignacio's ideas of professional propriety. He returned home from his first clinics with stories of the man who assaulted him when he thumped his chest to listen to his lungs, the woman who ran off at the sight of his stethoscope thinking it was made of snakes, and the little boy who clamped his teeth on the thermometer and ended up with a mouthful of mercury that nearly poisoned him. He complained that many of his patients spoke Nahuatl and that Padre Cáceres was too busy to translate for him. "Those people are impossible!" he concluded.

"Let me come with you," she said. "I speak some Nahuatl and I know many of the people in the parish, and if you have your wife with you they may be less inclined to assault you."

He resisted, but when he came home with a blackened eye given to him by the husband of a pregnant woman after he had touched her belly, he agreed.

"However," he said, "I insist on teaching you some basic principles of anatomy and physiology so that you will understand what I am doing." He smiled. "I need to knock Don Nacho out of your head."

Her classroom was the room in their suite at the palace that he had converted into his office and laboratory, much to her mother's horror. Miguel had reluctantly acceded to La Niña's insistence that they live with her after their marriage. "I am an old woman," she said. "You can't leave me to die alone in this big house." But after he moved his medical equipment into their apartment, she complained, "This is a family residence, not a tradesman's place of business." Only when he threatened to take Alicia and move did La Niña withdraw her objection.

For Alicia, however, the hours they spent in his office, where he instructed her in the body and its workings, were among the happiest of her marriage. He was a patient and kind teacher and she discovered in herself a thirst for knowledge. More than that, though, an intimacy arose between them that dispelled the awkwardness of having to play the roles of husband and wife and allowed them to resume their friendship, which had always been the strongest bond between them. Using his charts and models, he taught her the structure and parts of the body from skin to cells, explained the digestive and circulatory systems, and showed her a drop of his own blood beneath the microscope. He explained to her the causes and symptoms of various diseases and their treatments.

"Was this taught to you in the same way you teach me?" she asked.

"Ah, well, no," he said. "I attended many hours of lectures, of course, but the deeper understanding of disease came from the clinicals where we learned to match symptoms to causes by observing sickness in our patients and then studying their bodies after they died."

"You opened the bodies of the dead?" she asked, shocked.

He nodded. "We examined organs and tissues for disease. Only in that way could we confirm that our diagnoses were correct." Her distress must have been evident because he added, "Alicia, this is how medicine must proceed for new knowledge to arise."

She did not reply but thought that Miguel was virtually a different species than white-whiskered Don Ignacio.

One afternoon, as they examined a beautiful papier-mâché model of the brain, and he explained how its folds and convolutions contained the whole of human personality, she asked, "But in which part does the soul reside?"

"My dear," he said. "You know my views on that subject. Does this study of the body in all of its gross materiality shake your faith at all?"

She shook her head. "Not at all, Miguel! The wonders of the body you have shown me only deepen my belief because who could have made these ingenious things but God?"

A little boy of four or five in a calico shirt and droopy drawers ran up to Alicia and said, "*Feita*, the doctor wants you."

"Luis!" Reina scolded. "You must call her Doña Alicia."

"It's all right, Reina," she said. "He only repeats in innocence what others say about me."

"I have never called you *la fea*," Reina said. "To me you are beautiful."

Alicia smiled and patted the girl's head as she rose to go to her husband. She knew the people in the parish called her *la fea cariñosa*—the kind but ugly woman—just as they called Miguel *el guapo doctor*—the handsome doctor. But while his nickname was simply descriptive, hers, she understood, was affectionate and, softened by the diminutive *feita*, intended as an endearment, and she held it as such.

Miguel had carefully chosen the room he used as his clinic from all the other empty rooms that lined the garden and had been storerooms and priestly cells when the church was in its prime. This room, he explained to her, was sheltered from the wind and dust and had the largest window to let in the light. He had personally supervised its cleaning and even now the room smelled of carbolic acid, which, he had told Alicia, killed the tiny microbes that were invisible to the eye and the carriers of all disease. Try as she might, she could not help but picture these microbes as *diabolitos*—tiny demons—but she refrained from mentioning this to Miguel.

He was with a young girl—fifteen or sixteen, like Reina—who held in her arms a lace-wrapped bundle.

"Miguel, you wanted me?" she asked.

"The girl only speaks Nahuatl. Will you ask her about the baby?"

Alicia turned to the girl and asked, "What happened to your child, dear?" and then translated her answer. "She says her baby stopped crying two days ago. She doesn't know what's wrong. She begs for your help."

"Let me see the child," he said, and she translated his response.

She watched as the girl carefully unwrapped the lace coverings—which she realized were baptismal garments—to reveal the wizened, lifeless features of an infant. The girl fell to her knees and lifted the child above her head, presented Miguel with a tiny corpse—the skin of its fingers gray beneath delicate fingernails—and murmured, "Give my baby breath."

Alicia caught her gasp before it could escape her lips and glanced at Miguel, whose face showed as much distress as he allowed himself with a patient.

"Please tell her to stand up," he said.

Alicia addressed the girl gently and she rose from her knees. Miguel lowered his head and put his ear to the infant's face and then took its pulse.

"It's dead," he replied. "Tell her to bury it."

Alicia translated his response with soft words of sorrow and sympathy. Silently, the girl rewrapped the corpse in lace and slipped out of the room.

"I was harsh. I'm sorry," he said when she had left.

"It was shocking."

"Shock is a luxury of laymen," he said. "Doctors are not permitted to be shocked, but it was because it was an infant and it called to mind . . ." He looked at her. "Well, you know what it called to my mind."

"Yes," she said. "I know. I will go into the church and pray for her and her baby. Won't you come and sit with me and rest?"

He shook his head. "I have to find Cáceres. There's been an outbreak of smallpox in La Bolsa, and we are going out to try to persuade the local people to be vaccinated against the disease. It hasn't been easy. Their witchdoctors have been telling them that I want to infect them with poison."

She knew that what he called witchdoctors were the local *curanderos* who doctored with herbs and magic and who resented his presence because he charged nothing for his services.

"I could come," she said. "I could talk to the people."

"No, the priest and I have our little show where I inject him with saline to show that no harm will come from the vaccine. Poor Cáceres is beginning to look like a pincushion." He added abruptly, as if startled by the thought, "You could have been vaccinated. Why weren't you?"

"Oh, my parents would never have allowed Don Ignacio to take the liberty of injecting anything into my body," she said. "It was not the custom."

"Custom is the enemy of progress," he said. "Especially in our poor benighted México. When you pray for that child, pray also for an end to the ignorance that keeps our people enslaved to custom."

"Miguel, what was wrong with the man with the lump on his throat?"

"It's a problem with his thyroid," he replied. "It's a butterfly-shaped organ at the base of your throat. It makes a secretion, a kind of fluid called a hormone that helps control the body's metabolism, the rate that we burn the calories we extract from our food, like coal for a furnace. Sometimes the thyroid becomes diseased and makes too much of the hormone or not enough and so there is too much heat or not enough. I do not know from which this man suffers, but the goiter is interfering with his sleep and breathing and ability to swallow. I will have to cut it out."

"Is that dangerous?"

"No, I think I can perform the surgery here. But I may need your help."

She paled at the thought of it. She had helped him when he had had to extract a rotten tooth even though the sight of blood made her dizzy and the patient's pain was hard to bear, but then she observed how much better the patient felt afterward. Cutting into the flesh was something different, though.

"Will there be much blood?"

He grinned at her. "Not if I do it correctly. I must go. Cáceres and I will be on foot so you take the carriage home. Leave before dusk. These streets are not safe for you after the sun sets." He kissed her cheek. "Good-bye, my dear."

The interior of the church of San Francisco Tlalco was suffused with the mellow glow of Argand lamps and votive candles and scented with copal, the ancient incense of the Aztecs. She never entered it without being aware, more than in any other church, that its form was that of a ship, the nave like a keel surrounded by thick walls and a vaulted roof.

For here, she felt, was a refuge from the roiling waves of the city that lay just beyond the church's heavy wooden doors. Padre Cáceres had told her the church was founded by Franciscans when the parish was still a village outside the city limits. Over the centuries, the church had ministered to the descendants of those first converts and they had cared for it lovingly. Generations of neighborhood artisans had kept fresh the floral pattern of intertwining roses and marigolds painted on the humble plaster walls—the roses for Mary and the marigolds for Tonatzin, the mother goddess of the Aztecs. When Padre Cáceres had explained this to her, she asked whether it was not heretical to permit the symbols of the pagan religion to persist in a Christian church. He replied, "Tonatzin was a gentle goddess who did not demand human sacrifice but loved the humble common people. Mary has taken many forms, daughter, and who is to say that she did not come to the Indians in the form of Tonatzin even before her son arrived on these shores?"

Above the altar was a gilded *retablo* with five niches that held plaster statues of the patrons of the church. In the center was Jesus, not agonized on the cross but attired in simple linen robes with his arms outstretched to embrace his people. Above him, in the niches to the right and the left were two representations of his mother: Mary as La Dolorosa, the Mother of Sorrows, and Mary as the Virgin of Guadalupe. In the two niches beneath Jesus were Saint Francis and Saint Clare.

Alicia loved that three of the five figures were female. It seemed to her that their femininity permeated the manner of worship in the church. The harsh emphasis on sinfulness that she heard elsewhere in the city's churches was absent in Padre Cáceres's homilies. Instead, he spoke of fallibility and forgiveness and the passionate, unchanging and ever-present love of Jesus for his people whatever they did and in whatever circumstances they found themselves. At the end of each Mass, before the final blessing, he always reminded them that while Moses had given the Hebrews ten commandments, Jesus had promulgated only two: "Love God with all your heart and all your soul and all your strength and with all your mind, and love your neighbor as you love yourself. Children, that is the whole of the Gospel."

As she had predicted to Miguel, Alicia's sisters were horrified that she had chosen to marry in a church in the slums of the city. Her mother, surprisingly, accepted her decision with equanimity. "San Francisco Tlalco is a venerable church," La Niña said, overriding Nilda's fierce protests. "Your ancestors undoubtedly contributed money toward its construction. Of course your sister should marry there if she likes."

"Well, I for one will not risk being robbed in the streets or infested with lice in the church," Nilda said. "I will not come."

La Niña fixed her with a basilisk look and said coldly, "You will come. You will all come."

On the evening of the wedding, the small church was filled with *la gente de sangre*, the bluebloods, who knelt in their French silks and English wools on the worn tiles that usually received the scabby knees of the poor. Outside, a line of police officers formed a cordon between the gleaming carriages of the guests and gawkers from the barrio who had never seen such a display of polished wood and beribboned horses. Inside, waiting for the ceremony to begin, Alicia agonized over her decision to wear white. Her mother had insisted, rejecting her scruples.

"Mother, how can I appear before the altar of the Lord in the white of virginity when he knows I am not a virgin?"

La Niña fanned herself with a mother-of-pearl fan she had inherited from her mother and replied, "Phew! God is a gentleman. He will keep your secret."

"But Miguel also knows."

"Miguel is even more of a gentleman than God. Of course you will be wed in white. We will not have a scandal." She snapped shut the fan. "Besides, Daughter, do you really believe you are the first lady to miraculously recover her virginity on her wedding day? At least there won't be men in the church laughing into their hands as you walk down the aisle."

The gown she had chosen as her wedding dress was ivory silk damask with narrow sleeves and a high neck. The hem and sleeves were trimmed in lace that matched the lace jabot. She planned to wear a bustle but not a train. Her mantilla was to be fixed to her hair with a crown of white roses from the palace's garden.

Her mother and her sisters Eulalia and Leticia went with her to her fitting. When Eulalia saw the dress, she laughed. "Alicia, dearest, are you marrying Jesus? It's so modest. You have a lovely neck and shoulders and breasts. Why do you hide them under all this fabric?"

"They are for my husband to see, not the world."

Leticia said, "The dress is lovely, but what jewels will you wear with it?"

"None," Alicia replied. "It isn't proper to make a show of wealth in that humble church."

"Nonsense," said La Niña. "You will wear the diamond necklace and bracelets, and must you wear a crown of flowers when we have perfectly good tiaras gathering dust in the vaults of Saturino's bank?"

"Mother's right," Leticia said. "You are no ordinary woman, Alicia. Why pretend to be?"

"Because I want to be," she said. "An ordinary woman with a husband and children."

"Well, darling," Eulalia said, "on the stroke of midnight after your wedding you can become La Cenicienta again, but until then you must be the princess in the glass slippers. Your wicked sisters insist."

Alicia laughed. "Very well, wicked sisters, I give up. You may dress me as if I were a doll, but I draw the line at glass slippers."

Eulalia's French dressmaker replaced the long sleeves with short puffed ones, and dropped the neckline, which she bordered with white rosettes adorned with pearls. She replaced Alicia's short lace mantilla with a floor-length one made of silk tulle. It was in this gown and veil, ablaze with diamonds and a pearl-encrusted tiara of yellow gold that had belonged to her great-grandmother, that she married Miguel. At the dinner afterward at the Casino Español, he murmured, "You look like a queen, Alicia. I feel completely unworthy of you."

"This was my sisters' and my mother's doing," she said. "At midnight I revert to La Cenicienta."

"You have never been La Cenicienta," he replied and kissed her.

It was at that point, she remembered, that his cousin Jorge Luis had risen drunkenly from his seat at the table, knocking over his chair, and insisted on declaiming a poem he had written for the bride and groom. She recalled it was filled with images of swans and figures from Greek mythology, rambling and pointless, and that at the end he compared himself—the poet—to Narcissus who fell in love with his own image and wasted away waiting for his love to be reciprocated. He began to sob. Miguel excused himself and led him away. When he returned, she asked, "Is your cousin going to be all right?"

"He's drunk. I put him to sleep in the library. He'll be fine. I apologize for this disruption. He fancies himself a poet, but, as you heard, his aspirations are perhaps greater than his ability."

"I'm sure he meant well," she said.

At the end of the night, they returned to the palace, to their apartment, which was now also furnished with Miguel's few possessions. A maid undressed her and she put on the chiffon negligee that was part of her trousseau. She went into the bedroom, where the servants had lit lamps and candles and filled vases with roses. Miguel was already in the big four-poster canopy bed. He reposed on a pile of pillows. The lamplight shone on his naked chest.

"Are you nervous?" he asked.

"Yes," she said, approaching him. "For many reasons."

He kissed her hand. "I think I know all of them and I assure you, my dear, I will not fail to treasure you in every way. Come to bed."

She went around the room, extinguishing lights, until the darkness was impermeable. She slipped off her gown and into bed, where the shock of his body—naked, muscled, hairy, burning—made her gasp. His hands stroked her body, and she was glad that the disease that had pitted her face had concentrated its venom there. He leaned in to kiss her breasts, touch her nipples with the tip of his tongue as his fingers delicately opened her.

"Your body is lovely," he murmured.

Encouraged, she touched him, running her hand across the plated muscle of his chest and stomach with its ridges and contours, down through the rough hairs until she held his rod in her hand, hard and heavy and hot.

"Ah," he said. "Ah. Yes, take it in your hand and stroke it, up and down, like this."

He folded his big hand around hers and he moved it up and down. She felt a drop of fluid drip from the head of his rod.

"And now you," he said. He maneuvered them so that his head was between her legs and she could feel his breath as his tongue touched the tip of her opening and then plunged inside. Her body trilled with pleasure.

"What . . . what is that?" she managed to murmur.

"I love this taste," he said. "This taste of woman. Does it please you, Alicia?"

"Oh, yes, Miguel."

After a few minutes of his tongue moving inside of her, she felt herself flooded with sensations that were like an amalgamation of every good thing she had ever touched, tasted, or smelled, but more intense because its source was not outside of her, but within. And in the midst of it, suffused with bliss, she saw Anselmo's face above hers, his features tightened with the joy of release. But it was Miguel's body she felt pressing against her, the hair of his chest wiry against her breasts.

He entered her where she was still damp with his saliva and her own wetness. He pushed harder until he was completely encased in her flesh and he groaned with pleasure. His mouth grazed her nipples until they were hard buds that leaked a physical delight that coursed through her body, blunting the pain she felt from his penetrations. As he began to move, the pain subsided. His strokes became deeper and faster; she felt the sweat pour from his chest, and then he reared up and with a shudder he thrust one final time, pressed his lips together, and released his seed with an explosive breath.

And then it was over. He tumbled to her side, his breath hard and rapid.

She lay on her side and he pressed against her. "Thank you," he murmured.

Afterward, long after he was asleep, she lay awake. She could not deny her body's responsiveness to his touch, but this was different than it had been with Anselmo. Theirs had been a playful, mutual exploration of each other's body: sweet, funny kisses; licks and nibbles; and only then the shattering pleasure of release. By contrast, Miguel had performed upon her, as if she were a passive instrument for his need. He had not been unkind or inattentive. Indeed, he had been more attentive than she, with her scarred face, had a right to expect. But it had felt as if it were—she searched for the word—a duty, an obligation on his part. He had not once kissed her face during the act, nor even touched it. Was this, then, the only way he could bear the intimacy of the marriage bed? Tears streamed from her eyes, and she felt an old pang of self-pity for her condition that she thought she had rid herself of long ago. This once, she thought, she would let the tears flow, the sorrow well in her heart, but never again. For she was married, and to a good man, and if his revulsion was the price she must pay for her good fortune, she must humble herself and pay it.

A few nights later, she was awakened by the porter Andres tapping at the door and calling her name. She rose in the darkness, dressed in her robe, and greeted him at the door. The porter stood with a lamp in his hand and a worried expression on his face.

"Doña, the doctor's cousin is here and he demands to see him."

"Jorge Luis?" she said. "Where is he?"

"In the *sala*," he said.

"Take me to him."

She followed the porter into the sitting room, where she found Jorge Luis, disheveled and soaked with sweat, pacing the Persian carpet, his cigarette dropping ash and embers into it. He stopped short when he saw her, but his body trembled.

"Jorge Luis, what has happened?" she asked.

"I need to see Miguel, right away, please."

"But—"

"Please," he shrieked. "I need my cousin. Now."

"Of course," she said.

She took the lamp from the porter, dismissed him, and walked back to the bedroom, where she awakened Miguel and told him what had happened.

"I will see to him," Miguel said, dressing. "Go back to sleep."

She lay awake anxiously and had only just fallen asleep when she felt Miguel gently shaking her shoulder and saying her name.

"Miguel?"

"Is there money in the house?"

She sat up. "Money? Yes, of course, the household accounts. Why?"

"I need it," he said. "And whatever other money there is. Can you gather it up for me quickly?"

"For Jorge Luis?"

"He must leave the city tonight. I will tell you everything later. But now, we have to act quickly."

Alicia woke the majordomo and had him give her all the money in the strongbox. She brought the money to the *sala*, where the two men sat close together, heads bent in feverish but quiet conversation.

"This is everything," she said.

Miguel took the heavy purse, thanked her, and told her to go back to their room. Jorge Luis did not look up at her. She stepped outside the room but lingered just beyond the doorway and listened.

"Send a telegram when you have reached Veracruz to let me know you have arrived safely," Miguel said. "Book passage on the first ship out. Send word when you arrive at Le Havre. I will wire you funds. Don't look so frightened, Jorge Luis. You always wanted to see Paris. Now you will."

The younger man began to sob. "I've ruined my life," he said. "Disgraced my family. If I had honor left I would shoot myself, but I am too much a coward even for that."

"Don't be a fool," he said. "Go now and hurry."

"If the police come here . . ."

"I will take care of that. Go."

She hurried down the hall back into their bedroom. A few minutes later, Miguel entered the room, undressed, and got into their bed.

"If the police come tomorrow," he said, "and ask if my cousin was here, you will tell them no. Please make sure any servant who saw him provides the police with the same answer."

"Of course," she said. "Can you tell me what has happened?"

He was quiet for a moment. "My dear, what Jorge Luis has done is not fit for your ears."

"Did he kill someone?"

"No," Miguel said. "He is not a murderer. It is something worse."

"Worse than murder? But—"

At that moment, Miguel kissed her with a passion that shocked her out of her questions. He undressed her, and for the first time while he made love to her, he stroked and kissed her face. He locked his eyes on her eyes and with her name on his lips, he emptied himself into her. She later calculated that this was the night José had been conceived.

The police arrived the following afternoon. Not the street officers with their little capes and billy clubs who patrolled the intersections from doorways of *pulquerías* but two plain-clothed, hard-faced officers of *la seguridad*, Don Porfirio's private police. They interrogated her and Miguel together and then dismissed her. As she had the previous night, she listened from just outside the room. Their tone, respectful while she was in the room, now became menacing.

"Do you know why we are looking for your cousin?"

"Obviously I do not," Miguel replied.

"Your cousin is a sodomite. Did you know that?"

"That's absurd," Miguel said. "He is a perfectly normal man."

"Normal? We broke up a little party last night that your cousin was attending with his friends. All men, but half of them were dressed up like women. There were things going on in the bedrooms that would make you puke."

"I know nothing about this," Miguel said.

"You understand, Sarmiento, that if you lie to us you become an accomplice in his infamy?" one of them said.

"An accomplice to sodomy," the second added. "The crime against nature."

"Gentlemen," Miguel replied, "I know very little of that practice, but I am certain that one cannot be an accomplice without also being a participant, and I can assure you I was not."

"Don't be a smart-ass," the first officer snapped. "This is a matter of national security. If we find out you're protecting your cousin, no one's going to be able to help you, not the old lady who lives here or your uncle."

"Since when is sodomy a matter of national security?"

She heard the floor creak as they pushed back their chairs. "We're going to continue with our investigation," one of them said. "If it brings us back to you, our next conversation will be in Belem."

She hid in an alcove until they were gone and then went to Miguel and again asked him what Jorge Luis had done. He said, "The less you know the better. We will not speak of this again."

But she could not let it go. When she next saw Padre Cáceres, she asked him to confess her. After she confessed to having listened in on her husband's private conversations, she asked, "Padre, what is sodomy?"

She could feel his shock from behind the grille of the confessional.

"Why do you ask, Doña?"

"It was the subject of the conversation between my husband and . . . those to whom he was speaking. They told him that someone he knows is a 'sodomite.' I recalled the story of Sodom in scripture and I reread it, but I do not understand the meaning of the word when applied to my husband's . . . acquaintance."

"This is not a subject fit for the ears of a Christian woman."

"Padre, if it is in the Bible, then it is a subject for Christian women, if for no other reason than that I may take precautions to avoid whatever this terrible vice is."

"Women are physically incapable of this vice," he said.

"You will not tell me what it is."

"I will not," he said sternly. "I will, however, admonish you not to speak of this again to anyone as part of your penance for violating your husband's privacy. Do you understand me, Daughter?"

"Yes, Padre," she said.

Later, she again read the story of Lot and her eye fell on the phrase used by the men of Sodom who demanded that Lot bring forth the angels he was sheltering in his house "so that we may know them," and Lot's offer of his two virgin daughters to the crowd in response. She remembered the police officer's description of the party—all men, but half dressed as women—and his allusion to sickening acts in the bedrooms. From these fragments, she pieced together to her satisfaction an understanding of the crime Jorge Luis had committed. In some way he had either used another man as men use women or had allowed himself to be used in that manner. Her first response was not disgust so much as curiosity. How could this be? Surreptitiously, she consulted Miguel's anatomy texts examining the male body for some clue as to how two men might commit acts on each other that were similar to acts between a man and a woman. Eventually, however, she discovered her answer not in Miguel's texts but in her own forgotten experience. For she remembered now that the explorations that she and Anselmo had undertaken of each other's bodies went far beyond the bounds of propriety.

They were children, wild and curious and fearless and determined to give each other joy. She had discovered that nothing made him whimper with pleasure as much as when she took his private parts into her mouth. She remembered, too, that in his anxiety to preserve her virginity he had tried to penetrate her—and here, her face went beet-red with the memory—through her anus, but the pain was so great she had quickly demanded that he stop. Could these experimental gropings of impassioned children be the "crime against nature" that Jorge Luis had committed and for which he had had to leave México? It was too absurd and yet she could reach no other conclusion. The thought of two men engaged in these acts was repellent. Certainly God had not intended for men to abuse their bodies in that manner any more than he had intended them to become drunkards or gluttons. Nonetheless, she could not imagine any hierarchy of sin in which such acts could be deemed worse than murder. She was also surprised that her rationalist, non-believing husband would find common cause with a priest about the gravity of this indiscretion. She decided their extreme repulsion must arise from some deeper cause that was peculiarly male and, therefore, quite outside her understanding. Jorge Luis's banishment seemed to her an injustice and she pitied him his fate and prayed for his well-being and eventual safe return. As the days passed, and her pregnancy began to show, the incident faded.

That night, after Jorge Luis had gone, and after he had made love to his wife, Sarmiento lay awake for a long time, attempting to make sense of the night's events and worrying about their consequences. He realized that his sudden and fierce desire for Alicia had been, in part, a reaction to the repulsion he had felt at Jorge Luis's revelations about his own sexual irregularity. The thought of Jorge Luis's squalid practices, however, was not the cause of the anxiety that kept him awake. What kept him awake was the story his cousin had told him—that the police had raided a gathering of *pedes*—Sarmiento used the French word because he could think of no Spanish equivalent—at which one of the guests was Don Ignacio de la Torre, son-in-law of the president of the Republic. Jorge Luis had escaped by climbing out of a window and fleeing across the roofs of the city, but, he confessed, sobbing, he was well known in that circle and it was simply a matter of time before the police forced his name out of one of the apprehended men.

"The police will do whatever they have to do to protect Nacho de la Torre," he told Sarmiento. "They will throw the rest of us in prison or even kill us."

"Listen, Jorge Luis, when I was a student in Paris I was taken to *pede* clubs simply as an anthropological experience. Could de la Torre's visit not be excused in the same way?"

"To see the creatures in the zoo, you mean?" Jorge Luis said bitterly. "No, Miguel. He was no tourist. Don Nacho is a habitué of our little sect. He has had many lovers among us."

Sarmiento swallowed his distaste. "Your father is a senator. Surely that gives you some protection."

"My father's position is a sinecure. He has no power to interfere with police investigations and once this gets out, he will be ruined. I have to leave México, Miguel. Now. Tonight. Will you help me?"

He hesitated, but only for an instant. "Yes, of course," he said and they had concocted a plan.

In the days that followed, Sarmiento scanned the newspapers looking for reports about the raid, but found nothing. However, two weeks after the event, it was announced that Senator Cayetano Sarmiento had decided to leave public life, resigning his position in the Senate and retiring to his estate in Cuernavaca. Sarmiento went to see his uncle, who explained blandly that he had decided to spend his remaining years in the country on the advice of his physician. He said about his eldest son only that Jorge Luis had fulfilled his lifelong desire to travel in Europe and would be gone for an indefinite period. "But you probably already know that, Miguel."

"No, Uncle, I have had no news of Jorge Luis for some time. That is why I came to see you."

"Ah," the old man replied, clearly disbelieving him. "Well, now you are informed."

After a while, the vacuum of information was as anxiety-provoking to Sarmiento as the event itself. Then, at a family dinner, his brother-in-law Damian pulled him aside and said, "I hear your cousin is on a grand tour of Europe. If I were he, I would consider remaining there."

Sarmiento had learned that Damian's information, although rarely given directly, was always credible. "Why do you say that?"

"I would imagine that the salons of Rome and Paris are more to his taste than the cells of San Juan de Ulloa," he replied.

The name of the pestilential island prison chilled Sarmiento. "That is his alternative?"

Damian lit his cigar and puffed. "He might also be advised that Don Porfirio's agents are far-flung, and if he has any secrets that might be embarrassing to our president and his family, he should continue to keep them."

Sarmiento said, "If I hear from him, I will certainly pass along that message."

"Be sure that you do," Damian said grimly. "And Miguel, that advice applies to you as well." His brother-in-law's chilly tone was matched by the coldness in his bright blue eyes.

"There should no concern regarding my discretion," Sarmiento replied.

"And yet there is, so take care. The officials of *la seguridad* have long memories and suspicious minds. It is best not to attract their further attention."

There were no further visits from the secret police, and Sarmiento's life returned to its normal rounds, but it was only his joy at Alicia's pregnancy that finally allayed his residual fear. In Sarmiento's mind, the child they had created together would at last dispel the grief that each of them carried for the child each had lost. He threw himself into Alicia's care and into his work. Liceaga had commissioned him to write a thorough report regarding the problems of hygiene and sanitation in his district. With Cáceres's help, he interviewed dozens of residents about their medical histories, took and analyzed samples of food and water they ate and drank, measured the spaces of their hovels, and described in minute and unsparing detail the conditions in which they lived. Amassing this information, he produced an exhaustive report in which he made specific recommendations to improve the health of the residents of his district and, thereby, the health of the city as a whole. When he presented it to Liceaga, the public health director responded with characteristic ardency.

"This is exemplary, Miguel!" he said. "I will read it with great eagerness and see that it gets into the hands of those who have the authority to put your recommendations into effect."

"I would like to help in that effort."

"That goes without saying," Liceaga replied. "Indeed, Miguel, I have been thinking that your talents require greater scope than district sanitation officer." He removed his spectacles and cleaned them with a snowy handkerchief. "How would you feel about becoming my deputy?"

"What do you mean, Director?"

"I mean, I want to make you my second-in-command. You would have an office here and oversee the work of all the district sanitation officers. You would produce a comprehensive sanitation report for the entire city, not just a single district, and take the lead in its implementation. You would join me at international public health congresses and exchange ideas with our counterparts all over the world. We could turn our miasmatic city into a model of urban health and cleanliness, and then," he continued, warming to his subject, "we could turn our attention to the rest of México. Imagine, Miguel, we could foment a public health revolution! Do you accept?"

Caught up in Liceaga's enthusiasm, Sarmiento replied, "I would be honored."

On September 7, 1899, Sarmiento delivered his son, José Ramon Rodrigo Gavilán Guadalupe de Sarmiento, who would be, he hoped, the first of many sons. Later that month he was inducted into his new position, Deputy Director of the Board of Public Health for Ciudad de México. As the old century came to an end in an explosion of fireworks above the skies of the city, Sarmiento, holding his child in his arms with his wife by his side, knew what it meant to be happy.

Book 2

The Apostle of Freedom

1909–1911

8

The child sat in the mirador petting a small black cat in his lap as he recovered from his exertions. He had dug a deep hole in the palace garden, showering flower beds with dirt and uprooting a rose bush planted by his great-grandmother. The boy was short and slim and dressed in the blue cadet's uniform of an exclusive Jesuit school. From his stature, it was clear that he was eight or nine, and yet he seemed not so much a child as an adult in miniature. His uniform, with its brass buttons and martial cut, broad across the chest and shoulders, narrow at the waist, imposed upon his boyish form a soldier's silhouette. Moreover, his head was large for his body, and his face revealed the fully formed features of a man, only far more delicate. From his broad, clear brow, his face narrowed to a firm, round chin cleft with a shallow dimple that deepened irresistibly when he laughed. His complexion was simultaneously pale and dark, like a gardenia in the moonlight, framed by the inky blackness of his tumbled hair. His skin was flawless, as if it had been cut from a bolt of the finest silk ever spun. His eyes were an incandescent green, like a cluster of leaves with the sunlight shining through them, and his eyelashes were so long and thick that his eyes appeared to be ringed with kohl. To his grandmother, who was observing him from the garden gate, he was as beautiful as a child in a fable. She could never look at him without thinking he was not quite entirely human but was like a sprite, an elf-child, with his otherworldly beauty and his mysterious self-possession.

She entered the garden tapping her cane loudly against the walkway—the cane was an affectation, for she liked to appear frailer than she was—and approached him in a rustle of petticoats and black silk. The little cat, watching her progress with alarm, leapt from the boy's arms and ran into the bushes.

"Hello, Abuelita," the child said, rising and dusting the dirt from his uniform.

None of her other grandchildren would have dared address her as "granny." But José she allowed liberties she had allowed no other human because from the moment he had first gazed at her with his leaf-green eyes he had become the great love of her old age.

"José," she replied, "why are you destroying my garden?"

"Chepa told me there is an Aztec *teocalli* beneath our house, and inside there is a treasure room filled with gold the Aztec priests hid from the conquistadores."

The old woman sat down. "If the cook spent more time cooking and less time filling your head with Indian superstitions, her meals might actually be edible."

"They are not superstitions, Abuelita," he replied with a child's innocent adamancy. "In the national museum I saw stones from Tenochtitlán they found in the ground beneath the cathedral. Why couldn't there be a temple here, too?"

"And what would you do with this Aztec gold?"

"I would give it to you," he said.

She patted his hand. "You are a generous, foolish child. Come with me." She led him to the back wall of the mirador, where she used her cane to indicate the foundation. Unlike the marble from which the gazebo's visible parts were constructed, the foundation stone was *tezontle*, the volcanic rock from which Tenochtitlán had been fabricated. Faintly visible were the Aztec ideographs for water, motion, and reeds. "Do you see this stone?"

"Yes, Abuelita," he said, slipping his hand into hers.

"It comes from the Indian temple on which our residence sits. The temple was destroyed. Its rubble was thrown into the canal that once ran outside the walls of the garden, but the largest stones were used by your ancestors as the base of our house. Most of them are buried in the earth, beneath the walls, but this one you can see. Whatever gold there was in the temple would have been discovered and taken and melted down for coins. So you see, my dear, the temple was here all the time. It was not necessary for you to dig up Doña Esmeralda's roses to find it."

José knelt on the ground, running his hand over the ideographs. "Abuelita, do you think that the priests made human sacrifices in our temple? Do you think they ate human hearts?"

"I should hope not," she said with aristocratic disdain. "Where do you get such ideas? Come, José. You aunts will be here soon. Go and make yourself presentable."

He stood up. "I must fill the hole I dug."

"Leave it for the gardener. Say nothing about your excavations to your mother or father. They do not understand your romantic temperament." She linked her arm with his and they made their way through the garden. "So you would have given me the Aztec gold?"

"Oh, yes, Abuelita!" he said. "I would give you all the gold in the world if I could."

She kissed his head. "Silly child, you already have."

In the packed courtyard of the Jockey Club—the seventeenth-century Casa de los Azulejos famous for its blue-tiled exterior—Guillermo Landa y Escandón, the mutton-chopped governor of Ciudad de México, was concluding his speech to a gathering of expensively dressed men lounging beneath the panels of the immense skylight. His theme was the upcoming Centenario—the 1910 centennial celebration of México's independence. Sarmiento stood in the crowd, feeling absurd in the white uniform that Liceaga had insisted upon. Each year it became more elaborate, with gold-braided epaulets and wider bands of gold around the sleeves, the buttons larger, shinier, and more intricately engraved with the insignia of the Superior Sanitation Council, as the re-christened Board of Public Health was now known. Liceaga, in an even more martial uniform, stood behind the governor, in the semicircle of public officials and wealthy private individuals who formed the centennial committee. September 1910 was still sixteen months away, but the planning had been going on for years, and the city was in a frenzy of construction and expansion. Scattered around the courtyard were intricate models of buildings and monuments newly completed or being rushed to completion in time for México to receive the world on its hundredth birthday.

Among the models were the recently opened post office, a Renaissance palace with a double staircase that tumbled like a waterfall of marble and brass beneath the glass-enclosed ceiling; the stately House of Deputies with its facade of Roman gravity; the cenotaph to Benito Juárez, a semicircle of columns formed from snowy Carrara marble surrounding a seated statue of the dour Indian savior of his country; and the dizzying Column of Independence, the height of a twelve-story building, going up at the foot of the Paseo de la Reforma, where it would be crowned with a gold-plated sculpture of Nike, the goddess of victory. Surrounded by these symbols of Don Porfirio's reign, the wealthy men in the room, Mexican and foreign, nodded and murmured approval as the governor concluded: "Our days of backwardness are long behind us, our progress as a modern nation is assured. México is ready to step forward and assume its rightful place in the first ranks of the family of nations! *Viva México!*" The cry echoed in the vast room and then the crowd began to push upstairs into a private banquet room where a massive U-shaped table, festooned with garlands of flowers in the colors of the Mexican flag—red, white, and green—had been set for lunch.

Carried forward in the crowd, Sarmiento found himself behind the two Princes Iturbide, descendants of the short-lived Emperor Agustín I. In 1821 their ancestor had won México's independence from Spain and then made himself, briefly, king. He had ended his days, as had so many other nineteenth-century Mexican chief executives, in front of a firing squad. His young great-grandsons were popular figures in aristocratic circles, for they were, as Sarmiento's sister-in-law Eulalia liked to say, as "beautiful and dense as a pair of Sèvres vases."

One was saying to the other, "Don Porfirio is like the Conde de Orizaba who built this palace. His father didn't think he would amount to anything and told him, 'You will never build a house of tiles,' but he showed the old man. He took that proverb seriously and covered his palace with a fortune in Puebla tiles. The world told Don Porfirio, México will never be anything, and look, he has made us a great nation."

"And given us a handsome pension to build our own house of tiles," the other twin said, laughing.

He had no sooner entered the banquet hall than he heard Liceaga calling, "Sarmiento, over here. There are some people I want you to meet!"

Sarmiento found the director with two Americans. One of them was a short, stout, bald man with a white goatee, who exuded self-importance like a cloud of flatulence. The other was a shriveled, gray-haired, gray-faced man with an alcoholic tremor in his hands.

"Miguel," Liceaga said in English, "may I present Mr. J. Anthony King and his associate, Mr. Kieran McCarthy. They represent the interests of the Hearst family in México. This is Doctor Miguel Sarmiento, my deputy."

The man named King glanced at him and then past him, as if looking for someone more important to talk to. Gray-skinned McCarthy offered a trembling, moist hand.

"Doctor Liceaga was telling us about the important work that you are doing in the public health department," McCarthy said. "To prepare the city for all the visitors who will be arriving next year."

"I trust that your plans include giving the Indians pants," King said brusquely. "Or better yet, sweeping them off the streets altogether. The only way to deal with the Indians is what Díaz is doing with the Yaquis: round them up or wipe them out."

"Like your government?" Sarmiento asked.

King, glaring at him, said pompously, "It's a matter of scientific fact that the white race is the superior race, and it is our obligation as white men to ensure its triumph over the lesser races."

"As a scientist, I would have to disagree that any such fact has been established," Sarmiento replied mildly.

"I refer you, sir, to the work of Sir Francis Galton," King said. "England's preeminent eugenicist. Galton points out, and quite correctly, that if the morally and physically enfeebled are allowed to reproduce themselves, humanity will be dragged down."

"Even allowing that that is true, there are enfeebled individuals of every race, Señor King. Even among white Americans."

King's face reddened. "Sir, our subject is México, and I am telling you, until México eliminates its Indians, it will never be a first-rate power. Look, there's Rockefeller's man. Come along, McCarthy."

King stalked off without another word, McCarthy trotting behind him like a little dog.

"Why is it that Americans are either bombastic or puerile, I wonder," Liceaga said after the men had departed. "Not that I disagree with King's sentiments, however reprehensible his manner of expressing them."

"You would also exterminate thirty percent of our population?" Sarmiento asked, taking a glass of champagne from a passing, dark-skinned waiter.

"Come, come, Miguel. That's not what I meant. But it is true that our Indians seem utterly impervious to self-improvement. Surely your decade at the department has demonstrated that over and over."

"It is difficult to assess the Indian's capacity for self-improvement since he is never offered the opportunity for it," Sarmiento said. "He is forced to take the worst and lowest-paying jobs, eat food unfit for human consumption, drink putrid water, and live in squalor. His children must work rather than attend school, assuming there is a school available to them, and he is caught between the church and the *pulquería*, one offering the false panacea of a future heaven and the other the false panacea of intoxication to console him for his present misery. That's what I have learned in my ten years at the department."

Liceaga threw an affectionate arm around Sarmiento's shoulder. "You've obviously spent too much time in the field. You've 'gone native,' as the English say. I disagree with your analysis, Miguel, but your passion does you credit."

"Speaking of analysis, Eduardo, your report about the new water-works implies it will deliver potable water to most of the city, but we both know that only a few neighborhoods on the west side will actually benefit."

"The government wants to hear about progress, Miguel."

"And you tell them what they want to hear," Sarmiento replied.

"My dear boy," Liceaga said, "I refuse to be drawn into a quarrel with you, but I will say that your famous integrity does not come cheaply. I know because I'm the one who pays the price for it. We both want the same thing, a better life for all of our citizens, but we must do what is necessary before we can do what is possible." He dropped his voice. "Don Porfirio is almost eighty. This will be his last term, and then, perhaps, there will be new blood."

"According to Francisco Madero, our country cannot afford another four years of Díaz gerontocracy," Sarmiento said.

"Ah, I gather you read Madero's book."

"Yes, it was an eloquent call to a true democracy in México."

"A call that will not heard as long as the Sphinx is alive. They want us to take our places at the table. Let's pray we have not been seated with the Yankees. And don't mention Madero in this crowd."

José stood before the mirror, fresh from his bath, rubbing pomade into his hair. His room lay reflected around him, a large, high-ceilinged space with a single window, now shuttered, that opened out to a quiet side street off the *plazuela*. More than once, as a small child, he had gotten lost wandering the galleries and suites of his home. After one such adventure he had asked his grandmother, "Abuelita, do you know how many rooms there are in your house?" She had replied, "My dear, if I knew how many rooms there were, it would not be a palace."

The centerpiece of his room was a four-poster canopy bed in which, his grandmother had told him, many of his ancestors had breathed their last breath. Her story thrilled rather than troubled him. The bed was not merely his resting place, but a prop central to his imagination. He could pull the curtains shut and it became a theater stage or a ship on the high sea or a carriage on a bandit-infested road. Most often, it was the battlefield where he pitted his armies of lead soldiers against one another for hours at a time. The armies were now scattered across the room—soldiers from every era and every country and every rank in the infantry, cavalry, and artillery. He imagined himself a brave soldier in the army of Saint Louis fighting the infidels in Jerusalem, or with Charles I battling the French in Italy, or with Napoleon in Egypt. In almost every story he told himself, there was a moment when a fellow soldier was gravely injured and José carried him to safety, and when the boy survived, he vowed to José eternal love and friendship, always with the same words: "I will never leave you."

In actuality, José had no friends his own age. He had a solitary temperament but his solitude was not entirely temperamental. His grandmother coddled and protected him, but she also imposed her strict views of rank by which most of his schoolmates were deemed unsuitable companions for him. Those who met her high standards were boys he disliked because they were braggarts or bullies or dull. His cousins were all adults, the next youngest ten years his senior, and their children were infants.

When he was younger, his parents had taken him to the church of San Francisco Tlalco while his father held his clinic, and he had played with the children of the parish, but now he was at school during those hours. Some of those children were still his friends, but he saw them only on Sunday, after Mass. When he had proposed inviting them home, his grandmother responded with horror. He had resigned himself to living in a world of adults and to the wayward affection of his cat, El Morito, who crawled in from the garden every night and slept on his bed with him. He assuaged his loneliness with his lead soldiers, the novels of Jules Verne and Victor Hugo and Robert Louis Stevenson, and his stereopticon through which he viewed distant lands to which he hoped to one day travel with the one true friend he knew was awaiting him somewhere.

He brushed his hair back, dressed himself meticulously, and went to greet his aunts, who had gathered in his grandmother's parlor for tea. José privately thought of his aunts as the three stepsisters from *La cenicienta* dressed in their lavish gowns, faces powdered and rouged, on their way to the prince's ball. Each one had her predominant quality— Tía Nilda was caustic, Tía Leticia was melancholy, and Tía Eulalia was amusing. They had settled in their usual places in the pink-and-gold room with its enormous Velasco painting of the Valley of México on the wall above the sofa where his grandmother sat. When José entered the room, she patted the cushion, inviting him to sit beside her. Before he did, José approached each of his aunts, bowed from his waist, and kissed their hands.

"Ah, the Prince Imperial," Nilda said. He could taste the cream she used on her hands when he lifted his head from kissing her.

"No, no, *nieto*," Leticia said. "Give your old aunt a real kiss." She puckered her thin lips and he touched them with his. She smelled of rose water and tears.

"José, you are so pretty that if you were a girl, we would have to lock you up in a tower to protect your virtue," Eulalia said, but her tone, unlike Nilda's, was kind and affectionate. "As it is, you will lay waste to many female hearts before you marry."

He smiled at her because he liked her best, and also her dashing husband, Tío Damian.

"Bring my grandson his chocolate," La Niña ordered the young maid who hovered nervously in the corner. She took silver tongs and piled French lace cookies from a platter on the table before her onto a nearly translucent dessert plate and passed it to him. "Say nothing to your mother or I will be blamed for spoiling your appetite."

"I hardly think Alicia can blame you for anything having to do with the child," Nilda said. "You are more of a mother to him than she."

"Yes, Mother, where is Alicia?" Leticia asked.

"She has gone to seek the support of the first lady for a school to teach girls to become nurses."

"Really?" Nilda said. "Whatever for? There are more than enough nuns in this city to tend the sick."

"Oh, what do nuns do when you are sick but stand over you with their sour faces waiting for you to die so they can begin the novena?" Eulalia said. "Alicia wants girls who are actually trained to care for the sick."

"You seem to know rather a lot," Nilda said.

"Damian has pledged ten thousand pesos toward her school," she replied.

"What next?" Leticia marveled. "Women doctors?"

"Pigs will fly before that happens," Nilda said. "Women should desist from the occupations of men. That reminds me, I saw Carmen Rubio de Díaz at Sylvan's last week. She was dining with Limantour."

"The finance minister?" La Niña asked. "How extraordinary."

"Oh, from what I understand it's her hand at the till of the Republic rather than her husband's," Eulalia said. "Have you spoken to him recently? He loses his train of thought between one sentence and the next."

"Nonsense," Nilda said. "Don Porfirio may be eighty, but he is still *muy hombre*. As for Limantour, that man looks like he was squeezed out of a tube of ointment. And Carmen, well, I suppose she can't help meddling in affairs of state seeing how she is barren."

"She was a lovely girl," La Niña said. "I still think it was criminal that her father married her off to that man when she was only seventeen and he was already fifty."

"Well," Eulalia said quietly, "her father got a good price for her."

The sisters were silent, each thinking of her own arranged marriage, Nilda with a frown, Leticia with downcast eyes, and Eulalia with a slight smile.

"José," Leticia said. "Have you been practicing your piano? Won't you play for us?"

Alicia heard her son working his way through "Ave Maria" and reminded herself that she must find him a piano teacher. She had been his original instructor, but he had long since surpassed her. She paused and listened, picturing her beautiful boy's long, deliberate fingers on the keys, his face transfixed with the joy of making music. God in his infinite humor had given her a child endowed with the one disposition completely foreign to her—an artistic temperament. Her son was impractical but obsessive, distracted but disciplined, a silent, intense observer of others but completely self-absorbed. He drove his teachers mad with his inattentiveness in class, but she had watched him sit for hours maneuvering his toy soldiers in complicated formations, like actors on a stage, while quietly telling himself their story. As a small child he had often disappeared into the garden, where he picked flowers and arranged them with complete concentration by color, size, and type. He cheerfully practiced scales until the servants begged her to ask him to stop, but he could scarcely add or subtract, confused pesos and centavos, and could still not tell time or right from left. He had taken so long to speak that Miguel had worried he was deaf or feeble-minded, but then, when he did speak, it was in full sentences, not babyish babble. He still guarded his words though, a habit that made her heart ache because she wondered whether he kept silent out of fear of disappointing her and Miguel by speaking.

For she knew her ability to understand his character was limited by her own temperament, so different from his. In consequence, there were moments of misunderstanding between them, which she worried he took for lack of love. But she had carried him in her body and fed him with her milk, creating an intimacy between them that transient confusion could not impair for long. She knew, ultimately, that he felt secure in her devotion to him. Miguel, however, lacking that bond of body with José, could not always conceal the irritation he felt with a son so unlike his rational, methodical, and practical self. When he scolded José for his failures at school or inability to read the face of the clock, José shrunk back from his father and it pained her to see it.

"Miguel," she told him after such an episode, "you must be patient with him. He is not willfully disobedient."

"I know, I know," Miguel would say with a sigh. "I'm sorry that my frustrations show. I do not wish to perpetuate my own father's bad temper, but Alicia, he is an odd child. Almost an idiot savant, brilliant at some tasks, hopeless at others."

"Oh, Miguel, that is cruel! We are all better at some tasks than others. It is simply that you have little interest in the things he loves, music and stories and art. But those interests come honestly through my bloodline, as you can see in my mother, who lives for art. It is no wonder they are such great friends."

"Those interests may be acceptable in a woman who is not expected to shoulder worldly burdens, but José will have to take his place in the society of men. I would prefer he not enter it like a lamb among wolves with his head filled only with Chopin and Jules Verne."

"He is still a child, Miguel," she replied. "We both know the world will harden him. That is the nature of the world. Let him have his innocence while he can."

But she thought, as she listened to the last notes of his piece, José's innocence was not transient; it was deeply embedded in his character, the source of a freshness and vivacity that seemed more fitting for a girl than a boy. Miguel was, perhaps, justified in worrying how José would fare in the harsh world of men, but Alicia trusted that the God who had created her son as he was had a purpose he wished to express through José in the fullness of time.

"Bravo, José," she said as she entered the drawing room.

José scooted off the piano bench and ran to her. "Mamá!" he exclaimed, embracing her.

She kissed his forehead. "You are becoming such an accomplished musician. I will find you an instructor to help you advance even further."

"I liked it when you taught me," he replied, still holding her.

"Yes, I enjoyed that, too, *mijo*, but I have nothing more to teach you. Let me sit and visit with your aunts."

She sat on the sofa with her mother, José between them. He threaded his fingers through hers. His grandmother said, "José, stop pawing your mother so she can have a cup of tea."

"No, that's fine. I had tea with the first lady."

"Was she encouraging?" La Niña asked.

"Her views of a woman's place are very traditional," Alicia replied. "She regards nursing as a natural function of wives and mothers and the idea of paying women to perform that function is . . . a novelty to her."

She had chosen her words carefully. What Carmencita had actually said was that paying women to nurse would put them on the same moral level as prostitutes.

"She might feel differently if she had ever actually had to nurse a sick child or a sick husband," Eulalia said.

"Will you abandon your plan?" Leticia asked anxiously.

"No," she said adamantly. "The nursing that women do for their families is entirely different from the nursing required in hospitals. Hospital nurses are the physical senses of doctors when the doctors are absent. They must receive the same training as the physician's own senses so that they understand what they see, hear, smell, and touch. I regret that the first lady will not help create this school, but I will talk to Miguel about who else I should approach."

"Lovely speech," Nilda said. "You should run for president, sister. You and Señor Madero. Or, perhaps, you should spend more time with your child so that when he sees you, he does not cling to you like an orphan."

"You're a fine one to talk about motherhood," Eulalia replied. "You expelled your children from your womb directly into Swiss boarding schools."

"Oh, shut up, both of you!" La Niña said. "I have had enough. Go home now."

The three sisters rose, kissed their mother, and departed. As soon as they left the room, they began bickering again, their voices echoing down the corridor.

"Mamá," José said. "What is a womb?"

"It is the place in a woman's body where she carries her child until the child is ready to be born," she said. She touched her abdomen. "About here."

José put his hand on her hand. "Is that where you carried me?"

"Yes, *mijo*."

"How did I get in there?"

La Niña said, "That is not a suitable question for your mother, José."

"Your grandmother is right," Alicia said. "That is a question you must ask your father."

"No doubt he will give you the scientific explanation," La Niña sniffed, "and leave you more puzzled than before." She rose, adjusting the folds of her voluminous black dress. "Your sisters have once again exhausted me. I will take dinner in my rooms. Come and see me in the morning, José, and I will play for you my new recordings of Caruso singing arias from *Rigoletto* and *Aida*. They are marvelous!"

"Yes, Abuelita. Thank you."

After she left, José said, "Mamá, if you carried me in your belly, could you not carry another baby there? I should like a brother."

"Well, my dear, God, who judges these matters, decided that you were the only child I should carry."

"I shall ask God to change his mind," José said confidently. "When he understands how much I want a brother, I am sure he will put one inside of you."

Alicia sat before the mirror, brushing her hair, and saw Miguel reflected on the bed reading the letter that had arrived for him that afternoon from his cousin Jorge Luis. For the past decade, Jorge Luis's letters had arrived once or twice a year, postmarked from France and Italy, Spain and England. This one, she had observed, bore the postmark of the Mexican postal service. When she glanced at him again, Miguel had stopped reading and was watching her.

"What is it, Miguel?"

"Your face," he said. "It continues to heal. Have you noticed?"

She stopped midstroke and examined herself. Over the years of her marriage, there had been a change. The pitting had become less pronounced and the fiery psoriasis that had covered her cheeks and forehead had faded to reveal the natural shade of her complexion, which, like José's, was simultaneously dark and pale. She no longer caked her face with heavy powder or wore veiled hats when she went out. The pitying stares of strangers had become brief glances acknowledging the damage but not dwelling on it. The children of San Francisco Tlalco still called her *feita* but by rote, without understanding why she was so called.

"It is merely that age has softened the damage left by the disease," she said.

"No," he said. "I have seen the results of smallpox in other adults and your recovery is specific and rare. I cannot account for it medically."

"Then it is God who has had mercy on me," she said.

"I think it is happiness that has restored your beauty," he replied. "You have been happy, haven't you, Alicia?"

She rose from her mirror and went to bed, where she sat at his side and said, "It would have been enough to have been your wife and the mother of our child, but you gave me more than that. You have allowed me to be your student and a partner in your work. There is not enough space to hold my happiness. Have I made you happy, Miguel?"

"How can you even ask? I was prepared to end my life until you entered it. Each day I am still alive, I owe to you, Alicia."

He took her hand. They looked into each other's eyes, where they found not uxorious sentimentality but a love forged in a crucible. They knew they had saved each other. That knowledge and the accompanying gratitude each felt toward the other had created an unbreakable bond between them.

"Has Jorge Luis returned to México?" she asked as she went around the bed to her side and slipped in beside him.

"Yes," he said. "This letter is six months old, from Coahuila, where he has befriended Madero."

"Is it not still dangerous for him to have returned?"

"He writes that once Madero is president, he will pardon him for any offenses. He says he has explained himself to Madero and that Madero does not condemn him for who he is."

"You mean his love for men?" she asked.

Miguel had eventually and reluctantly told her the true cause of his cousin's departure from México without the details that she had puzzled out for herself.

"Jorge Luis has come to believe that the . . . aberration that inclines him toward those of own sex is not a mental disease or a moral deficiency, but that he and other men like him constitute a third gender, a male with a woman's psyche, and as such, are perfectly natural variants of the human species."

She sensed his distaste in the clinical tone he took.

"He thinks he is a man with a woman's soul," she said. "Where would he have arrived at such a notion?"

"It is a school of thought that began in Germany and was adopted by English pederasts who call themselves 'Uranians.' Jorge Luis spent a long time in England, where he evidently became their acolyte." He put the letter aside. "He says he will secretly come to the city and I should be on the watch for him."

"I would love to see him again, after all these years. He has never met his nephew."

"I'm not sure I would want José to associate with him."

"Oh, Miguel! He is our family."

Miguel shrugged. "He has been gone a long time. Madero's response to him is interesting, though."

"Do you think Madero will be president one day?" she asked.

"Our brother Damian, who seems to know such things, says no," he replied. "Damian says Díaz only allows Madero to make speeches against the regime to show foreigners that México is a democracy. The old man can't hang on forever, though. This will be his last term and then, perhaps, a different government will finally meet its obligations to the poor."

"We are all obligated to the poor," she said.

"Private acts of charity cannot change social conditions. As long as the poor are regarded as expendable parts of the machinery of the economy, they will continue to be ground into the dust. Our world must change, my dear. These conditions where a few prosper and the many are destitute cannot continue in a modern state."

"The Lord said the poor will always be with us," she murmured.

"One reason I am not a Christian," he replied. "Your Jesus should have spent less time teaching the poor to accept their lot and more time teaching the rich to share."

"His message was for the rich and poor alike," she said.

"What message was that?"

"As the poor stand in relation to the rich, so we all stand in relation to God. We are utterly dependent on his mercy, love, and generosity for everything we have. All he asks in return is that we love each other as he loves us. If every Christian takes that message to heart, there would be no poverty, Miguel."

With more rue than scorn, he said, "After nineteen hundred years, my dear, I'm afraid we must conclude the message has fallen on deaf ears and the experiment has failed."

He was obdurate on this point, so she left it and turned their conversation to a subject he would understand.

"Miguel, you must explain reproduction to José," she said.

"Why?"

She told him about her conversation with him about his birth. "He asked me for a brother. You must help him understand why that is not possible."

"I doubt whether the medical explanation would satisfy him," he replied. "It would be a hard thing to tell him about the brothers and the sister who were miscarried, even if he had the wit to understand it."

Following José's birth, there had been three other pregnancies, each ending in a bloody miscarriage, the last nearly costing her life. After that, at Miguel's insistence, she had submitted to a hysterectomy. There would be no other children.

"Still, you must try," she said. "I cannot evade the question again and it makes me unbearably sad."

"I will talk to him, I promise."

"But gently, Miguel," she said. "He is a sensitive child."

"You must not coddle him," he replied.

She opened her mouth to reply, but their disagreement about José's temperament was as longstanding and unresolvable as their disagreement about faith, so she said nothing.

9

Across the city, church bells clanged the hour, six o'clock in the evening the second day of Lent, at the beginning of March 1909. Sarmiento was locking up his apothecary cabinet after a long day of seeing patients at San Francisco Tlalco. As was their custom, his patients received his diagnoses with grave Indian silence, took the medicines he offered them, nodded when he prescribed a plan of treatment, and walked away on dirt-encrusted feet. He knew that most of them would sell the medicine for food or pulque and return next time with the same ailments. He had long since stopped hectoring them when they did this. He simply prescribed the medicines without comment. Since most of their diseases were variations of malnourishment, food and even alcohol were as useful to them as his drugs. He thought how Liceaga's comment had justified his misleadingly optimistic reports about the state of public health in the city—"we must do what is necessary to do what is possible." If sycophancy could soften the hearts of the powers-that-be toward the plight of the destitute, Sarmiento would have been licking their boots too. But Liceaga's sanguine reports only fueled the indifference of the authorities, while the situation of the poor worsened.

The evidence was all around him. Much of the beautiful garden of the old church had been converted from flowers to food. Squash, chili, melons, and corn had replaced the ancient roses to provide for the parishioners as the cost of these staples increased and their pitiful wages fell. The church, which had not been locked in the three centuries of its existence, was now sealed tight after sunset to prevent theft. When he walked through the neighborhood, the small businesses he had observed a decade earlier were shuttered because they were unable to compete with the factories that now turned out the same goods en masse.

Everywhere, he saw the symptoms of starvation as one economic crisis after another was balanced on the backs of the poor, while the city's anxious rich hoarded their wealth or sent it out of the country for safe-keeping in foreign banks. The eighty-year-old Díaz's refusal to name a successor created uncertainty about the future, while a series of bloody strikes in the mines and the factories seemed, even to the dullest and most self-satisfied plutocrat, a portent of things to come. It was as if, he thought, the nation was holding its breath and it was unclear whether the exhalation would be a sigh of relief or a death rattle.

"Doctor?" The voice, male, came from behind him.

"I'm sorry," he said without turning. "The clinic is closed but I will be back tomorrow afternoon at two."

"I don't need treatment, Miguel," the man said, the voice becoming familiar.

Sarmiento turned. The stranger was of medium height and stocky, his complexion darkened by the sun, his face shadowed by a broad-brimmed felt hat such as was worn in the north. He was dressed in an old but respectable suit and a collarless shirt. He removed his hat and in his broad, handsome face Sarmiento detected vestiges of his cousin's epicene features.

"Jorge Luis!" he cried. "Is it really you?"

"Yes, Primo, but I am only Luis now. Luis Parra." He stepped forward tentatively. "It is so good to see you, Miguel."

Sarmiento rushed to him and embraced him tightly. He felt the changes in his cousin's body, the aesthetic slenderness turned to hard muscle, the once smooth face now raspy with stubble. Even his breathing was different, deeper and harder.

"My God," he said. "You've become a man."

Luis broke off their embrace and smiled at Sarmiento. "Are you surprised? Did you think I would become a woman?"

His joy at their reunion seeped away at the memory of their last meeting. "Why have you changed your name?"

"For my safety," he replied. He reached into his pocket, removed a hand-rolled cigarette, and lit it. "And I have not really changed my name. I have simply rearranged it, taking my mother's name as my own."

"What are you doing in the city if it is still dangerous for you?"

"It is dangerous for Jorge Luis Sarmiento, not for Luis Parra. I have come to help organize Don Francisco Madero's anti-reelection club in advance of his arrival in May."

At that moment, Alicia and Padre Cáceres entered the room. For a moment, she gazed at the man beside her husband and then broke into a broad smile of recognition.

"Jorge Luis!" Alicia exclaimed, embracing him. "Thank God you are safe and well. Father," she said to Cáceres, "this is our cousin."

The priest extended his hand. Sarmiento observed that Luis took it with a sardonic glance in his direction, and in that glance, he saw that his cousin was less changed than he had first appeared.

"A pleasure, Padre," he said. To Alicia, he said, "Doña Alicia, I have so often wanted to stand before you and beg your forgiveness for every cruel remark I made about you, for my drunkenness at your wedding, and for failing to appreciate your virtues and your kindness."

She embraced him. "You owe me no apology, Cousin. I am so happy to see you healthy and sound." She stepped back. "There is a young man in the garden. Is he your friend?"

"Yes," Luis said. "His name is Ángel, an Indian boy from Coahuila who travels with me."

"You must both stay and eat with us," Cáceres said. "Our fare is simple, but we would be pleased to share it with you."

"Yes," Alicia said. "Please stay. We have so much to talk about."

"On some subjects," Luis replied quietly. "There are others that I need to discuss with my cousin alone. You understand, I hope."

"Of course," Alicia said. "You have been away for a long time. You and Miguel must have much to say to each other."

Over a meal of chicken stewed in red chili sauce, squash cooked with tomato and *queso fresco*, beans, and tortillas, Luis told lighthearted stories of his travels in Europe and the United States, turning his hardships into amusing anecdotes. For, as he explained, after his father died, his allowance was discontinued by his stepmother and he had been forced to earn his living.

"My only skill was versifying," he said with a laugh, "and Paris was not in need of another bad poet. When I was unable to pay my hotel bill, the management suggested that I work it off in the kitchen washing dishes in lieu of the city jail. What I observed about the sanitary conditions of the hotel kitchen made going hungry seem like a virtue rather than a grim necessity. Oh, and the characters I met there! The cooks screamed in French and Italian, the waiters in Russian, and me in Spanish. Fortunately, some physical gestures are universally understood."

"How did you escape?" Alicia asked.

"Friends liberated me. I had been too proud to ask for their help but they helped me nonetheless. Through them, I went to England and fell in with a circle of vigorous, mutton-eating Englishmen who thought nothing of brisk walks that took them halfway across their island and back between luncheon and tea. They were very kind to me." He paused and glanced at Sarmiento. "They turned me into a socialist."

"Ah," Cáceres said. "Are you then, like your cousin, a nonbeliever?"

"I believe that when God made man in his image he intended that there be no social distinctions among them. One man is as good as another, and all men are equally deserving of what Americans call life, liberty, and the pursuit of happiness—although, God knows, they themselves do not practice their creed. Still, it is my creed."

"You will find no quarrel in this church with those beliefs," Cáceres said.

"How did your association with Madero come about?" Sarmiento asked.

"I wanted to come home, but not to resume my old life, even were that possible," Luis said. "I went first to New York with letters of introduction from my English friends to a group of American socialists. They told me about the Flores Magón brothers, who published a radical newspaper called *Liberación* that they smuggled into México from their exile in the American city of St. Louis. I began to write for them about the true conditions that prevail in our country beneath Don Porfirio's gilt. I wrote about the government's seizure of ancestral Indian lands that reduced the Indians who had farmed them for centuries into peonage. I wrote about the extermination of the Yaquis in Sonora. I wrote about the sale of our mines and railroads and ports to foreigners who are immune from our laws, the suppression of unions, and, most of all, about the concentration of greater and greater wealth into fewer and fewer hands. After a while, it was not enough for me to write about these conditions; I wished to change them." He lit a cigarette, passed it to Ángel, and then, on the same match, lit another for himself. "I read Madero's book. He's no radical. His call for constitutional government, effective suffrage, and no reelection is the typical pallid fare of bourgeois liberals. Nonetheless, I sensed an underlying passion in his words that attracted me. I made my way to Coahuila and presented myself to him. I was not disappointed by the man." He grinned at the priest. "Intending no disrespect, Padre, I must say I did not understand sanctity until I met Madero."

The priest replied, "In what way is Señor Madero saintly?"

"In the way of complete self-sacrifice," Luis said. "Although he is a son of one of the richest families in México, he lives wholly for the benefit of others. The workers on his estate live decent, comfortable lives, and he pays for the education of their children. He has slowly been giving away his fortune to the poor, to the horror of his family. I heard him tell one of his brothers that he would not be like the rich man in the Gospels who turned his back on Jesus when Jesus commanded him to give all he had to the poor. Madero said, 'I shall pass through the eye of that needle, Brother, and I will bring you with me.'"

"Well," Cáceres said, "he must be a remarkable man."

"He is," Luis replied passionately. "He has bravely offered himself to speak against Don Porfirio's despotism, knowing the danger it places him in. I personally would follow him anywhere."

Sarmiento listened to his cousin's account of his transformation with growing amazement, for he remembered the effete young man who despised the Indians, worshipped all things French, and lived for pleasure. He glanced at the young Indian who had sat silently beside Luis while he spoke. There was more to this story, he thought, that Luis in his discretion had omitted in the presence of Alicia and the priest. He was impatient to speak to his cousin alone.

At last, the meal ended, the plates were cleared, and the priest brought out a dusty bottle of brandy.

"Gentlemen," he said to Sarmiento and Luis. "We will leave you now. Miguel, I will see that Alicia gets home safely. Ángel, if you are tired, there is room here for both you and your master to stay the night."

"Thank you," Luis said. "That is very kind." To Ángel, he said, "Go, *mijo*, I will come soon."

When they were alone, Sarmiento asked, "What is that boy to you? You called him 'son.'"

Luis poured brandy into the glasses the priest had set out for them. "He is my son and my companion and . . . my lover." He pushed the glass across the table. "Your expression, Primo! You had better drink this."

Sarmiento drank. "Thank you for not making that comment in the presence of my wife."

"Alicia knows," Luis said. "I could see that she had quickly surmised the nature of my friendship with Ángel. Did you tell her about me?"

"She listened to our conversation the night you left México," he said. "When the police came the next day and accused you of being . . . a sodomite, she listened to that conversation as well. Some time later, she admitted to eavesdropping, and we discussed the meaning of what she had heard."

"You spoke to her of it?" Luis asked, incredulous.

"Alicia is not like other women," Sarmiento replied. "She is my intellectual equal and I treat her as such. In any event, she had already pieced it together."

"What did she make of it?"

Sarmiento poured an inch of brandy into his glass. "Her sympathies are always with those whom she believes are treated unjustly, and she believes that about you."

"Notwithstanding the nature of my . . . offense?"

"She thinks it is a trivial sin of the flesh, like eating or drinking too much."

"In that case," Luis said, "her sympathy is greater than her understanding."

"That is equally true of me, Primo." Sarmiento said sternly. "I think you should explain yourself."

"Explain myself?"

"I knew you, Jorge Luis. You were a snob. I see you are transformed, but there is more to it than socialism," he said. "Your conversion is personal, not political."

Luis sipped his brandy. "You always were astute, Miguel. It's true that my politics are the product of my conversion, not their cause. I suppose my conversion began the night I left here disgraced and humiliated. Those first few years of exile, I wandered around Europe trying to re-create the life I had led here, but to achieve it I had to lie about who I was and why I had left México. The lies piled up like debts, creating a constant state of anxiety that drained my life of any pleasure." He lit another hand-rolled cigarette. "Not, in any event, that the pleasures were still so pleasurable. Another ball, another dinner party, another night at the theater. As I approached thirty, I realized that my life was without purpose and meaning, squalid and pointless. I don't suppose you would know how that feels."

"You would be surprised, Primo, but we are speaking of you now."

Luis cast a curious look at his cousin before continuing. "I was in Paris and my friends took me to meet a man who called himself Sebastian Melmoth, an Englishman living in filthy rooms at the Hôtel d'Alsace. I couldn't imagine why they had brought me to see him until he told me his real name. He was the writer Oscar Wilde, who fled to France after he was released from prison for sodomy in England. He told me he called himself Sebastian after Saint Sebastian, the martyr. There was a poisonous atmosphere in his rooms not simply of destitution but of despair and self-pity. I went back to my own shabby hotel, and I thought, if I follow this man's example, then I must live a life of self-hatred and die in fear."

"You mean, if you continued to practice . . . that vice?"

"No," Luis said. "I mean if I continued to accept the world's condemnation of my nature. It is my nature to love other men, Miguel. That may disgust you, but that night I decided I would no longer allow it to disgust me. It no longer does. I am at peace with myself."

His cousin's words were delivered so calmly and with such conviction that Sarmiento was forced to acknowledge either that they expressed a profound truth or were insane. He could not exclude the possibility of insanity, even though he saw no sign of mental illness in his cousin's serene countenance.

"Once I made that decision," Luis continued, "remarkable events occurred. I met a few men in Paris who felt as I did, and they introduced me to the work of the English Uranians. I began a correspondence with their leader, a man named Edward Carpenter. He turned his back on his bourgeois family to live with his lover on a farm in a small town. I went for a brief visit and stayed for a year, as his farmhand and his student. He is an honored figure among English socialists, but his socialism is motivated by love, not theory. Love, he told me, is the true leveler of distinctions. He always said you cannot love mankind and still wish to oppress men. For we homosexuals, that axiom is doubly true. You cannot love another man and still wish to oppress man."

"What was that word you used?" Sarmiento asked, frowning. "'Homosexual.'"

"'Homo,' from the Greek meaning same and 'sexual' . . . well you know what that Latinism means. The word was invented by a German writer to describe men who love other men."

"I see," Sarmiento replied skeptically. "Ugly word. Still, it has the virtue of clarity if not elegance." He poured some brandy into his own glass and his cousin's. "You really believe your behavior is normal?"

"It is for me," he said. He smiled. "Do you think I'm mad?"

"The thought has crossed my mind."

"I could say the same of you, Miguel."

"What are you talking about?"

"You said you knew me, but I knew you, too, better than anyone. You were an intellectual snob, an atheist, and the most melancholy of men. Yet here you are, tending to the poor, breaking bread with a priest, married to the least likely woman I would have imagined for you, and you even seem happy. Well, as happy as your nature permits. Someone less charitable than me might say you have taken leave of your senses."

"Touché," Sarmiento touching his glass to his cousin's.

"To madness," Luis replied.

José would always remember how he had watched from the railing as a boy—older, almost a grown-up—entered the courtyard, his eyes sweeping across the palace in awe, pushing a bicycle. José flew down the stairs and said breathlessly, "Is this your *bicicleta*? Will you teach me how to ride?"

The boy had a narrow, intelligent face and a mouth that, José soon learned, was habitually curled into a sweet half-smile. His hair was longer than the fashion, straight as an Indian's, and parted in the middle.

Beneath blunt, black eyebrows, his coffee-colored eyes were warm and friendly.

"You must be José," the boy said. "My name is David. I am your new piano teacher."

"I know how to play the piano," José replied impatiently. "But not how to ride a bicycle. Please, can I touch it?"

David surrendered the bicycle to José, who tentatively pushed it across the courtyard.

"You really don't have a bicycle?" David asked. José shook his head, and David said, with a sweeping gesture of his hand, "But you have all this. This . . . house."

José did not understand. "Do you belong to a bicycle club?" he asked, returning the bicycle to the other boy, who leaned it casually against the wall. "Do you race? I saw Juan Trigueros win the Independence Day race last year. He was fast as the wind! The seat is very high. How do you get on it? I—"

David clamped his hand over José's mouth. "Listen, peanut," he said with a broad, white smile, "Your *mamá* hired me to give you piano lessons. So if you take me to your piano and let me do my job, then maybe I will show you how to ride my bicycle. Okay?"

When he removed his hand, José was also smiling. "What does that mean, 'hokay'?"

"It's American for *de acuerdo*. Now, where is the piano, peanut?"

"In the *sala*," he said. Impulsively, he grabbed the older boy's warm, soft hand. "Come on, I'll take you."

When they entered the great salon, David stopped, looked around the vast room, and said, "This room is bigger than my family's apartment. Who are the people in those paintings?"

José glanced up at the twin portraits of the first Gaviláns.

"Those are my ancestors," José replied. "Don Lorenzo and Doña Teresa."

David ran his hand along the marble surface of the gold-and-white table at the center of the room and took in the immense Persian carpet that covered the floor in a muted explosion of reds and blues, the pink damask-covered furniture, the bronze wall scones in the form of caryatids, the Chinese vases, the vitrines displaying seventeenth-century porcelain, and a suit of armor from the time of Felipe Segundo.

"This is like the lobby of a fancy hotel," he said. "I can't believe anyone really lives here. Is that your piano? It's nicer than the one I play at the conservatory. Come on, peanut, let's start your lesson."

They sat at the bench. David pointed to the sheet music and said, "'The Raindrop Prelude'? Can you play that?"

"Yes," José said, running his fingers across the keys.

"Go ahead. Play."

José sucked in a breath and begin to play Chopin's piece, as his mother had taught him, touching the keys with soft fingers. He struggled with the denser passages, slowing the tempo to work through them, stopping once or twice in frustration, all the while conscious of the older boy's intent attention. He finished with a sigh of relief.

"Well, Josélito, you played all the notes, but I didn't hear the music."

José glanced at him and asked earnestly, "Is something wrong with your ears?"

David laughed. "Scoot over a little."

José moved to the edge of the bench. David glanced at the music and began to play. He touched the keys with confidence, smoothly untangling the passages that had stumped José. José found himself nodding in understanding as he watched David's hands sweep across the keys. His playing was thrillingly beautiful to José and he thought he knew what David had meant when he said José had played the notes but not the music. David could play both at the same time, the separate parts and the whole, the repeating A-flat holding the piece together like the sound of rain on a rooftop. When José wasn't watching David's hands, he was studying his face, where he saw—lips slightly parted, eyes tender— a look of love. It was the same look that José saw on his mother's and his grandmother's faces—even, sometimes, on his father's face—but he had never imagined that one could love an activity in the same way as one loved another person. As he continued to study the older boy's face, he felt flutters of pleasure in his belly such as no one had ever made him feel before.

"Do you understand what I mean about playing the music?" David was asking him.

"I think so," he said. "Can you teach me to play as well as you?"

"I thought you wanted me to teach you how to ride a bicycle?" David said, grinning.

"Will you teach me both?"

David threw his arm around José and said, "I will, peanut. Do you mind that I call you 'peanut'?"

"No," José said, his heart warm and happy. "I like it."

My feet cannot reach the pedals," José complained.

David, steadying the bicycle, replied, "I don't want you to pedal yet. I just want you to get used to the motion. Put your hand on the handlebars, not my shoulder. Come on, eyes forward."

Holding the bicycle, David ran down the stone path into the twilit green of the Alameda, past the half-completed cenotaph to Juárez, past the iron lampposts where the electric lights had just begun to flicker on, past the mortician's marble benches, past the bandstands and the formal gardens. José, clutching the handlebars, felt a surge of fear, then excitement, then joy.

"I want to pedal, David!" he shouted.

David slowed to a stop. "Next time. I have to bring a screwdriver to adjust the seat so your feet can reach the pedals. How did that feel?"

"I loved it!" José said.

"Okay, I need to get you home," David said.

José climbed off the bicycle. David got on and then José hopped up on the handlebars.

"Ready?" David asked.

"Okay," José said.

They plunged into the fashionable crowd promenading along the Paseo, eliciting shouts of "Hey, watch it!" and "Get off that thing and walk!" In response, David rode even faster and more recklessly, while José grasped the handlebars until his knuckles turned white.

The bells of the churches had been silenced for Holy Week, and the air was filled with the sound of the rattles that people carried to ward off evil spirits until the bells rang again on Easter morning. As they approached the Zócalo, David slowed down where the paving changed from macadam to cobblestone. The facade of the cathedral was draped in black. The streetcars jerked forward from the Zócalo station in a shower of electric sparks from the overhead wires. David darted among the *cargadores* carrying heavy trunks from the railroad station to the hotels on Calle San Francisco. He turned onto the side street that led to the palace and, too soon for José, arrived at the hulking doors, where the porter hurried out when David braked and José hopped off the handlebars.

"Won't you come and eat supper with us?" José asked.

David shook his head. "My family is expecting me. I will see you on Monday. In the meantime, I want you to practice that piece I gave you."

"'Claire de Lune,'" José said. "What a funny name for a song."

"Don't concern yourself with the title; worry about the notes. Goodbye, peanut," David said, and then he was off, disappearing into the Indian market in the *plazuela* and into the dusk.

"Come inside, Master José," the porter was saying. "Your grandmother is waiting for you."

Reluctantly, José went in. He found La Niña in her parlor waiting with his chocolate and plates of sweets.

"You are late, José," she said.

"David was teaching me how to ride a bicycle in the Alameda."

"Your piano teacher?"

"Yes," José said.

"He is not a suitable companion for you, José," she said. "He is only a servant, after all."

"He is not my servant," José said angrily. "He is my friend."

"Drink your chocolate before it gets cold," she said. "Next time he comes, I would like to meet this boy, your friend."

"I will introduce you, and you will love him as much as I do," José said.

"We shall see," she replied.

Alicia knelt before a painting on the stone floor of the empty church of San Francisco Tlalco. She did not know how long she had been there because the bells did not toll on Good Friday. She was aware only that the light had faded and the church lay deep in the shadows of dusk. Her knees ached and pain clawed the muscles of her back and shoulders, sending shuddering spasms that brought tears to her eyes. She was not certain she could rise, even if she wanted to, but she did not yet want to.

She had not intended for her devotion at the thirteenth station to become an exercise in self-mortification. However, as she gazed at the depiction of the death of Jesus that a self-taught Indian artist had painted three centuries earlier, she found herself rooted to the spot. In the background of Golgotha, the artist had painted the landscape of the Valley of México with its lakes and volcanoes and fields of blue agave. Jesus himself was no more than a half-naked Indian boy whose face was veiled with streams of blood that ran from a crown of cactus thorns. The horror and sadness of the moment of death was inscribed on his slender body, gaunt and exhausted and slack. His death cut straight to her heart, like a scythe, leveling the weeds of vanity. Her soul was naked before her God who loved her so much he had endured this death to bring her the grace of eternal life.

Miguel had once asked her what she thought about when she prayed. "Nothing," she told him. "But you spend so many hours at it, you must be thinking of something." "No," she insisted quietly. "I think of nothing." He had looked at her with the same frowning expression with which he regarded obstinate patients.

But she had spoken the truth. When she prayed, as she had for the past few hours, her prayer eventually shed the stifling cloak of language and became, instead, a pulse of yearning, grief, wonder, and gratitude. It felt, physically, as if her entire body and all its complex systems had become concentrated in her heartbeat. Mentally, where thought would have been, there was, instead, an enveloping sensation of light. Rarely was it as powerful as the light of sun. Rather, it was like the flickering of the flame of a votive candle, which, for as long as it lasted, suffused her with feelings of peace and well-being unrelated to any person or object in the world. She did not leave her body, as she had read that the saints did when they prayed. To the contrary, it seemed to her that she more deeply entered her body, until she touched the center of all existence, including her own, sometimes for no more than a moment, sometimes for a little longer. It was a place as still and quiet as the whisper that Elijah had heard on the mountain of Horeb, after the storm and the earthquake and the fire, which he recognized as the voice of God. She wondered what Miguel would have made of it had she answered his question about what went through her mind as she prayed by saying, "I listen for the whisper of God."

A groan involuntarily escaped her lips and she knew it was time to rise. She stood, crossed herself, and rested for a moment against a column before setting out for home. As part of her Lenten practices, she gave up her carriage and walked wherever she needed to go, overruling Miguel's concerns for her safety. Behind her, near the altar, she heard the frantic shuffle of footsteps and glimpsed Ramoncito, Padre Cáceres's mute Yaqui servant, running from the sanctuary. A moment later, she saw him and Padre Cáceres enter hurriedly.

"Are you sure he's dead?" Cáceres questioned frantically.

Ramoncito made a noise of affirmation.

"Take me to him."

They disappeared through the door behind the sanctuary that led to the room where the priest and his acolytes prepared for Mass. Alicia, stirred by concern, unthinkingly followed them, but the room was empty. It appeared that they had gone through another door, left open, through which she saw descending steps. She stood at the top of the steps, looked into darkness, and breathed the musty air of a crypt. She saw the flicker of a candle and heard Cáceres's voice again: "We can't leave him here. Let's take him to my room."

She stepped back, into shadows. A few minutes later the priest and his servant emerged through the door, carrying the body of a man.

"Padre," she said, stepping forward. "What is this?"

"Doña Alicia, what are you doing here!" he exclaimed.

"I was in the church and I heard you talking to Ramoncito,"

"Come," he commanded her. "I will explain everything."

She followed the men into the priest's cell, where they laid the corpse on his narrow bed. Cáceres lit the lamp and she saw the body was that of an emaciated young man, scarcely more than a boy. The priest knelt, laid his hands on the boy, and began to administer the sacrament of extreme unction. Alicia and Ramoncito knelt behind him. Silent tears ran down the Yaqui's face. When the sacrament was completed and the priest had covered the boy's face with a linen cloth, she asked him, "Who is he? What happened to him?"

The priest sighed, rose to his feet, and invited her to sit.

"His name was Diego. He was a tribesman of Ramoncito, another Yaqui, who had escaped from a henequen plantation in the Yucatán, where he had been enslaved. He got as far as here, but the privations he endured in slavery were too much for him."

"Why here?" she asked.

He paused, gave her a piercing look, and said, "What I am about to tell you must not leave this room."

"Whatever you say I will keep in the strictest confidence," she replied.

"In the days before the Americans fought their civil war, there was a system of sanctuaries that helped the black slaves escape from the southern part of the United States to Canada, where they were free. It was called the underground railroad. The sanctuaries were established by good Christians who knew that human slavery was abhorrent to the Lord."

She nodded. "Yes, it is."

"For twenty years, Yaqui men have been deported from their homeland in Sonora and sold as slaves to the henequen haciendas, where they are worked to death. Over time, we have created our own sanctuaries to help those who escape reach the American border. Our own underground railroad. This church is a station on that railroad. We shelter the men in the crypt until they are well enough to travel, and then we provide them with the means to reach the next station, in Guanajuato. Ultimately, they cross the border in the American territory of Arizona, where the Yaquis have set up their communities in exile."

She nodded. "This is commendable work, Father."

He shook his head. "Not in the eyes of the law, Doña Alicia. Legally, men like Diego are the property of the plantation owners. By helping them escape, we are committing theft. The penalties are very harsh. If we were discovered, I would be prosecuted and thrown into jail and the church itself shut down."

"Surely the archbishop would intervene on your behalf."

"The archbishop knows nothing of these activities," Cáceres said curtly. "If he did, he would personally surrender me to the civil authorities for prosecution."

"You mean . . . ," she began slowly, as the implications of his words sank in.

"Doña, power protects power. The church is no different. You see, we are quite alone in this work."

"Then you must allow me to assist you."

The priest shook his head. "No. You are generous and kind to offer, but the risks are too great."

"They are far less for me than for you, Father. I belong to an old family. My husband is an official in the government. My brother-in-law Damian is a confidant of Don Porfirio himself, and I am a friend of the first lady. I am above suspicion."

Ramoncito, who had remained in the room, made a rough noise. She turned to look at him. He pointed to her, tapped his heart, and nodded.

"Thank you," she told him and then addressed the priest. "If Ramoncito trusts my discretion, you should too, Father. Let me help you."

"All right," he said reluctantly. "Perhaps it was providential that you overheard me and discovered us. Now, our immediate concern is to give the boy a Christian burial."

"Padre," she said. "Do you shelter only Yaqui men? What of their women and children?"

His face turned to stone. "The children are taken from their families and placed in orphanages or given to Mexican families to adopt. The women are killed, so that they will not bear other children. It is the policy of our government to wipe these people off the face of the earth," he said. "God help us, but they are succeeding."

"But why?" she cried. "What is their offense?"

"Their offense?" he repeated angrily. "Their offense is that they refuse to surrender their ancient homeland to be partitioned among our president's cronies. Their offense is that they exist at all."

"God forgive México for this crime," she said.

10

Before he left the city to rejoin Madero's campaign, Luis had given Sarmiento a copy of Edward Carpenter's book *The Intermediate Sex*, which purported to be an explanation of homosexuals.

"You're a rationalist," Luis had challenged him. "You pride yourself on your scientific objectivity, but you think of men of my type with the same ignorant contempt as the most benighted parish priest. Acquaint yourself with the facts, Primo, before you draw your conclusions."

"A scientific fact is a conclusion based on measurable observations that can be reproduced by experimentation," Sarmiento replied pedantically. "Will I find those kinds of facts here?"

Luis smiled. "All I ask is that you keep an open mind. Isn't that also the way of science?"

One evening, Sarmiento opened the book and began to read. As he suspected, what Carpenter offered were not facts but a hypothesis: there existed a class of men who, although biologically male, were by temperament female—emotional, sympathetic, and kind—and, as such, were inclined to form romantic attachments with other men rather than with women. These homosexuals, Carpenter argued, were not pathological but anomalies, not mentally ill but simply a variation from the norm. As proof, Carpenter cited the historical persistence of such types, particularly among the ancient Greeks, who recognized and honored love attachments between men. He also claimed that certain famous individuals, including Michelangelo and Shakespeare, were homosexuals. These celebrated artistic personalities, Carpenter contended, typified the homosexual temperament in its highest form: passionate, sensitive, and creative. The only science he cited was a handful of studies of sex by the Germans Karl Ulrichs and Richard von Krafft-Ebing and the

Englishman Havelock Ellis that, to varying degrees, supported his hypothesis.

"What are you reading so intently?" Alicia asked, coming into the *sala* with her embroidery.

Sarmiento's first impulse was to hide the book, but he had always freely discussed his reading with her, whether it was a scientific monograph on public health issues or the poetry of the Nezahualcoyotl, the Texcoco philosopher-king. These conversations were invariably stimulating to him, her innate intelligence shedding a new or different light on the text.

"An Englishman's book that Luis gave me to explain . . . men of his kind. What the author calls 'homosexuals,'" he said, pronouncing the term in English. "A made-up word that means men who are attracted to one another."

"Men who love other men?" she queried, slipping a thimble on her finger, taking her needles and hoops from her basket. She was embroidering a bedspread with roses and lilies as a wedding gift for an Indian couple who were to be married at San Francisco Tlalco. Her fingers were a marvel of agility.

"You could call it that, I suppose, although I'm not certain that 'love' describes their physical activities."

"Of course that is a sin," she said, "but if they are led to it by real, if misguided, affection, like Luis and his friend Ángel, God will not judge them too harshly, nor should we."

"Carpenter makes the same plea for tolerance," he said, "although he wouldn't call what these men do a sin." He closed the book. "He would say, as Luis does, that what they do is natural to them."

She shook her head. "What is natural to them is the same as is natural to all men," she said. "To marry and to make children."

"But what of those marriages where children are not possible because of the sterility of the man or woman?" he wondered. "Is it unnatural for those spouses to have sexual relations for pleasure?"

She paused in her stitching. "If pleasure is the only reason for such relations, then they are merely expressions of lust. But for husband and wife, even those who cannot have children, those relations serve another purpose."

"Which is?" he pressed her.

She quietly worked on the bedspread for a moment before answering. "To deepen the bond of marital love."

"If that's true, why wouldn't it also be true of two men who have sexual relations out of real affection?"

"Because, my dear, two male bodies are not made for the natural expression of physical love."

He shook his head. "Carpenter would say men's bodies are quite capable of giving and receiving what you call physical love."

She looked at him. "Do you think that because something is possible it's also natural?"

"The very thought of two men attempting coitus repels me," he replied. "So I suppose the answer is no. There are many things one can do with one's body that could scarcely be considered natural. Still, if subscribing to Carpenter's theory helps Luis accept his . . . condition and preserve his self-respect, then I suppose it serves a useful purpose."

"Luis's condition is but a small part of who he is," she said. "And he is otherwise quite admirable." She smiled. "So, yes, I suppose we must accept his eccentricity."

"Even though he will go to hell for it?" Sarmiento joked.

"Don't be absurd, Miguel. He will have to repent in purgatory, of course." She added seriously, "But I'm certain that God will be merciful to him."

"Will I also have to repent my atheism in purgatory before I can join you in paradise?" he asked, smiling gently.

"Oh, Miguel," she said in exasperation, "do you think God cares that you say you don't believe in him? He created you, doubts and all."

At the end of May, a note arrived from Luis inviting Sarmiento to hear Madero speak in the city on San Juan's Day, June 24. "Madero," Luis wrote, "is anxious to meet the son of Rodrigo Sarmiento." The postscript startled him—how would Madero know his father?—but touched him, too, and swept away his misgivings about attending so public a protest against Don Porfirio's reign. Liceaga frequently reminded Sarmiento, sometimes jovially, sometimes with exasperation, that he was politically naive but even Sarmiento knew Madero was playing cat and mouse with the regime. Ostensibly, Madero's campaign to limit presidential terms was directed not at Díaz and the 1910 election but at whomever might succeed Díaz in 1914. His stated intention was not to challenge Díaz in 1910 but to persuade Díaz to appoint him as vice president and his likely successor in 1914.

Nonetheless, implicit in Madero's campaign was a devastating attack on the old man. His campaign slogan—"no reelection and effective suffrage"—was a denunciation of four decades of Díaz's system of fixed elections at every level of government from president of the Republic to the mayor of the lowliest villages. His book, *The Presidential Succession of 1910*, had ventured to criticize the effects of one-man rule, however tepidly, questioning the regime's brutal war against the Yaquis, its repression of labor unions, and its excessive concessions to foreign investors. The very mention of these topics had, for decades, sent newspaper editors to Belem jail and shut down their presses. That Madero had written about them extensively in a best-selling book was incendiary. Finally, in what was the most personal affront, were the intimations of Díaz's mortality, the assumption that by 1914 he would either be dead or too enfeebled to seek a ninth term.

Over drinks at the Jockey Club, Sarmiento asked his brother-in-law Damian, who was close to Díaz's inner circle, why the old man had not banned Madero's book and thrown him into jail.

His handsome brother-in-law smiled his feline smile, sipped his scotch, and said, "Tell me what happens in September 1910, Miguel."

"The Centenario," Sarmiento replied.

"And what does that mean?"

"The usual official bombast, I imagine."

Damian stopped a passing waiter. "Another." To Sarmiento, he said, "Yes, that, of course, but also, Miguel, the eyes of the world will be on México, and what do you think Don Porfirio wants the world to see?" He dropped his voice. "A dictatorship? No. México is, in theory, a democracy and that's what the old man intends to show the world. Free press, free speech, open elections. This is the only reason he hasn't crushed Madero," he continued, taking the heavy crystal glass the waiter offered him. "I would not want to be Don Panchito Madero on October 1, 1910, however." He frowned. "You're not thinking of getting mixed up in all that anti-reelection stuff, are you?"

"No, of course not."

Damian lifted a doubting eyebrow. "Some friendly advice, Hermano. When the Madero ship goes down, there won't be any lifeboats. *Entiendes?*"

Sarmiento smiled. "You know I'm not interested in politics."

"Good, because this is no time to become interested."

The summer rains began with a downpour that turned the dirt streets surrounding the railway station into sinkholes. The horses strained to pull Alicia's carriage through the mud. More than once, the man in the carriage with her—Padre Cáceres dressed as her servant—had had to get out and push the vehicle forward. Eventually, they reached their destination, a livestock pen at the edge of the station, guarded by soldiers. Inside the pen, a group of dispirited men sat in the mud as the rain came down. Alicia waited in the carriage while Cáceres looked for the captain of the guard. Her face was heavily veiled, but she had dressed richly and adorned herself with jewels. She knew that the success of her plan depended entirely on her ability to awe and intimidate. She steeled herself, assuming for her purposes her mother's imperious character.

Thick knuckles tapped the window. The captain's round, porcine face stared suspiciously at her. She lowered the glass.

"Señora," the captain said. "Your servant said you wished to see me."

"Come inside," she commanded, "but try not to ruin the upholstery with your wet clothes."

He flinched at her tone and entered the plush carriage almost apologetically. She caught the sour whiff of pulque on his breath. She let him sit for a moment and absorb the luxuriousness of the carriage, the sparkle of her gems, and the richness of her gown.

"Señora, how may I help you?"

"I wish to buy some of your Yaquis," she replied, as if negotiating for bolts of cloth. "I will pay gold coin—none of this worthless paper— and I will pay well, assuming you haven't starved or beaten the goods half to death."

The captain said, "Señora, that is not possible." His tone, she noted with relief, was deferential, that of a servant unable to comply with his mistress's request for an out-of-season fruit.

She made a dismissive noise. "Not possible? These men are destined to be sold to the henequen hacendados in the Yucatán. My family needs workers to harvest our maguey crop. Why should we not also benefit from the Yaquis' labor? I am told one Yaqui works harder than ten Mexicans."

"But, Señora, these men must all be accounted for when I reach Mérida." Now his voice was nearly a whine.

"Oh, come now, Captain," she sneered. "You have never had any escapes? Some of them don't die en route? We both know there are a hundred ways to put your thumb on the scales." She opened the purse she had brought with her, withdrew a dozen gold pesos, and tossed them into his lap. "This is a gratuity."

He picked up a coin. "Solid gold," he remarked.

"What did you expect? Tin?" She sighed loudly. "Make up your mind, Captain. I can't sit here in the rain all day."

He gathered up the coins and clanked them together in the palm of his hand. After a moment, he said, "I can give you ten without raising suspicion."

"Well, that's a start," she said. "But our fields are vast and we need a regular supply. Will there be other shipments?"

"Once a month," he said. "I will let you know."

"No, not me, Captain. My majordomo," she said. "Work out the details with him. Pedro!"

Cáceres came to the window. "Yes, Doña."

"Captain—what is your name?"

"Henriquez, Señora."

"Yes, Captain Henriquez has agreed to provide us with some livestock. Go with him and pick them and arrange for payment and transport. And remember, Pedro, strong backs!"

"Yes, Doña," he said.

"Thank you, Captain," she said, dismissing him. After he left, she fell back against the cushion and exhaled, her heart beating so hard she wondered how the soldier could not have heard it.

Rain dripped from the ceiling in José's bedroom into an eighteenth-century delft chamber pot depicting a trio of wispily bearded Chinese sages ascending a mountain path. He stood in front of his mirror, fingers glistening with pomade, which he worked into his tumble of hair until it lay flat on his head, and then, like David, he parted it in the middle. He imitated the older boy's habitual half-smile and ran downstairs to the *sala* to practice "Claire de Lune" before David arrived. El Morito was asleep on the sofa. As José began to play, the cat lifted its small black head and listened with sharply pointed ears. A moment later, José felt the cat rubbing itself against his ankles.

"Stop it, Morito," he said, but it was he who stopped to stroke his cat's soft fur. The cat jumped into his lap and purred.

"So you like Debussy," he said. "Can you see the moonlight on the roofs of the city? I can, but don't tell David. He says only girls make pictures in their head when they listen to music. He says music is mathematics."

"Are you talking to the cat?" David asked, behind him.

José turned so abruptly that El Morito, startled, hopped off his lap and ran beneath a cabinet. The older boy was drenched, rain having plastered his hair to his head and soaked his coat and trousers. He removed his mud-splattered coat and boots, hanging the coat over the back of a chair and setting his boots against the wall. José noticed the hole in his stocking where his big toe poked through. His shirtfront was wet, the white linen transparent against his chest, revealing two dark nipples and a triangle of wiry black hair. When he sat down on the bench beside José, he smelled of rain and sweat and tobacco, and heat seemed to rise from his flesh like steam. José scooted closer to him.

"You're dripping," he said.

"Brilliant observation, peanut," David replied. "I got caught in the rain on my bicycle and was nearly killed by a streetcar that sprayed me with mud. Come on, let's start, I want to get home to take a bath. Play for me."

José began the piece. David listened for a moment, stopped him, and had him replay a phrase.

"No, José," he said impatiently. "Like this."

Even though his fingers touched the same keys as José had touched, the music had a seamless quality that eluded José.

"I can't make it sound like that," José complained.

David got up, stood behind José, and then, leaning down, placed his fingers over José's, almost covering them. José could feel the subtle gradations in pressure as David pressed down on his fingers, manipulating them as if they were a part of the instrument. His breath grazed José's neck. For a second José imagined that David was going to kiss him, and he had to press his legs together to keep from squirming with pleasure.

"What is this?" At the sound of La Niña's voice, David snapped upright. "You use my chair as a clothesline and remove your boots as if you were in your own home?"

"Señora Marquesa," David stammered. "I am so sorry."

"You are covered with mud, boy! No gentleman would enter a house in such a state," she said, planting herself on a settee. "Please get dressed."

David pulled on his filthy jacket and boots. He bowed. "I apologize again, Señora."

"I should send you home," she said.

"No, Abuelita," José exclaimed. "It's not David's fault he got mud on him. We just started my lesson."

"Very well," she said. "Finish the boy's lesson, but mind my furniture."

David resumed his seat on the bench, but José could detect his anxiety. His grandmother's occasional appearances during their lessons had had that effect on David since the first time he met her. She had interrogated him about his family and his background so relentlessly that he was soaked in sweat when she finished.

"And your father, tell me again, what does he do?"

"He is a postal clerk, Señora Marquesa."

"A postal clerk." She repeated each word slowly and distinctly as if they described a species with which she was unfamiliar. "Where is your family's house?"

"In Colonia San Rafael," he replied nervously. "Not a house, but an apartment, in a building with other apartments. Nothing as grand as this."

She made a dismissive sound. "You study at the conservatory?"

"Yes, Señora Marquesa. I hope to become a concert pianist." He smiled at her and said with enthusiasm, "José is very talented. He could also become a professional musician."

"To play in front of strangers, for money? My grandson is being raised to be a gentleman, not an organ grinder's monkey."

"Yes, Señora Marquesa," David replied, completely deflated.

José had listened to the exchange and understood that David was being, in some manner, reproached by his grandmother, but he did not know how David had given offense and so could offer no excuses for him. All he knew was that David behaved with uncharacteristic formality when she was in the room. Now he asked José to continue playing "Claire de Lune," but instead of his usual caustic corrections, he said little, except to praise him loudly enough for La Niña to hear.

Your grandmother doesn't like me," David told him. They were sitting on a bench in the Alameda a few days later, on a Sunday afternoon. David's bicycle was propped up beside them. The rain had broken and the summer sky was crystalline. The volcanoes rose in the distance, still snowcapped in June. The tree-lined walkways of the gracious old park were filled with well-dressed strollers: men in summer suits and women corseted into the fashionable hourglass shape, carrying fringed parasols. Indian vendors patrolled the park selling ice cream out of pushcarts. José was finishing a cup of chocolate ice cream, while David had eaten strawberry.

"What do you mean?" José asked.

"She doesn't think I'm good enough to be your friend," he said. "Not the son of a postal clerk."

"But you are my friend," José insisted. "Aren't you?"

"Of course I am, peanut," he said, patting José's head. "Hey, look at those girls coming this way. *Qúe lindas, no?*" He threw his arm around José's shoulder. "Smile at them when they pass, okay?"

"Okay," he said.

The two girls, one dark, the other blonde, were David's age. They wore candy-colored lacy confections, the dark girl in pink, and the blonde girl in mint. The prettier of the two, the dark-haired, olive-skinned one, stopped when José smiled, exclaiming, "Oh, what a beautiful little boy!" To David, she said, "Is he your brother?"

Before José could respond, David said, "Yes, miss. This is my *hermanito* José."

"He's a perfect doll," the blonde girl said.

"My name is David," he said. "I have been teaching my brother how to ride a bicycle. Would you like to see him?"

"Well," the dark girl said, "I don't know. We aren't supposed to talk to boys. But all right, just for a minute. Josélito, show me how you ride a bicycle."

José, eager to show off his skill, mounted the bicycle. David pushed him down the path and whispered, "I want you to ride around the fountain and the bandstand very slowly." He let go. After a few panicked, wobbly seconds, José steadied himself and found his stride. He pedaled down the broad path, steering out of the way of baby prams and other cyclists. He reached the fountain where water roared from the mouths of stone lions, circled it, and rode back toward David, who, as José passed, was deep in conversation with the two girls and did not see him wave. He turned around again at the bandstand, where a police band was warming up, and when he came around the second time, David was waiting for him, alone. He caught the bicycle and helped José off.

"Did you see me go by? I waved at you."

"Of course, peanut, didn't you see me wave back?"

"No, you didn't. You were talking to those girls. Why did you tell them I was your brother?"

"Because you're like my little brother," David said and pecked the top of José's head. "Whatever your old witch of a grandmother thinks."

David had kissed him! He thought his heart would burst from happiness.

The last of the Gaviláns' lands that had not been confiscated or sold in the dark days after Maximiliano's fall was an ancient country house in the village of Coyoacán. In colonial days, the Gaviláns had used it as a summer retreat before the civil wars that followed independence made the roads impassable. By the time the roads had been cleared of bandits and mercenaries, the family was out of the habit of making the hour-long journey from city to country. For fifty years, the house had stood unused and dilapidated on a dirt road bordered by tall cactuses, the ochre-colored walls peeling, the carved doors worn away by the elements, the gardens turned to jungle, and the rooms filled with moth-eaten carpets and termite-eaten furniture.

Discreetly, Alicia had opened the house and hired workmen to repair the kitchen, prop up walls and pillars, and join the two largest rooms into a single long gallery that she filled with beds, converting it into a hospital ward. Cáceres found a cook and a half-dozen other trustworthy servants to staff the house. It was soon filled with the Yaquis whose freedom Alicia had purchased from corrupt Captain Henriquez. The manor's isolation and the status of its owners protected the men from prying officials and neighborhood gossip. The Yaquis remained sequestered at the house until they were fit to travel. They left at night, with forged identity papers, money, and a third-class railway ticket to the American border. All this had taken time to work out and it had to be done in the utmost secrecy.

Alicia, who deplored falsehood, had needed to become a convincing liar. The deceptions weighed on her conscience, particularly her lies to Miguel. She longed to tell her husband about the house in Coyoacán, but she refrained, fearing not his anger but his powers of reason. She had no doubt he would raise a hundred irrefutable reasons why she was acting foolishly. Even in her own mind, the faith that had inspired her to help the Yaquis wavered as she came to know them.

For as she heard their stories, she realized that, with a few exceptions, the men were warriors. Some of them had been fighting against the Mexicans for decades in defense of their homeland. In that long war, they had killed not only Mexican soldiers but the Mexican settlers to whom the Díaz government had given their land, including women and children. The men were grimly unapologetic for these atrocities and they made it clear that they intended to resume the war as soon as they returned to their land. She began to see how naive she had been. Not only was assisting these men treasonous but by becoming an accomplice to their violence, she endangered her soul.

She turned to Cáceres, her spiritual guide and confessor, as they sat at the kitchen table, where she peeled potatoes for the evening meal. He listened to her intently and then said, "Doña, do you not recall that the hardest teaching in all the Gospels is to love your enemies? 'Love your enemies, bless them that curse you, do good to them that hate you, and pray for them who persecute you.' Isn't that what you are doing here, for these men?"

"I can't believe that God intends for us to save their lives so they can return home and kill others."

"You must not presume to know the mind of God," Cáceres said sharply. "Of course, it is not his will to continue the cycle of violence between the Yaquis and ourselves." Then, more gently, he continued, "That is the very reason we are called upon to love them and to help them. We free ourselves from that cycle of killing by saving their lives, and in this way we follow Christ's directive to do good to those who would hate us."

"Is it not selfish of us to secure our own salvation by putting the lives of others at risk?"

"You assume these men will inevitably return to Sonora and make war on the Mexicans there, but hasn't your compassion taught them that not all Mexicans are their enemies? Can you be so certain that your example will not soften their hearts and stay their hands against violence?"

"How can I be sure?"

"You cannot," he replied. "We may never know what events our actions have set into motion, but we do know, from the mouth of Christ himself, what actions we must take. The rest is faith."

She paused in her peeling. "Before all this, my faith was as light as feathers but this weight I feel in my heart is terrible and ponderous."

He touched her hand. "What do you imagine the weight of the cross felt like on the naked shoulders of God as he trudged to his death on Golgotha? If the way of faith was easy, we would be living in paradise. Remember what our Lord told us. The gate we must enter is narrow, and wide is the road of the world that leads to suffering and destruction."

"My faith falters," she whispered.

"Then, like the father of the sick child in the Gospel, you must pray, 'Lord, I believe; help me in my unbelief.'"

"Yes," she said. "I do believe. Lord, help me in my unbelief."

The Teatro Coliseo was a shabby little music hall a few streets north of the Zócalo, where working-class audiences cheered ribald zarzuelas—comic operettas—like *Chin-Chun-Chan* that lampooned the nouveau riche. On the evening of June 24, 1909, the feast day of San Juan Bautista, the theater's well-worn seats were occupied by a different crowd. Sarmiento, glancing around the smoke-filled space, recognized types rather than individuals—humble factory workers, exuberant university students, frock-coated members of the petite bourgeoisie, the younger sons of cadet branches of old families, bon vivants seeking entertainment, cigar-smoking reporters, bespectacled intellectuals with nicotine-stained fingers, and plain-clothes officers of *la seguridad*. The tatty curtains had been drawn open, and on the bare boards of the stage there was a podium draped in red, white, and green bunting and flanked by tall arrangements of gladiolus. Behind the podium was a banner that proclaimed, "The Anti-Reelection Club of Ciudad de México." Sarmiento was standing at the back of the house, beneath the balcony, scanning the room for his cousin.

From behind him, Luis said, "Miguel, you're here," and clasped his hand on Sarmiento's shoulder.

Sarmiento turned and the two men embraced.

"Where is the man of the hour?" Sarmiento asked.

"Downstairs," Luis said. "Come, let me introduce you to him. I've told him all about you and he is eager to meet you."

To Sarmiento's surprise, Madero was not surrounded by the usual entourage that accompanied politicians. Rather, the little man was alone in the dingy dressing room except for an even smaller woman, who sat at a desk in the corner writing a letter. Madero was dressed simply in a dark brown suit; his hips were wider than his shoulders and he had a small potbelly. His receding hair, plastered across his head, emphasized his bulbous forehead, and his lips were lost in a luxuriant mustache and goatee. Beneath thick eyebrows his eyes were curious, intelligent, and gentle. He radiated kindness, even before he clasped his small hands over Sarmiento's and said, in a soft voice, "You must be Doctor Miguel Sarmiento. I had the honor of meeting your father many years ago. He is a great inspiration to me."

"Did you say this man is a doctor?" a male voice asked.

The man, who entered the room smoking a cigar, bore a family resemblance to Madero but was clearly cut of tougher cloth. He regarded Sarmiento with a fixed stare made disconcerting by Sarmiento's realization that his left eye had the lifeless glitter of glass.

"My brother Gustavo," Madero said. "Gustavo, Doctor Miguel Sarmiento."

"I thought perhaps you might be an alienist come to cart my brother away to the madhouse," Gustavo said, exhaling a plume of rich-smelling smoke.

Madero smiled. "My family thinks I have lost my mind and have commissioned my brother to be my guardian. My father says that I am like a microbe challenging an elephant. Don Porfirio being the elephant, of course."

From her desk, the drab little woman raised her eyes, paused in her writing, and in a high, grating voice declaimed, "Jesus's mother and brothers came and standing outside, they sent to him and called him. And a crowd was sitting around him, and they said to him, 'Your mother and your brothers are outside seeking you.' And Jesus, looking around him, said, 'Here are my mother and brothers. For whoever does the will of God, he is my brother and sister and mother.'"

"This is my wife, Sara," Madero said.

Sarmiento said, "You have great faith in your husband."

"It is not a matter of faith," she replied. "Francisco has been chosen for the task of restoring democracy to México."

"Chosen by the spirits," Gustavo sneered. To Sarmiento, he said, "They communicate with them on my brother's Ouija board."

"You are an idiot, Gustavo," Sara said without particular heat and resumed writing.

Sarmiento had no idea of what to make of this exchange. Madero laughed and said, "Don Miguel, you must think you really have entered an asylum. Let me explain. I am a spiritist, a disciple of the Frenchman Allan Kardec. You have heard of him?"

"I vaguely remember hearing the name when I was a student in Paris. He was a medium?"

"No," Madero said. "He himself, as he freely acknowledged, lacked the medium's gift, but he communicated through others with the spirit world. They taught him secrets that have, until now, been inaccessible to humans about the meaning of life and death. In summary, we are born, die, and are reborn again and again. In this manner we evolve spiritually until we are perfected and can achieve union with God. That is also the true message of Jesus of Nazareth and the meaning of his resurrection."

"*Do* you communicate with the spirit world?" Sarmiento asked, scarcely believing he was addressing this absurd question to the leader of México's opposition.

"We do, Sara and I, using a planchette. I fell into the habit after reading Kardec's autobiography. The first message I received was 'Love God above all things and your neighbor as yourself.' I believe it was a message from Christ himself. Later, another guide told me I must abandon my private philanthropy and enter politics for the salvation of our country. That message was conveyed to me by one 'BJ.'"

"BJ?" Sarmiento repeated.

"Benito Juárez," the little man said, "whom your father served as you will soon serve me, Miguel."

The sound of heavy feet rhythmically banging on the floor of the theater shook the ceiling of the dressing room and the crowd began to shout Madero's name over and over.

"Come on, then," Gustavo said. "Let's get the circus started."

"Good-bye, Miguel," Madero said. "We will meet again soon. I am sure of it."

As they made their way back to the theater, Sarmiento asked his cousin, in all seriousness, "Is he insane?"

"Listen to him speak," Luis replied, "and then answer that question for yourself."

They arrived at the floor of the theater just as Madero was taking the stage to loud, prolonged, and almost desperate applause. With difficulty, he quieted the crowd and began to speak. His voice like a flute—soft, clear, and intimate—reached to the farthest seats. He spoke first of himself, saying he was, in his heart and soul, a farmer who loved the country, its people, and its quiet pursuits. "I am not a politician," he told them, "but I am a man of México, and México, in her chains, has called to me, as she has called to every one of you and begs us to release her from the bonds of autocracy. Our mother México groans under the weight of foreign domination. Her children go hungry and die of disease and neglect. She cradles these dying children in her arms, and she begs us, 'For the love of God, save me!'"

A huge cheer erupted from the crowd. Sarmiento thought it a stroke of brilliance that Madero had invoked as a metaphor for México the image of a beggar woman holding a malnourished child. The streets of the city were filled with such women. They existed at the periphery of one's vision, a shameful sight that one ignored, quickening one's pace as they approached, bony hands outstretched, pleading, "Sir, for the love of God."

The beggar woman was a living reproach to the Díaz government's centennial slogan: Order and Progress. In invoking her, Madero allowed the people in the crowd to release the repressed guilt, anger, and shame that they felt at being part of a system that tolerated such inequality. Madero, it appeared, understood that human beings could not look away from human suffering indefinitely. Whether or not people were basically good, they were inescapably connected. Sarmiento himself had often thought that the suffering of others invoked a sympathetic response, as one nerve is sympathetic to the pain of an adjacent nerve.

For forty years, Don Porfirio's government had told its people to ignore their reactions to the degradation of their fellow beings, in essence, to deny reality. In the last decade, that reality had started to close in on México, as the inequalities became every starker and the sense of personal powerlessness increased—a feeling Sarmiento himself knew all too well. To continue to deny reality required greater and greater mental and moral contortions until, Sarmiento thought, the nation must go mad. Madero obviously understood that the critical moment had arrived, and his message was to face reality. Face reality and change it. As Sarmiento joined in the thunderous applause that proceeded to nearly drown out Madero's speech, he felt that he had been released from the web of lies that constituted the social fabric of Díaz's México and given back the most basic freedom of all: the freedom of thought.

"Is he insane?" Luis shouted over the crowd.

"No," Sarmiento replied. "He may be the sanest man in México."

11

La Niña emerged from the crypt beneath the altar of the church of San Andrés to rain pounding the stained glass windows and gloomy shadows flooding the sanctuary. The smell of incense permeated the still air—the odor of sanctity, she thought with distaste. She could not wait to escape it and fill her lungs with the miasmatic air of the city, that familiar mixture of fried foods, flowers, sewage, wood smoke, charcoal, horse manure, eucalyptus, and all the other innumerable fragrances, exhalations, odors, stinks, and emanations that proclaimed life. For the past hour, she had knelt beside the tomb of her husband while the obsequious pastor of the church led her in a rosary to commemorate the anniversary of his death. She droned her way through the Five Glorious Mysteries, nauseated by the musty air and the black smoke pouring from the candles. They provided the only illumination in the final resting place of three centuries of dull-witted, haughty Gaviláns. Her own family—hacendados from Durango—buried their dead in a hillside graveyard beneath canopies of oak branches where horses grazed and lovers picnicked.

Her maid hurried to her side as she prepared to leave the church. She pushed open the door for her mistress and unfurled an enormous umbrella at the very moment La Niña left the church. She took a dozen steps to her waiting carriage. The driver, with long-perfected timing, threw back the door just as she reached the coach and assisted her inside. Her maid entered behind her, arranged a fox fur throw across her lap, and then departed to join the driver for the three-minute ride to the palace. La Niña, who had been tended to by servants since infancy, was only peripherally aware of their activity.

She was in a nostalgic mood, for as she had knelt in the crypt beside the dust that had been her husband, her thoughts wandered back to her girlhood in Durango. She had been born in 1831, ten years after Iturbide secured México's independence from Spain. Her family's vast holdings had been unaffected by the change in government — the cattle continued to graze, the corn and wheat continued to grow, the veins of silver still traced their delicate lines through the darkness of the mines — and hers was the childhood of a princess. Not, however, a confined princess of the city. She was a country aristocrat who, by day, rode horses, raced barefoot in the dust, and swam in the cold streams of the mountains. At night, she sat at her father's table in silk and jewels, eating quail and fried squash blossoms off plates carried across the Pacific by the Manila galleons. Her childhood friends lived in the same careless opulence. When one of them, the son of a silver king, had married, the path from the bridal carriage to the church was paved with silver ingots. Silver was the foundation of all their fortunes and even the moonlight that filled her bedchamber seemed like a spray of silver.

It seemed, at first, that the romance would continue when she came to the city for her social debut. Her family had a fine house, a fine name, and wealth. The invitations poured in. There were candlelit balls, excursions to the Teotihuacán, where she stood at the peak of the Pyramid of the Sun, and long boat rides in the flowered canoes of Xochimilco. Although not as beautiful as other girls, she was fresh-faced and charmingly impertinent. She had a dozen suitors from which to choose a husband, but, as was the custom, her father made the choice: the dour Marqués of Gavilán, a widower fifteen years her senior. He was so arrogant that he spoke of himself in the plural, so dull in his conversation that she had to discreetly pinch herself to stay awake. She was crushed, but there was no question of defying her father. Moreover, she had loved the palace of the Gaviláns from the first time she entered it. Its immensity and decrepitude appealed to her romantic imagination and her patrician self-regard.

Forty-three years of marriage, three sons who died in childhood, four daughters who survived, and several reversals of fortune later, the *marqués* died. A prig to the end, he refused last rites from a priest whom he deemed unworthy of administering the sacraments to someone of his rank. She was secretly overjoyed when they sealed his casket in the crypt. Now, she thought, now she could begin to live again!

But something terrible had happened — she had become old.

The decades of her marriage had curdled her gaiety into scorn, transformed her charming impertinence into sarcasm, bent her back, whitened her hair, and withered her limbs. The spurs of life still dug into her flesh, but her flesh could not answer as it had when she rode through the forests of the Sierra Madre Occidental or danced until dawn at Chapultepec Castle. The only passions left to her were the vicarious passions of art—literature, music, opera, and theater. Art allowed her to be young and alive in her imagination, if nowhere else. As she steeped herself in those realms of the imaginary, her human connections withered and became mere social rituals. Until José was born. Her last grandchild was beautiful and sensitive, like a storybook character come to life. He awoke a passionate and protective love within her that she had not felt for her own children. She would have adored him even had he not reciprocated, but he was as devoted to her as she was to him, and he shared her passion for art. He loved nothing more than to lie in her vast bed in the morning, listening to her tales of country life while Caruso played on the phonograph. Or, at least, he had until he became infatuated with his piano teacher. Now all he spoke of was this boy, and she discovered that José had revived in her another emotion she had believed to be long entombed—jealousy.

The carriage came to a stop in the first courtyard of the palace. She waited. Her maid opened the door to the carriage and removed the throw. The driver assisted her descent as her maid held open the umbrella. She stepped through the gate into the second courtyard and began to climb the steps to her apartment when she heard the thrilling opening notes of the third movement of the "Moonlight Sonata." She paused and listened. The hands that played the piece were more practiced, confident, and experienced than José's. Waving her maid aside, she went to the grand *sala* and stood at the doorway. The musician was the boy—she could scarcely bear even to think his name, much less speak it aloud—David.

She was forced to admit that he made a charming picture, his long hair falling across his face as his fingers raced across the keyboard. He had a coarse kind of broad-shouldered good looks. She could understand why her fine-boned, delicately beautiful grandson might be drawn to him on the theory of the attraction of opposites. Of course, in ten years' time the boy's stolid muscularity would have turned to fat and his youthful effervescence faded into loutishness; such was the second sight of old age. But for now, she closed her eyes and allowed Beethoven's genius to quicken her pulse. When the boy reached an emphatic finish, she reflexively applauded.

He rose so quickly from the piano bench he nearly knocked it over. "Señora Marquesa, I did not know you had entered the room."

"I love that piece," she said and then, recovering her imperiousness, asked, "What are you doing here?"

"Your instrument is so much finer than anything we have at the conservatory that Doña Alicia gave me permission to practice on it for the competition."

"Competition? What competition?" she asked, seating herself.

The boy, who remained standing, replied, "The Centenario competition, Señora. The winner will be given a scholarship to study at the Conservatoire de Paris for two years."

"I see," she said. "This is something you aspire to."

"Oh, yes!" he exclaimed. "It is the finest conservatory in the world."

"Do you think you will prevail?"

"I do not know, Señora Marquesa," he said. "I started playing later than many of my classmates. That is why I need to practice, night and day."

"You started late? Explain yourself."

He looked down. "My family's means are such that we could not afford a piano, and I did not start playing until I was ten years old, at school. But, like José, many of my classmates began receiving lessons when they were five or six. I lost that time and I shall never recover it. In the end, that may be the difference between winning and losing."

A thought turned in her mind like a key opening a locked door, but to the boy she said only, "Well, in that case you had better resume your practice."

He bowed. "Yes, Señora Marquesa. Thank you."

"For what, boy?"

"For taking an interest in me," he said.

"I assure you," she said, rising to go to her room, "it was no more than a passing interest, and it has passed."

Sarmiento sat at his desk in his office reading a report about a typhoid outbreak in La Bolsa, a notorious *colonia* filled with flophouses and tenements. His department had imposed a quarantine, but the residents had refused to comply because it kept them from going to their jobs. The police were called in, a minor riot ensued, and three people were killed. Ultimately, the quarantine was established and the outbreak contained. The author of the report, a district inspector under Sarmiento's supervision, referred to the three violent deaths as "collateral damage," a masterpiece of bureaucratic dissemblance. He tipped back his chair and sighed. The poor had always resented the health department's agents, but in the past three years, as the economy had soured, their resentment had turned into resistance. His inspectors refused to enter certain neighborhoods without a police escort. The police themselves refused to enter the worst neighborhoods, and who knew what diseases were incubating in them.

An American colleague had sent him a copy of Jacob Riis's book *How the Other Half Lives*, about the tenements of New York City. It was filled with shocking descriptions and illustrated with even more shocking photographs. What was most impressive to Sarmiento, however, was that the plight of the destitute had even been deemed worthy of public exposure and discussion. He despised the Americans for their hypocrisy—defending democratic values in principle while behaving like the most retrograde colonialists—and their adolescent vulgarity. Still, he had to admit their imperfect democracy permitted, tolerated, and sometimes even rewarded scathing criticism of the status quo. A book like Riis's was unimaginable in México, where the government regarded the Indian poor as a state secret, and the upper classes dismissed their misfortunes as the fruit of racial degeneracy.

"The government?" he muttered aloud, casting a scornful glance at his big desk covered with papers bearing the seal of the Superior Sanitation Council. "I am the government."

He got up from his desk and walked to the window, gazing at the volcanoes that floated like mirages in the distance over the domes and towers and ochre-colored roofs of Ciudad de México. How beautiful his city was, how much he loved her, how hopeless he felt about her future.

"Señor Vice Director?"

He turned and saw his secretary standing at the door. "Yes, Juan."

"Sir, there is an Indian out here. He gave me this note to give you. The man cannot speak."

Sarmiento took the note, opened it, and immediately recognized his wife's handwriting. It implored him to come immediately to Coyoacán and to bring his medical bag and surgical tools. Sarmiento brushed past his secretary and saw Padre Cáceres's Yaqui servant, Ramoncito, standing in the anteroom.

"Did you just come from my wife with this note?" he asked.

The man nodded.

"Is she injured?"

He shook his head.

"But someone else is?"

Ramoncito again nodded.

"Very well, let me get my things."

She had sent her carriage and had evidently instructed the driver to race back because the journey was swift and bumpy. At last, they reached their destination, a decaying mansion at the outskirts of the village. When he alighted from the carriage, she was standing at the door to meet him.

"Alicia, what is this place? What are you doing here?"

"A family property," she said. "The rest I will explain later, but now I need for you to come with me."

In the overgrown courtyard, a half-dozen men were smoking and sunning themselves. They were all Indian and their kinship was obvious in their skin tone and features, but they were unlike the servile Indians of the city, for these men, even at rest, were coiled and watchful, like serpents or soldiers. They followed him with hard, wary eyes.

"Who are these people?" he asked her in a low voice.

"Yaquis," she said.

"What are they doing here?"

"This is their sanctuary."

Her response raised more questions than it answered, but he saw she was agitated and did not press her. They passed through a long room arranged like a hospital ward and into a smaller room where a man lay on a narrow, iron-framed bed, staring at the ceiling. His right leg beneath the knee was a swirl of searing red and putrid green. The air was foul with the smell of rot.

"Gangrene," Alicia said. "His leg must be amputated."

"This is why you called me? To chop off the leg of some stranger?"

"Miguel," she pleaded. "He will die unless you help."

"Before I agree to anything, I want an explanation of all this."

She nodded. "Come."

They stepped into a courtyard and sat on a stone bench beneath an ancient olive tree. She told him everything. He listened, with incredulity, then anger, and then grudging admiration at her courage and resourcefulness. When she finished he asked, "Do you have any idea of the trouble that you would bring upon yourself and our family if you are found out?"

"My rank will protect us from the harshest sanctions," she replied. "Carmen Díaz is my friend. She would not abandon me."

"And how long were you planning to continue this . . . I don't even know what to call it. Mission?"

"For as long as the government seizes these people and sells them into bondage."

The government, he thought. That word again. "I *am* the government, Alicia. I hold a public office. My commission was signed by Díaz himself."

"I know. That is why I kept this from you as long as I could. But you are not simply some bureaucrat, Miguel. You are a humanitarian. You could never execute orders that would cause the kind of suffering we have inflicted on the Yaquis."

He thought about the three people killed by the police to enforce his quarantine in La Bolsa. "Hard choices are sometimes required to achieve the general good," he said softly.

"What good is accomplished by driving the Yaquis from their land, killing their women, placing their children into orphanages, and enslaving their men?"

He was quiet for a moment. "The issue is more complicated than your question," he said. "We can discuss it after I operate. I have no anesthetic. This will not be easy."

"I will assist you," she said. "And Santiago—that is his name, Miguel—he is like the other Yaquis. They pride themselves on their ability to withstand pain without a murmur."

"Well," he said, rising and extending his hand to her. "This will put him to the test."

He explained to the Yaqui what he needed to do. The Indian gave a curt nod, took a long drink of the brandy that Alicia had brought for him, and clamped his teeth on a gag of rope. He did not flinch at the sight of Sarmiento's bow-framed saw. The operation was grisly but short and he made a clean cut. As he sutured the flap over the stump, he felt confident that his patient would make a good recovery. The Indian had endured the operation with scarcely a sound.

"You are a brave man," Sarmiento told him.

The Indian removed the gag from his mouth. "I am a warrior," he said in a guttural croak.

"Here," Sarmiento said, handing him the brandy. "Drink this. It will help with the pain."

The Indian took the bottle and, before drinking, said, "I bless you and your family for saving my life."

Afterward, as he and Alicia were driving back to the city, he said, "You were very good today."

She sighed. "It was all I could do to keep from fainting when you handed me Santiago's leg."

"But you didn't faint," he said. "You kept your head." He put his arm around her. "You must know that your project will be discovered. A servant will talk or the captain's superiors will become suspicious about the missing Indians. The villagers in Coyoacán will begin to wonder about your comings and goings. Or one of your patients will escape. You cannot continue this indefinitely."

"What would you have me do, Miguel?"

"I have never commanded your obedience in anything," he said. "I will not start now, but in this marriage we are not two people, Alicia, we are one. If you insist on continuing your work, I will have to resign my post. It is hypocrisy to take bread from Caesar with one hand and strike him with the other."

"No one knows better than I how little you have been able to accomplish in your position."

"Perhaps I have not done all I hoped," he conceded. "But I have been able to accomplish a little and there is a little more I hope to achieve. Particularly now. Díaz wants the city to be a showplace for the Centenario and he has given us more money this year than in the past ten. I hope to use some of those funds to actually make the city a better place to live. Besides, Alicia, Don Porfirio's time is coming to an end. Even he must see that, and accede to the demands of the people to make Madero his vice president. Then real change can begin." After a moment's silence, he continued. "I am asking you as your husband and your friend to give me a little longer in my work to do whatever good I still can."

Reluctantly, she nodded. "As soon as the men are recovered and well enough to travel, I will close the house," she said. "In the meantime, I will not take on any others. But I will find another way to help the Yaquis. I must."

"Tell me, why do they matter so much to you?"

"At first, I had no reason other than my sympathy for what they have suffered," she said. "But now that I have talked to them and learned something of their beliefs, I feel that they are . . . a kind of holy people."

He frowned. "I don't understand."

"The Yaquis believe God gave them their homeland. They say his angels came down from heaven and established the boundaries of their land with prayer and music. They describe a river valley at the edge of the desert that is like a paradise. In thanks, they make their lives into a constant sacrament of praise to God. When they are born, their mothers promise them to Jesus or Mary or one of the saints and they are expected to fulfill that promise by undertaking lifelong religious duties that would be onerous for anyone else. But they do it freely, gladly." A tear ran down her face. "In their minds, Miguel, our war to take their land is a war against their faith. If they are driven off their land, they will be driven away from God."

"My dear," he asked softly, "don't all combatants in wars say God is on their side?"

"The Yaquis don't say that God is their protector in this war. They say they fight to protect God. They would allow themselves to be exterminated before they would accept defeat."

"And you believe them?"

"Yes. They will die to the last man before they surrender their homeland. They must be saved."

"Very well, but next time, consult me," he said. "I will help you if I can."

José had known longing, but not loneliness, until his longing for a friend had been fulfilled by David. Only then did the hours he was alone take on the particular emptiness and weight created by the absence of the beloved. In that void, he was conscious of his solitude as he had never been before. The long galleries and empty rooms of the palace, which had been his playground, now seemed a kind of prison. School, which he had endured, was now unbearable because everywhere he looked he saw the friendships that his classmates formed and from which he was excluded. His parents seemed, more than ever, remote, benign giants who occasionally condescended to look down at him from their heights. As for his grandmother, with whom he would otherwise have filled the hours between his time with David, an estrangement had developed between them because of her dislike for his friend. Instead, he suffered those empty hours with thoughts and memories of David and anticipation at seeing him again. He imagined a future in which they would be together always, older and younger brother. They would live in the same house, where they would play piano duets and then go out and ride their bicycles and eat ice cream in the park before coming home to sleep in the same bed. When he dreamed of lying beside David, feeling his body's warmth, inhaling his distinctive scent, listening to the timbre of his voice as they whispered confidences, a feeling stirred in the pit of his stomach. Indescribably sweet, it seeped through him as if his body was a comb filling with honey. He had no name for this sensation, but even as it thrilled him, it also frightened him with its intensity. When it passed, his loneliness for David made him weep.

Returning to the palace from school one afternoon, he was surprised to see David's bicycle in the courtyard. It was not a lesson day nor had they made plans to see each other. Still, when he heard David's voice coming from the *sala*, he ran inside to see him. There he found David sitting stiffly at the end of the settee delicately holding a cup, while his mother sat on the other end.

Alicia saw him first and said, "José, we've been waiting for you."

"Hi, pea—uh, José," David said with his endearing half-smile.

"Sit down, José. It's early, but if you like you can have a cup of chocolate."

"No, Mamá," José said, sitting in a chair across from them. "Is everything okay?"

The Americanism puzzled her. David said, by way of explanation, "It means, 'is everything in order?'" He looked at José. "I have good news, José."

"Yes, what is it?"

"I'm going to Paris, to study at the conservatory!"

José nodded. David had often spoken of his desire to study in Paris. José sometimes imagined them together walking along its snowy boulevards. "Yes, but what is the good news?"

"That's the good news, peanut. I'm going to Paris."

Suddenly, he understood. David was not referring to a future event but to the present. "When?" José blurted out.

"I leave in a month," David said.

"Isn't that wonderful, José?" his mother prodded gently. "Aren't you happy for your friend?"

But all José could manage was a miserable question, "For how long?"

"The scholarship is for two years," David replied. "José, are you all right?"

He looked back and forth at the concerned faces of David and his mother, then jumped up and ran to his room, where he threw himself on his bed and burst into tears.

He was not aware his mother had entered his room until he felt her weight on the bed and heard her say, "José, you were very rude to our guest. That is not suitable behavior. When he comes for your lesson, I expect you to apologize and to tell him how happy you are for him. He is fortunate to have this opportunity, and he wanted to share his good fortune with you as his friend. You will be glad for him, and there will be no more scenes."

He rolled on his back, wiped his tears with his sleeve, and said, "I do not want him to leave. I love him."

She gazed wonderingly at him for a moment and then stroked his cheek with her palm. "Of course you love him," she said. "He is a sweet boy, and he has been kind to you."

The warmth of her hand and the sympathy in her voice consoled him, but there was a part of him that knew she did not understand what he had meant, but then he did not fully understand himself.

"No," he said emphatically. "I love him."

She sighed. "I know. But when you love another person you must want what makes him happy, not what makes you happy. Do you understand?"

"No, Mamá," he said dejectedly.

"All love comes from God, *mijo*, and God wants nothing from us except that we are happy. He loves us so much that he lets us choose our own paths to happiness, even when he would have us take another path, and even when our path leads us away from him. You love David and you want him to be happy. This is the path of happiness he has chosen, and, as you love him, you must let him take it, even though it takes him to Paris."

He laid his head in her lap and wept scalding tears of loss.

Later, after he had cried himself into exhaustion and fallen asleep, she kissed his tear-stained face and marveled at the extremity of this grief. She had observed that José was infatuated with the older boy, but she had thought it was merely a kind of hero worship. When José had said, "I love him," there was a nakedness in his declaration that had taken her aback because for a moment it seemed as if he was speaking of a lover. But, of course, she told herself, José was a nine-year-old boy who was innocent of such sentiments. No, she thought, José was simply an affectionate, sensitive, and emotional child who formed deeper attachments than other boys his age. She chided herself for letting him be alone too much. It was his loneliness that accounted for the depth of his affection for David. That was her fault, and she would correct it by seeing that José became more engaged with other boys his age.

At tea, her mother asked, "Where is my grandson?"

"He felt unwell and I put him to bed," Alicia said. "By the way, Mother, do you know anything about a scholarship donated to the conservatory for David de la Torre?"

"I am not familiar with the name," she said.

"José's piano instructor," she replied. "An anonymous benefactor made a gift to the conservatory to allow him to study in Paris. He thought I had made the donation and came to thank me. When I told him I was not his patroness, he thought it might be you."

La Niña raised a thin eyebrow. "Me? How extraordinary! The only time I've spoken to the boy was to reproach him for entering my house with muddy boots."

"Well, in any event, it's a wonderful opportunity for him," Alicia commented. Hearing voices approach the room, she said, "My sisters have arrived."

"With better gossip than the prospects of a postal clerk's son, I hope," La Niña said.

Only later did it occur to Alicia to wonder how her mother knew David's father was a postal clerk, and she meant to ask her, but the matter slipped her mind.

The *Imparcial* lay on Sarmiento's desk, its front page dominated by large portraits of Don Porfirio and his newly announced choice for vice president—Ramón Corral, the former governor of the state of Sonora. "Scourge of the savage Yaquis," the approving newspaper caption read. There was no mention of Madero, but the *Imparcial*, like almost all the city's newspapers, was subsidized by the government.

"I see you have been apprised of México's great good fortune," Liceaga said with heavy sarcasm, entering the room. He was the picture of summer elegance in his lightweight gray suit, blindingly white shirtfront and collar, and pale blue necktie.

"It is . . . unbelievable," Sarmiento replied.

"No, it is all too believable," Liceaga said, sitting on the other side of the desk. He lit a cigarette. "Corral is a corrupt, syphilitic Indian killer." He lightly exhaled. "Thus, no one wants to see him president, and, therefore, by choosing him, Don Porfirio guarantees that no one will intrigue to put Corral in his place."

"Which he feared would happen had he named Madero," Sarmiento surmised.

"Madero was never a real possibility. No one with any popular support was going to be named Díaz's successor. That's why he sent General Reyes off to Japan, because Reyes was being promoted for vice president by the army. That's why Limantour decided that now was a good time to visit London to renegotiate our loans with the English banks. The finance minister was being promoted by the technocrats and business interests." He waved his cigarette like a pointer. "Anyone who wanted to be vice president was automatically suspect in Díaz's eyes." He stood up. "So, it's Don Porfirio until 1914."

"At which point he will be eighty-four years old," Sarmiento said. "And when he dies . . ."

"*Après moi le déluge*, as Louis XV said."

"How do you know that Corral is syphilitic?"

"Oh, dear boy, everyone knows that. He's an investor in half the whorehouses of the city, and he has long enjoyed sampling the wares. Somewhere along the line, he got unlucky."

The note came from Luis within days, delivered by his silent Indian companion, Ángel, instructing Sarmiento to meet him at a *pulquería* in Indianilla called Valparaiso. At the appointed hour, Sarmiento pushed past the fringe of tattered *papel picado* at the doorway and passed from the brilliant sunlight into the tobacco-filled, alcohol-soaked darkness of the bar. Along one side of the room was a long, chest-high bar made out of cheap planks of wood and lined with schooners. Behind it were barrels of pulque painted carnival colors—red, pink, blue, and green—to suggest a gaiety that was nowhere else evident. On the other side of the room were tables and chairs hewn from the same rough wood as the bar. On the far wall was a painted ditty he had seen before:

> Do you know that pulque
> Is a liquor divine?
> It is drunk by angels
> Instead of wine?

As his eyes adjusted to the darkness, he saw his cousin with a glass in front of him, his personal, impeccable elegance like a bright light in the alcoholic dimness. Sarmiento went and sat.

"You want a drink?" Luis asked. "The stuff they sell here is less nauseating than the rot you get everywhere else."

"Not much of a recommendation," Sarmiento said.

Luis lifted the glass and took a sip. "I hated pulque before I met Ángel, but it's all he drinks. I've grown accustomed to it."

"How is it you and he travel together as companions without attracting attention?"

"It's simple, Primo, I am a gentleman and he is an Indian. It is assumed he is my servant and in public that is how we treat each other. Privately . . ." He shrugged. "I am sure those details would not interest you."

"Do you love him?" Sarmiento asked impulsively.

Luis said, "Do you really want me to answer that question?"

"I am trying to understand you, Luis. To understand what you are."

"I am a man like other men who love and suffer. Do I love Ángel? Yes, I love him. Do I suffer because of it? Yes. I suffer because my love for him must remain a secret and our life together enshrouded in lies." He swigged the pulque. "Can you imagine living in a world where there is no place in the sun for you, Miguel? Only a few rat holes like this one. Oh, hadn't you noticed? Those ladies over there? Beneath their heavy makeup are the shadows of beards. The barkeep with his gold tooth and thick neck? A woman. This is where those of my type gather, along with whores and thieves." He smiled grimly. "The Valley of Paradise."

Sarmiento cast his glance discreetly around the room and what had at first appeared a typical haunt of the sodden poor assumed a strange and furtive aspect.

"Don't stare, Miguel, it's impolite," Luis said.

"I think I will have that drink," Miguel replied and signaled to the barkeep. When he—she—brought the glass to the table, Sarmiento detected the wrappings beneath her shirt that bound her breasts, but even the loose trousers she wore could not conceal her womanly hips.

"These men who dress like women," he said softly to his cousin, "and this woman who dresses like a man. Your friend Carpenter claims that they represent only a small percentage of homosexuals."

"That is true," Luis said, "but without them, the rest of us would not know how to find each other. They are the red lights of the whorehouse, the cross on the church, the symbol of welcome." He lifted his glass. "Our beacons." He drank. "This is not why I asked you here. I assume you know about Corral."

"Of course," Sarmiento said. "It's appalling."

"Madero anticipated something like this," Luis said. "He will now drop the pretense that he was interested only in being Díaz's vice president and announce he is a candidate for the presidency."

Sarmiento said, "He must know that he will never be allowed to win."

"Yes, of course," Luis said impatiently. "He also knows that he will eventually be arrested, as will all the rest of us who are working for him. That will become the precipitating event."

"For what?" Sarmiento asked, though he feared he already knew the answer.

"A revolution," Luis replied. He lifted his glass and drank. "Everywhere he goes, we gather the local leaders of the disaffected. We tell them to be prepared to lead their followers into the street when the moment comes."

"The army will crush him," Sarmiento said, dropping his voice.

"That would have been true once," Luis replied. "But Don Porfirio knows only too well from his own coup that a powerful military is a threat to his security. For the last twenty years he has reduced the size of the army, decentralized its command, and paid the troops next to nothing. As a result, it is completely unprepared to stop a well-organized, well-armed rebel force."

"I cannot picture Don Francisco at the head of an army," Sarmiento said.

"Do not underestimate him," Luis said sharply. "He is a man of great personal courage, and while you may think that his talk about the spirit world is claptrap, it has given him an unassailable confidence in his mission." He looked at Sarmiento closely for a moment and then asked, "Will you be with us with the time comes, Miguel?"

"Until Don Porfirio, the history of México was a history of rebellions, invasions, civil wars, and insurrections," he said. "Is that you want to return to, Luis? Chaos? Destruction? Death?"

"I want a democracy," he said. "Don't you?"

"Of course, but—"

"But what, Miguel? Díaz will rig the election to secure his reelection, and we will have four more years of autocracy."

"He can't live forever."

"Díaz will die, but not the machinery of dictatorship. Another strongman will take over, but younger than Díaz, more energetic, and more ruthless. The moment to act is at hand."

"You are asking me to commit myself to treason."

"I am asking you to commit yourself to justice," Luis said. "When the time comes," he emphasized. "Not today or tomorrow. Not next month, but soon."

"I cannot give you an answer."

"But you will consider it?" Luis said. "Will you at least do that?"

Sarmiento took a deep breath. "Yes, I will consider it, as events unfold."

Then he swigged the milky, sour liquid and drained his glass.

12

A storm broke over the valley of Anáhuac on the night of September 14, 1910. Great swags of lightning illuminated the smoky sky and sheets of rain, like a downpour of darkness, blinded the city. Sarmiento sat in his study draining a bottle of brandy. Newspapers scattered on his desk proclaimed the reelection of President Porfirio Díaz with 91 percent of the vote, and previewed the Centenario parade—"a pageant of the history of México from the aborigines to the present day"—slated for September 16, Independence Day. He wondered whether Don Guillermo Landa y Escandón, the governor of the city, was also awake, wilting his costly bed linens with sweaty anxiety over whether the rain would spoil his twenty-million-peso party. As for Díaz, Sarmiento had no doubt he slept the peaceful sleep of one who knows that, whatever mishaps may occur, someone else will take the blame.

Sarmiento pictured the city's sewers overflowing and churning the dirt roads of the poor neighborhoods into a fecal stew. The floating gardens of Xochimilco would be sinking beneath the rising tide, and the heaven of saints and angels carved into the ancient facade of the cathedral weeping rainy tears. He imagined the vanquished lake on which the city was constructed rising from its grave. Good, he thought morosely, let the flood come and wash away the entire sordid enterprise that is the Republic of México!

Madero had been arrested in Monterrey just before the August 21 election. Five thousand of his supporters were also jailed, including Sarmiento's cousin, Luis. Luis was in the city at the time and was thrown into the prison at Belem with hundreds of other Maderistas. He got word to Sarmiento, who immediately went to the jail where he had met

Alicia so many years earlier. Outside the crumbling walls of the prison, the makeshift village he remembered was still there. Beneath multi-colored canopies, vendors sold food the families of prisoners took into the jail for the inmates and *evangelistas* wrote pleas for pardons to Don Porfirio on behalf of their illiterate clients. Sarmiento made his way past a cockfight and through a crowd of beggars and pickpockets, brushing away the graphic solicitations of drunk prostitutes. He presented his credentials to an unshaven guard, who waved him through the gate. He found his cousin in the same courtyard where Sarmiento's father had once been confined that preserved some of the serenity and loveliness of the ancient convent. It featured a small, well-tended garden and a fountain spilling clear water. The men who populated it were, like himself, clearly middle class by their dress and attitudes. They stood in small groups smoking and laughing. Among them was Luis.

"Primo," he called, breaking away from his friends. He embraced Sarmiento. "Welcome to purgatory. Cigar? They are excellent."

"No. Are you all right?"

"Perfectly," Luis said. "Other than being in prison, of course. But I am, at least, in excellent company." He waved his cigar at the men surrounding them. "We have lawyers, newspaper editors, university students, socialists, anarchists, and even a priest or two who take their faith seriously. We were all arrested at the same time."

"On what charges?"

Luis laughed. "On what charges, indeed, Primo! Madero was arrested for insulting the president and fomenting rebellion. The rest of us were simply rounded up. I assume we will be released after the election, or maybe when the Centenario is over. My only fear is that Díaz will apply the *ley fuego* to Don Pancho—you know, shoot him in the back and claim he was trying to escape. I think his family is rich enough to protect him."

"Under the circumstances, Luis, I admire your equanimity," Sarmiento said.

Luis led him to the fountain, where they sat on its broad edge, the water murmuring at their backs. "This is only a temporary setback. The revolution Madero has set in motion cannot be stopped." He grinned. "Stop looking at me as if I were delusional!"

"Aren't you, though?"

"If you had seen what I have seen in the last twelve months, Miguel, you would understand. Ten thousand welcomed Madero in Guadalajara, twenty-five thousand in Puebla. In Guanajuato, the mayor ordered the lights turned off at the railroad station, and we were met by three thousand carrying torches and candles. No matter how many thugs Díaz sent to break up our rallies, the people would not be intimidated. Madero was on fire, speaking with a passion and conviction that has not been heard in this country for forty years. They called him the Incorruptible, the Liberator, the Apostle of Freedom."

"But Díaz remains president," Sarmiento observed.

"No matter," Luis said, tapping ash from his cigar. "Porfirito may have won the battle, but he has lost the war."

"Because of the histrionics of the crowds? Come now, Luis, that's just Mexicans being Mexican. You can go to the Plaza de Toros any Sunday and see the *matadores* receive the same reception."

"It wasn't just the crowds," Luis said softly. "I saw with my own eyes that Díaz's México is a Potemkin village, Miguel. All facade with nothing behind it. I saw the real México. The *México profundo* where the poor are so hungry they eat grass and bark. I met Indians whose land is being devoured by Díaz's cronies, entire towns swallowed up, and the people reduced to peonage. I talked to Mexican railroad workers who are paid a fraction of what the American owners pay their own countrymen for the same work. And it's not just the poor or the laborers," he continued. "There are two generations of university-educated men who cannot find work anywhere but on the lowest rungs of their professions because Don Porfirio's clique of eighty-year-olds squat at the top. The conditions of México are ripe for revolution."

"Yet here you are in prison," Miguel said.

"For the moment," he said, smiling. "The old man will release us eventually and then the real fight will begin. Will you be with us, Miguel?"

"With you where? Back in jail? In front of a firing squad?"

Luis frowned. "Wouldn't even those fates be preferable to continuing to serve the dictator, Miguel? Or you still delude yourself that this rotting carcass of a government can be changed from within?" He stood up. "Come, let me introduce you to my fellow prisoners, the future of México."

His cousin's questions hit their mark. A year had passed since Sarmiento had asked Alicia to abandon her sanctuary for the Yaquis so that he could work within the government to make some improvement in the lives of the city's destitute. In that time, he had proposed extending new sewage lines into old neighborhoods, replacing the fetid tenements that housed half the city's poor with apartments that let in air and light, and inoculating children from the preventable diseases that carried thousands of them away each year. He presented his reports to the always-enthusiastic Liceaga only to receive his responses from the Ministry of the Interior—impossible, too costly, impractical, a waste of resources, no, no, no. Instead, the government spent a million pesos on a glass curtain designed by Tiffany for the stage of the new opera house. It spent millions more to finish the cenotaph to Juárez and to erect the Column of Independence at the foot of the Paseo de la Reforma. The government paid the expenses of the thousands of dignitaries from across the world who flocked to the city to witness the apotheosis of Don Porfirio Díaz on the occasion of the one-hundredth anniversary of México's independence. The poor were swept off the streets of the central city and kept away by battalions of police who enforced the cordon sanitaire with billy clubs and mass arrests. Luis was right—Ciudad de México was a Potemkin village, a make-believe European city designed for the tourists and the notables from abroad.

He had moved from his desk to the couch, where he lay with his eyes closed thinking about his father. He remembered the old man sitting in his cluttered room scribbling his diatribes against Don Porfirio and, for the first time, knew how he must have felt, driven into despair, half-mad with rage, and poisoned by his own ineffectuality.

"What can a man do?" he heard himself ask. There was no answer but the rain.

Alicia, awakened by the thunder, reached instinctively to Miguel's side of the bed and found it empty. She sighed. She knew she would find him in the morning asleep in his study, smelling of drink. This had been going on for weeks now, since his cousin had been arrested and imprisoned at Belem. At first she thought it was Miguel's concern over Luis's fate that kept him awake, but she had gone with him to visit Luis and found the younger man cheerful and in good health. In better health than Miguel, who subsisted on brandy and cigarettes. She knew generally the source of his distress was his frustration at his work, but not the particulars because in the last few weeks he had gone silent except for the occasional bitter remark. She worried about him, of course, but his self-absorbed misery also struck her as a form of spiritual vanity. For her, what men wanted and what God provided were often two different matters entirely. Once that was accepted, the task was to get done what was possible with the means that one had been given, not to lament the fact that those means were never enough to do everything. Miguel was a victim of his own rationality—if there was a solution to a problem, he could neither understand nor accept why it was not put in place. His inability to understand the world's irrationality drove him to despair. For her, the world was innately a fallen place—even Saint Paul had confessed, "The good I would do, I do not: but the evil which I would not do, that I do"—and redemption was a process, not a program.

In that spirit, after she had closed the sanctuary in Coyoacán, she had gone about her rounds of charitable work, while praying constantly for the opportunity to find another way to relieve the suffering of the Yaquis. Her prayers were answered when the first lady invited her to join a delegation of women touring the new orphanage.

The orphanage was housed in a massive brick building in a distant, sparsely settled *colonia*, where it was set behind a wide lawn and a high, stone wall. There were dormitories for the children, a chapel, kitchens, dining rooms, classrooms, and workshops where the *huérfanos* were to be taught trades to support themselves after they were released. Rows of windows filled the interior with light. The children swept the broad corridors and washed the walls, tended the gardens, worked in the kitchens and laundries, and served in the dining rooms. In the dormitories, the rows of simple iron beds were crisply made up and the children's possessions stowed in trunks at the foot of each bed.

The women in her party murmured approval at the brightness and modernity of the new orphanage, but Alicia found the orderliness of the place heartbreaking. Even in the worst slums of the city, the children flew through the streets like sooty little birds, filling the air with the hopeful warble of their voices. In the hushed atmosphere of the orphanage, the sunlight itself had an antiseptic quality and the white-smocked orphans drifted like little ghosts. As she sat in the chapel for the inaugural mass, looking at their composed, sad faces, she wondered whether some of them were the children of the Yaquis. Later, when they met with the director, she asked him. He told her some of the orphans had been sent from Sonora, but he could not tell whether they were Yaquis. In any event, he continued proudly, it was his mission to rid all of his Indian charges of their primitive ways, whatever their origins. When she asked him what he meant, he explained that these orphans were drilled in Spanish to purge them of their Indian dialects, steeped in Mexican history and culture, and imbued with orthodox Catholicism to rid their faith of any vestiges of pagan practices.

"We shall make good little Mexicans of all of them," he said proudly.

She had replied, "The Yaqui children come from a heroic race with ancient traditions. If you teach them to forget who they are that would truly be the end of their people."

The director was scandalized. "Señora Condesa, I beg to remind you that the Yaquis have been waging a long and savage war against the innocent settlers of Sonora. To civilize that impulse for violence in their children would be a blessing for them and for us."

The first lady, who happened to overhear the exchange, commented, "But of course, we must civilize these poor children, Alicia."

"You are both quite right," Alicia said, anxious not to call further attention to herself. "Thank you for enlightening me."

But later, she spoke to Padre Cáceres and told him, "If there are Yaqui children at the orphanage, they should be returned to their people. They are the only hope for the survival of their race."

The cleric was not encouraging. "Doña, if the children are here, their parents have been killed or imprisoned. There will be no one to return them to, even if it were possible to obtain information about their families."

"Yes, I have considered that," she replied. "But we know there are a few free communities of Yaquis across the border in Arizona. Would they not be glad to take these children?"

"Of that I have no doubt," he said. "The Yaquis are fiercely protective of their young. But still, how would we get the children out of the orphanage and to the border?"

"Could we not find families who would be willing to adopt them and then escort them to the border? I would, of course, pay all expenses."

"To put them on the underground railroad?" he said. "That is dangerous enough for full-grown men, but for children?"

"If they can be adopted, they could travel legally to the border with their adoptive families," she pointed out. "Quite unlike the Yaqui men who go in secret or with forged documents. As long as the children were in the care of people who could be trusted to return them to their tribe, they would be safe."

"Even if we can find families to adopt them, we would have to be assured that there would be someone to receive them at the border," he said. "Someone equally trustworthy."

"You know the Yaquis," she said. "You could find that person, Padre."

"Perhaps," he said thoughtfully. "I can promise nothing but let me send some messages to the border. I will see what I can do."

"I will return to the orphanage and find the Yaqui children."

"How?" he asked. "You must not be too inquisitive, Doña Alicia. You will only raise suspicions."

"I know," she agreed. "I will think of some plausible reason to account for my presence at the orphanage and pray for God's help in finding these children."

She volunteered to give the children piano lessons. The director was dubious, but he dared not refuse a friend of the first lady. Twice a week, for three hours a day, she sat at a piano and taught whichever children appeared. The lessons often devolved into simple noisemaking, the children pounding the keys as a release from the institutional silence that enclosed them. Word spread among the children about the rich doña with the scarred face and the kind smile who let them play. The children came and went, a few even acquiring rudimentary musical skills. More often, they simply wanted to sit in a maternal lap and tell their stories, recounting, in the guileless way of children, horrors that squeezed her heart. They came from all over México, some longing for home, others happy to have found refuge in the orphanage from destitution and death by starvation. But none of them were Yaqui.

A girl began to appear at the doorway of the music room. She stood with crossed arms, glaring at Alicia and whichever child she was teaching, but she would not enter or respond to questions. She was tall and thin, her skin the color of dried roses, and her hair black as widow's weeds. Her face was hard and plain, but beneath her formless smock, her body was beginning to show the contours of womanhood. Alicia thought she recognized in her features, coloring, and bearing the physiognomy of a Yaqui.

One afternoon, finding herself without students, Alicia began to play Chopin's "Prelude in E-Minor" for her own amusement.

"Make that music again," a harsh young voice said in a dialect of Nahautl that she immediately recognized as Yaqui. She looked up from the piano at the tall girl standing at the doorway. Alicia smiled at her and played the piece again. As she did, the girl edged her way into the room like a skittish cat until she was standing beside the piano, the hardness of her face softening as she listened to the music.

"Sit, Daughter," Alicia replied in the same dialect, to the girl's evident surprise.

"You speak my tongue."

"Yes, Daughter, I have known many Yaquis, and I have been their friend. My name is Alicia. What is yours?"

The girl hesitated, and Alicia thought she might leave, but after a moment, she said, "My name is Tomasa. I am a warrior."

Then she pressed her finger to a piano key and the sound it made startled a smile from her.

José had spent much of the storm beneath the covers, clutching his tattered, one-eyed Steiff teddy bear, a gift from his father for his second birthday. When the storm abated, he had lifted his head from beneath the covers and heard El Morito meowing from the floor beside the bed.

"Morito, come here," he whispered.

The cat hopped up on the bed, padded around in a circle, and then settled on José's chest, staring sleepily at him. He ran his hand along El Morito's back.

"You're wet!" he said. "Were you outside?"

The cat purred.

"I hope the rain doesn't ruin the parade," he told the cat. "Uncle Gonzalo promised to take us." He scratched the cat beneath its chin, which produced even louder purrs. "There will be real soldiers, Morito, and cannons and fireworks over the National Palace! I wish . . ." He finished the thought in his head, *David was here.*

He had hoped for a birthday message from his friend, but his tenth birthday had passed earlier in the month without a word. He had last heard from David in June, when he got a postcard of the Eiffel Tower and a quickly scribbled message he could only half decipher. He rarely touched the piano now, because playing alone made him sad. When his father had offered to give him a bicycle for his birthday, he had asked for skates instead because they were the rage among his classmates.

After David left for Paris, José's classmates began to invite him to their houses and birthday parties and on weekend excursions to Chapultepec Park to watch *béisbol* matches and look at girls and paddle the swan boats across the lake. He suspected their newfound interest in him had something to do with his mother's friendships with their mothers. At first, he was panicked to find himself among his classmates outside of school, where the Jesuits enforced silence and discipline and the boys were indistinguishable in their blue uniforms. Away from school, the other boys were alarmingly loud, profane, and physical. He quickly learned to become an unobjectionable companion by imitating them. He observed their gestures and figures of speech and practiced them when he was alone. He noticed their interests and pretended to share them so he could trade stories about the exploits of their favorite *matadores* and their *béisbol* heroes. His deceptions did not seem very convincing to him, but his classmates seemed willing to be deceived. They accepted him as one of them as long as he kept concealed from them the things he truly loved—his grandmother, opera recordings, his make-believe battles with his toy soldiers, Chopin and "Claire de Lune," his little black cat, his mother's embrace, Chepa the cook's stories about the Aztecs, marionette shows, the flower market beside the cathedral, walking through the Panteón Francés on the Day of the Dead, drinking chocolate with his gossipy aunts, his teddy bear, looking through his stereoscope at scenes of the Rhine and the Danube and the Nile, and David. Even as he acquired these new acquaintances—a pack of boys with which to skate along the paths of the Alameda on Sunday afternoons—his yearning for a true friend, a boy to whom to whisper confidences at night in a shared bed, was undiminished, and in the midst of his schoolmates he felt more alone than ever.

The sixteenth dawned clear and bright. José was up at sunrise, dressed and waiting for the clatter of horseshoes that announced the arrival of Tío Gonzalo and Tía Leticia. He ran downstairs through the gate and into the courtyard, where a knot of admiring servants was gathered around his uncle's custom-made vehicle. The white carriage was drawn by two white English stallions, tall and muscular, unlike the lighter, smaller horses of México. The white ostrich plumes they wore in their green velvet browbands would have seemed absurd on creatures less dignified. The seats of the carriage were upholstered in crushed velvet the same deep green as the uniform of the driver, a flame-haired, freckled young man. On the seat beside the driver was a wicker basket filled with food and drink. Enthroned in the carriage were his aunt and uncle, she thin and pale, he fat and dark, like a husband and wife from a nursery rhyme. Tía Leticia wore a white lace dress over a pale green sheath. Her hair was piled high on her head and adorned with pearls to match the ropes of pearl that hung around her scrawny neck. For once, the worry that usually pinched her face and the sadness in her eyes were absent as she fussed with Tío Gonzalo's collar. He wore a light-gray suit with a pale green tie and an enormous emerald stick pin. The fleshy folds of his fat neck spilled over his stiff collar. His fingers, thick as chorizos, were covered with rings. His platinum watch chain glittered in the sun, and he was smiling his "twenty-four-carat smile," as he called it, because it displayed his big gold front tooth.

José, in his sailor's suit, bounded into the carriage and planted himself between his aunt and uncle.

"Who is this handsome little mariner?" said Aunt Leticia, smelling of tuberose. She kissed his forehead.

"Yes, he's a looker," Uncle Gonzalo said. "Got a girl in every port, I bet."

"No, our little sailor is faithful to the girl he left behind," Leticia replied primly.

His uncle rolled his eyes, and, as was often true when he was with them, José was aware that their remarks were directed at each other, not him.

His parents entered the courtyard, much less gaily dressed, their wan faces straining to show cheerfulness. José knew they had talked deep into the night because when he had been awakened at two in the morning with the urgent need to make water, he had heard them in the drawing room on his way to the toilet. He didn't remember what they had been saying, but his father's voice had the serious tone it took on when he was trying to impart to José an important lesson, the significance of which, to his father's annoyance, José invariably failed to understand. José often misunderstood the grown-ups who surrounded him, although he could sometimes broadly surmise from their tones of voice what they were trying to communicate—humor, displeasure, curiosity, surprise— and respond to that. His father, however, had only two inflections: grave and graver. If José did not understand the meaning of his father's words— a frequent occurrence since the usual topics of his father's conversations, like integrity, honor, and selflessness, denoted nothing to José—he could only nod blindly and hope that assent was the right answer.

"Are you ready to go?" Uncle Gonzalo asked. "The crowds have been gathering along the Reforma since dawn. I have the perfect place picked out, right across from Don Porfirio's reviewing stand."

His father flinched. "We are both feeling slightly unwell . . ."

"Oh, no you don't," Gonzalo interrupted. "This is a once-in-a-lifetime event. You owe it to José so he can tell his grandchildren he saw the Centenario parade."

"Gonzalo is right, Miguel," his mother said, lifting José's heart, which had dropped like a stone at his father's words. "José has been looking forward to the parade for weeks."

"Yes, yes, fine," his father muttered. He helped her into the carriage and then climbed in himself. "Let's go see Nero fiddle while Rome burns."

"Cheer up, Miguel!" Uncle Gonzalo said, slapping his father on his knee. "This is a celebration, not a funeral. Sean, go!"

The redheaded driver shook the reins and the horses pranced out of the courtyard into the street and headed toward the Reforma.

José had never seen so many people, ten, twenty deep on either side of the Reforma. There were men perched in the boughs of trees and boys who had shimmied up lampposts or climbed the statues of the Illustrious Men, two from each state, that lined the broad avenue. When they reached the intersection with the Reforma, the crowds of Indians parted at the sight of the plumed white horses and fairy-tale carriage. They drove to the front of the crowd, where they parked along the roadway beside other elegant carriages, many of them enclosing the families of José's classmates. Across the wide boulevard, José saw a canopied platform raised high above the crowd. In the center of the platform was the presidential throne, its tall back surmounted by two carved eagles. An old, white-haired man in a dark suit sat in the chair as stiffly as a marionette waiting for its strings to be pulled. Beside him sat a stout woman in black, her face obscured by a heavy veil. Around them were men resplendent in military uniforms, red and blue, green and yellow, black and white, with rows of medals and sashes across their chests, wearing plumed and spiked hats. There was a tension in the crowd that José thought was like his own excitement as he waited for the parade to begin. The notes of the presidential anthem were struck by a military brass band. The old man rose, prepared to acknowledge the cheers of the crowd, but he was met by silence and then a single cry: "*Viva Madero!*" The roar of approval from the crowd behind José was quickly extinguished by a John Philip Sousa march and then by cries of "It's starting! Here they come!"

José looked in vain, but he could not see past the top of the driver's seat. He climbed up on the seat between his aunt and uncle.

"José, get down," his mother chided.

"But I cannot see!"

"Go up and sit with the driver," his uncle told him. "He has the best seat in the carriage. Sean, take my nephew and pass the basket down here."

The exchange was made, the pale, freckle-faced driver hoisting José to his seat. He was only a few years older than José, David's age. He grinned at him and said, in bad Spanish, "So, little man, your name is José?"

"Yes, sir," José said politely.

"I am named Sean," the driver said. "Juan in your language." His eyes were bright blue and his teeth were straight and white. A derby sat upon his thatch of red hair and his uniform, almost as tight as a matador's suit of lights, revealed a chest of heroic width. He threw his arm around José's shoulders, pulled him close, pointed to a group of men in the middle of the street that was slowly moving toward them, and asked, his breath grazing José's ear, "Now, that fellow, in the feathers? Is that supposed to be Moctezuma?"

José nodded, unable to speak, as excitement swooped through his body at the sights and sounds of the crowd, the weight of Sean's hand on his shoulder, his leg against Sean's leg, and the approach of the Aztecs. He was abruptly aware that his *pene* had become rigid and slipped through the opening of his undershorts. He looked down at his lap and saw it was sticking up beneath his trousers. He squeezed his legs together to conceal it and it rubbed against the woolly fabric of his trousers, creating a tickling sensation that was both abrasive and delicious. The air filled with the noise of drums, rattles, and whistles. Passing before him, in feathered headdresses and embroidered robes, was a group of Aztec musicians followed by warriors in even more glorious headdresses of iridescent quetzal feathers carrying feather-work shields. Behind them, on a canopied litter carried by six attendants, was an Indian representing Moctezuma.

The Aztec emperor was seated on a bench covered with gold cloth. At his feet was a jaguar skin. He wore a purple mantle and a gold, feathered headdress. He looked neither right nor left but straight ahead as he was carried toward the Zócalo where the National Palace occupied the site that had been his palace. José remembered Chepa the cook had told him that when the Spanish first laid eyes on the emperor, "their guts rose up and they were terrified at the sight of the god." There was a ripple of movement in the immense crowd and then the Indians began to fall to their knees as the cortege passed, only a few at first, then by the hundreds and soon, on either side of the Reforma, thousands were kneeling silently.

"What is this Indian madness!" his uncle exclaimed.

"It's not madness," his father replied. "They are honoring their king."

"Their king?" His uncle laughed. "Their king is King Pulque."

Trumpets sounded. There was the clatter of horses on the pavement and then, trotting behind the Aztecs, came a contingent of men in suits of armor surrounding a bearded man carrying the flag of Castile— Hernán Cortés. A wave of anger rose from the still-kneeling Indians, but from the carriages of the rich came the cry, "*Qué viva Cortés!*"

The armored soldiers stopped before the reviewing stand, dismounted, and bowed to Don Porfirio. He acknowledged them with a jerky wave and they continued on their way.

"Indian insolence," he heard his uncle say. "I blame Madero. When the Indians see dissension among the *gente decente*, it stirs them up. Thank God, Don Porfirio had the strength of character to lock up the little lunatic."

"And the Indians, Gonzalo," his father said. "Are they to eat cake?"

"Not my cake, Miguelito," his uncle said with a laugh. "José, try one of these chocolates. We received a shipment from Vienna." He passed a box of chocolates to José, who took one, offered one to Sean, and returned them to his uncle. He took a bite and chocolate liquid filled his mouth.

"Resigning from the department," his father was saying. "I can no longer serve this government. Díaz is a dictator, pure and simple."

"Only an iron man can rule México," his uncle replied. "Look at these savages! Do you think they're ready for democracy?"

"Not savages," his mother said. "Christians, like ourselves, Gonzalo."

José's attention turned away from the adult conversation back to the parade. A group of men in the powdered wigs and knee breeches of the age of the viceroys rode on a flower-decked float. On a dais was a throne occupied by an actor playing a Spanish king with a crown of Mexican gold on his head. Behind them were men in clerical robes mounted on black horses. They led another group of men in white robes carrying green candles.

"Mamá," José called. "Who are the men with the candles?"

It was his father who answered. "They are victims of the Inquisition on their way to be burned at the stake."

The penitents were followed by a dashing young man on a white charger in the costume of a Napoleonic general wearing a great, plumed tricorne. He was accompanied by two beautiful, similarly dressed young men.

"Iturbide," Uncle Gonzalo murmured. "And look, his grandsons ride with him."

A roar erupted from the crowd. José scanned the street and saw the cause. An actor dressed in the simple vestments of a country priest, carrying the banner of the Virgin of Guadalupe, walked alone in the center of the Reforma.

"*Viva Hidalgo!*" came the cries. "*Viva la patria! Viva México!*"

As Hidalgo approached, the crowd spontaneously burst into the national anthem. Everyone rose in the carriages, on the reviewing stage, even Don Porfirio, who, José saw, wiped tears from his eyes.

"See," his uncle said triumphantly. "See the president's tears! What dictator weeps out of love for his country?"

"My father once told me that Don Porfirio can cry on cue," his father replied.

"With all due respect, Miguel," his uncle said, "your father was a madman. Is that the path you intend to follow?"

"I am already well advanced on it," his father replied. "I support Madero. That is why I am leaving my post."

"And you, Alicia, are you also a Maderista?" Uncle Gonzalo asked.

"I am with my husband," she said.

Behind Hidalgo came a cavalcade of soldiers and sailors from a dozen countries, carrying the flags of their nations and of México.

"Papá, look!" José cried. "Japanese!"

"That's a queer lot," Sean said.

"There are the *inglés* sailors," José pointed out, testing his English. "Your country."

"I'm Irish, lad. The English are our enemies."

"Why?"

"That's a long story, to be told with tears and whiskey," the older boy replied. "Someday when you're older. Look, here comes your army."

A general with a handlebar mustache, ropes of gold braid, and a plumed helmet led the march of the cavalry. After the horsemen came the artillery, rank after rank of caissons loaded with cannons of every size and dimension and then the infantry, a great, silent mass of soldiers that filled the sky with bayonets. José was enthralled—here were his toy soldiers come to life, but the crowds of Indians fell silent as the army passed.

"That's your answer to Madero, Miguel," Uncle Gonzalo said.

There was a break in the ranks of soldiers and in the space between one unit and the next came a group of Indians chained together in iron collars, one man linked to the next by ropes of heavy iron. They wore the dirty white costume of countryside *peónes* but they looked angry, not frightened, and they carried themselves as proudly as their chains permitted. The lead man wore a sign around his neck and on it were the words *guerreros yaquis*.

José was astonished. *These* were the Yaquis, the fiercest warriors in México. In the newspapers they were depicted as savages in loincloths swinging axes and slaughtering men, women, and children for their scalps, which they wore on belts around their waists. These men looked nothing like that. They looked like the Indians of the marketplace.

"Papá, are they really Yaqui warriors?"

It was his mother who said, "This is shameful."

"No, it is a message to the mob," Uncle Gonzalo said.

The sight of the Yaquis had deepened the silence of the crowd, and now, as the next contingent appeared, José could sense fear.

"Who are they?" Sean asked as the horsemen approached.

"The *rurales*," José replied, awed. José explained to the young driver that the *rurales* were highwaymen who Don Porfirio had persuaded to protect the roads of the countryside instead of terrorizing them. They were clad in tight gray *charro* suits braided in silver, with yellow kerchiefs around their necks; the brims of their gigantic sombreros cast shadows that rendered them faceless and even more menacing. They rode beautiful horses on hand-tooled leather saddles heavy with silver studs and conchos. Their polished boots were fitted with silver spurs and rested in silver stirrups. Bandoliers crisscrossed their chests and their rifles were slung over their shoulders.

"Thieves and murderers," his father said. "Those are the kinds of men who keep your president on his throne. We've seen enough, Gonzalo. Take us home, please."

"But Papá," José protested. "There's more."

"Your father is right," his mother said. "Gonzalo, please."

"As you wish," his uncle said and curtly commanded the driver to return to the palace.

That night, José stood on the roof of the palace with his grandmother and watched the fireworks. They burst in the air above the Zócalo and rained fire in all the colors of the rainbow. When the last one had exploded, he stood in the darkness, thinking about the day, the parade, the redheaded, blue-eyed driver, the odd sensation in his *pene*, the quarrel between his father and his uncle, the Indians falling to their knees when Moctezuma passed, the thrilling, frightening ranks of the *rurales*, and he felt, without knowing how to express it, that he had been part of something momentous.

"Abuelita," he said, groping for words to frame his thought. "Was today history?"

"Today history?" she repeated incredulously. "You are too young to concern yourself with history." As the echoes of the last blasts faded in the air and the smoke dissipated above the city, the night birds began to sing again and the stars came out. In a softer voice she said, "History is simply the passage of time, José, so we are in history at every moment."

"History doesn't start after we die?"

"When we die, we are no longer in time," she said. "We are in eternity somewhere in the sky with God," she continued, somewhat disdainfully, as if imagining an unfashionable resort town. "On earth, we are simply the dead."

13

The Mexicans killed my mother." *Plink, plink, plink.* "I wanted to avenge her." *Plink.* Tomasa lifted her fingers from the piano keys and glanced at Alicia. "I know now that not all Mexicans are bad. Maybe they sent all the bad ones to Sonora to make war on my people." *Plink.* "That is why I left my brother in Arizona and followed the warriors home, so I could fight with them."

"You followed the warriors into the desert? Why didn't you go with them?" Alicia asked. She was teaching Tomasa to play by ear the Chopin prelude that had attracted the girl. She made it clear she did not wish to learn anything other than that piece and she refused to learn to read music. Alicia would play a few notes while Tomasa studied the placement of her fingers and then she would imitate her. The girl had intense concentration and fierce persistence, and she was well on her way to mastering the piece. As they worked together, she had begun to speak about herself in short bursts. She told Alicia her father was a warrior killed in battle against the Mexican army and that she had a younger half-brother. Her mother was hanged in a roundup of the Yaquis. She and her brother escaped with a band of refugees to an American border town in Arizona. Today, for the first time, she spoke of how she had come to the orphanage.

"The men would not take me," she said. "They said I was a child and a girl besides, but I am the daughter of a warrior." She pressed a half-dozen keys as if for emphasis. "They left at night. I waited and then tracked them. I planned to come into their camp the next day when we had gone too far for them to take me back."

"Weren't you afraid of becoming lost?"

She seemed surprised by the question. "I followed the road of the ancestors," she said. "Their souls burned in the night sky and lit the path to the homeland."

"The stars," Alicia said, grasping her meaning. "You were guided by the stars."

She nodded. "The men moved faster than I could follow and I lost them," she said. "After three nights I reached the homeland. I had brought no food or water, only the clothes on my back. When the Mexican soldiers found me, I was too weak to fight."

Alicia glanced at the girl. There was nothing special to distinguish her from all the other Indian girls Alicia encountered in the course of a day in the city, drawing water from communal fountains, selling lottery tickets, minding fruit and vegetable stalls in the markets, carrying tiny black-eyed babies in slings across their backs. But this girl had walked across the desert without food or water to become a soldier. She began to understand why, after thirty years of warfare, the Mexican army had been unable to defeat the Yaquis.

"The soldiers took me in chains to their fort at Potam. I was happy to breathe the air of the homeland again, even with an iron collar around my neck, but then they tried to . . ." She slammed her hand on the keyboard. "I fought them off but there were too many. Six of them held me while another put his thing in my mouth. I bit down so hard I could taste his blood. They beat me and threw me into a room with other Yaquis. They chained us together and marched us to a freight car and nailed it shut. We waited there for two nights before it began to move."

"Without food or water?" Alicia asked.

Tomasa nodded. "We drank our piss until we were dry. We licked our skin for the flavor of salt. We began to die." She added fiercely, "But we died like Yaquis, in silence or cursing the Mexicans." She played the first notes of the prelude before continuing. "After seven nights, we came here, to this town. They opened the doors of the car and the ones who were alive were put in a corral, like animals. Our feet were still chained together, but my legs are thin and I slipped out of the shackles. I escaped! But this town . . ." She shook her head. "There are so many people, more people than I have ever seen in one place. I did not know where I was or where to go. I stole some food from a market and wandered for a day until I saw a church that was like the churches of our villages, small and white and plain. I sought refuge there."

Alicia imagined the confusion and terror of the child as she wandered the streets of the city, hungry, thirsty, and alone.

"Inside there was an altar for San Miguel, the warrior. I prayed to him for help. The monks found me—the brothers of San Francisco. They fed me and let me bathe. I would not answer their questions because I was afraid they would return me to the soldiers. They brought me here." She gently pressed a key. "Now my mother comes to me in my dreams. She is very angry that I left my brother alone. She tells me I must return home to him. This is what I must do. As soon as I can, I will escape."

She spoke with certainty and Alicia did not doubt she would escape the orphanage on her own if she could find no other way to return home.

"I can help you, Daughter," Alicia said. "If you will let me."

"Why?" she demanded.

"Your brother needs you. Your people need you."

"I will leave soon," she replied, "for I have learned what I wished for you to teach me."

Then she played the prelude faultlessly.

Sarmiento reread the telegram. "Package safe in El Paso. When will you come to claim it?" It was signed by "LP." He smiled at his cousin's attempt at discretion. There was no need. All of México knew that Madero, released on bail, had crossed the border into the American state of Texas and issued a call to rebellion. Thus far, the call had not been heeded. Two months after the Centenario celebrations Don Porfirio seemed as entrenched as ever. There were reports of fighting in Morelos between the government and a ragtag Indian army that called itself the Ejército Libertador del Sur, the Liberation Army of the South, led by a self-appointed general named Zapata. The official press, however, assured its readers that General Huerta, called the "Indian butcher" for his ruthless suppression of the Mayas, had been dispatched to Morelos and would soon extinguish the revolt. Beyond that, the Pax Porfiriana kept the country in its iron thrall. The apparent hopelessness of Madero's cause should have made his cousin's invitation to join the rebellion—"When will you come to claim it?"—seem, at best, quixotic if not deluded. Much had changed for Sarmiento in the eighteen months since he had sat in the strange, squalid *pulquería* with Luis—it was called, he remembered, the Valley of Paradise. Even then, he had understood Díaz's government to be autocratic and corrupt, but he had held out hope that some incremental and positive change was possible, if only as a matter of the regime's self-interest. Don Porfirio's cynical motto—*Pan o palo*, bread or the stick—had once at least acknowledged some payment was due to the people in exchange for their freedoms. This was no longer true. Somewhere along the line the old man, hearing the cries of his people for bread, had muttered, like another autocrat, let them eat cake. Now there was only the stick, the billy club, the shackles. Díaz was a cancer on México and, if the patient was to survive, he must be carved out of its body. As a physician, Sarmiento saw his duty clearly. Now he must explain to his wife why it was necessary for him to leave her and their child, perhaps never to return alive.

José was mesmerized by the sight of himself in the long, gilded mirror. He loved his new evening clothes—black tailcoat with silk facings, black trousers with a satin stripe, glossy black pumps, white waistcoat, stiff shirt and wing collar, and a white silk bowtie. His suit had been made for him to accompany his grandmother to his first opera by Señor Vargas, the ancient tailor who had cut his grandfather's clothes. In his dusty shop, Vargas curtly instructed José to remove his cadet's uniform and to stand perfectly still while the old man took close measurements of every part of José's body, withered fingers brushing José's flesh, while mumbling to himself, "*Qué buena forma.*" The tailor's touch was discreet but approbative, as if José were a rare and particularly fine bolt of cloth, one with which he could make something extraordinary. The tailor's appreciative attentiveness to his body made José flush with pleasure. José did not understand his reaction, any more than he understood why he disliked it when his grandmother's confessor, Padre Juan Pablo, cupped José's face between his liver-spotted hands and lifted it as though he were about to kiss him with his fishy mouth. Yet both men, when they laid their hands on José's body, touched in him the same chord, one producing pride and the other repulsion.

Reluctantly, José tore himself away from the mirror to present himself to his grandmother. La Niña was dressed in her habitual black but not the rusty widow weeds she ordinarily affected. Rather, she wore a resplendent ball gown of jet, painstakingly sequined and beaded so that when she moved, it shimmered like starlight on black water. Her seamed cheeks were powdered smooth and rouged with a subtle tint of rose. Her mouth was painted in the same shade. She exuded lavender and jasmine. In place of her mantilla, her heavy white hair was piled on her head and adorned with a tiara. Around her neck hung a latticed necklace ablaze with diamonds, and diamond earrings dripped from her ears. José was amazed at her transformation from crone to queen, like a character in a fairy tale. She crooked a bejeweled finger at him and beckoned him forward.

"Old Vargas knows his business," she said approvingly. "You are as handsome as a prince. Come, let us go."

While they inched toward the entrance of the brilliantly lit theater, behind a long line of carriages and automobiles, La Niña provided detailed instructions on how he was to comport himself, but José's attention was captured by the sight of the beautifully dressed men and women alighting from their vehicles at the door of the great theater. When at last they reached the entrance, a uniformed usher rushed to open the carriage door, but La Niña waved him away in favor of her own footman. They descended the carriage to a red carpet. José offered his arm to his grandmother and led her beneath the great stone arch carved with the masks of comedy and tragedy into the foyer. The floor, white marble veined with gold, reflected the opalescent light of the dozen enormous lanterns and the massive chandelier. It was as if they had stepped into a pearl. The air was heavy with the scents of perfumes and colognes—in the garden of fragrances he detected rose, gardenia, clove, lime, and bay rum—and filled with the rumble of conversation. From fragments of conversation—"that beautiful boy? Her grandson," "one of the last grand ladies," "looking every minute of her age"—he realized that some of the talk was about his grandmother and him. A few women half-curtseyed as they passed, eliciting from his grandmother a curt nod of acknowledgement, but as he had been instructed, he looked straight ahead. He escorted her up the wide stairway to their box. A footman bowed at the sight of them, pulled back the heavy red drapes, and stepped aside to allow them to enter. Two gilt chairs had been set in the center of box, close to the railing. José stood behind his grandmother's chair, pulling it back slightly, and waited until she was seated before he took his own seat beside her. The vast theater was beginning to fill and José was again aware of the attention he and his grandmother attracted from the crowd, but he was too dazzled by all that lay before him to do more than dimly notice the fingers pointed at their box and the half-heard remarks.

Beneath a circular ceiling painted with plump putti, the Teatro de México was a rococo pile of white marble, pink damask, and gold. The facades of the tiered boxes were plastered with gold-leafed allegorical figures. Above the proscenium arch were two other massive arches thickly decorated with gods and angels. The proscenium itself was plastered with gilded fleur-de-lis. Enormous mirrors set along the sides of the house redoubled and echoed the decorative frenzy, and the soft light lilting down from the dazzling crystal chandelier added depth and dimension. The stage was hidden behind heavy gold curtains, the apron ablaze with footlights. As the musicians filed into the orchestra pit and began to tune their instruments, José's heart raced with anticipation. A few minutes later, the lights dimmed. The conductor emerged to a torrent of applause. His grandmother, who had been sitting beside him with regal indifference, now touched his hand. The moan of a single violin began the overture. Within moments, currents of music swelled through the still, scented, hothouse air. As the golden curtains slowly parted, José thought his heart would explode with excitement.

And then, he frowned. The stage was bare but for a row of battered papier-mâché palm trees against an immense painting of a dark stone wall and a pair of seated hawk-headed Egyptian gods. Two fat men stood near the center of the stage. One wore a long, white tunic, his arms covered with snake-shaped bracelets. The other was clad like a soldier in a leather skirt and breastplate, but his face was pink and jowly. José thought he looked more like a butcher than a general. The two men declaimed to the music in Italian, facing the audience rather than one another. The fat soldier burst into a song and when he finished, the audience applauded. He bowed and waved his hand. A stout woman emerged from the wings in a gold gown and a long headdress surmounted by a crown. She and the soldier sang for a moment and then another woman appeared, this one so fat that her chins bobbled like a windup toy. She wore a black wig that came down in a curtain of hair on either side of her face and a midnight-blue gown. The audience roared and there were cries of "Tetrazzini!" She and the two men sang for a moment and then a procession of singing soldiers filled the stage, followed by a man wearing the headdress of a pharaoh. The music grew loud and martial. José understood from the repetition of the word "*guerra*" that the soldiers were going to war. When the song ended, everyone departed the stage but the woman called Tetrazzini.

José knew that the opera was make-believe, but the make-believe seemed to him, who dwelled so deeply in his own detailed fantasies, shopworn and perfunctory. He could not bring himself to imagine that this porcine woman who looked like a cook was the beautiful Princess Aida. He slumped back in disappointment and began to fidget with the creases in his trousers. The opening notes of a lovely song drew his attention to the stage. Tetrazzini lifted her heavy arms, tilted her head, and, alone in the footlights, began to sing. The house was hushed as she cast her song into the silence. It was not the purity of her voice as much as her certitude that pierced his heart. With every cell in her body she communicated her conviction that she *was* Aida. He leaned forward, captivated, and he believed her. Her singing spun a web of enchantment that transformed the painted backdrop; the leaves of papier-mâché palm trees rustled with a desert breeze and the painted walls acquired the heft of stone. In the mesmerizing pool of her voice, everything had changed, not only on the stage, but in himself. He was still aware he was watching an illusion—paper trees, fat woman—but simultaneously he was transported to Egypt, where a beautiful young girl sang of love. He experienced something similar when he reread his favorite novel, imagining himself in a ship scouring the bottom of the ocean with Captain Nemo, but all that took place in the solitude of his mind. Here, his imagination was stimulated and intensified by the woman on the stage. When she reached out her hand as she ended her song, she seemed to be reaching for him, beckoning him to enter this marvelous fantasy. He reached back, his hand floating in the air, and in his mind their fingers touched.

"José, what are you doing?" his grandmother asked, breaking the spell.

"Applauding, Abuelita," he replied, raising his other hand and joining the deafening cheers and applause.

He had never felt such grief as he did when the opera drew to a close, Aida and Radames buried alive in the crypt, Princess Amneris prostrate above them. When the princess intoned her final "*pace*" to the imprisoned lovers, he could not see the stage for his tears. His head was filled not only with thoughts of the dying lovers but of David. He felt his grandmother's hand in his and glanced at her. She, too, was weeping. And then the music stopped, the curtain swung shut ending the tale, and the house exploded. The audience cheered, applauded, stamped its feet, and wailed the name "Tetrazzini!" He jumped to his feet and joined the cries, his grief transformed into wild joy. The curtains opened and Tetrazzini appeared on the stage, where she was soon ankle deep in roses flung from the crowd. He wished he had brought some gift to thank her for the journey she had led him on, but he could only beam love and gratitude toward her. He wept and applauded with the rest of the audience, demanding curtain call after curtain call. Tetrazzini burst into joyous laughter, her head bobbing with delight and cried out, "*Viva México!*" which incited the crowd to even higher peaks of delirium. "*Viva Tetrazzini!*" it roared back, in a single mighty voice that rattled the crystals of the chandelier. "*Viva! Viva! Viva!*"

His heart did not return to its normal beat until he was in his bed, hours after his last glance at the empty, flower-strewn stage. As he looked around his moonlit room in the deepening silence, he felt as if his feet had at last touched ground after descending the steps of a great height. Almost instantly, he was asleep.

Sarmiento lay on the sofa in the bedroom he had shared with his wife for over a decade, smoking. He pretended to read a medical journal while he watched her out of the corner of his eyes as she loosened her hair, shook it out, and reached for a silver-handled brush. She was the least vain woman he had ever met, but he assumed the pleasure she took in this nightly ritual derived in part from the matchless beauty of her long, black, glossy hair. The pinkish light of the paired Argand lamps that illuminated the mirror softened her facial scars. She wore a white nightgown, her shoulders covered with a beige cashmere shawl. Around her neck was the crucifix she never removed and on her fingers two rings, her wedding band and a gold ring set with a pearl. She brushed her hair with long, slow strokes. This is her place, he thought. She belonged here in this absurd but charming palace where the roof leaked, the servants stole, and La Niña refused to install electricity because she was convinced it would seep from the outlets and poison the household. This was her place in the world, but not his.

"Miguel, may I disturb your reading?" she asked tentatively.

"I am only pretending to read while I watch you," he said.

"Your journal must be very dull," she replied, smiling.

"What would you like to talk about?"

"There is a girl at the orphanage. Tomasa. She is a Yaqui who was captured by soldiers in Sonora and arrived here after terrible hardships. Her parents are dead. Killed by our soldiers, but she has a younger brother in Arizona for whom she is responsible. I promised her I would help her reunite with him." She paused in her brushing. "I told the director of the orphanage if he released her to my custody she could enter service here. He agreed. But I must still find a way to get her to the border."

He sat up. "How old is she?"

"Thirteen, perhaps. Not old enough to travel alone for such a distance, particularly without proper documents. Padre Cáceres said he would try to find a couple to adopt her and escort her, but his parishioners are . . ."

"Incapable of such an undertaking," Sarmiento said. "They are good people, but poor. Not the kind of people who travel for leisure. They could attract the attention of the authorities and be intimidated by them into confessing their true purpose."

"Yes," she said. "If Tomasa were an infant or even a small child, they could claim her as their child and who would question them? But a girl on the verge of womanhood is a different matter, and, well, she is rather fierce, Miguel. I'm afraid if she were questioned, she would run away."

He stood and walked behind her. "I will take her myself, Alicia."

With a puzzled expression, she said, "You?"

He placed his hands gently on her shoulders and said, "I will take her to the United States. Once I reunite her with her brother, I will continue on and join Madero, who has escaped to Texas, where he plans a revolution against Díaz."

She had been expecting this, or something like it since he had resigned his position at the Superior Sanitation Council. His restlessness and unhappiness had decreased, and he had begun to seem his old self again. Until this moment, she had not understood that this was because he had been coming to a decision and now he had made it. She knew she had the power to prevent him from leaving, although she doubted that even she would be able to restrain him for long. Once he was in thrall to an idea, he would suffer under its compulsion until he carried it out. This was their most basic difference. For her, ideas were phantoms that had only such power as one gave them, while humans were real with actual needs. Ideas were men's Moloch, the false gods they fabricated, clothed in purple, crowned, and to whom they then sacrificed themselves. Themselves and others, spilling real blood for an illusion. So she thought as he spoke of democracy and freedom and liberation.

"Miguel," she said, cutting him off. "Are you prepared to kill?"

Startled, he said, "I don't understand."

"Don Francisco wants to lead a revolution," she said. "Revolution is war. War, Miguel. Will you fight? Will you kill?"

She saw from his frown that this was not a question he had asked himself. He tipped his head back and closed his eyes. After a moment, he said, "No, I will not kill."

"How can you be sure?" she pressed.

"I have already killed once," he said softly, and she knew he was speaking of the servant girl who had died at his hand when he tried to abort their child. "That was enough for this lifetime. Besides, I am a doctor. I am sworn to preserve life, not to take it." With a resolute expression, he continued, "Yes, there will be war and death, but no man will die at my hands and I will save those who I can save." He reached for her hand, smiled sadly, and said, "Why couldn't you be like other women and throw yourself at my knees, weeping and begging me not to go? Instead, you ask me the one question that makes me doubt myself."

"I am like other women," she said unhappily. "I do not want you to go. I do not want you to be injured or killed, and if this revolution fails, I fear I will never see you again."

"If the revolution fails," he said, "I will seek refuge in the United States and you and José will come to me and we will begin a new life there."

"Oh, Miguel," she cried. "To give up everything for these ideas?"

"The suffering all around us is not an idea, Alicia, it is reality. Like the suffering of the girl, Tomasa. Don't you want to help more than one child at a time?"

She threaded her fingers through his and came to a decision of her own. "If you must go, I will go with you."

"War is no place for a woman," he said firmly.

"I don't mean that I will join your revolution," she replied. "But you will be less conspicuous if we travel as a family. We can go together as far as the border. I will take Tomasa to her brother and you will go to Don Francisco. And then I will return here to our home and wait for you."

"It's not necessary," he said quietly.

"It is," she told him. "I *am* like other women, Miguel. I know I cannot prevent you from going, but I am not ready yet to let you go."

He nodded, took her hands in his, and kissed them.

José felt a hand stroke his cheek and then gently shake his shoulder. He opened his eyes to the sight of his father sitting at the edge of his bed. A single lamp lit the room. His father was fully dressed in his habitual black suit. His face was grave but his eyes were filled with a tenderness José rarely saw in them.

"Papá, is something wrong?" José asked, sitting up in bed.

"No, *mijo*, just get dressed," he said quietly. "I'll wait for you outside."

His father left the room. José yawned and glanced at the window. He could see from the ashy pallor of the sky that it was near dawn. He drew the blankets around him to ward off the chill and considered the situation. He might have worried that he had angered his father except for the gentleness in his eyes and voice. Could his father be planning a surprise for him? This seemed unlikely because his birthday had passed and the Nativity was still two months away. Sleepily he tossed aside his blankets—waking El Morito, who hissed a complaint—and dressed quickly in his cadet's uniform, fastening its many buttons with icy fingers.

His father was waiting in his buggy at the doors of the palace. José climbed in beside him, wishing that his father had chosen to take his grandmother's carriage, which was large and warm and comfortable.

"Where are we going?"

"You'll see, José."

"Is Mamá coming?"

"No, what I have to show you is for your eyes alone."

José shivered, his mind filled with questions, but just then Chepa came running out of the palace with chocolate and *pan dulce*, a horsehair blanket draped over her shoulder. She chided his father for taking José out into the morning vapors without sufficient covering as she laid the blanket across José's lap and gave him his breakfast.

She concluded her scolding by saying, "And where are you taking him? Decent people do not go abroad at this hour. Only thieves and, well, worse, Doctor, and I'm sure you know what I mean."

Sarmiento smiled. "I will avoid the riffraff, Chepa. As a matter of fact, we are going to church."

She scowled. "Now you're mocking me!"

"No, I am sincere," he said. "I am taking my son to the cathedral."

She glared at him, decided he was being truthful, and said to José, "Remember to say your prayers for your family, Josélito. God loves the prayers of children above all others. And you," she said to his father, "I don't know what you're up to, but you might try a prayer or two yourself, if the words don't scorch your unbelieving mouth!"

His father laughed, shook the reins, and they trotted toward the Zócalo.

José sipped his chocolate and nibbled his gingerbread as his father drove them through the quiet streets, steering by the rows of red police lanterns in the middle of the roadway. The flicker of gas lights gave way to electric street lamps as they approached the great plaza. His father halted the buggy in front of the cathedral across from the streetcar kiosk where the big green and yellow cars were lined up in a double row readying for the day's runs. José looked at them longingly. He had never been on a streetcar, but he loved to watch them race along their tracks, sparking the electric lines overhead, the windows filled with the faces of their passengers. David had promised to take him on a streetcar to San Ángel, but then David had left.

His father, getting out of the buggy, said, "Here we are."

"Are we really going into the cathedral, Papá?" José asked.

He hadn't thought his father was serious when he told Chepa they were coming here because, as was well known, his father did not believe in the existence of God. José himself was quite satisfied that God existed, although his picture of God owed a great deal to the glowering portrait of his grandfather—long dead before he was born—that hung in the grand *sala*. That God was perpetually enraged but also quite remote, and José knew he was too unimportant to engage the deity's interest. He believed he was watched over by gentler spirits: by Jesus, whom Chepa called "*diosito lindo*" as if he were another of her grandchildren; by Jesus's mother, Mary, who had the same calm and loving eyes of his own mother; and by his guardian angel, whom he was always trying to catch in the corner of his field of vision, where Chepa told him he could be seen.

His father lifted him out of the buggy, as if he were a baby and not a ten-year-old boy. His protest died on his lips because the power of his father's body as he lifted and held him made him feel warm and protected.

"Not inside the cathedral," his father said. He crooked a finger upward. "To the top."

He followed the direction of his father's finger. Outlined against the sky's faded brocade was the west bell tower, where Santo Ángel de la Guarda lived. He was the little brother of Santa María de Guadalupe, who lived in the east tower. She was so immense that, when she was rung on a clear day, she could be heard all the way to heaven.

His father reached into the buggy for a lantern and handed José the blanket. "You may need this when we reach the top," he said. He stopped a passing Indian and gave him a peso to watch the horse and buggy.

He followed his father through the small, wooden door that led into the bell tower. His father lit the lantern and began to ascend the narrow stone risers. José tried to keep pace but the stairs were steep and the walls sweated a piercingly cold chill that made his teeth rattle. Cold and tired, he stopped. In a moment, he had lost sight of the lantern and stood in utter darkness.

"Papá!" he called, frightened. "Papá!"

His father came back down the stairs to where José was leaning, breathless, against the damp wall. "Do you remember when you were very little and rode on my back?" He stooped down. "Come on, *mijo.* Climb up and I will carry you the rest of the way."

He clambered onto his father's back, tucked his legs beneath his father's arms, and clasped his father's chest. He could feel the heat of exertion rising from his father's body, deepening the familiar scents of tobacco and bay rum. He leaned his cheek against his father's neck and closed his eyes, and he was a toddler again being swept off his unsteady feet by his enormous father, who slathered him with kisses and called him "*mi hombrecito*" — my little man.

José did not doubt that his father loved him, but it was the bodies of the women of his family from which he ordinarily received the animal intimacy that created love's profoundest bond. The smooth, soft, and yielding bodies of his mother, grandmother, and aunts swaddled him in flesh. His father's embrace was very different. His body was hard and his skin covered with bristly hairs. In his barbed embrace, José did not lose himself, as he did in his mother's arms, but remained a distinct entity. His mother's body sheltered him; his father's body challenged him. His mother's touch was imbued with the nostalgia of the womb, calling him back to a place of unquestioned safety. His father's strong hands had delivered him from that womb and continued to push him forward into the world.

They reached the cavernous room where a dozen lesser bells were hung and ascended a final flight of stairs to the top of the tower, where they stood on a platform beneath the three tons of Santo Ángel. José eased off his father's back. His father draped the blanket around José's shoulders, took his hand, led him to the east side of the tower, and said,

"*Mira*," as the eyes of morning began to open above the snow-shrouded peaks of the volcanos, Popocatépetl and Iztaccíhuatl.

He watched the light break across the valley, revealing the green and brown of farmland. The occasional flash of colored tiles marked the dome of a church of one of the outlying villages. He could see the silvery sheen of the five small lakes that, in ancient times, had filled most of the valley. His eyes traced La Viga, the last surviving canal from the time of the Aztecs, as it flowed toward the city from Lake Xochimilco. As it had in Moctezuma's time, it connected the countryside to the city, and its surface was clotted with barges and canoes laden with food and flowers for the markets. His father led him around the platform, and he saw the Paseo de la Reforma, almost deserted at this hour, cutting west toward the mossy forest and castle-covered hill of Chapultepec. He could see the domes and towers of the colonial city amid the marble structures of the Centenario, seventeenth-century tenements, and the new suburbs of the rich. Electric streetcars and horse-drawn carriages shared the same venerable cobblestone streets. Far off, a train crossed an iron trestle and plunged into a remnant of primordial forest. He saw everything all at once as the sun rose higher in the sky, and he could only murmur, "Oh, Papá, it is so beautiful. I never knew it was so beautiful."

"It is," his father said. "This is our patrimony, José. Do you know what that means?"

José, still astonished by the landscape unfolding beneath him, could only shake his head.

"This is México, Josélito. This is what our fathers have given us to love and protect and, if need be, to lay down our lives to preserve it for our sons. This is our world, José."

José's heart beat with pride for his country and love for his father, and he could not tell where one ended and the other began.

"Yes, Papá," he said, slipping his hand into his father's. "This is our world."

14

On the sidewalks of El Carmen, awed passersby stopped and pointed at the Silver Ghost. Even on the *colonia*'s gouged roadways the Rolls-Royce's engine purred, unlike the firework explosions of less opulent automobiles. The vehicle moved steadily forward in the direction of the polychrome-tiled dome of the church of Nuestra Señora del Carmen, visible above the row of palm trees that marked the plaza.

Tío Damian's new car had only recently arrived from England, complete with the broad-shouldered, hard-faced English driver whose black uniform gave him a martial look. The sensation of traveling in a coach not being pulled by horses made José feel like a character out of a Jules Verne novel. From his perch beside the driver, he turned to share his glee with his mother, but she and his uncle were deep in conversation.

"I can't believe you intended to come here unaccompanied," Damian said. "The streets are filled with thieves and worse."

"They are poor, not criminals," Alicia said shortly. "There is a difference."

"I do not see it," he replied.

She bit her lip. "It was good of you to escort us," she said.

"Well, since your husband has decided to run off and play the revolutionary, someone needs to watch over you," he replied and added, with feigned casualness, "Have you heard from him?"

"Not since January," she said. A month earlier. "He told me he would be traveling in areas from which he would be unable to send letters."

Damian nodded. "The Sierra Madre," he said. "That's where Madero and his people are holed up." He tapped his finger on the seat rest. "Twenty years ago, Díaz would have flushed them out and . . ."

She completed the sentence in her head—*and shot them*. Aloud she said, "But he has not. Even the government newspapers are filled with stories of fighting in the north and in Morelos."

He grunted. "A dozen tiny fires in a country the size of México do not make a revolution," he said uncertainly, as if trying to convince himself.

Alicia looked out the window and saw not the dusty barrio of El Carmen but herself embracing Miguel at the railway station in the American town of Douglas while Tomasa stood impatiently at her side. January in the Sonora desert was cold and bright, the winter sun refracted off the bare surfaces of rock and earth. The train station buzzed with activity. The conductor shouted, "All aboard," in the harsh syllables of English. Reluctantly, she released her husband.

"I will return to you," he said defiantly. "When I do, I will bring with me hope for a better México."

"I only care that you bring yourself home safely," she said.

"I must go," he said, picking up his satchel. "Good-bye, Tomasa."

The girl had slipped her hand into Alicia's. "Good-bye, Doctor," she said. "I will take care of Doña Alicia."

Miguel smiled. "I have no doubt of that."

And then he was gone. She stood with Tomasa at the platform until his train was no longer visible on the eastern horizon. She sighed, squeezed the girl's hand, and said, "Now we must find your brother."

The American town astonished her after the long journey across the vast expanses of dun-colored Mexican desert. When the train did stop, it was in villages where she witnessed scenes of poverty that still woke her at night. Packs of skeletal feral dogs, starving children, vultures swarming an unseen corpse, the slow parade of men and women so caked with desert dust they seemed to have sprung from the earth. She had always imagined that hell would be a place of caves and darkness, but here it was, brilliantly and cruelly lit, every horrifying detail laid bare beneath the relentless sun. After five days, the train pulled into Douglas, passing beneath an iron archway inscribed with the words "Welcome to America." Miguel, translating the words for her, had snorted, "America! Typical Yankee arrogance. We were America when these people were living in hovels."

As she and Tomasa rode through the streets of Douglas, she thought the days when the Americans lived in hovels were long past. The roads were wide and smoothly paved. In place of the familiar street markets of México were rows of dry goods stores, which displayed everything from shoes to hammers, sewing needles to candy confections, behind immense plate glass windows. As evening fell, the entire town was lit by electric lamps, creating a bright oasis in the surrounding darkness of the desert. The effect on Alicia was as disorienting as it was impressive. It seemed to her she had entered not simply a different country but a different time—the future. It was a future filled with the jangly language of the Americans, of which she spoke only a few carefully memorized sentences; with incessant mechanical noises—sputtering automobiles, ringing telephones, whistling trains, and water rushing through plumbing; with the acrid stink from the copper smelters at the edge of town; and with the Americans themselves, pale-eyed and sunburned, careening along the sidewalks as if cherub-sized demons prodded them forward with tiny pitchforks. She was both fascinated and repelled by the Americans, who, she thought, were like the food they served her, appetizing in appearance but flavorless.

Padre Cáceres had sent messages ahead to Douglas that Alicia was arriving with a daughter of the Yaquis. A message had returned that she would be met, but no details were given other than that she should wait. On her second evening in the town, the manager of the hotel knocked at the door to her room. Frowning, he communicated to her that she had a visitor downstairs. Leaving Tomasa behind, she followed him to the lobby filled with potted palms and horsehide furniture, where, to the manager's clear disapproval, a thin, hawk-faced, white-haired Indian with eyes like flints stood on the oriental carpet.

The Indian spoke in Spanish, saying, "I have come for Tomasa Flores."

"May I ask your name?" Alicia asked politely.

"Sacramento Matus," he replied. "I took custody of the girl and her brother after their mother's murder, and I brought them here. Where is she?"

Before she could respond, Alicia heard Tomasa, behind her, say quietly, "I am here, Don Sacramento." She walked past Alicia to

Sacramento. "I have returned to care for my brother as my mother wishes." After a moment, she added, "I only wanted to be a warrior, like my father."

A faint smile flickered across Sacramento's lips. "You have shown you have your father's blood in you, now you must show you have your mother's as well. Mateo needs you."

She bent her head slightly. "Yes, Achai. I will get my things and come with you."

She turned and went up the stairs, leaving Alicia alone with Sacramento. She was aware not merely of his physical strength—he was spare as a rod of steel—but of a spiritual power that glowed in the depths of his eyes. She felt, as she did with the Americans, that he occupied a different dimension of time than she, not the future, not the past, but a place beyond the reach of time.

"She called you 'father,'" Alicia said, recognizing the Yaqui word by which Tomasa had addressed him.

"I have tried to be a father to her and Mateo," he replied.

"Where will you take her?" Alicia asked.

"To her home," Sacramento said.

"Here, in this town?"

"Be assured, she will be safe," he said. "I am grateful to you for bringing her back to her people. Our children are so few that each one is precious to us."

"It is only a small restitution for what my people have done to yours," she said.

He cast a long look at her. The light in his eyes seemed to illuminate every cell in her body, every moment of her life. It was all she could do to endure his scrutiny.

At length he said, in a soft, kind voice, "Daughters of Jerusalem weep not for me, but for yourselves and your children."

She recognized the words that Jesus had spoken to the women who wept for him as he dragged his cross along the Via Dolorosa to Calvary.

"I do not understand, Don Sacramento."

"The women of México will soon enough know for themselves the suffering their soldiers have caused my people," he said.

He spoke without anger or malice. Before she could question him further, Tomasa came down the stairs clutching her carpet bag and went to Sacramento's side.

"Thank you, Doña," she said.

Alicia stepped forward, embraced the girl, and kissed her forehead. "You are my daughter now, Tomasa. I will remember you in my prayers, and one day perhaps we shall meet again in a different and happier world."

"Take this," Sacramento said to her. He removed from his neck a string of wooden beads that held a large wooden cross. The beads were carved in the shape of an eye. "It will protect you on your journey home. Come, child."

The man and the girl left her standing alone, her fingers attempting to decipher the meaning of the eye-shaped beads, and her mind the meaning of his quotation from the gospel.

The Silver Ghost came to a stop in front of a small warehouse. Painted on its facade was the faded word *mortuario*, and beneath that, in fresher paint, Teatro Palantino.

The driver turned and said to Damian, "We are here, sir."

Damian exclaimed, "This place! Are you sure?"

Alicia removed the cheap handbill from her bag, studied it for a moment, and said, "This is the correct address."

"You said it was a theater," her brother-in-law said.

"Teatro Palantino," she replied. "Just as it says on the building. It must be inside the mortuary."

"This is absurd," Damian said. He barked at the driver, "Go inside and see what this place is."

But Alicia had already opened her door. "No," she said. "I will see for myself."

"Alicia," he called after her.

"Mamá," José said, scurrying down from the front seat. "Wait for me."

She reached for José's hand and they entered the building. Aisles of plain pine coffins were stacked from floor to ceiling in a large, square room. The coffins were unlined and unpainted, except for the smallest—intended for infants and children—which were blue or pink or yellow or white. Cobwebs glittered in the dark corners and a heavy layer of dust covered the roughly planked wooden floor. The place smelled faintly like a forest. At the far end of the aisle, a lantern's glow illuminated the dimness.

"Come," his mother said, walking toward the light. José followed, running his finger in the dust along the sides of the coffins. At the back of the room was a wall with two curtained openings, one marked *Entrada* and the other *Salida*. Between them was a table, where a gaunt man sat behind a cashbox and a pile of pink slips of paper.

"Is this the Teatro Palantino?" his mother asked.

The man rose, bowed, and said, "Yes, Doña."

At that moment, José heard his uncle call, "Alicia!"

"This is the place," she told him. "I was just speaking to the proprietor." Addressing him, she asked, "The stage is behind the wall?"

"Not a stage, Doña. A stage is not required."

She pulled the handbill from her purse. "'Moving pictures of the Rebellion,'" she read. "Is that not the title of the performance?"

"Yes, Doña, but it is not a performance; it is the thing itself."

"The thing itself!" Tío Damian exclaimed. "What nonsense."

From behind the wall, a piano began to play a popular tune.

"Well, something is going on back there," his mother said. "How much for tickets, sir?"

"Five centavos for you and the gentleman. The boy can enter free."

She gave him some coins in exchange for three pink tickets. "Through this curtain?" she asked, indicating the *entrada*.

"Yes, Doña," he said.

"Alicia," his uncle said. "This is foolish. You have no idea what is in that room. We should leave now."

She took José's hand and, looking over her shoulder, said, "Are you coming, Damian?"

He sighed, rushed forward, pushed aside the dusty curtain, and entered first. José clutched his mother's hand, his stomach fluttering, as the curtain fell shut behind them. They found themselves in a dark room. A single beam of light shot through the musty air from the rafters and illuminated a large sheet of muslin hanging from a cord stretched across the front wall. A collection of chairs and benches faced the sheet. To its right was the piano, where a corpulent woman played a love song by the light of a candle. There were perhaps a dozen other people in the room, men mostly, laughing, talking, smoking, and drinking. The air smelled of sawdust, cigarettes, and pulque. José looked upward at the beam of light and followed it to its source, a small, square opening in the wall of a tiny room built into the rafters. He looked back at the sheet of muslin, white in the darkness, lit up like a ghost, and felt a shiver of premonitory excitement.

His uncle was saying, "This is hardly the place for a respectable woman," and he felt his mother waver. He grabbed her hand and said, "Mamá, I want to see what happens!"

After a moment, she said, "We are staying, Damian."

"As you wish," he replied curtly. "Let's sit apart from the rabble at least."

As the piano player thudded away, the room filled with still more people and the air grew warmer and thicker. His uncle put his handkerchief to his mouth, and his mother fanned herself with the handbill. When the room was at capacity, the pianist began to loudly pound the opening chords of the National Hymn. José saw flickering movements cross the muslin. He thought they were shadows, but then, as they came into focus, he gasped. He saw photographs of men in a dusty town and then—

"Mamá, *mira!*" José shouted. "The pictures are moving!"

The handbill slipped from her fingers, and she murmured, "Damian, look. It's Don Francisco Madero. He's walking toward us."

His uncle muttered, "*Fantástico.*"

Elsewhere in the audience were cries of disbelief and fear, one woman screaming, "Ghosts! Ghosts!" as she ran from the room. Others in the audience laughed with delight at the little figures of Madero and his advisors and generals. José watched raptly. The men were strolling on a wooden sidewalk beneath shop signs in English, their mouths moving in animated but silent conversation. They stopped and Madero seemed to look straight out at the audience, eliciting more gasps, for it was as if he were present. His image faded to a black square that occupied the whole of the sheet. Written in white lettering on the square were the words "*Vista de la revuelta.*" Cries of "Read it! Read it!" and "What does it say?" rose up from the illiterate audience. His mother stirred beside him, then stood up, and read in a clear, firm voice, "A view of the rebellion."

These words faded and another line of script appeared. She read, "The second battalion leaves Chihuahua to fight the rebels." The words died away to reveal a line of soldiers moving behind mounted officers across a desolate landscape. Visible in the background were the roofs of a small city. A horseman galloped toward the audience, growing larger and larger until he filled the sheet and it seemed that he was about to leap into the audience horse and all. There were screams and the clatter of overturned chairs as people threw themselves to the ground. José, who had remained riveted to his seat, felt his heart pounding in his throat.

Then the horseman receded, the scene faded, and another sentence appeared on the screen. As members of the audience got up from the ground and dusted themselves off, his mother read, "Rebels led by Francisco Villa prepare to fight the army."

There appeared on the muslin screen another desert scene, also filled by a group of armed men. Unlike the straight rows of the federal soldiers, these men did not march in formation nor did they wear uniforms. They were clad in the dirty white trousers and torn *zarapes* of the poor. They tramped in a ragged line behind a small, unshaven man on horseback wearing a dusty suit and a bowler hat, his chest crisscrossed with bandoliers.

José heard his uncle murmur, "There are so many of them."

In the back of the room, a man shouted, "*Viva la revolución!*" The pianist began to hammer out the presidential anthem, but other men in the audience took up the cry. His uncle glanced nervously around the room. On the white sheet, there was a single word.

His mother read the word. "Attack!"

A panoramic image filled the screen with the shapes of tiny men moving toward each other across a barren landscape fringed by distant mountains. The two lines of soldiers hurled themselves at one another across the desert scrub. Puffballs of smoke signified artillery shots, and men fell like puppets cut from their strings. Horses reared, tossing their riders, and galloped off toward the mountains. The audience was silent. Even the piano player had paused to watch the scene of slaughter that unfolded on the white cloth with the intimacy and the strangeness of a dream. José was transfixed. He felt as if the curtains of another world, a spirit world, had parted and offered itself to his gaze. It was a world so luminous and ephemeral he was afraid to breathe lest he dissolve it. And then the image faded, replaced by another mournful black box with another single word splashed across it.

Squeezing his hand, his mother solemnly intoned, "The dead."

An invisible eye slowly moved its gaze among the ghastly open-eyed corpses of dead soldiers of both armies lying on the ground while vultures strutted in the background. The image faded quickly and mercifully, replaced by more words.

"Madero in defeat."

Madero appeared in the field of dead soldiers, his face a study of sorrow. He was watching a man kneel at the side of a soldier, evidently trying to assist him. The man turned to speak to Madero and the camera recorded his face.

"Papá!" José shouted. He ran toward the sheet. "Papá!"

But, as he reached the front of the room, his arms open to embrace his father, the image faded, replaced by a final word: "*Fin.*"

Sarmiento watched his wife disappear into the desert landscape. Beneath a gigantic sky, flat plains of broken, tawny earth covered by low-growing, gray-green scrub rolled like a low tide toward distant barren mountains. The monotonous vista was broken only by gigantic saguaro. They were startlingly alive, thick-scabbed limbs twisting upward as if in supplication. The winter sun turned the dust to gold. It swirled upward from the ground and sprayed itself against the train, fogging the windows, slipping in through cracks and crevices, covering every surface with a thin layer of dirt. This is not the landscape of beginnings, Sarmiento thought. He glanced down at his dusty trousers and shoes and, in a spasm of panic, wondered, "What have I done?"

His misgivings were not allayed when he reached the American city of El Paso. It was separated from Ciudad Juárez by the muddy torrent of river the Americans called the Rio Grande and the Mexicans, the Rio Bravo. Luis's last telegraph had instructed him to check into the Pickwick Hotel. Sarmiento found the place, a modest two-story building off the main street. He entered, registered, went up to his room, and waited. A day passed, two, then three. He left his room only to eat in the downstairs restaurant, sitting at a table that gave him a view of the lobby. The hotel clerk supplied him with American newspapers, which he searched for news of Madero's progress. There were a few, brief reports of skirmishes and small uprisings, interspersed with official reassurances from Díaz's government that all was well. "Was there a revolution?" he wondered with dismay. The panic he had felt on the train again gripped him. By the fourth day, he was planning his return to México. And then, as he sat at lunch, trying to force himself to take a few bites of inedible pot roast, he looked up and saw his cousin stroll into the hotel lobby, smoking a cigar. Sarmiento nearly wept with relief.

By nightfall, he was back in México, drinking shots of whiskey with Luis at the table of a squalid cantina on a dirt backstreet of Ciudad Juárez, as his cousin recounted the story of the first days of the revolution. Luis had been among the small band of Madero's followers when the little man had first slipped into México from Texas. Madero had expected to meet a volunteer army that would carry him in triumph to the capital. Instead, Luis told Sarmiento, they got lost and spent a miserable night wandering through the bitter cold. The following day, when they kept their rendezvous, Madero's revolutionary army consisted of two dozen peasants armed with machetes and rocks.

At that point, Luis said, many of Madero's advisors—often, like Madero himself, the younger sons of wealthy families—tired of playing at rebellion and slunk home to their families.

"Madero persisted," Luis said. "We went from village to village all across the north, where he proclaimed the revolution, and, remarkably, Miguel, the revolution began."

"But where is it, Luis?" Sarmiento asked. He glanced around the room. A few rough-looking men sat at other tables, drinking and talking loudly above a band of musicians led by an accordionist playing a kind of harsh, country polka. "Is this it? A roomful of men getting drunk?"

"Yes, Miguel," Luis replied. "These men and men like them *are* the revolution. Common people with nothing to lose but their misery. They fight the same way they drink, hard and grim. They're not like the toy soldiers Don Porfirio parades down the Reforma on Independence Day. We are a people's army."

"When does it plan to start fighting?" he asked dryly. "There was almost nothing in the American newspapers about the rebellion."

Luis sneered. "The Americans think we are an inferior race, lazy, ignorant, and vicious. The prospect of Mexicans killing each other does not disturb them. Of course, they do not take Madero seriously. To them, he is simply another 'greaser.'"

"You didn't answer me."

Luis signaled for another round. "When we started, we made the mistake of attacking the big towns where the *federales* are dug in. They destroyed us. We changed tactics, raiding isolated army outposts and haciendas and establishing ourselves in the villages where Madero is a hero. Now we control the countryside and the *federales* are squeezed into the cities. The time has come for us to bring the fight to them, here in Juárez. If we can take this town, the north will be ours."

"Are you a solider now, Luis?"

"I am whatever Don Pancho needs me to be," he replied with a smile. "Tonight, I am a spy."

"A spy?"

"Together we will take in the sights of Ciudad Juárez." Their drinks had arrived. He raised his glass and said, "To your first assignment in the people's army, Miguel. *Salud.*"

A few shots of whiskey later, they left Sarmiento's bag with the barman—a friend of the revolution, Luis explained—and went out into the soft spring darkness. Unlike its American counterpart on the other side of the river, whose electric lights blazed into the night, Ciudad Juárez was illuminated by gaslight or lanterns in those neighborhoods where there was any light at all. Luis led them to the western edge of the town, where from a shadowy distance they observed soldiers shoveling earth by lamplight.

"If they detain us, act drunk," Luis murmured.

"That won't be difficult," Sarmiento replied, feeling the effects of the rotgut on his empty stomach. "What are they doing?"

"Digging trenches," Luis replied. "Defense lines. They're digging them east and south of the city, as well."

"What about the north?"

"The north is the river and 'Uncle Sam,'" Luis remarked. "Natural barriers."

"How many are there? *Federales?*"

"A thousand. Twelve hundred. We greatly outnumber them, but they have better weapons. Come."

Sarmiento followed his cousin through primitive streets where the mud houses could have been constructed in Sumeria and into the center of the town. The austere Gothic cathedral, with its two tall bell towers, faced the thick walls of the army garrison across the cobblestoned plaza. The heavy doors seemed impenetrable. After inspecting the garrison, they walked to the customs house at the edge of the river. Now and then, Luis murmured a comment about the number of soldiers in the streets, the placement of entrances on the public buildings, the presence or absence of street lamps, as if fixing these details in his mind. To Sarmiento, Juárez was nothing more than a dusty provincial town caught between the unforgiving desert and the outstretched talons of the American eagle. He was reminded of the one witticism of Don Porfirio that even his foes liked to repeat: "Poor México, so far from God, so close to the United States." Sarmiento's stomach growled.

"When did you last eat?" Luis asked.

"Not recently enough," Sarmiento replied.

"Our last stop is the railroad station. There should be some food there."

At the station, they ate greasy tacos, seasoned with the hottest salsa Sarmiento had ever tasted. They were filled with meat, the origins of which he preferred not to think about, although there was a noticeable absence of the feral dogs who ran in packs elsewhere in the city.

"No soldiers," Luis commented, as he spat out some gristle.

"What?" Sarmiento said, his tongue blazing. Was it foolish, he wondered, to hope that the chilies incinerated any bacterium in the meat?

"The station is unguarded. We're done. Let's go."

As they walked back to the cantina, Sarmiento asked, "Why is this town so important? It seems completely insignificant."

"Guns and money," his cousin replied. "Guns from the garrison, money from the revenues at the customs house. Juárez is the biggest town on the border. If we take it, we have a base of operations in the north, where Díaz has never been popular. If we beat him here, the entire north will soon fall."

They returned to the cantina. The barman put them up in a tiny, filthy room with straw mats on the floor and a chamber pot that needed emptying. Exhausted, Sarmiento stretched out on the *petate* and reflected with amusement upon his first day of the revolution—bad liquor, worse food, and the droll company of his cousin—before sleep fell upon him like a wall.

The National Palace of the Revolution was one of the fifteen adobe buildings that comprised the village of La Santisima, a short distance west of Ciudad Juárez. It was an evening in the last week of April 1911. Sarmiento sat at the long table where Madero's staff was assembled for a dinner of stewed pork, beans, and tortillas. He glanced around at the improbable collection of revolutionaries—farmers and lawyers, university students and horse thieves, men with great names and men who could not spell their names. All of them were united by the slight, balding man at the head of the table who was saying to an American journalist, "I have been chosen by Providence. Neither poverty nor prison, nor even death frighten me."

"By Providence, sir?" the journalist asked skeptically.

"Yes," Madero replied calmly. "Like your own Abraham Lincoln."

"*Quién es este* Lincoln?" the man beside Sarmiento asked him. He was Pascual Orozco, formerly a muleteer, now a general. His ruthless fighting skills had been honed in a series of Don Porfirio's prisons.

Sarmiento looked into Orozco's cold blue eyes and explained that Lincoln was the American president who had liberated the black slaves during the American civil war.

Orozco asked, "You knew this Lincoln?"

"No, he was killed before I was born. I read about him."

Orozco smiled contemptuously. "Someday, when the real work is done, you must teach me how to read."

Orozco's disdain for Madero's civilian advisors was shared by the other rough-hewn generals, like Francisco Villa, who had recruited the men who fought and died for Madero. They had no interest in the long, legalistic debates about how to conduct the revolution and the form the government should take after Díaz was deposed. They only wanted to exterminate Díaz's army and to stick his head on a pike in the middle of the Zócalo. To the educated men, the peasant generals were ignorant, impulsive, and dangerous, useful as cannon fodder, but not to be entrusted with the future of México. Without Madero, the two factions would have been at each other's throats, and, as it was, he controlled them only with the greatest of difficulty.

"Do you really believe you can defeat President Díaz's troops with your army?" the American journalist asked, not masking his incredulity.

Madero replied, "There is less to Don Porfirio's army than it seems. His soldiers are kidnapped off the streets and impressed into service. His generals are toothless old men who were promoted precisely because they are too incompetent to pose a military threat to his rule. The people have long since turned against him. Díaz is a head without a body. I tell you, sir," he concluded confidently, "in three months, General Díaz will be on a boat to exile in Paris, and we will be eating our tortillas in the National Palace."

He had been speaking English to the journalist, but for this response Madero had switched back to Spanish and spoken loudly enough to silence the clatter of the table. When Madero shook himself out of his habitual, kindly vagueness and spoke in these passionate, commanding tones, Sarmiento would have followed him anywhere. Glancing around the table, he saw he was not alone in this sentiment. Madero's peasant generals and frock-coated advisors alike listened with something like reverence, and when he finished, broke into a lusty round of *Viva Madero! Viva la Revolución!*

Sarmiento missed his cousin, who, he imagined, would have responded to this enthusiasm sardonically. The steadiness of Luis's allegiance to the revolution did not require such displays of emotionalism, which is why, Sarmiento thought, Madero had entrusted him with the confidential mission on which he had departed almost two weeks earlier.

Dinner over, Sarmiento stood in twilight watching the army settle in for the night. Around dozens of tiny campfires, the *soldaderas* prepared meager meals for their men. Sarmiento had been startled at all the women who traveled with the soldiers, but he had come to understand that, without them, there would have been no army. The women scrounged for the food and water that kept the soldiers alive in the un-forgiving desert, and, when necessary, took up arms and fought beside their men. Seeing them, he recalled with amusement how he had so confidently told Alicia war was no place for a woman, and then felt a pang of longing for her. Their separation gnawed softly at his heart day and night. He found relief only in sleep when she was united with him in his dreams.

Three soldiers passed by. One wore overalls, another dirty white cottons, a third an ancient frock coat and tight vaquero trousers; all were barefoot. They were armed, respectively, with a machete, a rifle, and an enormous antique revolver. Not far away, someone playing a guitar began to sing a *corrido* about Madero's escape across the border. These ballads were the newspapers of the illiterate soldiers recounting important events. There would be a skirmish in the morning and by nightfall, the soldiers would be singing about it. As he listened, he wondered whether Homer's great poem of war had had its beginnings in the campfire ballads of the Greek soldiers at the walls of Troy.

Many of the soldiers were Indians who, like their generals, were suspicious of men like him. The soldiers called his ilk the "*perfumados*" — the scented ones, for the colognes and *eaus* they affected, even in the wilderness. Just a few days earlier, as he dug a bullet out of the thigh of an old Yaqui captain, the Indian told him, "If I die, Señor Doctor, my men will kill you." As Sarmiento performed the painful excision of the bullet, the old man's eyes remained trained on his face like a pair of pistols. Madero had promised the Yaquis he would return their home-land in Sonora to them. They fought for him with a ferocity so legendary that their mere appearance on a battlefield could cause opposing troops to take flight.

He thought of Tomasa and then again of Alicia and sighed.

"You sound so sad, Primo," he heard the familiar voice say. "Cheer up. Imagine our triumphal entry into the capital."

He turned. "Luis!" he exclaimed, embracing his cousin. "When did you return?"

"Just this minute," he said, and looked it. The dust of the road clung to his clothes. "I cleaned out a pharmacy in El Paso to bring you medical supplies."

"I am grateful," Sarmiento replied. "But you haven't been gone for two weeks shopping for me."

Luis offered him a hand-rolled cigarette, took one himself, and languidly lit them, as if they were sitting at Luis's favorite French restaurant in the capital over postprandial brandies.

"No," he said. "I had, as the Americans say, 'bigger fish to fry.' A mule pack is making its way through the desert from Arizona with five hundred Winchester rifles, a half-dozen Hotchkiss machine guns, and crates of ammunition."

"How did you get past the gringo embargo?"

Luis rubbed his fingers together in the universal sign for bribes. "How goes the revolution?"

Sarmiento spread his hand across the encampment. "As you see. Everyone is waiting for something to happen."

"They won't be waiting much longer." Luis flicked his cigarette to the ground. "Ángel has pitched a tent for us somewhere in this chaos," he said, "I'm off to find him and beg a couple of tortillas from a *soldada*. I'll come by later with a bottle of American whiskey."

"It's good to see you, Luis," Sarmiento said warmly. "To see family."

"Don't worry, Miguel, you'll be back in your wife's bed by the end of the month." Luis slipped into the darkness, whistling a waltz.

15

Alicia sat in her parlor embroidering an altar cloth for the altar at San Francisco Tlalco. In past times she would have been at the weekly luncheon of the Daughters of Jerusalem hosted by the first lady at Chapultepec castle. Soon after she had returned from Arizona, however, and it became common knowledge that Miguel had joined Madero's rebellion, a stiff note had arrived from Carmen Díaz revoking Alicia's membership in the charitable organization. The other ladies of Señora Díaz's circle quickly followed the first lady's lead and dropped Alicia thoroughly and completely. Even her sisters were reluctant to appear with her in public and her brother-in-law Damian had told her that only a direct appeal from him to Don Porfirio had spared her an extremely unpleasant visit by the officers of *la seguridad.*

"I assured him you know nothing of Miguel's activities," he said.

"But that is entirely true," she said.

He had sat on the sofa where she now sewed and given her a long, hard look. "You accompanied him to the border," he said accusingly.

"On business of my own," she replied.

"Business that involved a young Indian girl you removed from the orphanage, who traveled with you and did not return when you did."

His words disquieted her for she had told no one about Tomasa. "How do you know this?"

"These old walls have ears," he said, with a gesture that encompassed the entire palace. Then, softly, he added, "Servants can be bribed, Alicia. I warn you that even your rank will not protect you if you continue to involve yourself in—indiscretions." He stood up, leaned casually against the chiffonier, and said, "Like your adventure in Coyoacán."

She looked up sharply. "How . . . ?" Then she understood. "Your money bribes my servants."

"Better me than Díaz," he replied. "Far better, believe me."

"For how long have you spied on us?" she demanded.

"For as long as I have been married to your sister," he said. With a tight, humorless smile, he continued, "Spare me your indignation. Saturino may fancy himself the head of this family, but I am the one who works ceaselessly to preserve its status and prosperity. Listen to me, Alicia. I like your husband, and I am your greatest admirer, but I will not have either one of you endanger what I have labored so hard to create and maintain. Labors, which, by the way, support you, your mother, and this absurd residence." He withdrew a cigarette from his gold-plated cigarette case and lit it. "Don't misunderstand me. I have never begrudged that support. Indeed, I find this fairy-tale world that you and your mother inhabit to be rather charming. I advise you to remain in it and leave reality to those, like me, who are capable of directing it. Henceforth, you will quietly devote yourself to your child and to your charities. No more mysterious trips to the border. No more hospices for Indians. Is that understood?"

"What about Miguel?"

Damian shrugged. "I cannot help him now that he has turned himself into a renegade. When this charade is over, I will do what I can to prevent him from ending up in front of a firing squad."

She paused in her work and remembered how shaken the conversation with Damian had left her. It had forced her to realize that one form of her spiritual vanity was the unacknowledged pride she took in her disinterest in worldly affairs. Damian's words had emphatically impressed upon her that her inattention was a luxury she could no longer afford. For, while she had been regarding with mild contempt the world of men like Damian and their machinations, that world had been insinuating itself into her existence. She had been spied upon by her own servants and been made, by her own actions, an object of suspicion to Don Porfirio himself. She had drawn herself into the spider's web, where her only hope for survival now was to remain still. All she could do was pray night and day for the success of Madero's rebellion.

Neither a soldier nor a lawyer, Sarmiento's seat at Madero's daily staff meetings reflected his symbolic value as the son of Benito Juárez's personal physician. By the beginning of May, the meetings had devolved into profane shouting matches between the peasant generals and the *perfumado* civilian advisors. The fuse that had exploded the divisions between the two groups was the arrival of secret emissaries from Díaz offering a negotiated settlement. Díaz promised to appoint Madero his vice president and successor and to retire at the end of his term in 1914 in exchange for the disbanding of Madero's forces. Orozco and Villa demanded that Madero allow them to lead their soldiers in a frontal attack against Ciudad Juárez, while the *perfumados* insisted that he continue negotiations with Díaz.

"Díaz is shitting his pants," Pascual Orozco proclaimed. "Now is the time to strike Juárez, Don Francisco."

"But if we attack and fail," replied a portly lawyer, "Díaz will lose any incentive to continue to negotiate. No, I say we use his fear to wring some more concessions from him."

"What shit are you talking, fatso?" Orozco replied contemptuously. "'Incentive'? 'Concessions'? What the fuck do those words even mean?"

"They mean, you bastard cowboy, that you're not going to take Juárez using machetes against machine guns and bows and arrows against artillery guns."

"Gentlemen," Madero said, raising a small, pale hand. "There is no question about the bravery and dedication of our troops, but Don Gerardo is right. The *federales* have a huge advantage in weaponry. We will only have one opportunity to take Juárez, and if we fail, well, it's the gallows or the firing squad for all of us, and an end to our dreams of a better day for México. For now, we will continue to talk with Don Porfirio's emissaries." He faced down the angry shouts from the generals. "You are courageous fighters," he told them. "And I know you love your men. Knowing that, I must ask you, why would you sacrifice their lives to achieve what we might yet achieve without bloodshed, the end of Porfirio Díaz?"

Luis said, "Pardon me, Don Francisco, but Díaz is a soldier. Whatever his emissaries may tell you, the only thing he really respects is force. He will not resign until it is clear that his army can no longer guarantee his survival. I agree with Don Pascual and General Villa. We should attack now. Díaz has sent his best troops into Juárez. If the city falls, his regime will be exposed as defenseless and his government will collapse."

Now it was the *perfumados* who shouted. Sarmiento felt Madero's mild eye fall upon him and his throat tightened.

"What do you say, Doctor?" Madero asked. "You are doubtless the most impartial man in the room."

"Not so impartial as ignorant," Sarmiento replied, temporizing.

But Madero would not have it. "Come, Miguel. No believes you are ignorant. Tell us what you think."

"My job is to save lives, not to endanger them," he said. "But since you ask, I would say that I don't know if our men can take Juárez, but I know they are ready to try."

"And risk failure?" the fat lawyer pressed him.

"My father was a man of many sayings," Sarmiento replied. "And one of them was '*A mas honor, mas dolor.*' No risk, no reward. He said he learned that *dicho* from Don Benito Juárez himself."

His invocation of the hallowed name of Juárez momentarily silenced the room, but then the men resumed their quarrel, each side loudly claiming that Juárez would have supported their position. After another half hour of this, Sarmiento slipped out and walked out into the desert to smoke a cigarette and clear his head before he began his day of doctoring.

"Did Juárez really teach your father that saying?"

He turned to find Madero smiling at him. "Honestly, I do not know, Don Francisco. If Don Benito said even half the things my father claimed he said, then the man never stopped talking. Is the meeting over?"

"For now," Madero said. He touched Sarmiento's shoulder. "Of course, another one is about to start, so I must go. I'm glad you're here, Miguel. You are the most civilized of men."

"That doesn't seem to be much of a virtue under the circumstances."

"War is destruction and destruction is easy," Madero said. "I will need the civilized to rebuild México."

When Sarmiento arrived at the staff meeting the next morning, the air in the room was charged. He took his customary seat by the door.

Madero was standing in front of a large map of México with a pointer, indicating a spot just south of the capital.

"Gentlemen, early this morning we learned that General Zapata and his Army of the South have taken Cuautla from Don Porfirio's Fifth Calvary. The road to the capital now lies open to our brother revolutionaries from Morelos. Therefore, I am ordering an attack on Ciudad Juárez to begin tomorrow morning." He paused and waited for the outcry in the room—cheers from the generals, groans from the civilians—to die down.

One of the generals called, "Why wait for tomorrow? My men are ready to kill the bastards now!"

Madero put out his hands and quieted the room. "I have just informed President Díaz's emissaries of my decision, and it only seems fair to give them time to consult with the government and respond. General Garibaldi will explain the plan of attack."

Madero stepped aside for his chief of staff. Garibaldi, grandson of the liberator of Italy, came forward dressed, as always, in a Norfolk jacket, jodhpurs, a Tyrolean hat, and a red shirt and tie, like a country gentleman about to go out on a shoot. Tall, bespectacled, and mustached, he resembled the American president, Theodore Roosevelt. He was one of a number of foreign soldiers who had joined Madero out of idealism or for the adventure. In his heavily accented Spanish he set out his strategy to take Juárez. Orozco's men would attack from the east along the Rio Bravo and make for the railway station, Villa's army would attack from the south and advance to the cathedral in the central plaza, and Garibaldi would move from the west with the customs house as his objective. Once inside the city, the three groups would join forces and capture the federal garrison.

"But the *federales* are entrenched in ditches around the city," a civilian advisor objected. "Their machine guns will slaughter you."

"They have not had time to complete their trench work," Garibaldi replied. "There are weak spots where they have barricaded themselves behind brick walls and in old houses. We will blast our way through those defenses."

"With what?" the same man asked skeptically. "We have no artillery."

"We have dynamite," Garibaldi said. "Not as precise as artillery shells but quite as effective."

As the discussion continued, Sarmiento slowly realized what the attack would mean for him. He was the only physician in the entire camp, and he had yet to experience battlefield conditions. The patients he had treated were more often sick with one of the diseases that festered in overcrowded and unsanitary conditions than wounded from the brief skirmishes with the *federales*. Dread gripped him as he imagined the carnage to come.

He spent the rest of the day setting up a field hospital in a copse of alamo trees on a slight rise that gave him an unencumbered view of Juárez. Luis, seeing him packing and moving supplies, sent Ángel to help him. Sarmiento had rarely seen his cousin's young companion since arriving at camp and had never been alone with him. The boy—for Sarmiento guessed he was no more than nineteen or twenty—was slender, but when he removed his shirt against the midday heat, Sarmiento saw he had the long, hard muscles of someone accustomed to hard labor. There was a patch of discoloration on his left shoulder that looked like a healed bullet wound and across his back were faded scars that could only have been made by a rawhide whip. Ángel's reserve bordered on hostility, and Sarmiento knew better than to ask the boy directly about his wounds. Still, he was curious not only about the scars, but whether Ángel shared Luis's understanding of what he was, an invert, a homosexual. For there was not the slightest hint of effeminacy about Ángel, nothing to distinguish him from the hundreds of other young Indian soldiers at the camp. Like them, Ángel had the soft features of a child and the wary eyes of a coyote.

Working in silence, the two men set up tents for the wounded to be brought into when they first arrived, as well as tents for surgery and recovery. Sarmiento stocked his supplies in the surgical tent—basins, bandages, chloroform, morphine, and whiskey. They filled immense water jars at the small tributary stream of the Rio Bravo that ran at the edge of the camp and carried them up the hill. Sarmiento knew he would need help once the battle began and, on an impulse, asked Ángel if he would stay.

The young Indian, who was setting up cots beneath the alamo trees, replied without looking at him. "Tomorrow I fight with Luis." A moment later, he added, "I will tell him to send some women to help you."

Ángel spoke his cousin's name with a familiarity that surprised Sarmiento. He had expected that the boy—who addressed him with the formal "*usted*"—would call Luis by something equally formal and distant. Instead, he referred to Luis as an equal, a friend, a companion. Sarmiento was unexpectedly moved.

"Is there anything else you want me to do, sir?" Ángel asked.

Sarmiento looked around. Everything was in order. "No, thank you, Ángel. You can go now." But before the boy could leave, Sarmiento said, "Ángel, tomorrow . . . watch out for yourself and for Luis. I love him as if he were my own brother, and as you are his friend, you are also my friend."

The dark, inscrutable eyes gazed at him; the unreadable expression on his face did not change. "I would die myself before I let harm come his way," the boy said, turned, and slipped away.

Through a pair of field glasses, Sarmiento watched the battle of Ciudad Juárez begin at seven o'clock the next morning when, disregarding Garibaldi's orders to launch an infantry attack, Pancho Villa sent his cavalry charging the trenches of the *federales*, where they were annihilated by machine gun fire. At the same time, Sarmiento heard the earth-shaking explosions of artillery shells and dynamite. Pillars of dust, Biblical in girth and density, rose out of the assaulted desert like furious wraiths. By seven-thirty, the first casualties had begun to arrive and thereafter, Sarmiento's view of the battle was of the mangled bodies of the wounded.

Months later, Sarmiento would remember the strange idea that had taken hold of him on that endless day in Juárez as he worked on the soldiers. It had begun to seem to him that the bullets that had maimed the men were not inanimate metal projectiles but imbued with tiny, malignant spirits that directed their destructive courses with an evil humor. Thus, a bullet sheared off the nipple on one man's chest, nearly, but not quite, severing it, before it interred itself in his neck, where it would cost him the power of speech. Another took out a general's eye but did no further damage, while a third tore a tuft of hair from a soldier's scalp and buried it in a furrow that it dug between his shoulders. A fourth made a precise, clean hole in a soldier's armpit from which it sailed whimsically into his heart. There was the bullet that nicked a fingertip before shattering a collarbone; the bullet that caromed within the body like a billiard ball; the bullet that efficiently perforated the bowel and departed, consigning its victim to an agonizing death from peritonitis; the bullet that chose to burrow into the soft, warm folds of the thirteen-year-old soldier's brain, blinding him, but leaving him alive. As he removed the bullets that he could, Sarmiento cursed them as if they could hear and understand his epithets. Tears of exhaustion and grief ran down his dusty face. Blood dripped into his shoes from his blood-soaked trousers and his feet squished with each step. That was how Madero found him at the end of the day when the little man appeared to console the wounded. He took one look at Sarmiento and embraced him, smearing himself with the blood of his soldiers, and whispered into Sarmiento's ear, "You are the bravest of all, Miguel, to face this unbearable suffering and to work to alleviate it."

Sometime later, in the darkness of a night he thought would never fall, Luis appeared. He led Sarmiento away from the charnel house that his hospital had become. Luis took Sarmiento to his room, where he helped him clean himself up and change into fresh clothes. From there, they went to the mess, where Luis made him eat a plate of beans that he washed down with whiskey. He returned Sarmiento to his room and put him into his bed.

"No," Sarmiento said hoarsely, trying to get up. "The wounded are still coming in."

Luis pressed down gently on his chest, forcing him to lie down. "You'll take better care of them when you're rested," he said. "Get some sleep. I'll wake you if you're needed."

Sarmiento wanted to raise his voice in further protest, but his eyelids felt as if they were weighted with stones. With his fading vision he saw that Luis's shirtfront was smeared with blood.

"You are wounded," he croaked, touching his hand to his cousin's shirt.

Luis shook his head. "No, it's not my blood. It's Ángel's. He died in my arms this morning." Luis stroked Sarmiento's face. "Sleep now, Primito. Tomorrow will be a better day."

"How could it be?" It was a cry of agony.

With a melancholy smile, Luis replied, "We are victorious, Miguel. Ciudad Juárez has fallen."

Alicia could almost hear the collective gasp of shock from her circle when news reached the capital that Ciudad Júarez had fallen. In the days that followed, the shock deepened to dismay and then panic as rich refugees from the northern states began to trickle into the city with tales of marauding revolutionaries and the mass desertions of federal troops to Madero. She could not help but be affected by what looked to be the imminent collapse of Don Porfirio's regime. Such a thing was almost unimaginable to the generations of Mexicans like hers that had never known another president. He had seemed as solid in his place as the National Palace itself, but the loss of a single city had revealed him as he was, an enfeebled, old man of eighty clinging by his fingertips to his throne as a whirlwind bore down upon him. Day after day, the Zócalo was filled with protesters against whom the police and the army were vastly outnumbered. The once docile press began to publish stories about the actual conditions of the country and call for vast social and political changes. The government issued contradictory communiqués, some promising reforms, others stubbornly rejecting any need for them, that no one believed. Madero's portraits began to appear everywhere in the capital and beneath them the caption "The Apostle of Freedom," while Don Porfirio's were discreetly removed. Meanwhile, the once conspicuous rich deserted their usual playgrounds and retired to their mansions or quietly made preparations to leave for Europe or the United States after first shipping their assets to foreign banks.

Alicia also observed, with bemusement, the sudden surge in her popularity among the very friends who had turned their backs on her after Miguel had joined Madero. She was courteous but reserved toward them, deflecting their invitations to tea, listening without comment to their sotto voce jabs at Don Porfirio and intimations that, in their inmost hearts, they had been Madero sympathizers all along. "After all," they would say, nervously, "Don Francisco's family is very wealthy, *gente decente* like us, isn't that right, Alicia?"

She passed off these little hypocrisies and tried to remind herself that the ingratitude shown to Don Porfirio by her circle was spurred by fear, not malice. The only old friend toward whom she directed any sympathetic thoughts was the first lady. There was a longstanding bond between the Gaviláns and the Rubio family. Alicia had known Carmen Rubio as a girl before she was married off to Don Porfirio when she was seventeen and he was fifty-one. Her mother had once shown Alicia a letter she had received from Carmen on the eve of the wedding seeking counsel from La Niña on how to be the wife of a man so much older than she. Alicia still remembered the large, girlish writing and the anxiety and sadness between the carefully composed lines—the choice to marry Don Porfirio had not been Carmen's and although she did not complain, her unhappiness was plain to see.

The marriage proceeded. After thirty years, Carmen had gone from being a slender, beautiful bride to a stout matron. Her childlessness was the subject of uncharitable speculation about her fertility because Don Porfirio had had several children by his first wife. As if to compensate for her failure to give him children, Carmen became her husband's fiercest political partisan. As he grew older and distracted, she began to openly involve herself in affairs of state, much to the displeasure of Don Porfirio's ministers, who took exception to receiving orders from any woman, much less one with no more than a convent education.

A few weeks after the fall of Júarez, a message arrived from the first lady to La Niña informing her that the weekly luncheon of the Daughters of Jerusalem had been moved from Chapultepec Castle to the Díaz's private residence on Calle Cadena. When Alicia asked her mother if she intended to go, La Niña had not even lifted her head from the novel she was reading.

"Of course not," she said.

"Mother, she is an old family friend."

"The invitation is mere bravado, Alicia," La Niña replied. "She can't possibly expect her friends to risk their lives by trying to get through the mob at the Zócalo to dine on chilled shrimp as if the world were not collapsing around our ears. No, I shall stay home."

On the day of the luncheon, Alicia called for the carriage and ventured out in the direction of Calle Cadena. On Avenida de San Francisco, her brother-in-law's department store was shuttered and guarded by armed, private police. The carriage took the narrow back streets behind the cathedral in order to avoid the protestors at the Zócalo, but their chants demanding Díaz's resignation resounded through the entire central city. A double line of soldiers had sealed off Calle Cadena. Her carriage was stopped, and she was harshly interrogated before she was allowed to proceed to the president's heavily guarded residence. In the foyer, at the bottom of a marble staircase where in the past she had been met by an English footman in livery, there were even more soldiers, all of them in battle dress. One of the men conducted her to the drawing room. A dozen small tables held elaborate place settings. A row of maids was lined against the wall, some of them visibly frightened. A small orchestra played a waltz behind a screen of potted palms. The room was otherwise empty. Alicia had been distracted from her feelings by the surreal journey from the palace to the residence. Now, however, she looked at the lavish, deserted room and the brilliant, un-occupied tables and the reality of the moment sank in; this was the end of Don Porfirio! The shock made her fingers tremble.

She heard the rustle of silk behind her and turned. Carmen Díaz approached in a pale green gown with ropes of pearls around her neck. Beneath an upswept crown of dark hair, her heavy, double-chinned face was tired almost beyond recognition.

Alicia embraced her, whispering, "Carmen, my dear."

The first lady shook her off without returning the embrace. "I am surprised you would choose to show your face in this house."

"I come as an old friend concerned for your well-being."

"An old friend," Carmen repeated bitterly. "Your husband would have my husband hanging from the gallows in the Zócalo, old friend."

"No," Alicia protested. "Not Miguel. He acts out of principle, not out of animosity toward Don Porfirio. As for me, you know I have never wished you or Don Porfirio the least harm. Can we not set aside the arguments of our husbands and be as we were before all this began?"

Carmen gave her head a weary shake. "That is not possible, Alicia, as our fates are inextricably tied to theirs. But I am wrong to visit your husband's sins upon you. You are a good woman, probably the best in our set. You may be the only one of us who deserves to be called a Daughter of Jerusalem. You might actually have attempted to console Christ on his journey to Calvary unlike the rest of us, who would only have seen a peasant justifiably punished for his insubordination."

"You have been tireless in your charitable work," Alicia said.

"What else was I supposed to do?" the first lady asked. "Sit at home and knit? Sit down, Alicia, let's have tea. You shouldn't stay long though. It is only a matter of time before word gets out to the mob that we are here."

They sat. A maid rushed over and poured tea.

"Why did you leave Chapultepec?" Alicia asked. "Isn't it safer there?"

"One road up and one road out," Carmen said. "We would've been trapped and then what? The mob is calling for our blood. Here, at least, there are escape routes."

"How is the president?"

"Ill," she said. "The doctor extracted a tooth and an infection set in. He's been in bed for a week, leaving me to deal with all . . . this."

"I am so sorry."

A ghost of smile crossed the older woman's face. "Porfirio felled by a toothache. It could be the title of an opera buffa, don't you think?"

"I find the entire situation most distressing," Alicia replied.

"It will soon be over for us," Carmen said. "We have been negotiating with Madero since Juárez fell. Tomorrow my husband will resign. As soon as he can travel, we will leave this ungrateful country and set sail to France."

"I hardly know what to say."

"What is there to say? The king is dead; long live the king!" She narrowed her eyes and added bitterly, "May the reign of Francisco I be short and sour."

Luis had been right about Ciudad Juárez. Within days of Madero's victory, the governors of the northern Mexican states had declared themselves in revolt against Díaz and put their militias at Madero's disposal. Meanwhile, Emiliano Zapata had continued his advance on the capital from the south. The army collapsed as battalion after battalion abandoned the government. At the beginning of June, Díaz resigned and departed from México on a German steamship. Madero began his triumphant progress to the capital. With his sense of history, Madero had decided to travel not by train but in a small black carriage like the one in which his hero Benito Juárez had entered the city following the expulsion of the French. As the long line of horse- and mule-drawn carriages and wagons passed through still another dusty Mexican village, Sarmiento administered a shot of morphine to the Apostle of Freedom in the curtained privacy of Madero's closed carriage. The wagon bounced violently as it hit a rut in the road. Madero groaned and vomited into a chamber pot. He had begun suffering from headaches of such intensity that Sarmiento had begun to fear a brain tumor.

"Excuse me, Miguel," Madero said, wiping his mouth with his handkerchief.

"Don't apologize, Don Pancho. Try to make yourself comfortable. The drug should start working momentarily."

"You didn't give me too much, did you? I have to speak later."

"You can scarcely stand; I don't know how you to expect to speak."

"Nonetheless," Madero said, arranging himself in a half-recumbent position on the seat, "I must speak. The people would be disappointed if I did not."

Sarmiento wondered. Half the villages they stopped in were so isolated their inhabitants still thought Don Benito was president if they had any idea at all of what a president was. In others, Madero had been met more with puzzlement than enthusiasm. His stirring phrases about democracy, freedom, and universal suffrage might just as well have been addressed to the empty fields.

"Perhaps so," Sarmiento said, "but you are ill. It would be better if you took a train into the capital immediately, where you could be properly examined."

"These headaches, you mean? They are a gift from God to keep me humble."

"You can't really believe that."

Madero smiled. "Of course I do, Miguel. Every illness, every disease, has a spiritual function. I have—what is the expression in English—a 'swollen head' because of our success against Don Porfirio. These head-aches are merely God's way of deflating me."

Then, as the drug began to take effect, he closed his eyes and fell asleep.

In the early morning hours of June 7, 1911, the capital was shaken by an earthquake that filled the air with the clamor of church bells. Two hundred died, crushed in the rubble of their homes, and in the poorest districts of the city, entire blocks were reduced to dust. That afternoon, behind a procession of flags and banners, Francisco Madero entered the city astride a white horse. Sarmiento was not with him. As soon as he had reached the outskirts of the city, he had left Madero's entourage and gone home to his wife and child.

Book 3

Tragic Days

1912–1913

16

Beneath the summer sun, the air was as warm as flesh. It released the scents of earth and water as long, flat-bottomed vessels—*trajineras*—drifted beneath stone bridges among the ancient floating gardens on the still, green waters of the canals of Xochimilco. In La Niña's childhood, the canopied *trajineras* of the great families were guided along the placid waterways by Indian gondoliers to the tiny villages that dotted the banks of the canals. Indian women rowed out on fragile skiffs selling flowers and fruit and food, and other canoes carried musicians. Back and forth, too, went the innumerable punts that carried vegetables, fruits, and flowers from the floating gardens—the *chinampas*—to the city's markets. The banks of the canals were lined with *ahuejote*, the native junipers. The scent of flowers—for the name Xochimilco meant garden in the language of the Aztecs—was deep in the air, a sweetness that La Niña had imagined was the scent of Eden. She remembered herself on her eighteenth birthday: long, black hair loose around her slender shoulders, sinking into a pile of silk pillows while a band of floating musicians serenaded her.

She had described this scene to José so often it seemed to him that he must have been there with her. He watched his grandmother settled by her maid on a throne of cushions at the back of the *trajinera*. It was another birthday, her eightieth. She had commanded the family to join her on this outing. There was not enough room for everyone on her vessel, so it carried only his aunts, his mother, himself, and servants, while a second vessel carried his father and his *tíos* Damian and Gonzalo—Tío Saturnino, the banker, had gone to Paris after Don Francisco Madero had become president and he had yet to return. In the warm air his thoughts drifted and he smiled as he recalled his friend, the funny little man whom he knew as Don Panchito.

When his father had told him that the next president of the Republic was coming to the palace for dinner, José had expected someone old and frightening, like Don Porfirio. But Don Panchito was boy-sized, scarcely taller than José himself, and he had a boy's giggle and soft, high voice. Emboldened by the man's small stature and kind eyes, José had offered to show him his room, as if he were a classmate. José had performed for him a version of *Aida* in the toy theater his grandmother had given him for his birthday until his father came to remind Don Panchito there were other guests who wished to meet him. The next time José saw Don Panchito was at a reception at Chapultepec Castle, after he had become president. The president and his sad-eyed wife, Doña Sara, were in the receiving line shaking hands with dignitaries. When he saw José, the president scooped him into an embrace and told José he still owed him the last two acts of *Aida*. A few days later, José had received a package from Chapultepec. Inside, he discovered an Italian-made toy theater, an exquisite miniature La Scala, with papier-mâché casts of three Puccini operas. José was perplexed by the terrible things that were said about his friend in the newspapers. He asked his father, who told him they were lies.

"But why would the newspapers lie about Don Panchito?" he asked.

His father sighed and said, "Because he gave them that freedom," an answer that left José even more perplexed.

The gondoliers dipped their oars into the canal and the water slid beneath them as the boat began to move. José was fascinated by the *chinampas*, the tiny plots of land built on twigs and branches that dotted the canals and were farmed by the Indians. Some held a single row of pumpkins or a solitary rose bush yielding tall columns of blood-red roses. Others were spacious enough for a small thatched hut and a pretty little garden where naked Indian babies watched their mothers harvest chilies and corn. He was dimly aware of the buzz of his aunts' complaining voices like mosquitos in the background. His grandmother crooked her finger at him, and he joined her on her pile of pillows. He lay against her bony shoulder and watched the sunlight flash between the shaggy branches of the juniper trees.

"Abuelita, do the gardens really float?" he asked her.

"They did once," she replied, "but now they are so old they are rooted to the canal beds. When I was little girl, some of them still drifted, and it was lovely to see. What are your aunts saying?"

"They say the water smells and the insects bite them."

"Cows," she commented. "I wish my sons had lived."

"Why, Abuelita?"

"Because they would have left," she replied. "Unlike daughters. Daughters never leave. Promise me, *mijo*, that you will go and see the world."

"I do not wish to leave you," he said.

She stroked his hair. "You are my precious boy," she said. "But you will leave. Men cannot help it. Restlessness runs in your veins. What book is your mother reading?"

"I think it is the life of Santa Teresa de Ávila."

"Ah," she said. "Seeking instruction for sainthood, no doubt. Well, at least she does not complain, and she has in her own way lived."

"What do you mean, Abuelita?"

"To visit God in his heaven is to go somewhere even if it is only in her mind. Where would you like to go, José?"

"Oh," he murmured drowsily. "Everywhere."

Alicia, overhearing the conversation between her mother and her son, smiled to herself. They spoke to each other like old friends across the decades that separated them. A kind of innocence united them, but while José's was born of wonder, La Niña's was the product of world-weariness. Alicia's childhood memories of her mother were of a woman who labored grimly and ceaselessly at the innumerable tasks required to preserve her family's status in the tumultuous times that followed the expulsion of the French. The Marquesa María de Jesús had been sharp-tongued and humorless, a social arbiter and a stickler for propriety who raised her daughters in the language of threats, proverbs, and admonitions. That woman had decamped, leaving in her place La Niña, an old widow who was by turns sentimental and tactless, caustic and tender, conniving and selfless, and utterly indifferent to the social mores that she had once fought to preserve. This elderly edition of her mother was easier to love, but there was no greater understanding between them than when Alicia had been the unmarriageable and pious thorn in the *marquesa*'s side.

Her mother's essential and unchanging quality was her worldliness. From her mother's perspective, Alicia knew her religious devotion had always seemed like a way to avoid the painful reality of her disfigurement. La Niña could not understand that the point of Alicia's faith was not to project herself into a distant heaven to escape the actualities of life on earth. To the contrary, as Jesus had insisted, the kingdom of God was to be found on earth, in the day-to-day life of flesh and blood. God had not descended from heaven and lived as a man so that men might awaken in paradise when they died. He had lived as a man to make human life sacred. She could not be a true follower of Christ without living as though every moment on earth was luminous.

She glanced across the water at her husband, engrossed in conversation with his brothers-in-law, his broad back turned to her. Upon his return from the north, they had discovered a depth of desire for each other that had surprised them both. Her relief that he had returned alive, and his gratitude after the horrors of war for the life she provided for him, had renewed their marriage. Night after night, they explored together the intense animal comfort of bodily closeness and the joy of giving and getting pleasure. Her avidity had startled him at first. He had imagined she would feel constrained by what he awkwardly called her "piety." She had laughed and told him, "We are husband and wife, Miguel. There is no shame between us." Inspired, he had introduced new ways for them to wring every last drop of bliss from each other's body. Now, as she watched him, she was imagining the familiar body naked atop her, the prickle of his chest hair, his warm, smoky breath, his hard buttock muscles contracting and relaxing beneath her hands as he drove into her. A flush of longing heated her breasts and colored her throat. She looked down at her book and fell upon the words with which Santa Teresa described her union with God: "The pain was so sharp that it made me utter several moans; and so excessive was the sweetness caused me by this intense pain that one can never wish to lose it."

Sarmiento sat beneath the canopy of the *trajinera* that carried him and his brothers-in-law alongside the women. It was named *La Sirena* and decorated with primitive paintings of large-breasted mermaids wearing seaweed tiaras. The canal had narrowed and the Indian oarsmen stopped pulling to let the vessel fall back for the women to pass. He watched Alicia disappear with a pang in his chest and a twitch in his groin as his tongue recalled her briny savor, like a pearl freshly cut from an oyster.

"Miguel! Pay attention!"

He returned his gaze to Gonzalo and the deck of cards laid out on the table before him. His brothers-in-law were attempting to teach him how to play a gambling game, but he kept losing the thread of the explanations, which involved French and English phrases and a complicated system of betting.

"He's hopeless," Damian said with a smile. The small, handsomely formed man was impeccable in a white linen suit and straw boater. "Let's just drink, shall we?"

"And eat," gluttonous Gonzalo chimed in. He snapped his fingers and a servant brought a picnic basket stocked with imported foods from his department store and a bucket holding a half-dozen bottles of champagne on ice. "We must keep up our strength for our encounter with our mother-in-law."

"I am very fond of her," Miguel protested.

"Of course, you are her favorite," Gonzalo replied. "She barely suffers me and Damian. I wonder what our father-in-law would have made of you."

"I never had the pleasure of meeting him," Sarmiento replied.

Damian laughed. "It was no pleasure!" He turned to Gonzalo. "Did you get the lecture on the ranks of nobility?"

"Ah, yes," Gonzalo replied. "A duke outranks a *marqués*, but a *marqués* outranks a count, who in turn outranks a viscount . . ."

"Duke from *dux*," Damian quoted, "meaning leader in Latin, and *marqués* from the Old French *marchis*, the ruler of a frontier."

Gonzalo paused midbite and said to Sarmiento, "The old man took all that crap quite seriously. He fancied himself the last civilized man in barbaric México."

"Yes, he was a real bastard," Damian said. "Let's eat."

The food was served, the wine poured. Damian, sampling the wine, said, "It's just as well that we don't teach Miguel to play faro. With his luck, he'd clean us out."

"My luck?" Sarmiento asked. "I've never been good at gaming of any kind."

"You bet on Madero," Damian said. "He was what the Americans call 'the long shot.' 'Long shots' pay off quite well, yet you seem reluctant to collect your winnings."

Sarmiento set his glass down. "You're being typically obscure."

"He means," Gonzalo said, his mouth full of bread and ham, "Madero owes you for sticking your neck out for him."

"Exactly," Damian said, smiling. "He is in your debt."

"I supported Madero on principle. I don't want anything from him."

"Then you are the only man in México who doesn't," Damian said.

"What do you want, Damian?"

He shrugged modestly. "Nothing specific, Miguel, but in my business, it is often useful to have well-placed friends. I would like an introduction."

"To Madero? I don't think—"

"No, of course not," Damian said soothingly. "Not to the president, but you must also know his brother, Gustavo."

"Yes, speaking of bastards," Sarmiento replied.

He had last seen Gustavo Madero, the president's one-eyed brother, holding forth at the Madero family's mansion in Colonia Roma when he had gone to examine Madero before his inauguration. As a functionary led Sarmiento to Madero's third-floor bedroom, he heard Gustavo say, "In a family filled with clever men, the family fool is going to be president."

"He is someone I could do business with," Damian said.

Sarmiento had found Madero in a large, sunny bedroom filled with congratulatory baskets of fruits and flowers. He sat with ink-stained fingers at a little writing desk wearing a maroon robe with a white silk scarf knotted at his throat. Just as on the first day they had met, the little man was alone; not even his wife with him. On a table beside his bed was the famous Ouija board. There were scraps of paper on the floor on which were answers from the spirits to the questions Madero and his wife propounded to them.

"Miguel," he said, rising from his chair. "How good of you to come."

"How are you feeling?" he asked.

"Wonderful!" he exclaimed. "The headaches are gone, but Sara wanted you to take a look at me to reassure her that my parts are in good working order."

"Where is Señora Madero? I didn't see her when I came in."

"She is calling at the French and German embassies. Evidently the life of a first lady is endless cups of tea and chatter."

Sarmiento doubted that Sara Madero would find that life to her liking for long. As intense as her husband was amiable, and ambitious enough for both of them, she had been the only woman admitted to Madero's staff meetings, where she sat, in her dark, dour dresses, like a tiny, venomous spider.

As he examined Madero, he was aware of the little man's bright eyes following him. Those eyes—large, dark, and kindly—were his most compelling feature. He suffered the examination cheerfully and halfway through, Sarmiento knew he would find nothing irregular.

"Am I well enough to take up the duties of my office?" he asked when Sarmiento had finished.

"From a medical perspective," he replied.

"And from other perspectives?" Madero said with a smile.

"The newspapers say that Pascual Orozco has gone into rebellion against you. He is a dangerous man," Sarmiento said, remembering the ex-muleteer's icy eyes and cold contempt for the *perfumados*.

Madero frowned. "He expected me to make him governor of Chihuahua, when he cannot even write his own name. Of course, I had to refuse."

"And Zapata has also refused to lay down his arms. And the Yaquis . . ."

"Have renewed hostilities against the government. I know," he said, knotting his scarf. "You haven't mentioned Díaz's loyalists in the government who have never stopped plotting against me, or my brother who calls me a fool." He smiled. "Gustavo has repeated his little witticism in every parlor in Ciudad de México."

"I worry about you," Sarmiento said. "As your friend."

Madero patted Sarmiento's shoulder. "Arjuna, do thine allotted task."

"I beg your pardon, Don Pancho."

"Those are the words that Krishna speaks to the great warrior king, Arjuna, in the Bhagavad Gita on the eve of the great battle Arjuna must fight with his kinsmen. Arjuna looks down upon the camps of the two armies and he asks Lord Krishna what good can come from brother slaying brother."

"And Krishna's answer is 'do thine allotted task'?"

"Yes, but there is more." He dug through the pile of books on his writing desk and found a small book bound in blood-red leather with gilt lettering. He opened it without hesitation to a particular page and read, "'Such earthly actions do, free from desire, and thou shalt well perform thy heavenly purpose.' Do you understand, Miguel?"

"I am not a spiritist."

"This is not occult knowledge," the little man replied. "It is simple wisdom. We are like arrows shot from a bow. Our course is determined, but whether we hit our mark or miss is not for us to know. Therefore, we need have no anxiety about our destination. Our only task is to stay the course."

"I would not think the arrow has much choice in the matter," Sarmiento observed.

Madero laughed, a high-pitched child's laugh. "Precisely so. To believe otherwise is mere vanity."

Miguel. Will you introduce me to Gustavo?" Damian asked again.

Sarmiento replied, "I won't need to. You and he are birds of a feather. You'll find each other soon enough."

His brother-in-law raised an eyebrow. "One bastard to another, you mean? I suppose you're right. When I do find him, may I mention our connection?"

Sarmiento shrugged. "For whatever good it does, of course. Now, more champagne."

The two boats drifted in and out of the cana...
gardens. Birds swooped through the air, the whir of t...
in their passage. The scent of flowers and leaf meal rose...
of the water. The sounds of flute and guitar approached and t...
as the musicians' boats came and went. The *trajineras* docked a...
inn, where, at a long table shaded by a white canopy, the family...
brated La Niña's eightieth year over a long and festive meal. At the en...
of the day, over darkening waters, they were rowed to their carriages
and driven home.

Miguel twitched and muttered in his sleep. Alicia put down her book
and stroked his head. When he had first returned to her, their sleep had
been shattered by nightmares in which he wandered through heavy
smoke in a sun-scorched landscape, his hands dripping blood. A year
later, he no longer woke her with his cries, but sometimes the terrible
images of battle still seeped into his dreams. As she threaded her fingers
through his hair, she was aware that he had awakened.

Without looking up at her, he said, "I dreamed I was on the train,
pulling away from the station, and you were standing on the platform,
getting smaller and smaller. I did not know where we were, or where
I was going, but the sky was blood red." He sighed. "I felt so lost, so
hopeless."

"You were remembering how we parted in Arizona," she said.

"Yes, that was the loneliest moment of my life. I didn't know if I
would ever see you again."

"All of that is over," she said soothingly. "You have a gray hair. Just
one. Shall I pluck it?"

"No, I think I have earned it," he said.

"My hair will be completely gray before I am fifty," she said. "And
when we go out together people will assume that I'm your mother."

He sat up and looked at her, smiling lewdly, and murmured, "*Mi
madrecita*." He slid her nightgown from her shoulder, exposing the top
of her breast, and kissed it. "You taste like cinnamon."

She laughed. "What, like a cup of Chepa's chocolate?"

He continued to lower her nightgown and she felt the cool air on
her nipple and then his warm mouth. The stroke of his tongue made

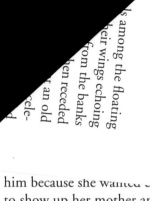

eyes at once imploring and demanding.
...s she sank into the bed, her book fell to

...l in his arms, her back against him, he

...e replied.

...y had spoken to each other in the first
...ey were both still cautious of each other's
...leceive nor hurt the other. She knew he
...spected and admired her. She had married
him because she wanted ...lren and, she could now admit to herself,
to show up her mother and her sisters and all the society women who
had pitied or scorned her for her ruined face.

"When did it become love?" she said softly, only half-intending to
speak the words aloud.

He pressed against her, his hands resting on her belly. "For me, it
was after the last miscarriage, when I realized I could lose you."

"For me, it was watching you care for the poor of San Francisco
Tlalco," she said.

"I would never have done that without you," he said. "You have
been the making of me, Alicia. I am the man I am because of your
example of kindness and generosity."

"Oh, Miguel, don't make me sound like a saint," she said with mock
irritation. "I hear enough of that from my mother and my sisters."

He slowly slid his hand down her belly and, with a practiced touch,
slowly and gently parted her and pressed his finger into her flesh. A
flush crept up her neck and her eyes glazed over with pleasure. When he
finished, he rested his hand familiarly between her thighs and said, "I
think we have established that you're no saint. I hope when you pray
you remember to thank God I saved you from a life of celibacy."

"Don't mock, Miguel," she sighed. "And yes, I do remember to
thank him in my prayers for your skillful and beautiful body." She
shifted away from him. "I'm cold."

She slipped out of bed to retrieve her nightgown and heard the
crinkle of paper beneath her feet. Once she had dressed, she reached
down for the newspaper that Miguel had been reading. On the front

page was a photograph of the president of the Republic and a map of México that depicted the rebellions against him in the north and south.

"Even after a year, it is still strange to me that Don Francisco is president," she said, folding the newspaper and placing it on her night table. "Don Porfirio was president for so long he seemed more like a monument than a man."

"A monument with clay feet."

She got back into bed. "Did you think he would fall so quickly?" she asked.

"No," he said. "Like everyone else I thought the army would fight to the death for him, but Madero knew better. Díaz's army was a bunch of boys abducted from the streets and forced into uniform. They had no loyalty to him."

"Will they fight for Don Francisco?" she asked.

"Against the rebels? Yes, if only because the generals prefer Madero to either Orozco or Zapata. Madero is a gentleman; those two are peasants."

"Don Francisco is also a man of peace," she said. "I felt that when I met him. I know he would like to end the fighting."

"The rebellions will burn out eventually," he replied. "At any rate, it is no longer our concern. I had my brush with history at Ciudad Juárez. Whatever happens now will not affect us. We are not important."

"I thank God for that," she sighed as she lay her head on his chest and closed her eyes.

Sarmiento had not been entirely honest when he had told his brothers-in-law he wanted nothing from Madero. After Madero's election, he had sent him a copy of the report he had written recommending improvements to the city's public health. He had hoped Madero would be more receptive than Don Porfirio to the needs of the poor. Madero had responded with a note thanking him for the report and promising to read it. Months had passed and Sarmiento had heard nothing since. Curious about the fate of his report, Sarmiento asked his cousin to meet him for a drink. He had seen very little of Luis since their return to the city, though he read about him often enough in the newspapers. Luis had been appointed to the prominent position of sub-secretary of government. He and his boss, Abraham González, who had also fought in the desert, were the daily subjects of scurrilous attacks in the opposition press.

Sarmiento waited for Luis at a sidewalk table at the Café Colón on the Reforma in the shadow of the immense monument to the explorer for whom it was named. His was one of the four shrines Don Porfirio had erected in the last years of his reign along the Reforma—the others, equally ostentatious, commemorated Cuauhtémoc, the last Aztec king; memorialized Benito Juárez; and culminated in the Angel of Independence. The monuments were Don Porfirio's retelling of the history of México in marble and iron—a history that combined the fortuitous but peaceful discovery of the new world with the heroic resistance of the indigenous people and the mixture of bloodlines, Spanish and Indian, that produced a great and free people. Two sumptuous carriages filled with beautifully dressed women passed beneath Columbus's monument. They were the advance guard of the daily procession of the rich that wound its way up the boulevard and around Chapultepec in a stately and pointless show of opulence. Meanwhile, ragged Indian men swept the sidewalks with branch-and-twig brooms, bent over at their labor and ignored by the passersby. The distance between the silk women and the pauper Indians was the true history of México, Sarmiento thought.

"Primo!" The familiar voice hailed him. Luis came toward him, emerging from the dappled shadows of the eucalyptus trees that lined the boulevard. His face showed the strain of long days and too little sleep. Beneath the physical weariness, Sarmiento recognized the deeper pall of loss. Sarmiento had helped Luis bury his lover in the desert. He remembered how tenderly Luis had opened the boy's mouth and pressed a gold coin on his tongue.

"Why?" Sarmiento had asked.

"For the ferryman who will row him across the river to Mictlan, the underworld." His entire body shuddered. "Oh, Miguel, I will never see my boy again." He fell to his knees, keening like a wounded animal.

"Thank you for meeting me," Sarmiento said. "I know you are busy."

"Never too busy for you, Miguel," he said. "Come, let's go inside. After all those months in the desert, I prefer the reek of cigars and alcohol to fresh air."

The café was dark wood and mirrors and small tables in shadowy corners where well-dressed men talked in low, conspiratorial tones over cut crystal glasses filled with imported whiskey. As they wended their way among the tables, the flutter of soft, pale hands detained them as the café's patrons—some of them opposition leaders who fulminated daily against the president in newspaper columns and on the floor of the Senate—reached out for a word with a member of Madero's inner circle. The combination of the dead eyes and wide smiles of Café Colón's habitués reminded Sarmiento of the gaping expression of skulls. At last, they reached a back table where a waiter had already poured Luis's absinthe and brought Sarmiento's scotch along with small dishes of nuts, olives, cured meats, cheeses, and crackers that Luis gobbled as if he hadn't eaten in days. A broad-shouldered, bald, and dark-skinned man in an army officer's uniform lay face-forward on the adjacent table, snoring. A bottle of brandy and a half-filled glass sat within reach.

Sarmiento glanced at him and then looked questioningly to his cousin.

"Ah," Luis replied, in a low voice. "That, Primo, is the fearless Indian killer, General Victoriano Huerta with his favorite companion, Mister Hennessey. Díaz sent him to deal with Zapata's peasant revolt in Morales. Unfortunately, the general is more of a thug than a strategist and only succeeded in increasing Zapata's numbers. Madero took away his command. Now he sits in the drool of his self-pity."

"Huerta," Sarmiento repeated. "Didn't Don Porfirio send him to fight the Yaquis?"

"That was one of his commands. He was more successful with the Yaquis than the Zapatistas because all he was expected to do was to exterminate them."

"Not entirely successful," Sarmiento observed. "I read that the Yaquis have taken up arms against the government."

Luis sipped his absinthe. "That is so. They sent a delegation to Madero and demanded that he return to them the entire river valley they claim as their homeland. They say God gave it to them after Noah's flood."

"I don't recall any Yaquis being taken aboard the ark."

"They have supplemented the Bible with their own legends to make themselves the center of God's creation," his cousin replied. "For example, one of their towns is called Bethlehem. Madero asked them why and they told him it was because Jesus was born there."

"They can't possibly believe that."

"But they do," Luis replied. "They say Jesus walked among them practicing his arts as a healer and was crucified in the arms of his mother, who had transformed herself into a tree to embrace her son at the moment of his death." He sipped his drink. "Some of their stories are actually quite beautiful. They appeal to what is left of the poet in me."

"Enough to advise Madero to return their property to them?"

"No. Díaz stole their lands and resettled them with Mexican colonists. Some of those families have been there for thirty years now. Madero can't just force them to pack up and leave, but the Yaquis will not accept anything less than everything. So . . ." His voice trailed off and he finished his drink in a gulp, summoning the waiter for another.

"The Yaquis fought for Don Francisco in Chihuahua."

"Fought with, not for," his cousin corrected. "They fought for themselves, for their own objectives. That, as it turns out, was the case with most of the army of the revolution."

"I did sometimes wonder about the depth of their loyalty."

"In that case, you were more prescient than most, including Madero. He thought he was leading a movement, but as it happens he was only leading a faction. So, Zapata in the south, Orozco in the north, and now the Yaquis." He shrugged. "But enough about that. You wanted to know about your report."

The drunken general roused himself and, attempting to stand, overturned the marble-topped table on which his glass and bottle had rested. The bottle shattered and a stream of brandy puddled at Sarmiento's feet.

He glanced at the man, expecting an apology, but the soldier said, "What are you looking at?"

Sarmiento, who despised public drunkenness, said, "A fool."

The general weaved toward him aggressively. Sarmiento stood up and found he was half a head taller than the other man, who stared at him through blue-tinted glasses that gave him a sinister appearance.

"You call me a fool," he said thickly. He pulled a pistol from his waistband and waved it in Sarmiento's direction. "You *perfumado* cocksucker! No one calls Victoriano Huerta a fool."

Half a dozen waiters had rushed toward the back of the room, but at the sight of the pistol they froze and all conversation stopped. Huerta unleashed a stream of curses while he tried to fix Sarmiento in his sights. Swiftly, Sarmiento stepped toward the little man as he fumbled with the trigger of his gun and struck him in his jaw. The blow threw Huerta back and off-balance. The gun fired as he dropped to the floor, the bullet striking the tin ceiling. Sarmiento pressed his foot down on Huerta's right wrist, forcing him to release the pistol, then kicked it aside and retrieved it.

The waiters came forward. Two of them assisted Huerta to his feet. He had lost his glasses and his eyes were tiny and weak. As the surge of adrenaline ebbed, Sarmiento was embarrassed that he had allowed himself to be drawn into a scene with the drunk.

One of the waiters found Huerta's glasses. A lens was shattered, but he put them on, looking even more absurd.

"Give me my gun, you bastard!"

Sarmiento removed the bullets from the pistol and returned the weapon to the man. "Señor," he said, extending his hand. "Shall we put this behind us?"

Huerta glared at Sarmiento and said, "I have no idea who you are, but today you have made an enemy. A powerful enemy."

Before Sarmiento could respond, the other lens dropped out of Huerta's spectacles. The café rocked with laughter. Huerta turned on his heel and marched out. The waiters cleaned up the spill and Sarmiento sat down with his cousin, who had observed the entire incident silently.

"A ridiculous little man," Sarmiento said.

"Most soldiers kill out of duty, but Huerta is a murderer who was fortunate enough to find the army," Jorge Luis replied. "Now, your report."

"I had hoped to hear some word by now," Sarmiento said.

"I know Madero has read it," Luis replied. "He mentioned it to me, but his mind and his time are otherwise occupied. The health and well-being of the poor is not something he can worry about when his presidency hangs by threads."

"Is the situation that tenuous?"

"Yes," he said simply and finished his drink. "I must get back to work. I will speak to Madero and try to arrange an audience with him. But don't expect too much, Primo."

The summons to the National Palace came a few days later. On a rainy afternoon, Sarmiento approached the Puerta de Honor, one of the three entrances into the block-long labyrinth. The soldiers who guarded the door inspected his pass and ominously and unapologetically searched him for weapons. Afterward one of them escorted him up a broad stairway to the presidential offices. Purposeful men carrying sheaves of papers bound in leather folders walked down the corridors. Voices rose from the courtyard below, one of seven, where a statue of Pegasus presided over an assemblage of would-be petitioners awaiting their moment with a government bureaucrat. The guard deposited Sarmiento in the presidential waiting room.

Beneath a massive painting of the signing of the Constitution of 1857, the room was packed with other men, some alone, some in groups, who regarded this new supplicant with suspicion and annoyance. One man had fallen asleep in a corner chair and his snores filled the air. In another corner was a delegation of sandal-shod Indians, conspicuous in a room filled with dark coats and silk ties. One of the Indians clung to a bundle of battered paper tied with twine. Heavy smoke from the innumerable cigars and cigarettes rose like a fist and squeezed the oxygen from the air. Sarmiento considered the number of people in the room ahead of him and sighed. His appointment was in ten minutes, but he doubted he would even see Madero that day. He found an empty seat near a window that he managed to pry open for an inch of fresh air.

A thin, supercilious young man wearing a monocle stepped into the room. The various conversations quieted and all looked at him expectantly.

"Señor Doctor Miguel Sarmiento," he droned.

"Yes, I am he," Dr. Sarmiento said, rising from his chair. He could feel the resentment of the other men in the room like a physical blow.

"Your pass, please," the young man said.

Sarmiento handed him the thick card he had received in the mail that had called him to the palace. The young man raised it to his monocled eye and studied it briefly.

"Come with me, Doctor."

They passed through a room hung with a heroic life-sized portrait of Hidalgo and then through another chamber with red walls, where beneath an enormous chandelier a dozen other young men worked at large desks. They entered a third, smaller room, papered in blue and white.

"Wait here," the monocled boy said and exited through a heavy, richly polished door.

Sarmiento paced the little room, studying the three large landscape paintings that depicted a panoramic view of the valley. Ten minutes passed, then fifteen, then thirty. He had begun to wonder whether he had been forgotten when he heard voices on the other side of the door. Two men entered the room. Unhappily, he recognized both of them. One was Gustavo Madero, the president's cynical one-eyed brother. The other man, now sober and resplendent in his dress uniform, was Victoriano Huerta, the drunken general he had last seen fumbling for the exit at the Café Colón. He had repaired his blue-tinted spectacles.

"Ah, Miguel," Gustavo said. "Good to see you. Do you know General Huerta?"

"I don't believe we have ever been properly introduced," Sarmiento said, extending his hand. "General."

Huerta took it and held it only as long as politeness required. "Señor Doctor," he said.

"General Huerta is being dispatched to Chihuahua to deal with Pascual Orozco." He patted Huerta's back. "An exterminator to rid us of a pest."

At Gustavo's touch, contempt flitted across Huerta's face, but he said, "I am at the service of my country and my president."

"Just the right proportions of arrogance and servility," Gustavo said, laughing. "That's why I love soldiers."

Sarmiento said, "I wish you success in your campaign, General."

Huerta bit off a "Thank you," and then turned to Gustavo. "Again, my deepest gratitude to the president for his confidence in me."

"Make certain it's not misplaced. You are expendable," Gustavo said mildly. "Here, take this stairway, General. You will avoid the unwashed mob out there."

After Huerta took his leave, Gustavo slipped his arm through Sarmiento's as if they were old friends and led him out of the room, remarking, "Huerta's a savage, of course, but savagery is what is required to deal with the likes of Orozco. My brother is very anxious to talk to you."

Sarmiento nodded. He was disturbed that Gustavo—who had never bothered to conceal his contempt for his brother—now appeared to have his confidence.

They entered the presidential office, the famous yellow room. The walls were hung with yellow brocade satin and the ceiling had fleur-de-lis adornments. In one corner was the long table used for cabinet meetings. At its head was the president's chair with a gilt eagle of México carved above the back. The same eagle was worked into a deep green carpet that covered the floor. The carpet's green was echoed by the velvet drapes on the tall, narrow windows that looked out on a small, private courtyard. In the center of the room was a massive desk where a silver inkstand bore the monogram of Emperor Maximiliano. Madero was behind the desk, dwarfed by its polished splendor.

He sprang up and came around the table. "Miguel, how wonderful to see you again."

"You are a long way from La Santisima," Sarmiento said.

Madero laughed and embraced him. "So it would seem, but appearances can be deceptive. The debates that you used to find so tedious during our staff meetings in the desert have followed me here. How is my *amigito*, José?"

"My son is well. He was very excited when I told him I was coming to see you and asked to be remembered to you."

"You must give him a kiss from me," Madero said.

Madero wore a plain brown suit but his vest was peacock blue. He seemed as indomitably cheerful as ever, but Sarmiento's practiced eye detected a deepening in the lines around his eyes and the furrows across his forehead that seemed to him to be a sign of chronic pain.

"How is your health, Don Francisco? Have the headaches returned?"

Madero laughed. "They have never left! Didn't you see them in the reception room?" He motioned Sarmiento to a chair. "It's because of them that I haven't been able to talk to you about your fine report, Miguel. I have every intention of instituting your reforms to make life more bearable for the poor, but first the country must be pacified. You know our old friend Pascual Orozco is leading an army in the north."

Sarmiento said, "His betrayal must be painful."

"I have learned not to take these things personally. I wield this power for the people, not for myself. On the day my term expires, I will gladly surrender this power and return home. Until then, I am obligated to defend my position. Only I can't do it alone. I need the help of my friends. I need your help, Miguel."

Confused by the turn in the conversation, Sarmiento murmured, "Of course, Señor Presidente, I am at your command."

Madero glanced at his brother.

Gustavo cleared his throat and said, "Old Senator Murgia from Quintana Roo dropped dead last week. He was a dyed-in-the-wool Díaz partisan and a pain in our ass. Now we have the opportunity to elect someone more sympathetic to our goals. That's where you can assist us."

"I'm afraid I don't know anyone in Quintana Roo," Sarmiento said. "I've never even been there."

"I want you to run for his seat," Madero said.

"But that's absurd," Sarmiento said. "As I said, I have no connection to that state. I am not a politician and I—"

"Nor was I until it became my duty," Madero said. "Miguel, we need the Quintana Roo seat in the Senate to give the government a majority. Without it, none of the reforms I hope to enact, including your public health reforms, will be adopted."

Sarmiento shook his head. "I can't believe you don't have a better choice than me, someone who knows politics. As you yourself said, I have no patience for political debates."

"Do you remember that day in the desert when I came to see the wounded soldiers after Juárez had fallen?" Madero asked quietly. "When I found you, you were drenched in their blood. I will never forget that moment, Miguel."

"I remember, Don Francisco," he replied softly. "But I fail to see—"

"I don't want another politician in the Senate," Madero said, with surprising asperity. "I want someone who knows the price we paid in blood to rid ourselves of Díaz and to restore democracy to México. I want a friend, Miguel. I want you."

Sarmiento was at a loss for words, and for a moment there was silence in the opulent room. He remembered the slosh of blood in his boots, the pile of amputated limbs in the corner of the surgical tent. He looked at the little man who looked back at him with magnetic, melancholy eyes.

"I know nothing about campaigning," he said, a last weak protest.

That drew a sharp laugh from Gustavo. "You won't need to campaign, Miguel. I can guarantee your election."

Madero grimaced, and in the look that passed between him and Gustavo, Sarmiento realized that electoral fraud was back.

"Did you not just talk about restoring democracy to México?" he said to Madero.

"Sometimes," Madero said softly, "the ends do justify the means. I implore you, Miguel. Do this for me."

The mask of cheerfulness had dissolved, and Sarmiento saw the fatigue and desperation eating into the little man's flesh.

"All right, Don Francisco," he said. "I will do this for you."

"And for México," Madero added.

Sarmiento shook his head. "For you."

"Forgive me," Madero said with a sigh.

17

Slivers of silvery light illuminated the tangle of trees. The branches were leafless and twisted. They ended in nubs like the amputated limbs José had seen in one of his father's medical books. His heart pounded in his chest, and a spasm of nausea constricted his throat. His feet sank into soft, squishy ground. Each step released another jet of the stench of rotting meat that filled his nostrils and clung to his clothes. As he edged his way among the trees there suddenly appeared in his path a man-sized, winged creature covered in fecal-colored feathers. Its face, framed by a mane of greasy hair, was half-human, half-avian. It turned black, irisless eyes on José and croaked menacingly. José staggered back away from the creature, and, as he did, tore through the gnarled branch of a tree. From a dozen broken twigs, voices shrieked, "Why do you hurt us, boy!"

José screamed. El Morito's startled green eyes glared at him for a second and then the cat jumped off the bed. His breath was hard and shallow and his heart pounded in his chest. His bedclothes were damp with sweat. He reached to the bed table and turned on the lamp. The light flickered on, dispelling the shadows in which he half-feared the bird creatures were lurking.

His door creaked opened and his mother entered the room in her nightgown and robe. Her long, thick hair, falling loosely around her shoulders, reminded him of the birds, and he shuddered as she approached him.

"José," she said gently. "I heard you shout. Did you have another nightmare?"

"Yes," he said in a quavering voice. "I dreamed of the Wood of the Suicides."

She sat at the edge of his bed and sighed. "I wish you had obeyed me and stayed away from the Palantino."

"I'm sorry, Mamá," he said sobbing, as he threw himself into the cradle of her arms. "I shall never disobey you again. I will never go back there."

For weeks after he had gone to the coffin maker's theater, the flickering shadows on the muslin had replayed themselves obsessively in his mind. He had repeatedly asked his mother if they could return, but her only interest in the Teatro Palantino had been to learn about his father. When he asked to go alone, she told him El Carmen was not a safe neighborhood for an unaccompanied child.

"But I am not a child," he whined. "I am almost twelve."

"José, that is enough," she said in a tone that brooked no further argument. "I forbid it."

His grandmother, noticing his moping, asked him the cause. He tried to explain to her what he had seen and why it was so urgent that he return. "The pictures moved like a dream, Abuelita, and I want to see them again, but my mother says no."

"If it is that important, I will send Santos with you," she said, "but you are not to tell your mother."

"Thank you, thank you," he said, kissing her powdered cheek.

One afternoon, while his mother was away, he slipped out of the palace with Santos, his grandmother's majordomo. Santos hailed a cab and they wandered the streets of El Carmen until they found the *mortuorio* just as José had remembered it. José trotted down the coffin-stacked aisles to the table where the man sold tickets, Santos at his heels. Santos bought tickets and they went into the close, dark room that smelled, Santos complained, like the privy in a cantina. José chose a bench closest to the screen, near where the fat woman pounded away at her out-of-tune piano. As before, they waited until the room was filled and then, like the purest and most intense moonbeam, the white ray of light materialized above their heads and filled the muslin sheet.

A black box was projected upon the screen and words appeared in white lettering—*La voyage dans la lune*—and beneath those words, "Geo. Méliès, Star Films, Paris." José had no idea what the latter words meant, but the first phrase filled him with excitement because it conjured up the title of Jules Verne's *From the Earth to the Moon*. He hoped that the similarity between the titles was not a coincidence. His hope was rewarded when the title faded. A long-haired, snowy bearded man, clad like a medieval alchemist in robes bespangled with stars and planets, appeared before a gathering of similarly dressed men. Illustrating his scheme on a blackboard, he proposed a journey to the moon. José clapped his hands, earning the suspicious stares of the sodden crowd that surrounded him.

With increasing wonder, José saw that the story unfolding on the screen was just as Verne had told it: the forging of a bullet-shaped chamber, which was loaded into an enormous cannon and fired into the night sky to carry six of the men—astronomers—to the moon. In images that words could never have captured, the moon grew larger and larger until its cratered surface filled the screen. It revealed the craggy face of the man in the moon, just as José had always imagined he would look. His astonishment turned to laughter when the projectile pierced the moon's eye. He gasped in amazement at the lunar terrain the astronomers encountered when they emerged from their vessel, arabesques of pale stone spiraling against the moonless sky. As the exhausted astronomers slept, seven stars rose in the sky above them, each with the face of a woman. The stars faded and the moon goddess appeared swinging on a crescent, while Saturn, like the Ancient of Days, looked down at the astronomers from among his rings.

In his conscious mind, José knew, as he had known at the opera, that he was looking at painted backdrops, not stars and planets, and human beings, not celestial creatures. But the flicker of shadow and light where image tumbled upon image, magically fading in and out, enchanted him. It was as if he had been carried to the screen and deposited there, unseen but present as the astronomers, fleeing a sudden snow, escaped into a tunnel that led to a subterranean landscape filled with enormous mushrooms. He shared their terror when they encountered the Selenites, insectoid moon people, moving like contortionists across the frightening topography. When the astronomers ran from the hostile Selenites to their vessel, José's heart raced as if he were running with them. When they reached their capsule, he lurched forward, silently urging them into the chamber. The capsule was poised at the edge of the cliff. One of the astronomers threw a rope over the cliff, climbed down, and loosened the vessel so that it fell from the moon and dropped like a stone through the sky. He watched it plunge into the ocean, scraping the bed of the sea. Only when the capsule floated to the surface where it was towed by a steamer to port did José expel his pent-up breath. On the screen the word "*Fin*" released him from the film's spell. Dazed, he found himself back in the loud, squalid room beside Santos, who was doubled over, eyes shut, muttering prayers.

Later, his grandmother summoned him to her bedroom and said, "Santos told me that you took him to a haunted mortuary filled with ghosts and devils! He was so frightened I asked your father to give him something to calm his nerves."

"They were not ghosts, Abuelita, they were moving photographs that told the story of a journey to the moon."

She looked at him with complete incomprehension. "Whatever it was, he refuses to go back. I am sorry, José, but perhaps your mother was correct to forbid you from this . . . activity."

José did not protest. He knew now how to find the theater and he had every intention of returning.

José," his mother said, stroking his hair, "what you saw were only images, photographs. They are no more real than the book that first described them."

He lifted his head from her breast. "But they *were* real. The people on the screen were real."

"Actors," she said. "They were only actors, *mijo*."

He wanted to believe her, but he could not shake the residual images of the tormented souls in hell that filled his head when he shut his eyes.

Several weeks passed before he was able to return to the Palantino. He had set out from the palace under sunny skies, but the capricious summer weather turned stormy as he retraced his path to El Carmen. He was caught in a downpour of warm, oily rain. He sheltered in a dark, dusty shop called La Huesana. Its walls were lined with shelves that held the store's small stock of candles, religious statues, *milagros*, and jars and jars of dried herbs. He shook off the rain and read the labels on the jars. Some he recognized—rosemary, basil, spearmint, *epazote*, rue, sage. Others were strange in name and appearance—withered flowers, scaly bark, and dried twisted roots in jars labeled wolf bane, angel's trumpet, and devil's claw. Copal burned at an altar in a dim corner of the room where seven candles, each a different color, flickered before a robed and hooded statue of the Virgin of Guadalupe. As he approached the altar, he was conscious of the shuffle of his footsteps on the dusty floor and the pounding rain on the roof. The objects laid out on the table among the colored candles—glasses of water, vials of oily substances, hand-scrawled notes, a bottle labeled Agua de Florida—mystified him. The statue was clad in a rainbow-hued robe the same seven colors as the candles—gold, silver, copper, blue, purple, red, and green. He looked up at the hooded face, expecting the stern but loving visage of Guadalupe, and gasped when he saw, instead, a skull. Only then did he realize that the figure held a scythe in one hand and a globe in the other.

"La Santisima Muerte," an old voice rasped, making his heart jump. "Our lady Mictecacihuatl, the Lady of the Dead."

José looked at the person who had spoken, a woman dressed in the garb of the poor of the city—full calico skirt, dusty at the hem, a stained embroidered blouse, a black, frayed rebozo draped across her shoulders. She seemed ancient, older even than his grandmother, who was the oldest person he knew. Her white hair was piled into a bun and her face was creased, careworn, and dotted with moles, warts, and age spots. She studied him with rheumy eyes, glistening and damp.

"She is the most powerful of the gods," she continued, in the same rasp that he imagined was what his cat would sound like if it could speak. "Everyone must come to her. The world is her field, the cutter is her harvesting tool." She reached out a withered hand and touched his face appraisingly. Her fingers were as brittle as the leaves of an old book. "You are a pretty boy," she said. "A two spirit. What is your name, child?"

"José, Señora. I came in from the rain. I did not mean to disturb you."

"The Lady called you," she said, gesturing toward the skeleton she had called Saint Death. "Some peril must await you, but she will protect you if you give her reverence."

He wanted to run from the incense-scented shop, but he felt rooted to the floor.

"Give me a coin, two-spirit child," the woman said.

José dug into his pocket and pressed a silver coin into her hand, thinking he would buy his way out. She took it and commanded, in a tone he dared not disobey, "Wait here."

She disappeared behind a beaded curtain he had not noticed before. He heard the beating of wings, a soft cooing, and then she shuffled into the room holding a pigeon in her hands. She lifted its head to him for him to touch. Mesmerized, he stroked the tiny, feathered head. The pigeon turned its head toward him, eyes black and hard, like the beads of his grandmother's rosary.

"What is a two spirit, Señora?" José asked as he continued to nervously stroke the pigeon's head.

"The two spirit combines the male and the female in a single body and is desired by all. Men and women both will burn for your touch. To incite such desire is a dangerous thing. I will implore the Lady's protection for you, but the cost of her protection is life. Not yours, child, but someone near you."

José was now confused and terrified. "I must go, Señora," he said.

"You will stay until the ritual is over," she commanded.

He wanted to leave but could not make his legs move. Horrified, he watched her take the pigeon and with a swift twist break its neck. At the altar of Santisima Muerte, she plunged a little knife into the pigeon's breast and caught its blood in a shallow dish. She began an incantation. José ran out of the shop into the rain and did not stop until he came to the theater.

He sat on the bench in the front of the room, staring at the muslin sheet, still shaking from his encounter with the old woman. He realized she was a *bruja*, a witch. Chepa had told him about such people, men and women who could cast spells and speak to the dead. He had always thrilled to the cook's stories but now he remembered anxiously that she warned him never to give a *bruja* his true name or any item he had touched, and he had done both. Would the *bruja* find him and cast a spell on him? He waited for the film to start and to distract him with its magic from his fears.

The moonbeam shot across the room above him, the sheet filled with light, a black box materialized, and then the words:

> Midway in our life's journey, I went astray
> From the straight road and woke to find myself
> In a dark wood. How shall I say
> What wood it was! I never saw so drear
> So rank, so arduous a wilderness!
> Its very memory gives a shape to fear!

This was followed by the words "*L'Inferno del gran poeta Dante.*"

The film was Italian, and as José quickly gathered, depicted the journey of the poet Dante into hell guided by the spirit of another poet named Virgil. The opening scenes were dark and ominous, but thrilling in the way that José had come to expect from films. The play of shadow and light drew him into the story so thoroughly it seemed he had left his body and was following the two poets. Every emotion and sensation they experienced ran through him as well. So completely had he surrendered to the film that when he followed the poets into the circle of gluttons, a spasm of shock passed through him.

Naked men writhed and twisted on the stony ground beneath torrents of rain and clouds of mist. José had never seen a naked man before, but as he watched, he felt that some corner of his mind had longed for these images. He did not understand why the sight of their muscled chests and thighs, lean buttocks, and the mysterious triangles of hair that cloaked their genitals both mesmerized and mortified him. All he knew was that his skin prickled with excitement and shame.

The poets descended further. The images of hell became darker and more frightening. He felt himself sinking into their horror as if water were closing over his head. The two men entered the Wood of the Suicides. The bare trees and the filthy bird creatures hopping along the blasted ground rose up in his imagination like vomit he could not expel. Having surrendered to the power of the film, he could not stop it as he could close a book that frightened him, nor could he control the images that flooded the screen as he could control his own imagination. He was as beguiled, as hypnotized by the flickering images of hell as he had been by Tetrazzini's voice when she sang *Aida*. Some part of him knew this hell was as illusory as Aida's Egypt, but the illusion was like a threshold that, once crossed, drew him into a reality so saturated with emotion it consumed him.

So, unwillingly but unblinkingly, he followed the poets into the trenches of hell, to the flaming tombs in which the heretics burned for eternity and to where the blasphemers lay beneath a rain of fire. The poets crossed a narrow bridge across a gorge where, in the river of filth below, the dissolute tried in vain to wash away their sins. José watched the poets approach the slow procession of hypocrites weighed down by robes of lead, past Caiaphas, Jesus's condemner, now himself crucified on the floor of hell. The lake of ice was like a vast chessboard where the treasonous were frozen to their necks. It was here that José, surfeited by the images of horror, was aghast at the sight of one man feasting on the brains of another and at last had to turn his head aside. When he could finally bring himself to look at the screen again, it was filled with the three-headed image of Satan, himself frozen in the lake. In one of his mouths was the wriggling body of Judas. José watched the enormous jaws bite down on the struggling legs and torso. Satan's eyes, beneath eyebrows as thick as malevolent caterpillars, looked surprised at Judas's resistance to being eaten. His clawlike fingers tore at Judas's parts, like a man dismembering a roasted chicken. The poets climbed his hairy hide to the surface of the earth, where, their backs turned to the mouth of hell, they beheld the stars. The film ended.

It was dusk when José left the theater, the sky above El Carmen shading into the darker blue of evening. He stumbled home, frightened by the shadows deepening in the doorways, by the gaunt faces of the beggars who approached him with outstretched hands crying, "*por Dios, por Dios,*" by the skeletal burros shaking beneath their heavy burdens, and by the painted faces of the women who accosted him from the alleys with lewd hisses. By the time he arrived home, his heart was like a bird beating its wings against its cage. He ran to his mother and confessed that he had disobeyed her, willing to risk punishment in exchange for consolation. That night the nightmares began.

His mother kissed his forehead and again reminded him, "What you saw was not real, José."

He wanted to believe her, and yet he wondered how could hell have been imagined in such detail if someone—Dante or the man who made the film—had not been there? "But there is a hell, isn't there, where bad people go? I don't want to go there. Please don't let me go there."

"Are you a bad boy, José?" she asked gently.

He sniffled. "No," he said, but the image of the naked men passed through his head with the shameful memory of his excitement. "I'm not a bad boy, am I?"

"No, *mijo*, you are a good and gentle child. You do not have to worry about hell. Now, say your prayers and ask God to help you cast these images out of your head. Think, instead, of the sweetness of his heaven."

"Will you stay with me?" he pleaded.

"Of course," she said. "Always."

The renovated Senate chamber was one of Don Porfirio's more ironic public works because in his time the Senate was a collection of elderly sycophants so responsive to his whims he called it his *caballada*, his stable. In the dowdy old chamber, furnished with spittoons, moth-eaten drapes, and frayed carpets, ancient ex-comrades-in-arms of the president enjoyed a peaceful retirement rubber-stamping his decrees between naps. The potted palms, it was said, were livelier than the solons, and when one senator quietly died at his desk, it was several hours before anyone noticed. With the approach of the Centenario, it was decided to renovate the chamber in anticipation of the foreigners who might wish to observe Mexican democracy in action.

The spittoons were gone, the drapes and carpets replaced. The marble dais from which the president of the Senate presided over his colleagues was cleaned and polished. The old battered desks were replaced with new ones complete with sterling silver ink sets—these quickly disappeared—and red, white, and green bunting was hung along the edges of the ceiling.

When Sarmiento entered the Senate, it was no longer a place of repose but one of buzzing, even violent, activity aimed primarily against Madero's government. Opposition senators heaped scorn and calumny on Madero in vicious speeches that were faithfully reprinted in anti-government newspapers and accompanied by scabrous cartoons. Madero's Senate enemies, partisans of the old regime, were emboldened as Madero's inability to satisfy the competing demands of his partisans destroyed his popular support. The opposition senators were determined to depose Madero and reinstate, if not old Don Porfirio, another strong man who could govern México with the iron hand they believed it required. Some opposition senators favored General Huerta, recently returned in triumph from Chihuahua, where he had put down Pascual Orozco's rebellion. The old Indian killer, however, continued to profess his allegiance to Madero. Others had encouraged General Bernardo Reyes, Díaz's minister of war. He had launched a rebellion that was quickly quashed, and Reyes now awaited trial for treason in a military prison in the capital. What had drawn the Senate into special session was yet another rebellion.

Sarmiento slipped into the chamber just as the president of the Senate had begun to speak. "We are informed by the government that Señor Félix Díaz, nephew of the former dictator, has landed at the port of Veracruz at the head of a rebel army and declares himself the provisional president of the Republic."

Cheers from the opposition were immediately drowned out by cries of "Treason!" from Madero's partisans. On the dais the president slammed his gavel ineffectively as the clamor grew, accusations and counteraccusations filling the air. A hand clasped Sarmiento's shoulder. He spun around and faced his cousin.

"Come," Luis said. "There's a meeting. Madero asks you to attend."

He followed his cousin out of the chamber and through the labyrinthine corridor of the National Palace to the president's offices. Luis walked briskly and said nothing. His hair, Sarmiento observed, was threaded with gray and his suit draped a thinner body. He had left the Ministry of Government and been assigned to the Ministry of War, where he operated what was called the counterrebellion division. It kept him busier than ever, snuffing out rebellions large and small against the first democratically elected president of México in almost fifty years. As for Sarmiento, he had hoped to enter the Senate inconspicuously, serve Madero quietly until his term expired in 1914, and return to private life.

His suspicious election, however, had immediately made him a target of Madero's Senate enemies and the opposition press. Moreover, as Madero's fair-weather supporters abandoned him, he clung all the more closely to those, including Sarmiento, who had been with him in the desert. Inevitably, Sarmiento had been tugged into Madero's inner circle.

He followed Luis into the yellow room where Madero, his brother Gustavo, a few other civilians, and a battery of uniformed army officers stood around the conference table covered with maps. Sarmiento recognized the minister of war and the leader of Madero's faction in the Chamber of Deputies, but of the generals, he knew only Huerta, who glared at him briefly from behind his blue-tinted glasses. He felt out of place among the soldiers whom he instinctively distrusted, even as Madero's government was increasingly reliant on the military for its survival. The maps, he observed, showed the topography of the city of Veracruz and its environs.

One of the generals, pointing to a spot above the city, said, "We could move our artillery here, fire on the barracks, and then send in a force."

"And turn the streets of Veracruz into a battlefield," Gustavo Madero said sharply. "Political suicide."

"An invasion by sea, then?" another general offered.

"Don Félix commands the coastal defenses," the minister of war said. "We couldn't get close enough to land without exposing ourselves to his guns."

"Then we have no choice but to surround the city and lay siege," Gustavo Madero said. "How long can they last?"

The minister of war replied, "They have enough food for weeks, but if we cut the water supply, days."

Sarmiento said, "If you cut the water supply, you will be inviting a cholera epidemic."

All eyes were upon him. Gustavo Madero said, "We can't take the city without some casualties. Microbes are cleaner than bullets."

Huerta cleared his voice and growled, "A government incapable of taking one of its own cities except by siege looks weak."

No one spoke until the president said, "I would rather look weak than soak the streets of Veracruz in the blood of its residents, General."

The generals exchanged hooded looks before returning their attention to the maps.

"A siege by land, then," the president said, "and a blockade of the port. Don't cut the water except on my instructions."

"And Félix Díaz?" Huerta asked. "When he surrenders, do we shoot him on the spot?"

"No, General," Madero said, "you bring him here for trial."

His minister of war said, "Don Francisco, I urge you to reconsider. We don't need a trial to establish that Félix Díaz is a traitor who should be stood against a wall and shot. You bring him here and he will become a magnet for other would-be rebels."

Gustavo Madero chimed in, "Like Bernardo Reyes. Reyes sits in his very comfortable prison cell writing long letters to his partisans justifying his treason. You can read them in the opposition papers. You should have executed him, Francisco. Shoot Díaz and show the world you have some balls!"

Even the generals seemed startled by Gustavo's audacity in expressing what they were surely thinking themselves, but Gustavo was the president's brother. Unlike them, he could speak his mind without fearing the loss of his command or a transfer to a backwater post in the jungles of the Yucatán.

Madero looked at this brother and said, "An eye for an eye ends in blindness. I will not countenance extrajudicial murder. Reyes and Díaz will be tried, convicted, and punished according to the laws I have sworn to protect and preserve. That's all, gentlemen."

Two weeks later, Félix Díaz surrendered and was brought to the capital, where he was comfortably lodged in the new penitentiary to await trial for treason.

José's school had been founded as a military academy three hundred years earlier by Spanish Jesuits who in the tradition of their founder, San Ignacio de Loyola, conceived of themselves as God's infantry. Now it was operated by French Jesuits more interested in civilizing their charges than in preparing them for holy warfare. All that remained of the school's martial traditions were the cadet's uniforms its students wore and twenty minutes of drilling each morning in the courtyard.

Shouldering wooden rifles, the boys marched to the beat of a drum and fife under the gentle gaze of Frère Reynaud.

On the morning of February 2, 1913, José was treading the ancient cobblestones of the courtyard with his classmates in a disheveled formation not remotely military. The boys laughed and chattered, arms thrown around each other's shoulders, wooden rifles dragging on the ground behind them. Fatty Marquez thought it was funny to use his rifle to poke José in the butt. José turned, glared at him, and hissed, "Stop it, Fatty!"

"Would you rather I poke you with my *pinga*, Josélito," the older boy chortled.

José made a vulgar gesture and heard Frère Reynaud's high, soft voice admonish him, "José Ramon, would you want your mother to see you do that?"

"Fatty started it," he complained. "He—"

A sharp whistling noise shrieked in the air above them, and a tall stone urn, overflowing with red and white geraniums, exploded, spraying the boys with dirt, rocks, and petals. The boys ran screaming to the classrooms just as another shell gouged a crater in the center of the courtyard. José took refuge in the classroom where Frère Martin taught geography with beautiful colored maps that fueled José's daydreams when he should have been learning about the chief exports of Bolivia and French Indochina. Frère Martin ordered the boys to duck beneath desks and tables. Another shell struck the courtyard, blowing the door off the classroom. Fatty Marquez, crouching beside José, whimpered and a puddle of urine spread beneath him. José felt his heart pounding in his throat. The sound of gunfire and screaming penetrated the room from the streets just beyond the walls of the school. After what seemed to José to be an eternity, the violent noises stopped. Frère Georges, the white-haired principal of the school, entered the room. He spoke to Frère Martin in rapid French and then told the boys to stand. They got out of their hiding places, some of them wiping away tears.

Frère Georges said, "Boys, circumstances beyond my control compel me to close the school until further notice. Your families have been notified of this fact, and when they come for you, you will be allowed to leave. Until then, you must remain as you are."

"What is happening, Frère Georges?"

"There has been an attack on the National Palace against President Madero."

Some of the students, sons of rich anti-Madero families, cheered.

"Is he dead?" one of them asked.

"The situation is unclear," the principal replied. "The rebels have retreated from the Zócalo to the Ciudadela, where they remain at this moment. No more questions. I leave you to Frère Martin."

When he had left, Frère Martin said, "It is wrong to cheer a revolt against President Madero. He is a true Christian. One who has regard for the poor. Now, let us pray for him and for the safety of all. Come on boys, 'Our Father . . .'"

José tried to say the familiar words but kept losing his place in his anxiety for Don Panchito and for his father, who had gone to the National Palace that morning for a meeting of the Senate. The hours passed slowly. One by one, the boys were released into the custody of their families. José was among the last left and fear gnawed at his belly. Had something happened to his father? But then his father arrived, looking old and tired.

"Papá!" José exclaimed, running to him. He threw himself into his father's arms and only then saw that his coat was damp with blood. José recoiled. "You're bleeding! Are you hurt?"

"No, José, it's not my blood. There were wounded in the Zócalo; I stopped to help those whom I could. That's why I'm so late. Are you all right?"

"There were explosions. Juanito Marquez wet his pants. Papá," he said, grabbing his father's arm urgently. "Is Don Panchito dead?"

"No, *mijo*, he's fine. Come, let's go home. Your mother and your grandmother must be sick with worry."

They drove to the palace in his father's buggy through deserted streets, skirting the edge of the Zócalo, where José saw people stretched out beneath the trees as if sleeping on the cobblestone. The National Palace was surrounded by soldiers. They were not the ceremonial soldiers who usually guarded the doors in the splendid dress uniforms that José loved for their gold buttons and spiked helmets. These soldiers were armed and in battle dress. He watched a line of artillery guns being wheeled by horse cart down the Avenida de Cinco de Mayo, just as they had during the Centenario parade. But this time there were no cheering crowds. In the resounding silence, he could hear the clip-clop of the horses' hooves and the scraping of the wheels on the pavement. He looked again at the prone bodies scattered around the plaza.

In a trembling voice he asked, "Papá, are those people dead?"

"Yes, José," his father replied, taking his hand. "They were killed in the fighting this morning."

"Why did the soldiers attack Don Panchito?"

"They want someone else to be president," his father replied.

"Why don't they wait for the elections?"

His father sighed. "Don Pancho is the first freely elected president in almost fifty years. Before him, presidents have more often been installed by violence or by fraud. I thought, I hoped, that we had outgrown that history, but . . ." His voice trailed off. "Everything depends on the loyalty of the army," he said, more to himself than José.

"I'm frightened," José said, seeking reassurance.

His father, lost in his own thoughts, did not immediately reply but then, as if remembering José was present, said unconvincingly, "Don't worry, *mijo*. Everything is fine."

At the palace, he was greeted with kisses from his grandmother and his mother, but as soon as they had assured themselves of his well-being, they sent him to the kitchen so they could talk to his father. Chepa gave him a cup of chocolate and a *concha*, his favorite *pan dulce*, but it tasted like dust. The porter Andres opened the gates, and he heard his cousin Luis in the courtyard, asking for his father. The porter told Luis that the doctor was in the library. While Chepa was distracted, José stole away from her worried care. The library door was half-open. José stood outside, straining to hear. He knew it was wrong to listen uninvited to the conversation of the adults, but his fear overcame his scruples. He felt the urgent need to understand what had happened that morning, and he wanted the hard words the grown-ups spoke to each other, not the gentle evasions they addressed to him.

"It was Díaz and Reyes," Luis was saying. "They conspired in their prison cells with some old Díaz generals, who sprang them from jail and provided the troops. Reyes was shot when he tried to charge the palace. Díaz has retreated to the Ciudadela."

"I was leaving the Senate chamber when I heard the shooting," his father said. "We lacked a quorum because almost none of the opposition senators showed up. I suppose they had been warned. Don Francisco had not yet arrived at his office."

"He rode down the Reforma from Chapultepec on a white horse," Luis said. "The poor grabbed at him, wailing and praying, as if he were the second coming of Jesus. When he reached Avenida Juárez, there was gunfire and a policeman standing next to him was hit in the head. Madero's guards hustled him off into a shop until the shooting stopped. That's where they told him Bernardo Reyes had been killed. He actually wept. Fool. He should have killed the son of a bitch when he had the chance."

"That leaves Félix Díaz," Sarmiento said. "Not a military man. Why would the army follow him?"

José peered into the room just as his father took the brandy bottle and filled his cousin's empty glass. Luis looked like a man who had seen his own grave.

"The generals know Díaz is a fool, but his uncle's name is a rallying point, for now. General Villar was seriously wounded repulsing the attack on the palace."

"I know. As soon as the casualties started to arrive, I went to see how I could help. He had a head wound. Very bad." Sarmiento sighed. "It was like Ciudad Juárez all over again."

"It gets worse," Luis said. "You know who Madero appointed to replace Villar as the new military commander of the city? Your old friend, Huerta."

"No! Not Huerta!"

"Yes, the butcher," Luis replied, draining his second glass. He reached for the bottle and poured another. "Huerta spread his arms and embraced the little man and told him he would give his life for the president of the Republic. That made Madero weep again."

"Huerta cannot be trusted," Sarmiento said adamantly.

"I know, I know. Army men are behind the coup and now that Reyes is dead, they'll need a new leader. Díaz is a figurehead, useful for the time being, but ultimately the army will want one of its own. Some-one like Huerta."

"Did you warn Madero?"

Luis said, "Madero smiled and told me I was too mistrustful. He seemed, I don't know, resigned. Almost peaceful."

Sarmiento, remembering Krishna's words to Arjuna on the eve of battle that Madero had quoted to him, said, "Don Pancho believes we have our destinies and they cannot be altered. What's the situation now?"

"Díaz and his rebels have dug in at the Ciudadela and the sur-rounding streets," he said. "There are about fifteen hundred of them. They are well equipped with artillery and guns and the Ciudadela has enough ammunition to keep them in business for weeks. Huerta is moving troops into the Zócalo. Madero has slipped away to Cuernavaca to gather reinforcements. The city is about to become a battleground. You might want to consider removing your wife and child."

"What will you do?"

"Stay at my post, of course. What about you?"

"Stay. I have a feeling that doctors will be in short supply." After a moment, he said, "What do you think will happen, Luis?"

His cousin shrugged. "Díaz's force is small. A sustained attack on the Ciudadela would drive them out into the open, where they would be annihilated. But this is not a military situation, Miguel, it's a political one. Madero's support has been falling for months. His enemies have grown bolder. If they suborn Huerta and he goes over to their side, our little president is finished. As are we all." He stood up. "I have work to do. I will see you again." The two men embraced.

José hurried out of their path, back to his room. He lay on his bed and thought about what he had heard. The rebels had captured the Ciudadela. The ancient armory lay a mile and a half south of the Zócalo. José knew it well from weekend excursions with his classmates. The long, low building lay behind thick walls with entrances at the four cardinal points. Outside its walls was a park that had some of the best skating paths in the city. Among the park's fountains and flowers was a monument to José Morelos, one of the fathers of Mexican indepen-dence. Morelos had been imprisoned in the Ciudadela by the Spanish and executed against its walls, the bullet holes still visible a century later. Don Porfirio had turned the building into a military museum, where José and his friends had examined the massive cannons that had been used against the Spanish in the War of Independence.

José could not imagine that the quiet, musty corridors of the Ciudadela housed real soldiers or that its ancient guns could be fired. But Primo Luis had spoken of ammunition and artillery. It occurred to José that his Ciudadela, a playground where he raced his classmates on skates and ate ice cream while a military band played in an ivy-covered gazebo, was not the real Ciudadela. His thoughts wandered back to the dead bodies in the Zócalo, which was another of his playgrounds. The city itself had always been for him benign and familiar. Was it all an illusion? What was happening? And abruptly the images of the inferno rose in his mind, and he ran from his room in a panic to seek comfort in his mother's arms.

In the evening, his aunts arrived at the palace to plead with La Niña to leave the city and retire to the family's house in Coyoacán. José sat beside the old woman, who listened impatiently to her daughters.

"And you?" she asked, when they had finished. "Are all of you leaving the city?"

"Yes, of course," Tía Nilda replied. "There are soldiers in the streets! There are dead bodies in the plaza. You cannot remain here. It is too dangerous."

"Don't speak to me of danger," La Niña replied. "I have lived through worse. The French army bombarding its way into the city, the rabble that invaded my home after the French left and seized your father. I pled for his life at the point of their bayonets. You think I am afraid of a little fireworks? How ridiculous! This is my home and I intend to remain in it."

His mother had slipped into the room during La Niña's little speech. Now Nilda addressed her. "What about you, Alicia? Surely you will not remain here with your child?"

"I will not leave without Miguel, and Miguel does not intend to leave. In any event, someone must remain with Mother." She looked at José. "But perhaps it is best if you go with your aunts, José."

"No!" he cried without thinking. "I want to stay with you and my *abuelita*."

Tía Leticia said, "Come now, José, don't you love your aunties? We will take good care of you until it's safe to return to the city."

He was afraid to say what he feared—that if he left, something might happen to his parents or La Niña because saying it aloud might make it come true—so he shook his head and said, "No, I want to stay." He looked at his mother. "Please let me stay with you, Mamá. Don't make me go."

"It may be frightening for you," his mother said.

"I promise I'll be brave," he replied, even as he trembled inwardly.

"He proves his courage with his desire to remain here," La Niña said. "Let the boy stay."

His mother looked at her sisters and said, "My family will remain here. God protect us and you."

At ten o'clock the following morning, Huerta began a bombardment of the Ciudadela. The rebels responded in kind, and for the next ten hours an artillery duel shook the city to its bones. Inside the palace, the family, including Sarmiento, sheltered in La Niña's apartments and pantomimed normality. She read a yellow-bound French novel, while José and his mother sat at the piano and practiced the "Moonlight Sonata."

Another shell struck nearby and José's fingers faltered for a moment. Sarmiento looked up from the German medical journal he was pretending to read and watched his wife and child. He could scarcely begin to assess his emotional state, a confusing brew of fear, anger, and disbelief overlaid by simple shock. He had been in battle before, but he had never thought the battle would follow him into his very home. This invasion of his family's private world by the machinery of warfare felt like a nightmare from which he struggled to awaken. But it was no dream. He and his family had been reduced in an instant from autonomous human beings with free will and personal histories to ciphers on the battlefield. They were of no greater significance to the generals lobbing bombs above the city than stray dogs. His fury was equaled only by his despair. *Let it end soon*, he thought, not caring on what terms or for which side. *Let it end.*

The battle continued for a third day. The servants, like cats, disappeared into the crevices of the palace, ignoring La Niña's summonses. She stalked them until she found each one of them, cursed them for their laziness, and threatened to turn them out into the inferno if they did not return to their duties. Late in the morning, the pastor of San Andrés church pounded at the doors of the palace seeking refuge. One of the rebels' explosive shells had struck the bell tower and leveled it. The debris had collapsed the roof of the rectory, leaving him without a home. He was admitted and later, with trembling hands, said Mass in the family chapel for the entire household. Even Sarmiento attended.

As the day wore on, the rattle of machine gun fire joined the explosions of shells. Soldiers' voices could be heard shouting above the din, loudly and then trailing off as they ran through the streets. The old families who had lived in the neighborhood for generations and over whom the Gaviláns had once exercised suzerainty now also appeared at the gates. La Niña instructed the porter to let them in. Soon the elegant courtyards were filled with men, women, children, and infants surrounded by the piles and bundles of their possessions. There were wounds to tend to and hands to hold, keeping Sarmiento and Alicia busy. La Niña and Chepa inspected the larder and discussed how to stretch the food to feed the masses in the courtyards. José leaned on the walkway of the second floor and looked down at the silent Indians crowding the courtyards. Their appearance in the palace was more frightening to him than the explosions and the machine guns outside the walls. After a few minutes, he went into his room. Almost mechanically, he began to collect his dozens of tin soldiers. He dropped them into his toy box and shut the lid.

Alicia rose early the next morning. After dressing in old clothes, she went into the kitchen to help prepare food for the families crammed into the courtyards and the lower rooms of the palace. Chepa smiled when she saw Alicia. At the far end of the room, where the entire wall was taken up with adobe stoves, ovens, and fireplaces, scullions stirred pots and turned tortillas. The cooking fires illuminated walls hung with braids of garlic and chilies and the high ceiling, a rich, greasy brown from the smoke of generations of meals.

"Are you hungry, *Hija*?" Chepa asked.

"No, I came to help you feed our neighbors who are staying with us."

Chepa replied tartly, "What shall we feed them? José's little cat? There's not enough food."

"Remember what Jesus did with five loaves and two fishes," Alicia replied mildly. "Everyone will eat, if only a bowl of beans and tortillas. Give me an apron and put me to work. What do you need done?"

Chepa said reluctantly, "Well, the *molendera* ran away during the night, but grinding corn for tortillas is no work for a lady."

"Show me her place," Alicia replied, reaching for an apron hanging on a peg on the wall.

When Sarmiento came into the kitchen looking for her, she was soaking the ground corn in lime water. He took her aside and said, "I'm going to go out while the guns have stopped."

"The streets are dangerous, Miguel," she protested.

He lifted his hand, showing her his black bag. "I'll take this," he said. "A doctor will be safer on the streets than a senator."

"No one is safe in the streets."

"I've been in battle before," he said.

"But where will you go?"

"To scrounge whatever medical supplies I can and go to the National Palace," he said. "To see if Madero is still president." He kissed her forehead. "I'll be back soon."

"Won't you eat something first?"

He took a roll, warm from the oven. "This is enough."

"Please, be careful."

He kissed her brow. "I will return alive and in one piece. I promise."

The damage from the previous day's bombardment was apparent as soon as Sarmiento stepped outside the palace. There was a crater in the *plazuela* where the bandstand had been. Flower urns had been overturned and shattered on the cobblestone, spilling black soil and red geraniums. The body of a soldier lay in a pile of debris in a corner. Sarmiento approached. The soldier had been shot through the head, and his shoes and rifle had been taken. He closed the boy's eyes and began walking toward the Zócalo down narrow streets that seemed suddenly foreign and treacherous. The devastation was worse as he approached the great plaza. The sides of buildings looked as if giant bites had been taken out of them. Walls were collapsed and roofs had fallen in. Lampposts were bent down and ruptured telegraph and telephone wires festooned the deserted roadways. The Zócalo was strewn with rubble and bodies. A half-dozen green streetcars had been blasted into burned-out shells. Trees still smoldered from the shells that had hit them. In front of the National Palace, soldiers lay on their stomachs guarding the entrances, and there was a row of artillery guns in front of the cathedral. He willed himself to be calm as he walked through the wreckage toward the entrance of the National Palace. At the door, a captain stopped him and said, "*Quién vive?*"

Sarmiento took a guess. "Madero."

The captain nodded. "Who are you, Señor?"

"Doctor Miguel Sarmiento," he said. "I am the president's personal physician and a senator of his party. So he still governs México."

The captain sighed. "Who governs México is anyone's guess, but the president is still in the palace. You may enter."

Once inside he was confronted by other soldiers who detained him for nearly an hour until, to his surprise, Gustavo Madero himself appeared.

The president's brother wore a wrinkled suit and a collarless shirt. He was unshaven and his hair uncombed. His glass eye was bright and round as a marble but his natural eye was bloodshot and fatigued.

"Sarmiento," he said wearily, "perhaps you have not been told, but the Senate is not in session today. You should get back to your family. Díaz may attack again at any moment."

"I'm your brother's physician. I want to check on his well-being."

Gustavo hesitated, but then said, "All right. Come. He is fond of you. Perhaps seeing you will raise his spirits."

He followed Gustavo through the labyrinth of the palace to the presidential suite. In Madero's private office, cots had been set up and the room smelled of food, sweat, and fatigue. The president, as formally attired as his brother was casually dressed, sat in an armchair by a window reading. When he saw Sarmiento, he rose, set the book down on his desk, and went to embrace him.

"Miguel," he said. "Thank God you are all right! And your family? Josélito? How are they?"

"Frightened, but unharmed. And you?"

"The rebels shelled my house, but fortunately it was not occupied," he said. "My wife is at Chapultepec and they will not attack there." He smiled. "This will soon be over."

"Yes?" Sarmiento asked.

"Reinforcements are on their way. Once they arrive, the rebels will be vastly outnumbered and General Huerta can begin his attack . . ."

"An attack he should have launched this morning," Gustavo grunted.

Madero threw him an exasperated look. "I have complete confidence in General Huerta."

Sarmiento could tell this was an ongoing debate. He sided with Gustavo. "But surely the army outnumbers the rebels at this moment."

Madero said, as if quoting, "The Ciudadela is a venerable fortress, Miguel. Overwhelming force will be required to take it." He smiled his gentle, beneficent smile. "You must not worry about the situation too much. When I rode to the palace from Chapultepec, the people came out and threw flowers in my path. The people are still with us, Miguel, and as long as they are with us, all will be well. Your cousin is here. He has been doing good work for us."

"Luis? May I see him?"

"Yes, of course." He embraced Sarmiento again. "*Hasta luego*, Miguel."

"*Hasta luego, mi presidente*," Sarmiento said. From the corner of his eye, his glance fell on the book Madero had been reading. *The Bhagavad Gita.*

A young secretary escorted him down the hall, past soldiers and scurrying clerks, to Luis's office. Luis came out from behind his desk, held Sarmiento in a long, tight embrace, and, after inquiring about his family, asked, "What is it like on the streets?"

"Silence and horror."

His cousin nodded. "This morning the rebels blew a hole through the wall at Belem prison, freeing all the scum of the city. Their thugs set fire to the offices of newspapers friendly to the government. Our thugs set fire to theirs."

"Our thugs?"

He shrugged. "Don't look so surprised. Don Francisco doesn't know about them or pretends not to know, but without them we would be defenseless."

"Madero says reinforcements are arriving for an attack on the Ciudadela?"

Luis looked disgusted. "So Huerta tells him, but then he disappears to his favorite bar, and our soldiers sit in the streets being picked off by the rebels. If Huerta fails to attack tomorrow, perhaps even Madero will come to the end of his patience. Until he opens his eyes to the actual situation, there is nothing anyone can do."

"What is the actual situation, Luis?"

"Huerta is a traitor. I believe that he is exchanging secret messages with Díaz through the American ambassador but I cannot yet prove it. Gustavo has men watching Huerta and in the embassy."

"Why would the Americans help the rebels bring down a democratically elected government?" Sarmiento asked incredulously.

"Dictators are better for American business," he said. "While Don Porfirio was in power he made enormous concessions to the American mining and railroad companies without consulting anyone. Madero has been looking at those deals and making noises about revising their terms so that México gets more than a few pennies on the dollar. Wilson, the American ambassador, is determined to prevent Madero from interfering with American profits. He has been attacking Madero privately for months, and now he sees his chance to get rid of him. We have intercepted his cables to Washington telling his government that Madero is finished and urging them to recognize Don Félix. So far, their fat President Taft has been cautious, but Wilson is pushing for intervention."

"An American invasion? On what grounds?"

"All it would take is a misplaced shell or the accidental killing of one of their citizens and they would have their pretext to invade in support of the rebels."

"This situation—it seems unreal, unbelievable, Luis."

Luis sighed. "México's history is a series of coups and rebellions, Miguel. I know we hoped it would be different, but evidently political violence is in our blood." He forced a smile. "Well, one way or the other it will all be settled soon. Perhaps in a day or two we will meet for a drink at the Café Colón."

Sarmiento could not respond with equal gaiety. Instead he embraced his cousin, kissed him, and murmured, "Take care of yourself, Primito."

"Go home to your family," Luis said. "I will see you soon."

The shops were closed, but Sarmiento found a looted pharmacy. He entered and took whatever had been left of value he could use to doctor. As he emerged from the wrecked building, a long car slid imperiously through the bloody streets on its way to the National Palace. American flags fluttered from its corners and he saw in the back seat the profile of the American ambassador.

For the next three days detonating shells and bombs echoed through every quarter of the city. To José, the silence in the lulls between the bombing was even more frightening than the bombings themselves. The ordinary noisiness of the city to which he was accustomed was human noise, from the songs and cries of the street peddlers to the pleading whispers of the beggars. Those voices were utterly still, as if the city were empty. He sat at his piano, playing every piece he knew, trying to fill the silence with something other than his terror.

The courtyards of the palace continued to fill with refugees from the neighborhood, many sick or wounded. Miguel saw to their injuries and Alicia nursed them afterward. During pauses in the fighting, she went out with Chepa to forage for food and medicine. The sights of destruction and death were searing. Bodies had been piled into mounds, doused with gasoline, and set on fire. The corpses twitched as they burned, and the smell of roasting human flesh made her dizzy with nausea, but she dare not stop. In the rubble of a collapsed building, she heard a child whimpering. She dug through the brick until she found it, an infant clinging to her mother's corpse. She carried the baby to the palace, but Miguel was unable to save the child, and they buried her in the garden. In stolen moments, she went into the chapel and prayed, with more passion that she had ever prayed for anything, saying again and again, "Dear God, let it be over soon."

At dawn on the sixth day of the battle, soldiers marched through the streets proclaiming a twenty-four-hour truce. Sarmiento wandered through once familiar streets that had been pummeled beyond recognition. Thousands of residents piled their possessions into carts or on their backs and began walking out of the city. Red Cross vans went around the Zócalo picking up bodies. These were taken to the plains of Balbuena and incinerated. A few stores reopened and were immediately mobbed by crowds looking for food and drink. Barricades of broken furniture and overturned carts were put in place to seal off the streets to the Zócalo. Artillery guns were wheeled into place. The rebels remained ensconced in the Ciudadela and the government clung to possession of the National Palace. In the late afternoon, a delegation of opposition senators was admitted to the Ciudadela ostensibly to negotiate with Félix Díaz. When they emerged, they announced that Don Félix had demanded Madero's resignation as the price of peace. This news was conveyed to the National Palace. Madero refused. At five in the afternoon, the bombing resumed.

18

On the afternoon of the seventh day of the battle, Alicia returned from visiting families who had chosen to remain in the neighborhood. She hurried to the toilet, where she gushed watery diarrhea. She composed herself and started toward the kitchen to help the cooks, but she did not get out of the room before she again had to seek the toilet. By now, with the onset of a headache and nausea, she was forced to admit she was ill. The symptoms were familiar — she had seen them among the poor of San Francisco Tlalco — but she hoped she was wrong about what they indicated. She changed into a light shift and lay down, but every few minutes, she was back on the toilet, the expulsions progressively more painful as there was less and less to expel. The headache throbbed in her temples. She thought back to the cup of tepid, muddy tea she had accepted two days earlier from a woman in Tepito to whom she had brought food. The woman — Luz, she remembered, her name was Luz — had poured her gratitude into the cup, and Alicia could not refuse to drink even though it was a near certainty the water had come from the fetid communal well she had passed earlier. A simple cup of tea, no more than two swallows — how fragile the body was, she thought. She was convulsed by abdominal cramps and staggered to the toilet. As she tried to make her way back to the bed, she was overcome with dizziness and fell to the floor. Her last conscious thought was *cholera*.

Sarmiento had been working at a Red Cross field hospital set up in the Alameda, but on the morning of the seventh day, restless to see the damage to the capital, he had gone out in one of the vans. The city was a sepulchre. The police had abandoned their corner posts, the priests locked up their churches, and even the doors of the great cathedral were closed against the importuning of the faithful. The thirty boxcars of pulque that slaked the thirst of the city did not arrive at the Estación de Colonia, and the fruit-, flower-, and vegetable-laden *trajineras* did not skim the surface of La Viga. The big green and yellow *tranvías* remained parked at the station in the Zócalo. The stables were filled with restless, hungry horses. The familiar trucks of the Buen Tono cigarette factory were nowhere to be seen, and the factory was shut down. The great department stores along the Avenida San Francisco—the Port of Veracruz and the Iron House—and the lowliest dry goods shops on the dirt streets of Colonia San Sebastían were shuttered and barred against looters. Theaters were closed, the billboards of cancelled performances still splashed across their entrances. As they passed through the Colonia Guerrero, Sarmiento heard a cellist playing Bach's second cello suite, the "Sarabande." The complex, mournful music crossed the courtyard of a once grand building, now pockmarked with bullet holes, and spilled into the clear, still air. The light, as always, was dazzlingly pure, and above the roofs and domes of the city, Popocatépetl released white puffs of smoke and Iztaccíhuatl spread her snowy body beside him.

The van approached the streets surrounding the Ciudadela, where the rebels remained firmly ensconced despite the government's superior numbers and weapons. As it approached an army checkpoint, Sarmiento observed a truck flying the American flag laden with food and water. The soldiers waved it through. At first, he thought the Americans were bringing food to the starving civilians as a humanitarian gesture, but to his astonishment, the truck drove up to the gates of the Ciudadela. They were thrown open to receive it without any interference by the government soldiers. The same soldiers who had casually allowed the rebels to be provisioned with food and water detained the Red Cross wagon for an hour before they finally admitted it into the battle-torn streets. While he stood with other volunteers at the side of the road waiting to be cleared to enter, Sarmiento saw two other supply trucks admitted into the Ciudadela. He began to understand why the rebels had been able to hold out. Instead of starving them out of their citadel, government soldiers were helping to feed them. The sheer brazenness of the treason made it clear to Sarmiento that the orders to assist the rebels came from very high in the army. He needed to get a message to his cousin, but that would have to wait until he helped scour the area for the wounded or the dead.

In the long evenings, Sarmiento had been passing the time by re-reading Bernal Díaz del Castillo's account of the Spanish conquest of the Aztec empires. He had last read the Spanish soldier's eyewitness account of the destruction of Tenochtitlán as a boy. Then all his sympathies lay with Cortés's men, who were, after all, his people. This time through the narrative he found himself mourning for the defeat of the Aztecs. Sarmiento did not sentimentalize the Aztecs—Bernal Díaz's horror at their practice of human sacrifice was too vivid and unguarded to have been a falsehood planted by the conquerors to justify their bloody annihilation of the Indians. But Sarmiento knew something that Bernal Díaz did not know: the annihilation of the Indians would continue for centuries after the conquest, by war, disease, enslavement, and destitution, until their population had been reduced to a tenth of what it had been when Cortés reached the shores of México. Sarmiento saw in the streets of the capital that the degradation of the Indians continued to this very moment. At least, as Cáceres had argued, the Aztecs' practice of human sacrifice was ritualized and had served a religious purpose, however benighted. The human sacrifice inflicted by the Spanish had been indiscriminate and pointless. Moreover, it seemed to him that the Spanish had infused their own casual cruelty and contempt for the native people into the Mexican race that emerged from the conquest. Because this Mexican race was half-Indian, this in turn created a nation permanently divided against itself, driven by a self-hatred that expressed itself in paroxysms of violence such as that which now filled the streets of the capital with corpses.

The Red Cross wagon entered the neighborhoods surrounding the Ciudadela, where bodies festered and rotted like the fallen leaves of a ghastly autumn. Gaunt survivors flitted like shadows from one ruined building to another. Sarmiento remembered the passage from Bernal Díaz describing the entry of Cortés's soldiers into Tenochtitlán after forty-five days of siege: "When we returned to the City we found the streets full of women and children and other miserable people, thin and afflicted who were dying of hunger and we found in the streets gnawed roots and bark of trees, the most pitiable thing in the world to see."

Sarmiento could have left behind his black bag because all he did that day was help collect bodies and stack them like cordwood in the wagon for incineration.

Sarmiento asked to be let off at the Zócalo. Since it was no longer possible to penetrate the barricades that surrounded the National Palace, he and Luis had worked out a way to communicate by leaving notes in the shattered masonry of the arcade that surrounded the great plaza. He scribbled his observations of provisions passing through government checkpoints in the Ciudadela, stuck it in the crevice they had designated for the exchange of messages, and then hurried home before the fighting resumed.

José lay on his bed looking through his stereoscope at peaceful scenes of the French countryside. By habit, he reached out his hand to pet El Morito, but the cat had disappeared on the first day of the fighting and had not returned. His grandmother had assured him that El Morito was simply hiding somewhere and would emerge when the gun blasts stopped shaking the walls. José believed her, if only because the alternative was too terrible to think about. He tried not to think at all, but unlike the adults who seemed frantically occupied, José had nothing to do with the long hours of the long days. His parents were gone most of the day to help where they could. His grandmother commanded the remaining servants like a household general, keeping them at their work even as the bombs rained down a half-dozen blocks away. The people of the neighborhood who had sought shelter the first days had either returned to their homes or fled the city. José was alone. He had always enjoyed his solitary pursuits, his soldiers and books, toy theater and marionettes, but that solitude was an oasis from the routines of school and family. Those routines had been shattered, and his current solitude felt more like a prison than a garden.

He was no longer as frightened as he had been after he and his father had driven through the Zócalo and he had seen the dead bodies and the menacing soldiers. He took his cue from the grown-ups. His father was still his father, brisk and energetic; his mother had become, if anything, even gentler; and his grandmother was more imperious. It was if they were actors playing themselves, exaggerating their basic qualities to mask their fear. José imitated their attitudes as well as he could and played himself. But at a deeper level, he was enraged by the grown-ups, by all grown-ups. They had created this horror. They were the ones who slaughtered people in the streets and turned the world upside down for reasons that no one—not even his brilliant father—could satisfactorily explain to José. He could not understand why it mattered so much whether Don Porfirio or Don Panchito wore the presidential sash, that ordinary men and women should pay the price of their lives to decide the issue. For once, he knew his lack of understanding was not because he was unintelligent in adult matters—it was because the carnage in the streets was pointless. The adults had started this stupid fight and inflicted it upon him. José hated them for it. He would never again accept their words with the same credulity as before the war. He promised himself he would not grow up to be like them.

In the meantime, he pretended the sound of the guns was thunder and distracted himself from his anxiety with his toys and books and the piano. But a low, ever-present thrum of fear still ran through his body and fed itself on his thoughts. What if a bomb fell in the palace? What if the fighting never stopped? What if El Morito never returned? And worst of all, what if something happened to his parents or his grandmother? The only way he could overcome these thoughts was by imagining in exacting detail being somewhere other than where he was and removing himself completely from the present.

He put another card in his stereoscope—a hand-painted scene of the endless lavender fields of Provence. He imagined himself walking through the aisles of lavender. He felt the sun on the back of his neck, the soft ground beneath his feet. He imagined a breeze stirring the purple tips of the plants, creating a cloud of fragrance, and the smoky sweetness of lavender filling his lungs.

When Sarmiento found Alicia collapsed on the floor of their bedroom, he thought she was dead, killed by an errant bullet or bit of shrapnel. Then her body moved with her breath and he dropped to his knees beside her. Her skin was cold and clammy and she had soiled herself. He called for her maid, Catalina. Together they cleaned and changed her. He carried her to their bed.

"Alicia," he murmured. "Darling, can you hear me?"

She opened glazed, unfocused eyes. "Miguel?"

"I found you on the floor. How long have you been like this?"

"The water was bad," she whispered. "Cholera, I think."

He had guessed as much. "How long have you been sick?"

"Today. It started today." She grimaced. "Toilet."

He helped her up and settled her on a chamber pot, where she expelled another blast of fishy smelling ordure. When she was back in bed, he emptied the pot but kept a specimen. While she slept, he examined the specimen under his microscope and saw the rice-shaped bacterium—*Vibrio cholerae*—that was the agent of cholera. All he could do for now was restore fluids to her body to avoid death by dehydration. He was hopeful she would recover—she was strong, seldom ill, and he was there to nurse her—but outbreaks of cholera in the city had claimed thousands of lives so he did not deceive himself about the gravity of her condition.

After he had made her comfortable, he went into his mother-in-law's apartment, where he found her at her desk going over the household accounts.

"Alicia is ill," he said. "Cholera. She drank tainted water. If she drank it here, the household may be in danger of an outbreak."

La Niña blanched. "But I instructed the servants to boil all of the drinking water as you directed." She stood up and came around to him. "How is she?"

"She's still in the first stage," he said, casting about for a euphemism. Finding none, he said, "Extreme diarrhea. There is little I can do until these episodes end except to give her fluids."

La Niña frowned. "What do you need?"

"Pure, unadulterated water," he said.

She nodded. "I will personally supervise the boiling."

"All of our water containers must be cleaned and purified," he said. "The latrines should also be cleaned and scoured with carbolic acid. If anyone else begins to show any signs of the disease, you must let me know immediately. I will stay with Alicia."

"Have you told José?"

"No," he said. "Perhaps you can talk to him. I prefer he not visit his mother in her current state. It would be too distressing for him."

She nodded. "Yes, but you must let him see her as soon as she can receive him. He is already badly frightened. Once I tell him his mother is ill, he will be even more fearful."

"This barbaric rebellion!" he exclaimed. "How can civilized men in the twentieth century be tossing bombs across a city filled with their own people? What madness has poisoned México!"

She looked at him for a long moment. "In the years since you took up residence in my house, I have become very fond of you, Miguel. I am grateful for the happiness you have given my daughter and for my exquisite grandson, so what I say now I say without malice. You are not a Mexican."

"I beg your pardon, Señora. I was born here."

"Yes, but you are a full-blooded Spaniard like your father, a *gachupín*."

"Surely, those colonial classifications are irrelevant in modern México."

A knowing smile wrinkled her lips. "That you speak of modern México only reveals that you do not know what it is to be Mexican."

"Then what is it to be Mexican?"

"To live in the friction of being half-civilized and half-barbaric, the one half always at war with the other. This revolution is not about politics. Nothing in México is ever about politics. The bombs that explode around us are the sound of our self-hatred."

"You are a fatalist, Señora."

"No. I *am* a Mexican," she said. "Go and care for your woman. I will see to José and to the household."

Sarmiento slipped his stethoscope from his ears and touched his wife's pale face. The room filled with the pink light of dawn. Alicia slept beneath thick blankets packed with hot water bottles. Her skin was cold; her lips were cracked. Twelve hours had passed since he had discovered her collapsed on the floor. The diarrhea had abated and she had entered the second, graver stage of the disease. The loss of fluids had caused her blood pressure to drop dangerously, and her pulse was fast and weak as her heart tried to push the diminished supply of blood through her exhausted body. She had vomited the sips of water he had given her earlier. When she awakened, he would have to try another tactic to keep her alive. He slumped into a chair. He had not allowed himself to consider the possibility of her death even as it hovered in the air. When José had come to see her and burst into tears, Sarmiento had sent him away with furious words that had expressed his own terror. Life without Alicia was unimaginable, now more than ever as the world collapsed around them in the thunder of artillery shells and the rattle of machine guns.

"You must live," he whispered.

"Miguel?" Her voice was a dry husk.

"I'm here, darling," he said, standing, stroking her face.

"I see only white. Am I going blind?"

"No, darling, that's the disease. It will pass."

"The guns have stopped."

He thought at first she was describing another symptom, a loss of hearing or cognizance, but then he realized that it had been hours since the sounds of battle had echoed in the air. Had another truce been declared? Not that that mattered. All he cared about was keeping her alive.

"Miguel, if I am dying, I require a priest."

"You are not dying, Alicia."

A thin smile pressed itself on her lips. "I have seen this disease before."

"Then you know it is not invariably fatal." He smiled back. "Place your trust in your physician."

"More than trust . . . love." Her eyes closed, then opened. "I am so thirsty."

"You can't keep water through the mouth, but there is another way. Unpleasant and painful, I'm afraid."

"Do what you must," she said. "I want to live."

Late in the evening, a servant appeared with a plate of food for him. He wolfed down the beans and rice, his first food in more than a day. He set aside the plate and stroked Alicia's hair. He had been giving her rectal injections of water, tannin, salt, and gum arabic. The first injection had simply flowed back out, but he had continued, reasoning that whatever she could absorb would help her. The treatment was working. The third time he injected her, she retained the fluid. Her skin was detectably less desiccated, and her breathing, once rapid and shallow, had deepened. He was exhausted, not merely from lack of sleep but from the grinding anxiety that he might lose her. He lay down beside her and closed his eyes.

He was awakened by the clamor of bells so loud it seemed as if every bell in every church in the city had been struck by lightning at precisely the same moment. He shook off his fatigue. Alicia was still sleeping. Her breath was deep and slow but that she had slept through the explosion of bells was evidence of her deathly debilitation. Her pulse, still erratic and weak, confirmed this. When she awoke, he would give her more fluids, orally if she could tolerate it. Perhaps a crust of bread? She had gone forty-eight hours without food.

The bells still clanged. He went to the door and called for Alicia's maid, Catalina.

"Why are the bells ringing?" he asked her.

"They say the fighting is over, doctor."

At last, he thought. The Ciudadela has been taken. He heard Alicia murmur his name. "Bring me water with a little lemon in it," he told the maid. "Bread if there is any in the house."

"The doña?" the maid asked hopefully.

"Yes," he said with a tired smile. "We may have more than Madero's victory to celebrate. And Catalina, send my son to us."

José stepped tentatively into his parents' room. He was still scalded by his father's reproaches from when he had last visited his mother. When he had seen her on the bed, waxen, he thought she was dead. Convulsed by grief, he had doubled over, sobbing wildly. His tears had driven his father into a fury José had never seen before.

"Why are you whimpering like a little girl?" he had snapped. "Do you think this helps? My God, you have been treated too gently by your grandmother. She might as well put you in dresses and braid your hair. Get out of my sight until you can compose yourself like a man." He had grabbed José by the collar, thrown him out of the room, and slammed shut the door.

It was the first and only time his father had laid a violent hand on him, and he had slumped to the ground, weeping out of shame as well as grief. The anger and contempt in his father's voice had seared him.

Even though the words were spoken in anger, José knew they were not words his father would have used at all had he not already believed them to be true. His father was brisk, disciplined, decisive, and rational. By contrast, José knew he was lazy and soft and emotional. He and his father had had many quiet talks about José's poor showing in school and what his father called his "daydreaming." If what it meant to be a man was to be like his father, José knew he was a failure. He could not bear the thought that his mother might die and leave him alone to be a continual disappointment to his father. He prayed for her recovery as he had never prayed for anything else in his life.

Come in, *mijo*," his father said. "Your mother is feeling much better."

José tentatively approached the bed, where his mother lay propped up by pillows, eyes open and shining with love for him. He bit back the sobs, but he could not prevent the tears from falling.

"Mamá," he whispered, taking her hands. "Mamá."

"Don't cry, Josélito," she said in a tired voice. "I'm going to get well."

"I prayed for you," he sniffled.

"Thank you, *mijo*. Now you must thank the Lord for hearing your prayers." She smiled. "So few people remember to thank him that I know he will appreciate your gratitude."

"Yes, Mamá," he said, wiping his nose with his sleeve.

"Where's your handkerchief?" she asked, still smiling.

"I forgot."

His father said, "Your mother needs her rest now, Son. You may return later."

"Yes, Papá," he said, reluctantly pulling himself away.

His father walked him to the door, his hand on José's shoulder. "José, I am very sorry I lost my temper with you before. Your mother was so ill that I . . . forgot myself. Do you forgive me?"

"Yes, Papá," José said. "I am sorry I disappoint you."

His father kissed him. "You have never disappointed me, *mijo*."

It was the first time his father had ever lied to him.

She had kept down the water and the morsels of bread and now she was sleeping again. Sarmiento thought he should bathe and change his clothes and report to his mother-in-law on Alicia's condition. He stretched and wandered out into the corridor. He heard voices, Catalina's and a man's voice, insistent and weary. It was Luis. He looked down to the courtyard, where his cousin was demanding to be allowed to talk to Sarmiento.

"Primo, what are you doing here?" Sarmiento called down.

Luis looked up and said, "Madero's been overthrown. I need a drink."

"Catalina, go and stay with my wife. Luis, come up to my study."

He had heard the words—"Madero's been overthrown"—but he had not truly absorbed them until he sat across from Luis looking at his cousin's stricken face, reading a depth of grief he had not seen in him since he had buried Ángel. Then his own hand began to tremble.

"I heard the bells," he said, as if that explained anything.

"The church celebrates the end of Madero," Luis said bitterly. "The archbishop hates Madero because he actually practices what the church professes. Humility, charity, peace . . ." His voice broke, but when he resumed it was with fury. "If Jesus appeared in the Zócalo, the Catholic Church would nail him to the cross all over again."

"Luis," Sarmiento said, extending his hand to the other man's. "Tell me exactly what happened."

"Huerta turned on him," Luis said, draining his glass. He poured another drink. "Gustavo's spies followed Huerta to a secret meeting with the American ambassador and Félix Díaz. Gustavo had Huerta arrested and brought before Madero. I was there. I told Madero that you had seen food and water being allowed in the Ciudadela. I advised him to shoot Huerta on the spot."

"But he didn't," Sarmiento said. "He wouldn't. It's not in his nature."

"He asked Huerta for an explanation. The bastard got on his knees weeping and said it was all a misunderstanding. Yes, he had met with Díaz only to arrange a truce. No, he had no idea that food and water were getting to the rebels, but he would put a stop to it at once. Madero lifted him to his feet and looked into his eyes and said, 'I believe you.' He let him go with orders to take the Ciudadela within twenty-four hours or lose his command."

Sarmiento groaned. He admired Madero, perhaps even loved him, but his naiveté approached . . . foolishness. "Maybe Gustavo was right," he muttered, remembering the cynical remark Gustavo had made about the family fool having been elected president. "Couldn't you and Gustavo stop him?"

"Madero's faith in his judgment about people is not open for discussion," he said sourly. "When Huerta left, Gustavo said, 'You have just released your assassin.' Madero smiled and said, 'I looked into his eyes and I saw his soul.' Four hours later, Huerta sent Aurelio Blanquet into Madero's office with ten soldiers and informed him he was under arrest. Huerta's such a coward he couldn't even come himself. There was a firefight at the palace and Blanquet's men gained control. I just managed to escape."

"Where is Madero now?"

"In a prison cell at Lecumberri," Luis said. "He is still president, Miguel. I know him; he will not willingly resign. That is the only card we have to play to save his life. He must be persuaded to resign in exchange for a guarantee of his personal safety."

"A guarantee from Huerta?" Sarmiento said incredulously.

Luis shook his head. "Huerta knows that without Madero's resignation, his government would be illegitimate. No country will recognize him and Madero's supporters in the army will revolt. I have been to see the Chilean ambassador. He has agreed to negotiate the deal."

"Who will persuade Don Francisco to resign? You? Gustavo?"

"I urged him to shoot Huerta," Luis reminded him. "If I show my face, I will be arrested. Gustavo has disappeared and I fear the worst. You must go, Miguel. You are his friend, perhaps the only friend who never asked anything of him. He will listen to you. Don Salvador, the Chilean ambassador, will arrive within the hour to take you to the prison under his protection."

"Luis, my wife has been deathly ill. I cannot leave her."

"If Madero cannot be persuaded to resign willingly, Huerta will torture his resignation out of him. He will murder him, Miguel. Our friend, our leader. Only you can save him."

Sarmiento sighed. "All right. I will go. You stay here until I return. I don't want to be anxious over your safety while I am trying to negotiate Madero's."

Luis nodded. "I will immerse myself in this delicious bottle of cognac. Bring back good news, Primo."

At dusk, a black Rolls-Royce, flying the blue-and-white flags of Chile from its grille, pulled up to the palace gate where Sarmiento was waiting. A chauffeur opened the door for him. The Chilean ambassador, Salvador Gossens, a white-haired, avuncular man, greeted him. "Senator, it is always a pleasure to see you, although I wish we were meeting under happier circumstances." A thick plate of glass, inset with a small sliding window, separated the back seat from the front. Gossens slid the window open, barked, "To Lecumberri" to the chauffeur, and then closed the window.

The darkening sky was pink and gold. The deepening shadows could not conceal the gouged walls, shattered windows, and collapsed roofs of shops and houses, churches and factories as the car bumped over the rubble-strewn roadway. The streets were empty except for a few dazed civilians picking their way through the ruins. The conspicuous absence of soldiers manning the makeshift barricades brought home to Sarmiento even more than the silence of the guns that the battle for the city was over and Madero had lost.

"México is the eldest daughter in the family of nations created from the old Spanish empire," Gossens said. "This ancient, beautiful city is the spiritual capital of all of Spanish America." He looked at Sarmiento beseechingly. "Tell me, Senator, how could this have happened here? The city in ruins, the president in prison? Tell me, so I can make sense of this horror and explain it to my government, to myself."

Sarmiento, recalling Bernal Díaz's description of the capture of Tenochtitlán by Cortés, said, "Perhaps we are haunted by the ghosts of the Aztec city that the Spanish razed and buried in the swamps beneath us."

"That was in another time, primitive and cruel," Gossens said. "This is the twentieth century, man! The age of progress and order and democracy. You can't believe that a curse lies on this city because of something that happened almost four hundred years ago."

"No," Sarmiento said. "Of course not. I was being fanciful." He sympathized with Gossens, the representative of a peaceful, stable, and prosperous nation, for whom México must have been a sinecure, the capstone of his career. "I have been caring for my wife, who is ill, and I just learned this afternoon of the president's arrest. Is there a plan in place to guarantee his safe release?"

"I hope your wife is improved," Gossens said automatically. "There is a plan, but it hinges on the president's willingness to resign. Once he delivers his letter of resignation to me, I will keep it until he and his family depart from Veracruz to Cuba, where they have been offered sanctuary. At that point, I will hand over the letter to the minister of foreign affairs, who is next in line in succession for the presidency."

"Pedro Lascuráin? Madero trusted him. Is he a traitor too?"

"Most assuredly not," the ambassador replied. "He is an honorable man acting under duress. I need not tell you from whom."

"Huerta," Sarmiento said.

Gossens gave a sharp nod. "General Huerta," he said, not concealing the contempt in his voice, "is determined that his ascendance to the presidency accord with the requirements of your constitution. Once Lascuráin becomes president, he will appoint Huerta the minister of the interior, who, as you know, is next in the line of succession. Lascuráin will then resign and, voilà, General Huerta becomes the president of the Republic."

"With all the legal formalities properly observed," Sarmiento said. "Very neat. A complete farce, but very neat. What if Don Francisco refuses to resign?"

"Then I'm afraid Huerta might be tempted to choose expediency over formality. I'm sure you grasp my meaning, Senator."

"Only too clearly," he said. They had reached the outskirts of the city, where the only lights were the campfires of the destitute living in the ruins of their former residences. "What about the Americans? Their ambassador engineered this coup and Huerta is his creature. Wilson could guarantee Madero's safety."

A flash of anger crossed Gossens's placid features. "The American ambassador takes the position that the fate of President Madero—to whom he is still accredited—is strictly an internal Mexican affair. He takes no position on the subject."

"That bastard!" Sarmiento said. "Wilson brings down Madero's government and now he washes his hands of him."

"Do you know Rubén Darío's 'Ode to Roosevelt'?" the ambassador asked and then, without waiting for a reply, began to recite, "'You are the United States, future invader of Spanish America.'" He tapped a heavy gold signet ring against the window. "Nothing good comes out of the North," he said. "From that furnace of aggression and greed and self-righteousness. All of Spanish America feels its heat, but only México roasts on its spit."

Miguel?"

"No, Alicia, it's Luis. Miguel has gone on an errand. He will be back soon."

Luis's broad face and features came into focus. He looked melancholy and he smelled of drink.

"Something has happened," she said. "The guns. They've stopped."

"Thankfully," he said with a sad smile, "the battle for the city is over. Unfortunately, Madero lost."

"Where is Miguel?" she asked, suddenly panicked. "Has he been arrested?"

"No, nothing like that. He has gone to talk Madero into resigning so that he and his family can safely depart from México." He grasped her hand. "Alicia, all will be well. You need not worry about Miguel. You need only think about recovering. Are you feeling better?"

"Yes, quite weak, but I'll live," she said, returning the pressure of his touch. She studied his face. Beneath the hard worldliness there remained an implacable sensitivity. She remembered that, while she had hovered between life and death, she had made a connection between Miguel's cousin and her own son. She did not trust it because it had been the product of delirium, but now she felt compelled to take up the subject. "Luis, there is something I want to ask you about your . . . condition."

He looked puzzled for a moment, then said, "Ah, my condition. Yes. Ask anything, Alicia."

"When did you know that you loved men?"

He grinned. "Miguel is right about you. You don't mince words. It's rather terrifying."

"I don't ask out of mere curiosity," she said.

"No? Then why?"

"José," she said quietly.

"You think he may be like me? Why?"

She stirred, trying to sit up. He helped her, arranging pillows behind her, covering her with a blanket. "I must look a fright," she said. "More than usual, I mean." She cut off his protests with a smile. "I know you haven't written verse in many years, but you have retained a poet's sensitivity. It's the same type of sensitivity I see in José, unusual in men in its depth and sweetness."

He laughed a low laugh. "Sweetness is not a quality most people associate with me, Alicia."

"I saw you with Ángel," she replied.

A shadow of grief crossed his face. "Yes," he allowed. "There was sweetness there. Many men are sensitive, Alicia, but not all sensitive men are homosexuals. Your husband, for example, although he would deny it, is a very sensitive man. Perhaps José has inherited that quality from Miguel."

"No, it's different," she said. "And there was a boy, David, José's piano teacher. I think José fell in love with him. He was only nine at the time, too young to understand what was happening to him, but I recognized the signs. He is twelve now and he will eventually meet someone else and fall in love again. How old were you?"

"Younger than José is now," he said. "But like him, I did not understand what it was. Not for many years did I understand." He looked at her. "What will you do if he is like me?"

"What should I do, Luis?" she responded pleadingly.

"You must help him accept his nature," Luis replied forcefully. "Do not let him do as I did and stumble for years in the darkness trying to make sense of his feelings and his shame. Can you do that, Alicia?"

"I do not know if I can teach him to accept what I feel is . . . a sin," she said apologetically. "A small sin, but nonetheless, a sin."

"Sins are volitional, are they not, Alicia? A choice. Yet you yourself recognize that this quality is woven into José's nature. If that is so, then did God not make him as he is?"

She considered him for a long moment. "You give me much to think about, Luis. I can make one promise to you about José. I will not love him any less, no matter what his nature is."

"That may be enough," Luis replied.

Lecumberri penitentiary was new, but it resembled a medieval castle with its thick, windowless walls, towers, and parapets. After anxious negotiations with the terrified warden, Sarmiento and Gossens were led across the prison yard, past the circular guard tower, to the small cell where the president of the Republic was sitting at a table in his shirtsleeves writing letters. He sprang to his feet when the iron door was opened and clapped his hands happily when his visitors entered the room.

"Don Salvador! Miguel!" He embraced each man. "I have never been happier to see either one of you than I am now."

"Señor Presidente," Gossens said, bowing a bit. "How are you being treated? Are you well?"

Madero shrugged. "They feed me and leave me alone. But yes, I am well."

"I should examine you," Sarmiento said.

"Unnecessary, Miguel. There is nothing wrong with me except, of course, for my unlawful detention." A troubled look crossed his face. "They took me from the palace before I could speak to Sara."

"I spoke to the first lady earlier," Gossens said. "She is safe at Chapultepec for now. Don Francisco, we don't have much time. We must speak of your future."

"Please, sit," Madero said, indicating the room's single chair and the narrow bed. He perched at the edge of the writing table and in a mildly curious tone asked, "What do you have in mind for my future, gentlemen? Resignation? Exile? Am I to join Don Porfirio in Paris? Or," he said with a smile, "is it back to that dreadful American city, El Paso?"

"Havana," Sarmiento replied, smiling back.

"Ah, the Cubans have agreed to take me in." He smoothed his goatee with slender, pale, beautifully formed fingers. A saint's fingers, Sarmiento thought.

"Cuba," he repeated. He looked at them, shook his head sadly, and said, "No."

"Of course we could make other arrangements," the ambassador said quickly.

"That's not it, Don Salvador," he said. "I mean, I will not resign and I will not leave México."

There were sounds of shouting and rushed footsteps. Sarmiento reflexively cringed, but then there was silence. Madero poured himself a glass of water from a carafe on the table and sipped it.

"Señor Presidente," Gossens said softly. "You must not think of this as a defeat but as a tactical retreat. As soon as you are out of México, you can renounce your resignation. I can assure you my government will not recognize . . . the usurper. You will remain the legitimately elected president."

"The Americans have a saying I learned when I studied at the university in Berkeley," he said. "'Possession is nine-tenths of the law.' I could call myself president of the Republic or like one of my predecessors, emperor of México, but once I leave the country, it will belong to Huerta, and your government, Don Salvador, and all the other governments will eventually be forced to recognize him."

Sarmiento watched Gossens struggle to find a diplomatic response and interjected, "Do you still not understand what kind of man you are dealing with? Huerta will kill you if you try to stay in México."

Madero eased himself off the table. "I have always known what kind of man Huerta is, Miguel. Vicious, unintelligent, murderous. But also shrewd, fearless, and respected by his troops."

"You should have had him arrested when Gustavo told you about his meeting with the American ambassador," Sarmiento said.

Madero focused his magnetic gaze on Sarmiento. "Arresting Huerta would not have solved the problem because the problem is not Huerta, it's the army. Huerta's replacement would have also schemed behind my back and his replacement and his replacement. Don't you understand, Miguel? Until the army finally submits to civilian control, México will never be a real democracy. The army must stop thinking of itself as a branch of the government. Its generals must stop thinking of themselves as presidents-in-waiting. Until then, México will be condemned to repeat the last one hundred years of coups, countercoups, civil wars, and military dictatorships until Jesus arrives in the glory of his second coming and puts an end to it."

"Did you think you could turn Huerta from his treason?" Sarmiento asked.

"I had to try!" Madero said fervently. "If I had succeeded, he would have ruthlessly suppressed any further rebellion in the army." He paced the room. "I spent so many hours with him, explaining, threatening, cajoling, and praying. There were moments when I believed I had persuaded him to join me in building a true democracy for México. In the end, his vicious instincts won out over his decent ones. The prize of being president was too great a temptation. Poor, lost little man."

Gossens spoke. "Don Francisco, your compassion is, as always, commendable, but the senator is right. You are not safe in México."

Madero stopped midstep, dug into the pocket of his trousers, and then rolled a shining orb across the table toward Sarmiento, who stopped and inspected it. It was a glass eye.

He gasped, "Gustavo?"

"It was delivered to me as an inducement to resign," Madero said. "Don Salvador, whether or not I resign, I will never be allowed to leave México alive. Huerta does not like loose ends."

"You will be protected by the weight of the entire diplomatic corps," Gossens replied.

"Except for the Americans," Madero said, with a sad smile. "Their opinion is the only one that matters to Huerta. So if I am to be killed, let it be the assassination of the elected president of México and not the back-alley slaughter of a disgraced politician who tried to save his own skin by running away from his responsibilities."

Gossens rose heavily from his chair. "Don Francisco," he said, "I had hoped I would be spared the burden of what I must now tell you." He cleared his throat. "If you do not resign, your wife, your mother, your father, and every member of your family within reach of General Victoriano Huerta will be murdered. One member of your family for each day that you refuse to resign." In a broken whisper, he concluded. "Your mother first."

"No!" Sarmiento protested. "No! He can't be serious."

"Look in your hand," Madero said, "and tell me he is not serious."

Sarmiento opened his hand. Gustavo Madero's glass eye stared back at him; it was both comical and horrifying. He dropped it, and the orb rolled back toward Madero, who scooped it up.

"My brother saw more clearly with one eye than I saw with two," Madero said. He sat at the table, pulled a fresh sheet of paper, and quickly began to write out his letter of resignation.

The idling locomotive expelled puffs of steam that quickly dissipated in the cool night air. A small group of people huddled on the platform. There were no other trains that night, only the locomotive and two passenger cars of the Interoceanic Railway. Soldiers patrolled the empty station and prevented anyone from entering. Sarmiento glanced at his pocket watch. It was closing in on midnight and Madero had still not arrived. At the far end of the platform, Don Salvador was in an agitated, whispered conversation with Sara Madero while other members of the Madero family gathered around them. Their stiff postures indicated anxiety and anger.

More than twenty-four hours had passed since Madero had handed his letter of resignation to the ambassador. After Gossens had had his car drop Sarmiento at the palace, the ambassador had gone to present the letter to the minister of foreign affairs, Lascuráin. Huerta had been waiting and he had insisted that the ambassador hand over the letter to him, ostensibly to authenticate Madero's signature. Surrounded by Huerta's bodyguards, exhausted and in fear for his own safety, Gossens surrendered the letter. In the morning, Sarmiento had awakened to the news that Madero had resigned and Huerta was the new president; Lascuráin's presidency had lasted forty-five minutes, just long enough for him to appoint Huerta minister of the interior and then step aside. Sarmiento had hurried to the Chilean embassy, where Gossens had described the meeting with Huerta.

"I exacted his promise that Don Francisco will still be allowed to leave the city," the ambassador said. "He has arranged for a train to depart tonight to Veracruz."

"His promises are not exactly binding," Sarmiento observed.

"The ambassadors of Cuba and Argentina are at Lecumberri even as we speak," Gossens replied. "They will not let Don Francisco out of their sight until he is safely on the train. Will you come to the train station and be a witness to his safe departure?"

"Yes," he said. "Of course."

That was how Sarmiento had come to be standing on the platform. Madero had been expected shortly after nine. Three hours late. With every passing second, Madero's safe passage from México became less and less likely, ambassadorial escort or not. Gossens disengaged himself from the Madero family and strode to Sarmiento's side.

"I am going back to the National Palace to speak to Huerta," he said. "Will you stay here until I return?"

Sarmiento nodded. "What will you tell our new president?"

"I will demand that he release Don Francisco from wherever he is being held and allow him to leave, as he promised, or I will make my personal mission to see to it that not a single country in Spanish America recognizes Huerta's government. I will make him a pariah."

"Do you think he will care about his international reputation?"

"He will care about the ability of México to borrow money and export its goods," Gossens replied. "Those things are much harder to do when your government is an international outlaw."

Before Sarmiento could reply, they were interrupted by the screech of wheels and shouted voices outside the station. A moment later, several men dressed in the dark clothes of the diplomatic corps rushed in with soldiers on their heels. One of them, tall and bulky, came breathlessly to Gossens. Sarmiento recognized him from receptions at Chapultepec as the Cuban ambassador, Carlos Salvatierra.

"Don Salvador, we lost him."

"What! How?"

"The military escort insisted that we travel separately from the prison," Don Carlos replied. "Our car left first and then the car with Don Francisco. There was a barricade. We were detained, but his car continued on. I demanded that we be allowed to continue, but by the time the soldiers waved us on, he was gone."

"When was this?" Gossens asked.

"A half hour, forty-five minutes ago," he said. "I came as quickly as I could but the city is difficult to travel."

"I am going to see Huerta," Gossens said. "Come with me."

Don Carlos nodded. "I hope it is not too late."

The two men hurried off, Gossens calling to Sarmiento over his shoulder, "Wait here, Miguel."

They bustled off. He sensed Sara Madero's spidery presence before he heard her demand, "What happened?"

He told her. She stared at him with her black, perpetually aggrieved eyes, as if her husband's abduction were his fault, but instead she said, "Your wife has always been kind to me."

"Señora?"

"The rest of them, all the society women, they scorned me and closed their doors to me, but not your wife. I will not forget her kindness," she said, stepping away from him and fading into the darkness like a wraith.

After that, the blackness seemed to deepen rather than lighten as night crawled slowly toward dawn. When he next heard the approach of vehicles outside the station, it was without the urgency of the Cuban ambassador's earlier arrival. Wheels ground to a stop, footsteps labored across the empty station, and then he saw the defeated figures of the two ambassadors as they climbed the steps to the platform, eyes downcast and faces grim. They brushed past him and went directly to Sara Madero. When she began to scream, he knew Madero was dead.

19

The casket carrying the body of Francisco Madero was gently lifted onto a funeral tram. The sides of the car were draped in black bunting, and it flew the flag of México as it made its way from the Zócalo to the Panteón de Dolores, where Madero would be laid to rest. The mob of mourners that surrounded the car shuffled slowly on the tracks, impeding the vehicle's progress. Sarmiento observed that the church bells that had clanged so jubilantly at the news of Madero's fall were silent. José clutched his hand, and he glanced down at his son. José's eyes were rimmed with red and his expression was more of shock than grief as he watched Sara Madero fall upon the casket, her small body quaking with sobs. Observing the boy's distress, he questioned his decision to bring him to the funeral. José had never experienced the death of a friend, but Sarmiento had hoped that witnessing the terrible pomp of this moment would help José understand the larger tragedy that Madero's death symbolized for México. José, however, seemed dazed and lost in his private misery, and Sarmiento did not know how to comfort his son. He wished Alicia had been well enough to come, but she was still bed-ridden and weak.

A group of musicians materialized out of the crowd—trumpeters, violinists, guitarists, and an accordion player—and began to play a slow, harsh, mournful ballad. It was a song about a departed lover, more appropriate in its lachrymose sentimentality—"My tears will deepen the waters of the sea"—to a corner cantina than the funeral of a Mexican president. And yet Sarmiento thought it was fitting that the common people who had embraced Madero would send him to his rest with a song from the streets. Some of the mourners, recognizing the tune, began to sing:

No volverán, mis ojos a mirarte,
ni tus oídos escucharán mi canto.
Voy a aumentar los mares con mi llanto.
Adiós mujer, adios para siempre, adiós.

As the rest of the crowd picked up the song, he heard José's voice, thin at first but gathering strength as he joined it to the chorus of the mourners: "Good-bye, my love. Good-bye, forever, good-bye."

His father's arm rested on his shoulder, steadying José as he watched Don Panchito's casket carried into the crypt. Then the iron gate was closed with a clang and a great key turned in the lock. Afterward, his father stooped down, murmured instructions for José to wait for him while he spoke to someone, and left José standing at the tomb as the crowd melted away.

Not far from the tomb was a stone bench. José made his way over to it. Sunlight shifted through the branches of the cypress trees, dappling the great city of the dead with its miniature Gothic cathedral mausoleums, grieving stone angels, and brightly tiled graves packed together as densely as the most crowded *colonia* of the city. Patches of weeds, thorny brambles, and a few early wildflowers were scattered across the ground. A breeze carried the smell of damp earth and vegetable decay. The chatter of the birds and the sibilant swoop of their wings as they flew among the trees echoed in the air. On many of the graves were broken vases, flowers withered to brown, the dust of offerings left from Día de los Muertos commemorations. José shed a few final tears for his friend.

That morning, taking his chocolate and *pan dulce* in the kitchen, he had asked Chepa whether Don Panchito was in heaven. The old cook had nodded vigorously and said, "He is in the highest heavens."

"Isn't there only one heaven?" he asked her, between bites of his *concha*.

"No, *mijo*," she replied, drinking her milky coffee. "There are thirteen heavens for God and all his saints. The good people like Don Pancho Madero, who fought bravely for México, they go to the heaven of the warriors, where they walk in the trail of the sun."

He looked up at the sky, squinting against the sun, which was half-hidden among feathery leaves, and tried to feel Don Panchito's spirit in the beneficent warmth. He thought of the conversation he had with his mother, who told him, even though his friend was gone, José could still love him. "But, Mamá, if he's not here, he can't love me back," he had replied, weeping.

She had murmured some consolation, but for once her consolations failed him. Loss had entered into José's heart and taken up a dwelling there. The loss was not only of his friend Don Panchito but of the world he had known before the fighting and of his faith in the grown-ups. The fighting had ended and his old routines had begun to be reestablished—even El Morito had reappeared, skinny and flea-ridden—but nothing was as it had been. He was like someone who had stepped into a long, dark, and frightening tunnel and, coming into the light, could not blink away the darkness that continued to cloud the periphery of his vision. The world was a more arbitrary and crueler place, and even though his family surrounded him, he knew now that he was essentially alone in it. This sense of his separateness had frightened him at first, but there were moments now when it felt like a kind of freedom too, a space where he could begin to dream about a future that owed nothing to the customs and expectations of his family. A future that belonged to him alone.

The familiar voice had whispered into Sarmiento's ear, "We must talk, Primo. No, don't turn around. There is a tomb nearby, for the Gutiérrez Ojeda family. I will wait for you there."

Sarmiento nearly sobbed with relief at the sound of his cousin's voice. He told José to wait for him, and as inconspicuously as he could, slipped away. Luis was leaning against the back of the tomb—a small, fanciful replica of the Parthenon—smoking a cigarette. The stubs of three others on the ground belied his seeming insouciance. Dressed in a laborer's rough clothes, his goatee shaven off and his hair shorn, Luis was barely recognizable. His eyes were exhausted. He embraced Sarmiento and said, "It's good to see you, Primo."

"Thank God you're safe," Sarmiento answered. "I feared the worst after the president was murdered. What happened?"

"Friends hid me."

"Why didn't you come to me?"

Luis shook his head. "Our association is too well known. They would have come looking for me. No, my fellow inverts are much better at making themselves invisible in plain sight, and they are loyal to each other as only the despised can be."

Sarmiento bristled. "I am loyal to you, Luis. You are like my brother."

Luis clamped his shoulder affectionately. "I don't doubt your loyalty, but your brothers-in-law are opportunists and reactionaries who would have surrendered me to gain Huerta's goodwill." He shrugged. "In any event, here we are. I have come to say good-bye, Miguel."

Although he had expected something like this, Sarmiento's heart fell. Luis's departure would seal the end of Madero's era. "Where will you go?"

"North, to Coahuila. The governor there, Carranza, is on the verge of declaring himself in rebellion against Huerta. Once he does, others will follow." He lit another cigarette. "It's back to the battlefield for me, Miguel. Huerta won't fall as easily as Don Porfirio, but he can't last. The army is already divided, Zapata continues to harass him from the south, and Carranza has the state militia to do his fighting, not the ragtag army Madero put together. Six months, a year, and I will be back."

Wearily, Sarmiento said, "And then what, Luis? Who is this Carranza? Another would-be dictator?"

"Carranza is an old liberal," Luis replied with a resigned shrug. "A harder man than Madero, but a democrat, like him. He's our best hope against Huerta. Our only hope."

"Can any democrat succeed in México?" Sarmiento wondered. "Perhaps it is true that México only responds to a strong hand at the till. To a minimum of terror and a maximum of benevolence, as one of my fellow senators said in praise of Don Porfirio."

Luis exhaled a plume of smoke and leaned back against the tomb of the Gutiérrez Ojedas. He closed his eyes and basked in the warmth of the sun for a moment before responding, "*L'amor che move il sole e l'atre stelle.*"

Sarmiento recognized the language—Italian—but not the quotation. "I don't understand, Luis."

"The last line of Dante's *Paradiso*," he replied. "'The love that moves the sun and all the other stars.' At the end of his journey, Dante discovers that love is the engine of the universe. Men are forced to respond to fear, but they want to respond to love. It is love, not fear, that gives us courage and hope and changes our lives for the better. I know this is true because it changed mine. Yours too, Miguel."

"You are speaking of personal sentiments, not a political program," Sarmiento said.

Luis shook his head. "You think, even after what you have just seen, that politics is rational? No, it is all about feeling. Madero may have failed in his programs, but he brought the force of love into politics and that cannot be extinguished by an assassin's bullets. After Madero, no one will be able to govern México by fear alone." He flicked his cigarette to the ground and smiled. "You think I am being romantic. Well, you are the scientist and I am the poet, but in this case I am right." He embraced Sarmiento and kissed his cheeks. "I advise you to fade into private life for now. Protect yourself and your family. Until we meet again, Primo, good-bye."

Sarmiento felt hot tears in his eyes and could scarcely trust his voice. "Promise me that we will. I could not bear to lose you, Luis."

Luis embraced him again and the two men clung to each other like the boys they had once been. "I promise, I promise."

A painful fit of coughing left Alicia breathless. She retrieved the rosary that had slipped from her fingers to the bedspread and tried to remember on which bead she had left off as she prayed the decade of the First Joyful Mystery, the Annunciation. Her thoughts wandered to the words of the Magnificat, Mary's serene words of surrender and reverence, a prayer that had always inspired and consoled Alicia.

She began to whisper the words: "My soul magnifies the Lord and my spirit rejoices in God, my Savior. For he has looked with favor on his lowly servant and from this day all generations will call me blessed. The Lord has done great things for me and holy is his name . . ."

There was a change in the atmosphere. A moment earlier, the room had been the familiar jumble of walls, windows, light, furniture, and linens that the weariness of illness had made as oppressive as a prison cell. Her body had been weighted down by pain, her senses were dulled, and her mind turned inward. But now, as if she had been jolted awake, the room seemed illuminated by a fresh, auroral light in which every object glowed with sentience. The light entered her, suffused her, and her pain and fatigue melted away. She touched the green brocaded coverlet on the bed and felt each strand of the silk fibers in the cloth, felt the small fingers that had separated the threads from the cocoons and even the wriggling silkworms spinning the threads of the cocoons. Startled, she lifted her hand from the bed. A low thrum filled her ears. It was the sound of her blood moving in her veins. The intensity of her perception was terrifying, for each touch, scent, sound, sight, and even the taste of her own saliva was like a series of doors flying open through which she was falling, faster and faster. She thought she must be going mad. She opened her mouth to call out for her maid, but then the sensation of falling gave way to a deep calm. She touched the coverlet again. She could still sense every strand of activity that had created it — from the unfolding of the leaves of the mulberry bush that fed the silkworms to the wrinkled fingers weaving the brocade on a hand loom — but her fear vanished. In its place she felt awe and then an immense love for everything, from the wriggling worm to the old woman at the loom in a small room in a port city in Belgium.

Everything is one. The thought rose in her mind like a bubble rising to the surface of a stream. *Everything is one.* As she meditated upon it, she began to understand the doors of her senses flying open, the feeling of falling. The doors were barriers she herself had created as she constructed the rooms of her personality and her life. *In my father's house are many dwellings.* Is that what Jesus had meant? Was he speaking not only of heaven but of this life in which each person carved out of the vast, unified reality of existence the little houses of personality they inhabited? She had a vision of children making sand houses at the edge of the sea and of waves gently spilling over and eradicating them. The little sand houses were like the houses of self, and the waves were the fingers of

God drawing the sand back into himself. For one moment, God had reclaimed her and blown open the doors of the little house in which she had sealed herself. In that moment she experienced the shattering, unmediated knowledge of God: *Everything is one.*

She thought of Mary and of Mary's prayer that had been on her lips when this vision—for she knew that this *was* a vision—had begun. Mary, a girl, scarcely more than a child, to whom an angel had come. How terrified she must have been, Alicia thought. Had she closed her eyes, thrown herself upon the floor, tried to run away? Even after she had calmed herself, the angel's message could not have been welcome. For what woman could bear the weight of carrying in her womb the son of God? She must have felt confused, frightened, and overwhelmed by the angel's words, and yet she had been given the grace to respond, "I am the servant of the Lord."

"I am the servant of the Lord," Alicia said.

"Fear no evil, Daughter, for I am with you, always." The voice that spoke these words was low and sweet, male or female, she could not tell. It poured over her like honey and wrapped her in womb-like warmth. For what seemed both an instant and an eternity, she rose out of her body like a stirring in the air, like the fragrance of a rose, and united with God. The ecstasy was beyond words, thoughts, feelings, beyond any happiness she had ever felt on earth.

When she reluctantly opened her eyes to the familiar room, she experienced the pain of her exile as she never had before. She also knew a moment of evil was coming. Yet she was not afraid because that moment, like every other moment of her life, was only a door, which once opened led to where all doors ultimately led. To home.

In the days following Madero's funeral, Sarmiento's anxiety over Alicia's health distracted him from public events. Still weakened from the effects of cholera, she developed bronchitis. He feared it would turn into pneumonia and in her exhausted state prove fatal. He kept her under virtual quarantine until she began to recover. He remained at her side constantly, treating her, monitoring her condition, and allowing only the briefest visits from her sisters. He bore their resentment with equanimity—they had always seemed a gaggle of clucking hens to him, loud but harmless. It would be weeks, even months, before Alicia regained her full strength, and he was determined to protect her. In this, his mother-in-law was his ally, herding the sisters out of the room when Alicia began to falter, overseeing the details of her diet, even bathing her. He came to appreciate that, in her unsentimental way, the old woman was a devoted mother. José slipped in and out of the room, trying to conceal his obvious anxiety as he sat on the bed beside his mother, threading his fingers into hers, his head against her shoulder. In the evenings, Sarmiento helped Alicia into the drawing room of their apartment, where José played the piano, La Niña read her novels, Sarmiento attacked his stack of newspapers, and Alicia worked at her embroidery. For those precious, lamp-lit hours, life appeared almost normal. At such times, Sarmiento imagined he could follow his cousin's advice and fade into private life, but then the newspaper headlines recording Huerta's consolidation of power and the toadying tone of the stories beneath them filled him with rage.

One evening in the drawing room, when it was just the two of them, Sarmiento crushed the newspaper in his hands and tossed it to the floor.

"Miguel, what is it?" Alicia asked, looking up from the pile of José's discarded clothes she was examining for mending before she sent them to San Francisco Tlalco. She wore a heavy robe over a thick nightgown, and her thin face showed the effects of illness.

"Is the world insane, Alicia, or is it just me?" he replied. "Does no one notice that a murderer governs México? My God, to read the newspapers you would think Madero never existed."

"Of course you are not insane," she said. "At times like these, I find it useful to meditate on what the Lord said, 'The prince of the world is coming, but he has no power over me.'"

He shook his head. "I am amazed you persist in your faith even as the archbishop licks Huerta's boots."

"My faith has nothing to do with the archbishop," she replied.

"I can't let Madero's murder pass with a prayer and shrug that the world is an evil place."

She sighed. "You know how much I admired Don Francisco, and I think he would have understood me better than you, Miguel. What is false does not become true simply because people shout it. What is right does not change because it is inconvenient. Don Victoriano is a murderer. That is the truth whether or not the world acknowledges it."

Abashed, he said, "I apologize, darling. Yes, that is the truth, but the truth is not self-executing, it would seem."

She set aside a pair of trousers that needed patching and said, "Then perhaps, Miguel, *you* should stand up and tell the truth."

At her remark, his skin prickled with fear and he waited until it passed before he spoke. "There would be consequences," he said.

She looked up at him. "We can bear them."

"Alicia, Huerta ordered the murder of the president of the Republic. He would have no qualms about eliminating an obscure senator."

"You left the city once before, to fight with Don Francisco," she said. "If you had to, you could leave again to fight Don Victoriano. I would go with you."

"You have no idea of what you are saying," he replied. "The hardships, the separation from your family."

"You are my family, Miguel. As for hardship, if the choice is between hardship in the service of what is right and comfort purchased at the expense of my conscience, there is no choice." She reached out her hand and folded it in his. "You think I have not been aware of your restlessness, but I am, and I share your horror at what was done to Don Francisco, to México."

He raised her hand to his lips, kissed it, and smiled at her. "I thought Christians turned the other cheek."

"They also die for their beliefs," she replied. "And they are not the only ones. Francisco Madero died for his. Leaving the city for a time would be a small price to pay for yours." She pulled a shirt from the pile of clothes and inspected the collar and the cuffs. "This shirt is too frayed to give away, but the material is so fine, I don't want to discard it. Perhaps I can cut it up and make a smaller garment from it." She held it out. "What do you think?"

Later, when he was alone, Sarmiento mulled over his wife's words. It was not her courage that astonished him—her life was a lesson in courage—but her placid certitude. While he was tormented with anxieties, fears, ambivalence, self-doubt, and self-loathing at his cowardice, Alicia was calmly prepared to leave the life she had always known for an uncertain exile with a man who, once he denounced Huerta, would almost certainly have a price on his head. Now that she had spoken, his path became clear to him. He set about writing what he knew would be the last speech he ever delivered in the Senate chambers.

Sarmiento entered the Café Colón and stood for a moment to allow his eyes to adjust to the darkness of the bar. Presidents come and go, he thought with grim amusement as he surveyed the scene before him, but the Colón never changed—the same richly dressed men huddled over the round, marble-topped tables whispering conspiratorially. He saw Damian sitting at a table in the back of the room, not far from where Victoriano Huerta, then a drunken, disgraced general, had pulled a gun on Sarmiento. Now Huerta was president of the Republic and Sarmiento, as he passed among the tables of politicians, high-ranking bureaucrats, and plutocrats, could have been invisible for all the attention they paid him. He remembered what Luis had once told him: "Politicians don't have permanent friends, only permanent interests." Even so, the crudeness with which he was dismissed by the men in the bar who had once cultivated him because of his friendship with Madero astounded him. He made his way to his brother-in-law. He had sought out Damian because it had occurred to him that his speech would affect his wife's entire family and, potentially, their fortunes. He hoped to make them understand why he felt he must speak out. He thought Damian, who had had his own ties to Madero through Gustavo, would be the most sympathetic.

"Miguel," Damian said, rising.

They embraced and sat. A white-coated waiter came, took their order, and left them to consider each other through the haze of Damian's cigar, burning in the heavy obsidian ashtray on the table. Sarmiento had not spoken to Damian since his brother-in-law had left the city with the rest of the family before the Ten Tragic Days that had preceded Madero's fall.

"You look well," Sarmiento said, and Damian did look as inscrutably handsome as ever. "Alicia tells me that your house was undamaged in the fighting."

He picked up his cigar and puffed it. "Fortunately. Don Francisco's house was burned to the ground."

"Yes, I saw the photographs in the newspapers," Sarmiento replied. "That had to have been deliberate."

The waiter brought them their drinks. After he left, Damian said, "Of course it was. You were at the funeral, Miguel." He smiled at Sarmiento's unspoken question of how he knew. "I read the newspapers, too. You were photographed."

"Yes. You were not." It came out as more of a challenge than Sarmiento had intended.

Damian lifted his drink to his lips, a frothy mix he favored called a Brandy Alexander, and sipped it, leaving a thin line of cream along his moustache. "You blame me?"

"You were friends with Gustavo." Again, his tone was unintentionally accusatory as if all the anger he felt at those who had abandoned Madero—the roomful of men around them—was seeping out at Damian.

"I did business with Gustavo," he replied mildly. "If you've come to reproach me, Miguel, don't waste your breath. I am not a politician, much less an idealist like you. I'm a businessman. I adjust to circumstances. You should try it. One sleeps better at night."

"I have not come to scold you but to tell you," he dropped his voice, "that I am going to make a speech on the Senate floor denouncing Huerta. I am fully prepared to accept the consequences for myself, but for you, Eulalia, the rest of the family—well, I wanted you to know so you could prepare."

His brother-in-law lifted his cocktail glass by the stem and turned it in his fingers, thoughtfully. "And you are going to commit suicide when? Because you realize you will be killed."

"We will leave the city. Alicia, my son, myself. We will go north."

"To join Governor Carranza's rebellion?" Damian asked. He sipped his drink. "I've met the old man, Miguel. A pompous windbag who would like to be dictator himself. He's no Madero."

"There was only one Madero," Sarmiento replied softly.

"Ah, the legend begins," Damian said scornfully. "Madero, the martyr of democracy." He drained his glass and held it up for the waiter to see before setting it on the table. "Your certainties are like those of a child, Miguel, the product of blissful ignorance and misplaced hero worship." The waiter brought his second drink. "You want to know the truth about Francisco Madero? I will tell you. He was as corrupt as Don Porfirio."

"That's slander. I knew Madero and a more honest man never lived."

"And I knew Gustavo," Damian retorted. "His brother's right hand. Gustavo, who doled out government jobs to Madero's supporters and collected the kickbacks on government contracts for the Madero family. Gustavo, who organized the *porra*—the band of thugs that threatened opposition politicians and burned one of the opposition newspapers to the ground. You think you're the only legislator who owes his office to election fraud? That was Gustavo too, but everything Gustavo did, he did with his brother's knowledge and consent."

Sarmiento remembered the meeting with Madero and his brother when they proposed his election into the Senate. His face must have shown his discomfort because Damian pressed on relentlessly. "You do know what I am talking about, don't you, Miguel? How could you not? You voted for Madero's bill to impose press censorship."

"It was a temporary measure," Sarmiento murmured. "The opposition newspapers were attempting to foment a rebellion against the elected government."

"The road to dictatorship is paved with temporary measures," Damian replied mockingly.

"Madero was no dictator."

"Agreed. He was far too inept for that," Damian said. "Look, Miguel, what did the man really accomplish? He brought down the most stable government México has ever known and replaced it with a weak regime whose days were numbered from the beginning. He gave us Huerta, a drunkard and a murderer." He waved his cigar. "Don't look so surprised. The fact that I despised Madero doesn't mean I admire his assassin. I am simply realistic. Huerta is president now. One has to do business with him. It won't make life easier if you insist on attacking him in public. I would advise you not to."

"I did not come to you for advice, Damian, only to warn you."

"Then I will return the favor," his brother-in-law said. "If you do this, you will be completely on your own. No one in the family will defend you or assist you. To the contrary, we will denounce you, and if necessary to prove our loyalty to the government, help capture and prosecute you. So whatever your plan of escape is, Miguel, you might wish to keep it to yourself."

Shocked, he gasped, "You would really do that to me, Damian, to Alicia?"

"My God," Damian said, his anger breaking through his composure. "Are you Don Quixote? This is not your absurd, chivalrous fantasy of the world, Miguel; this is the actual world, where real people have real things to lose if you persist in your foolishness. I will not risk my family to protect yours." He smiled humorlessly. "It's survival of the fittest, not the most virtuous."

"And if I return to the city with a triumphant Carranza, Damian?" Sarmiento said, with equal anger. "What will you say then?"

He shrugged. "All hail the conquering hero."

The Senate chamber was half-empty and even the senators who were present behaved more like casual acquaintances at a social event—smoking, laughing, aimlessly pacing the thick, burgundy carpet in the well of the chamber—than legislators. It was a very different scene than Sarmiento remembered from the last time he had attended, when Maderista senators and opposition senators hurled invective at each other while the president of the Senate futilely called for order. His entrance into the chamber was met with murmured comments and a few raised eyebrows. None of his colleagues approached him except for Marciano Trejo, the ancient senator from the state of Jalisco. Senator Trejo was a remnant from Don Porfirio's era, nominally in opposition to Madero, but for all that a kind and gracious man who had known and admired Sarmiento's father.

"*Chico*," he said in his old man's croak. "Thank God you are safe and well. Although I must say, I am a little surprised to see you here." He glanced around the room. "The other lambs have all run off, leaving only us wolves."

Sarmiento, too, had observed that the only senators present were those who had opposed Madero. "Has it been like this since . . . the change in government?"

Trejo shrugged. "At first a few of your lot showed up and made speeches against Huerta, but after soldiers were sent to fill the gallery, discretion became the better part of valor. Why are you here, Miguel?"

"I too have a speech to make."

The old man frowned. "Unless you have converted to our side, that is not a good idea. Belisario Domínguez was the last senator to denounce Huerta and three days later he was beaten to death in his hotel room. By persons unknown, of course."

"I heard," Sarmiento said. "The old days are back, Don Marciano."

Trejo dropped his voice. "Huerta is to Díaz what a butcher is to a surgeon. These are not the old days. These are different days, worse days. I am only glad I will die before they are over. Miguel, think carefully before you deliver yourself to Huerta's hands."

The president of the Senate called the body to order. Trejo clasped Sarmiento's shoulder affectionately and shuffled to his desk. Sarmiento took his own seat, surrounded by the empty desks of his absent colleagues, and listened to the president drone on about routine matters. He heard footsteps in the gallery above the chamber, brisk and orderly. He glanced up. A row of soldiers, fully armed and in battle dress, arranged themselves silently against the wall of the gallery. The president seemed to falter for a moment, then recovered, and went on. When he finished, Sarmiento stood and asked to be recognized. He was grateful his desk hid his legs because they were shaking uncontrollably.

"For what purpose?" the president asked.

"To speak about the recent events that have disturbed the tranquility of our country," Sarmiento replied, forcing his voice to remain steady.

His colleagues began to whisper among themselves and one shouted, "Out of order!"

"I am not out of order," he declared, anger dissolving his fear. "It is the privilege of any senator to speak on whatever issue he chooses."

"Nonetheless, Senator," the president replied, glancing at the gallery, "it is my responsibility to maintain decorum in the chamber."

Sarmiento said, "Are the rules that govern this body not still in effect? Or has the constitutional guarantee of freedom of speech been suppressed even in this room?"

There were shouts of "Sit down!" and "Expel him!" The president anxiously called for order.

Sarmiento's heart raced. His hands were damp with sweat. Then Trejo stood up and silenced the chamber with an upraised hand.

"Señor Presidente," he said, addressing himself to the dais. "You look unwell. May I suggest you retire to your office for a moment to recover? I offer my services in your place."

The president nodded quickly. "Yes. Something I ate disagrees with me. I must rest. Senator Trejo will preside until I return."

All activity stopped as the president departed and Trejo slowly made his way to the dais and seated himself there. He looked at Sarmiento, who had remained standing. "Does Senator Sarmiento still wish to be recognized?"

"I do, Senator."

He sighed. "So be it."

Sarmiento reached into his coat for his speech and laid the papers on his desk. He drew a deep breath and began to speak. "Señor Presidente, I read with deep interest the statement of Don Victoriano Huerta to this body upon his succession to the presidency." The chamber was utterly still. He thought about the soldiers in the gallery and forced himself to focus on the page before him and continued. "In that statement, he asserted that the resignation of the legitimately elected president of the Republic, Don Francisco Madero, was necessary to pacify the nation, restore the confidence of foreign governments in México's ability to govern itself, revive the economy, and bring order to the streets of this city. Every one of these statements, Señor Presidente, was a lie." He paused, waiting for the outcry, but the silence only deepened. "These statements were nothing more than justifications for one of the darkest episodes in the history of our beloved country. These justifications fail, sir. The people of México will never accept Victoriano Huerta's claim to be its legitimate president knowing, as they do, that he seized control of the government by means of betrayal, and that his first act after taking office was the assassination of the lawful president in a cowardly act—"

The clamor began. Shouts of "Treason!" and "Lies!" filled the room.

"A cowardly act," Sarmiento continued, shouting now, "committed in the dead of night. By this act, Victoriano Huerta demonstrates he is prepared to shed the blood of innocents to maintain power, and he will." The shouting grew louder. Ominously, the soldiers in the gallery headed toward the exits. "He will cover México in the corpses of its own people and bring the nation to ruin to satisfy his personal greed—" The doors of the chamber burst open and the soldiers poured in. "A murderer!" Sarmiento shouted as the soldiers surrounded him. "A common criminal!"

"Sir," a captain shouted into Sarmiento's face. "You are under arrest!"

"On what charge?"

"Insulting the integrity of the president of the Republic."

"Integrity?" Sarmiento spat. "Your master is a thug."

"Take him," the captain ordered.

Sarmiento was pulled away from his desk and dragged out of the chamber, shouting, "*Viva la República de México! Viva Presidente Madero!*"

Outside, he was slammed against a wall. The captain said to his men, "I've got it from here, boys." He grabbed Sarmiento's arm and jerked him forward.

"I am a senator!" Sarmiento said. "I have immunity! Take your hands off me." But the adrenaline that had fueled him through his speech had begun to subside and he felt terror rising in his chest.

The captain pushed him through a door into a narrow corridor and then released him.

"Relax, Señor Doctor. I am getting you out of here," he said in a low voice.

Sarmiento looked at the soldier in amazement. "What?"

"You don't remember me, of course," he said. "You dug a bullet out of my shoulder at Ciudad Juárez that I received fighting for Don Francisco. Come, there is no time to talk."

Sarmiento followed the soldier through back corridors of the National Palace he had not known existed. They came to an obscure exit.

"You have perhaps twenty-four hours before they discover I did not take you to Lecumberri. I suggest you leave the city."

"What about you?"

"I'm leaving now, to join the rebels up north. God bless you, Señor. Go."

For a moment Sarmiento stood unmoving as the eddies of street life rushed around him. The day was cool and clear. The light fell crisply on the facades of the ancient buildings that surrounded him, picking out, here and there, a weathered adornment. The cathedral bells chimed the quarter hour. It was time. Time to go.

20

Sarmiento plunged into the crowded streets behind the National Palace. When he and Alicia had discussed the possible consequences of his speech, they had agreed the likeliest outcome was his arrest and confinement in Lecumberri. She would seek him at the prison when he did not return home. Should he return home? He thought not, at least not until he had time to work out another plan. But where could he go? He glanced down the street and saw a pair of priests, deep in conversation, walking toward him. Cáceres, he thought. Cáceres would take him in. He moved swiftly and purposefully south, toward San Francisco Tlalco.

The priest was in the garden tending his remaining rose bushes. Sarmiento paused at the gate and watched him. The first time he had entered the garden it had seemed to him an unlikely slice of paradise in a blighted neighborhood. Cáceres had shown him, however, that San Francisco Tlalco was not a human refuse pile but a community. Its inhabitants were the vestigial descendants of the ancient race of the Aztecs, and the parish garden was a lingering breath of the garden city of Tenochtitlán. When he had first come into its streets in his white uniform and his citation book, Sarmiento had seen only the degradation of the Indians. Cáceres had taught him to see the triumph of their survival after centuries of violence, disease, and destitution. Sarmiento did not pretend to understand everything that the survival of the Indians meant for México, but he knew México would never achieve wholeness until it embraced the heritage they represented. It was, he thought, as the American president Lincoln had said in the passage of a speech Madero liked to quote: "A house divided against itself cannot stand." Until México accepted the past that its Indians represented, it would have no peace, and without peace the future of México, like Ciudad de México itself, would be constructed on a swamp.

"Pedro," Sarmiento called, entering the garden.

Cáceres looked up, saw him, and grinned. "Miguel, have you come to help me? If so, you are overdressed."

"I have come to ask your help," Sarmiento said.

The priest put down his shovel and gazed at him with concern. "You are distressed, Miguel. What has happened?"

"Can we talk in private?"

The priest wiped his hands on his trousers and approached him. "Yes, of course. Come."

In her anxiety, Alicia went to the one place in the palace where she had always been happiest—the kitchen. Chepa, seeing her shuffle slowly into the big, warm, fragrant room, clucked, "*Mija*, you should be in bed! How thin you have become! What can I feed you? Graciela, bring the lady some of that fresh bread you have just taken out of the oven. Juana! Butter and honey. Quickly."

Alicia eased herself onto the bench at the long table where the women of the kitchen plucked and chopped, ground and skinned, mixed and kneaded. Sunlight glinted off the copper pans hanging from racks near the big, tiled stove. She drew her rebozo over her thin shoulders and relaxed to the smells and noises of the kitchen. She smiled at the little altar to San Pascualito, the aproned kitchen saint, who held a wooden spoon in one hand and a bowl in the other. Instead of flowers, the altar was decorated with garlic, onions, beans, flour, and peppers. As she defeathered a chicken, one of the girls sang a song Alicia had sung as a child, "*Tengo una muñequita vestida de azul, zapatitos blancos, camisón de tul . . .*" Chepa brought Alicia thick slices of warm bread spread with butter and dripping honey, and a cup of sweet, milky coffee.

"You must eat!" she said fretfully.

Alicia knew the cook was thinking of the many meals she had sent up to Alicia's room during her convalescence, only to have them returned almost untouched. To appease her, Alicia picked up a slab of bread, its warmth tingling her fingers, and took a bite. It was delicious! Surely, she imagined, when Jesus broke the bread he passed to his followers at his last supper, it had tasted like this bread—dense and substantial—not like the flat, tasteless hosts the priests handed out at the Eucharist. She licked honey and butter from her fingertips to Chepa's evident delight.

"Another bite, *mija*," the cook said. "You must regain your strength."

She sipped her coffee, nibbled at the bread, and said, "My dear, if ever I had to leave this place, I believe I would miss you the most."

"Leave this place?" Chepa snorted. "Why would you leave this place? What troubles you, Daughter?"

She smiled, kissed the older woman's fingertips. "Nothing. At this moment, I am very happy."

Quarreling male voices followed by banging on the door to the palace startled the women into silence. Alicia rose from the table and went out into the courtyard, followed by the cook. The front door flew open. The porter Andres stumbled backward and fell to the ground. A group of men brandishing rifles and pistols poured into the courtyard. Although they were dressed in ordinary clothes and were neither police nor soldiers, they appeared organized and purposeful. *Ladrones*, was Alicia's first thought, but what kinds of thieves would dare such a brazen daylight assault on the palace?

"Who are you?" she demanded, swiftly barring their way forward. "What do you want?"

She was addressing an older man—the others seemed like boys, barely out their teens—who wore a black suit, sombrero, and collarless white shirt.

"Sarmiento," he growled. "Where is he?"

"If you are referring to my husband, he is not here. Leave now, or I will call the police."

"Move!" he said, and pushed her aside so roughly she stumbled and fell into Chepa's arms.

"Stop, you devils!" Chepa shouted. "Do you not know you are in the palace of the Marquesa de Guadalupe Gavilán?"

The leader ignored her and called out, "We want Sarmiento."

He and the other men moved toward the second gate, into the family's courtyard. Alicia, recovering her balance, rushed ahead of them and threw herself before the gate.

"Unless you are the police, I will not allow you to enter."

The leader drew his pistol and pointed it at her. "Lady, if you do not move, I will shoot you."

Chepa screamed. Startled, he spun toward her, and shouted, "Shut her up!"

One of the other men struck the cook with the butt of his rifle, knocking her to the ground.

Alicia, shocked by this violence, pressed herself more tightly against the gate. "Leave, I tell you!" she commanded. "Leave my house!"

She heard footsteps running across the courtyard behind her. She glanced back to see Santos, the majordomo, running toward her with a pistol in his hand. The leader of the invaders raised his own pistol and aimed it at the servant.

"Santos, no!" she screamed and threw her body between him and the shooter. There was an explosion and she felt molten heat sear her insides. Her hand went to her belly and blood gushed between her fingers. She fell. Screams and shouting filled the courtyard. She saw the boots of her attackers as they fled the courtyard. Then she saw nothing.

Cáceres should have returned by now, Sarmiento thought anxiously, though in the dim recesses of the church crypt he had no real sense of how much time had passed since the priest had left for the palace. He sat on a cot at one end of the long, musty room. Illuminated by torches were rows of tombs. Along the walls were shelves lined with skulls and bones that reached from the stone floor to the vaulted ceiling. The tombs held the remains of three centuries of parish priests. The bones along the walls were the Indians who had been buried in the church cemetery, long since dug up as the neighborhood—once its own small village—was engulfed by the city. Ordinarily, human remains inspired neither fear nor reverence in Sarmiento, for whom death was simply a cessation of biological functions and not the portal to an afterlife. At the moment, however, with his own mortality seemingly hanging in the balance, the staring sockets of the dead, the smell of bone crumbling into dust, and the skittering of rats made him shiver from more than the damp and cold. He pulled an itchy blanket around his shoulders and resigned himself to waiting for the priest.

He had fallen asleep. His eyes fluttered open and a cobweb of images from a dream clung to his consciousness—Paquita, the girl he had killed; Alicia's face; a bloody hand, perhaps his own. Some of the torches had gone out and darkness encroached upon him like a rising tide. The priest, he thought, where was the priest! Had he been caught and detained? Was Sarmiento's hiding place being tortured out of him? Had he seen Alicia? He could wait no longer, he decided, but would go home, whatever the risk. At that moment, the door to the crypt was thrown open. A square of light appeared at the top of the stairs followed by a rush of footsteps that belonged to more than one man. He sprang up and looked for something, anything, with which to defend himself. He grabbed an iron candelabrum and prepared to swing it at the intruders, when he saw Cáceres and Damian. His brother-in-law was, as always, impeccably groomed and dressed, but he was red-faced from exertion.

"What is this?" Sarmiento demanded of the priest. "Why have you brought my brother-in-law?"

"Doña Alicia has been shot," Cáceres gasped.

Sarmiento dropped the candlestick. "No," he moaned. "No."

Damian stepped forward. "Huerta's thugs invaded the palace. She tried to prevent them from shooting a servant." He laid his hand on Sarmiento's shoulder. "She's not dead, Miguel, but she is badly wounded. You must come."

He shook off Damian's hand. "Why are you here? You told me if I challenged Huerta you would abandon me." He looked at Cáceres. "Is this a trap? Did he force you to bring him? Are there soldiers waiting for me upstairs?"

"No, Miguel," Cáceres said. "I swear on my vocation. Your wife lies gravely wounded. She begged me to bring you to her and Don Damian heard. He insisted on accompanying me, to help if we were stopped."

"Look, Miguel," Damian said. "I know what I told you, and had it been you they had shot . . ." He faltered and when he spoke again his voice shook with feeling. "But it was Alicia. Please, this is no trick."

Confused and horrified, he hesitated. Was he still dreaming?

"If you fear Huerta's men will return to the palace, don't," Damian said. "The whole city knows what happened today. The palace is surrounded by a mob of Indians who revere your wife. They will not permit entry by anyone who would harm her. Come, there is no time to argue further." He grabbed Sarmiento's shoulders and begged, "You must trust me, Miguel."

He shook himself into alertness. "Take me to her."

Outside the palace, as Damian had said, an immense crowd thronged the gates. He recognized people from the neighborhood and from San Francisco Tlalco, but others he had never seen before. They let him pass, accompanied by Damian and Cáceres, in mournful silence. A group of nuns in white habits knelt in the first courtyard, praying the rosary. In the second courtyard, society women mingled with street vendors and maids, and richly robed cathedral priests stood with Franciscan monks in brown habits and sandals. Their murmurs of consolation followed him as he passed among them and climbed the stairs to his family's apartment. In the parlor, his sister-in-law Nilda was deep in conversation with a surgeon named Terraza. Sarmiento knew him. He was a butcher. Nilda looked at him and hissed, "You! This is all your fault."

"Quiet, woman," Damian said curtly.

Terraza approached, hand outstretched. The man's shirt cuffs were soaked in blood. Her blood.

"Miguel," Terraza said, grasping his hand. "Such a tragedy."

He jerked his hand out of the surgeon's. "How is she?"

"A bullet to the abdomen," he said. "It perforated the bowel. There was a great loss of blood. I removed the bullet and sutured. But as you know, in these cases the real threat is sepsis."

Sarmiento stared at the bloody cuffs. "She is already weak, recovering from a serious illness. Even a minor infection will kill her."

"Yes. I'm sorry. I did all I could. I did my best."

Sarmiento nodded. "Thank you."

He turned his back to the others and wept.

The numbness in her fingertips was slowly spreading through her fingers and soon she would be deprived of the sense of touch. The other senses would follow—taste, smell, hearing, sight—and she would leave the world blind, deaf, and insensate. Her anxiety was mitigated by her subtle awareness of doors opening—the same doors through which she had tumbled in her vision of unity. They opened now more slowly, deliberately, inviting her to step across their thresholds. She hesitated, knowing that once those thresholds were crossed, there would be no turning back. So this was dying—the pause between two realms of existence that allowed the soul a moment to compose itself before death, like gravity, tugged the leaf from the branch.

A fleshy blur above her resolved itself into the features of Pedro Cáceres. The priest's careworn face and white hair were luminous. He squeezed a bit of sensation into her failing hand.

"Daughter," he murmured. "My dearest daughter."

She heard herself croak, "Where is Miguel?"

"Safe at the church. I will go and bring him here."

"First, confess me," she whispered.

"Of course."

"Father, forgive me for I have sinned," she said, but she abandoned the familiar formula and cried, "Pedro, I am afraid of dying!"

"That's no sin, Alicia. Even Christ in the garden was afraid of dying. I assure you, *mija*, you should have no more fear of damnation than he did."

"I am not afraid of hell," she whispered. "I am afraid of heaven."

She saw his confusion and wished she had the strength to explain that the source of her anxiety was the annihilating purification that awaited her.

"The body," she said laboriously. "Everything it loved, gone. What will be left of me?"

He smiled lovingly. "The cup that holds the water and the lantern that shelters the flame are only vessels, Alicia. Discard them and water is water, fire remains fire. The part of you that loves has never been your body. It is your soul and that will not be extinguished."

She nodded. "Yes, yes. Of course."

"I will bring Miguel. Will you wait for him?"

"Yes," she said. "But bring him quickly."

The familiar scent of lavender and roses and the rustle of silks stirred her into consciousness, and she opened her eyes. Her mother sat beside her. Her face, unlike the priest's, was not illuminated but desolate and withered. It was the face of an ancient animal trapped, uncomprehendingly, in old age and infirmity. She knew, looking into the other woman's bleary eyes, that death was already sinking its tendrils into her mother's flesh and would not be kept waiting for long. Her heart surged with compassion.

"Mother," she said, lifting her hand to La Niña's face.

"You fool," La Niña said bitterly. "Did you think Santos has more value to me than you? Servants can be replaced. Not my child." Tears streamed from her eyes. "You had no right to martyr yourself. You should have stood aside."

"Forgive me," she said, taking her mother's hand. "I could not."

"Do not die and there will be nothing to forgive."

"If God wills it . . ."

"If you had listened less to God and more to me," her mother said with some asperity, "you would not be lying here. One does not make old bones by being virtuous. Could you not have spared a thought for your own well-being, Daughter? Did you have to open your purse to every beggar who stretched out his hand to you?" Grief crumpled her face. "What did you achieve?"

"I have been happy," Alicia replied.

La Niña sighed. "Happy? Does that matter so much?"

"It is everything, Mother."

Alicia? Can you hear me?"

His voice was warm and soft, like a drizzle of honey.

"Miguel!" She opened her eyes. His face was furrowed with worry. He stroked her face tenderly, biting back tears. "Thank God, you are safe."

"I came as soon as I could." He stood and pulled back the covers. "Let me look at the wound."

She heard him gasp when he undid the bandages and saw where the bullet had entered her. She could smell her putrefying flesh. He had explained septicemia to her—an uncontrollable bacterial infection that often followed traumatic wounds. She had already guessed from her failing body that something like this was happening to her, but his shock confirmed it. He carefully rebandaged her.

"How much time is left to me?" she asked him.

"Don't talk like that," he said, avoiding her eyes.

"We have always been honest with each other, Miguel."

"Not long," he said reluctantly. "A day or two. How do you feel? Are you in pain? I could give you morphine."

She shook her head. "Morphine dulls the senses. I would rather bear the pain."

"Oh God, Alicia, this is my fault," he said, breaking down. "I brought this upon us." He sobbed. "I am so sorry."

She stroked his hair, now threaded with gray, coarser than it was the first time she had touched it so many years earlier. The beloved body, she thought, once so hard and strong. Time's depredations had begun to soften it, loosening the skin on his neck, rounding his shoulders, raising the veins in his hands. The realization that she would not grow old with him stabbed at her heart.

"We agreed," she said softly. "You did the right thing."

"Then I should bear the consequences," he said, lifting his head. "Not you." He was like a little boy, entreating his mother.

"You will have your own cross to bear, Miguel," she told him.

He nodded. "This was not what I expected."

"God does not care about our expectations," she said. "He sends us the suffering we need, not the suffering we are prepared to endure."

"How can you speak of God when he is going to take you away from me?" he said bitterly.

She kissed his fingers. "After Anselmo, after my disfigurement, I did not think another man would ever love me or that I would bear another child. What a miracle you have been for me, Miguel! Still, even in our happiness, we were fated to part. Only the moment of parting was unknown. Now that it is here, I prefer to be grateful for the miracle rather than angry it is over. It makes our separation more bearable." She stirred; the pain was great. "You must take José and leave México. You aren't safe here."

"Without you, there would be no reason to remain, in any event."

"You must marry again," she said quietly.

"Never!" he cried.

"My dear," she said. "You need a woman to soften your solitude. You must also think of José. He is a sensitive and gentle child. He needs a mother."

She saw from his face that only now was he thinking about the effect her death would have on their son. It was a look of terror.

"He will look to you when I am gone," she said. "Be brave for him."

He pressed his face into her breast like a child seeking comfort and wept fresh tears. She kissed the top of his head. Her words had failed to assuage his grief, but they had quelled her own lingering fears because their truth had resonated in the depths of her heart. Parting had always been inevitable and now that the moment had arrived, there was nothing to be done about it except to be grateful for what had been and for what was to be. Jesus on the cross must have felt such release, she thought, turning his eyes at the end from the suffering of the world at his feet to the limitless serenity of the sky where his father awaited him like the father in the parable of the prodigal son: "For this son of mine was dead, and now he is alive again!" She heard a voice in her head, slow and sweet as honey on the tongue: "Peace I leave with you; my peace I give you. Not as the world gives, give I to you. Let not your heart be troubled, neither let it be afraid." As he sobbed, tears sprang to her eyes too, quick and hot, but while his were tears of sorrow, hers were tears of joy.

José Ramon!"

Frère Martin's sharp tone woke José from his daydream and brought him back into his geometry class, to the itchy wool of his uniform against the skin of his thighs, to Fatty Marquez's smirking assumption that José was in trouble again for his inattention. José readied himself for the teacher's reproach, but instead, in a softer voice, Frère Martin continued, "Come, José. The rest of you, keep working."

José followed his teacher into the courtyard, where Tío Damian was waiting for him.

"José," he said, in a strained voice, quite unlike his usual amused tones, "I have come to take you home."

José's confusion was increased when Frère Martin crouched down so that they were eye to eye. He took José's shoulders in his hands and said gravely, "God bless you, child."

"Come, José," Damian said, extending his hand.

"What's wrong?" José blurted out.

"We will speak in the car," Damian replied.

But as Damian's driver negotiated the dozen blocks between José's school and the palace, his uncle remained silent until the Rolls-Royce had stopped at the palace gate. A crowd was gathered in front of it. Damian turned to José and said, "Your mother was injured this morning when some men invaded your home looking for your father."

Nothing in that sentence made sense to José, who, only a few hours earlier, had left the palace with his mother's kiss lingering on his lips and his father's admonition to concentrate on his studies echoing in his ears. As he passed through the crowd to enter the palace, José heard sympathetic murmurs of "*Pobrecito.*" In the first courtyard, one of the housemaids was on her knees scrubbing dark stains from the cobblestone. She glanced up at him, her face streaked with tears. Chepa came running from out of the kitchen. Her head was bandaged. She squeezed him in a tight embrace. She, too, was weeping. Damian separated him from the cook. By now, José was terrified.

"Where's my mother!" he demanded.

Chepa drew a shaky breath. "The doctor just finished. She is in her room."

"What doctor? Where's my father?"

"Come along, José," Damian said. To Chepa, he said, "Bring two brandies, would you?"

They stepped past the maid on her knees—José glanced into the pail beside her, its water red—into the second courtyard and sat on a bench facing the fountain. The warm sun, the familiar fragrance of roses, the trickle of water from the stone tiers of the cantera fountain into the pond calmed him a little. He waited for his uncle to speak.

"Your father went into the Senate this morning and made a very dangerous speech," Damian said. Chepa came with the brandy; he took one and gave one to José. "Take a sip, boy."

He made a face at the liquid's sour taste. "What did my *papá* say?"

"He called the president of the Republic a murderer," Damian replied. "It is nothing less than the truth, of course, but you don't walk into the lion's cage to taunt the lion and expect to walk out uninjured." He gulped his brandy. "Your father knew he was risking his life by speaking out—"

"Then why did he?" José cried.

Damian gazed at him appraisingly. "You are nothing like him, are you?"

José looked down and prodded the moss that grew between the cobblestones with the tip of his shoe. "I disappoint him."

"You must continue to do so," his uncle replied. "It may save your life one day."

"Where is he?"

"I don't know," Damian said. "After he made the speech, he disappeared. Huerta sent men here to find him. They came into the house and were going to shoot one of the servants when your mother tried to stop them. She was shot instead. She was not killed, José, but she was seriously injured. The doctor removed the bullet, and she is resting now. I will take you to see her, but you must be brave." He tugged at the collar of José's cadet's uniform. "Can you be brave, little soldier? For your *mamá*?"

José, biting back tears, nodded. "Where is my *abuelita*?"

"I think we will find her and your aunts with your mother. Come on, then."

His mother was lying in bed, encircled by his aunts and his grandmother. When he entered the room, they lifted their heads and looked at him, their faces raw with grief. His grandmother held him in her thin arms, and he was aware of her fragility. His aunts moved away slightly from the bed to make room for him. He sat on the edge of the bed and looked at his mother's sleeping face. He touched the faded scars she had once told him were God's gift to cure her of vanity, stroked her thick, soft hair, and listened to her ragged breathing. She seemed small and spent, like an exhausted child.

She is dying.

The words formed in his mind with a certainty that left no room for fear. Instead, he was enshrouded by a strange calm, not the calm of acceptance, but the bleaker calm of fate. When she had been ill before, and he had thought she might die, he had been wild with fear and grief because her death would have ruptured his reality—the reality of a cosseted child, a little prince living in a palace whose greatest challenge was the boredom of surfeit. Since then, however, his city had disintegrated around him, shattered buildings and the glassy-eyed dead transforming familiar landscapes into a circle of hell. He had felt the fear of the adults whom he had once believed were impervious to fear and invincible in their certainties. The world had taught him there are no certainties and ultimately no safety. Terrible things happened without warning or explanation. His mother could die.

He blinked back his tears. He was not yet a man, at least not like his father or Tió Damian, but he could no longer be a child. As he watched his dying mother, he felt the world's enmity and he responded not with a child's grief but a man's defiance, as if his blood were being infiltrated with threads of iron.

He sat there for a long time until she opened her eyes, which were clouded with pain, and whispered, "*Mijo.*"

He clasped her hand and smiled. "Mamá."

Dinner was morose, the servant girls unable to hide their tears as they served the courses and cleared the dishes. Exasperated, Gonzalo muttered, "How can I enjoy my food with all this sobbing?" and was met by a cold stare from his sister-in-law Nilda and an admonitory one from his wife, Leticia. The ordinarily gay Eulalia quietly rearranged the food on her plate without eating. Damian simply drank through the meal, waving away the platters of food offered to him. At the head of the table, the wizened *marquesa* sat sphinx-like, casting unfriendly glances at her family as if they were uncouth strangers whose company had been inflicted upon her. Sarmiento observed the table silently, lifting forkfuls of food into his mouth but tasting nothing.

"This is all your fault," Nilda said to him, not raising her eyes from her plate. "You killed our sister."

"Alicia's not dead!" Leticia cried.

Now Nilda looked up, not at him but at her sister. "She will die and he is to blame."

No one spoke in his defense and the truth struck like a slap. He had no friends at this table. His connection to the family had been entirely through Alicia, and once she was gone, the connection would be severed. Without excusing himself, he rose from the table.

"Stay," La Niña commanded.

"I am not welcome here," he said stiffly. "I will go to my wife."

"The rest of you, go," she said. "You sit, Doctor. There are matters we must discuss."

In a clatter of silverware and heavy chairs skidding resentfully across tile, the room cleared and he was left alone with his mother-in-law. She indicated her wineglass and he filled it and then sat beside her.

"Nilda is a fool," she said. "Alicia has achieved what she has always wanted."

"What is that, Señora?"

She sipped her wine, grimaced, and spat out, "Martyrdom," as if it were a curse.

His remonstration died on his lips—her anger was her way of grief. Instead he said quietly, "Her actions were consistent with her character."

"As were yours!" La Niña barked. "The two of you, peas in a pod, she looking to heaven in the sky and you to heaven on earth. Striving after things that do not exist and never will. Had either of your feet touched the ground instead of walking on clouds, we would not be sitting here. Why could this life not be enough for you?"

"We dreamed of a better world," he said.

"A better world? For whom? Not for me," she said. "This world is quite sufficient to my needs. I do not wish for it to change." In a softer voice, she said, "You think I am a selfish old woman, but the truth, Doctor, is that I have seen the disasters dreamers like you inflict upon the rest of us. Do not forget, I lived through the civil wars that followed independence, the French invasion, the coups, and the countercoups after Juárez died. Bloodshed and misery, and all of it in the cause of someone's idea of a better world. Díaz was a peasant with an appalling accent, but he was a realist who understood México. He imposed peace and order. You and your friend Madero have only succeeded in bringing down the roof."

"It was not Madero," he mumbled, "but the forces of reaction. He never had a chance."

She shrugged. "I have said my piece. Now we must be practical. You must leave soon, to protect yourself and this house."

"Yes, I know. I will." He paused, expecting an argument, then added, "José must come with me."

She nodded slowly. "You are his father." With a bleak smile, she asked, "Did you think I would demand that he remain?"

"I know how much you love him."

"It is because I love him that I would send him away," she replied. "If he remained here, he would become the family's poor relation after I die. He would only end up in some miserable marriage arranged by one of his uncles to bring money into the family. Take him to Europe or the United States, where he will be free to become himself, whatever that may be." She creaked out of her chair. "I only regret I will not live long enough to see him become a man."

"Whether you live to see it or not, he will do you credit," Sarmiento replied.

She paused at the threshold and looked back at him. "I wish I could be as certain as you, but I cannot foresee what will become of him. His gifts are useless in the world I have known." She sighed. "But my world is passing away and perhaps in the world to come, there will be a place for him."

Day gave way to night. The moon filled the window above José's mother's bed and then passed on. The electric lamps cast orbs of light too frail to penetrate the shadowy recesses of the big room. Chepa had come and lit candles, tall and thick and yellow. Father Pedro had arrived and administered last rites as the family gathered at the foot of the bed, their faces as still as the ancestor portraits that lined the walls of the palace. One by one they departed, even his father, but José remained at his mother's side, refusing food or sleep. For once, his wishes were respected, and he was allowed to remain.

His mother had not opened her eyes for a long time now. Sometimes her arms jerked into the air and then just as abruptly fell back upon the bed. Her raspy breath filled the room, subsided into a nearly imperceptible stream of air, then began again loud and labored. José had imagined death was like sleep—you closed your eyes and it was over—but dying, it appeared, was hard work. He wept silently at times, but for the most part he experienced not grief but an immeasurable compassion for his mother.

This was a new emotion for him, deeper than the quotidian love of mother and child. That love was personal and possessive, a web spun from the filaments of their moment-to-moment intimacies that went all the way back to his first heartbeat in her womb. The love that swelled and broke his heart as he sat beside her was forged in suffering—her suffering as she lay dying, his as he maintained a helpless vigil—but it transcended the particular event and seemed, to José, to comprehend every moment of loss that had ever been suffered by anyone. It was as if he were standing at the summit of the volcano Popocatépetl and he could see, in every direction, the vast terrain of human loss. But beyond that landscape, at the far rim of his vision, there was a blur of light where, without knowing why, he knew that all suffering and all loss came to an end. Then came the startled realization: this was God. The deep sense of peace that held back his torrent of grief was the presence of God in the room.

His mother was looking at him with tired but serene eyes.

"Josélito, bring me the silver box on my dresser and the little pair of scissors," she said in the calm, loving voice he had always known, as if today were like any other day, and her request like any other request.

"Yes, Mamá," he said and went to retrieve the items.

She had managed, with great effort, to prop herself up on her pillows and placed the box in her lap. She took the scissors from his hand and clipped a lock of her hair. Then she cut a bit of the satin ribbon from her nightgown. Slowly, with clumsy fingers, she tied the lock of hair in the ribbon. Then she opened the box and removed a ring set with a large, yellowed pearl and a necklace formed of wooden beads and a rough cross.

"Give me your hands, *mijo*," she said.

He put out his hands.

"This is your inheritance from me." She strung the necklace—which he now saw was a rosary—between his fingers. "This was given to me by a man whose people have been hunted down but who still survive because they believe God has not abandoned them. It represents faith." She placed the lock of her hair in his palm. "This is my promise to you that you and I will be reunited through the grace of our Lord, Jesus. It represents hope." Lastly, she gave him the ring. "This pearl was given to me by my first love, a boy named Anselmo. I looked into his eyes and saw God there, because God is love, and love is God, José. All love, *mijo*. Whoever you love, love fearlessly, no matter who he may be. Do you understand?"

"No, Mamá," he said haplessly. "I am sorry to be so stupid."

"You are not stupid, my dear. You will one day remember my words and understand them. Faith, hope, and love," she whispered. "These three things remain. But the greatest of these is love."

"Yes, Mamá."

"Put these in their place," she said, indicating the silver box and scissors.

He took them from her lap and carried them to the dresser. When he returned to her bedside, she was gone.

He stood beside her bed, wracked by heavy involuntary sighs, as if his soul were trying to catch its breath. When he regained his composure, he slipped the rosary over his neck, the ring on his finger, and the lock of her hair into his pocket. Then he went to find his father.

Epilogue

Welcome to America

May 1913

At every station between the capital and the border, Sarmiento saw fresh evidence that México was disintegrating. The train was running two days behind schedule as it made its way to Arizona, diverted from bad track that had not been repaired because once again the countryside was filled with robbers and rebels. The first-class tickets he had purchased for José and himself bought few amenities—the food was barely edible, the service erratic. But poor service and bad food were the least of it as the train huffed slowly north. In the northern states, where Madero's revolution had first taken root, a new rebellion against Huerta was shaking the arid landscape. At Torreón, federal soldiers had ripped out the seats of the second-class cars and packed themselves in, on their way to reinforce vulnerable garrisons in the border towns. At dun-colored villages the train was met not with the usual food and trinket vendors but frightened crowds anxious for news from the capital. He saw telegraph poles felled by the rebels to disrupt communications, deserted ranches where the corpses of cattle lay bloated in the sun, and in the swirling dust of the Chihuahua desert, men, women, and children walking along the tracks, refugees seeking shelter in the towns. Far off, low clouds of dust kicked up against the horizon marked the movement of rebel battalions.

Sarmiento watched it all with a weariness that sank into his bones. War was coming, if it had not already started, in the mountains, valleys, and deserts of the north. This time, though, unlike Madero's revolution, there would be no quick resolution because Huerta was not Díaz. In the end, the old dictator had lost his taste for bloodshed and slipped away, but Huerta would soak the earth in the blood of his soldiers before he was killed or exiled. Among the rebels, there was no new Madero, no saintly figure to inspire and unite the little warlords rising up against Huerta. Carranza, Villa, Zapata. Each now fought for himself, for his own ambitions. Once they succeeded in defeating Huerta, they would turn on each other. Sarmiento could not see how this war would end, but with the memories of the Ten Tragic Days fresh in his mind, he knew it would bring a level of destruction to México not seen since the Spanish had razed Tenochtitlán. And who would suffer the most? As always, the Indians, the poor, the disenfranchised. He could have wept for his country, but the wells of pity had run dry in him when his wife had been murdered. What a fool he had been to have believed he could stir men's consciences with his speech. He should have taken his cousin's advice and slipped into the woodwork until the combatants had beaten each other bloody. Luis, he thought with a pang. Where was Luis? Would he ever see him again?

It was night. He stood at the front of the car smoking a cigarette beneath the brilliant desert sky. He had left José sleeping in their compartment. He had worried that the scenes of war would send his son into a panic, but on the journey the boy had shown the same stoicism he had displayed at his mother's funeral, where, dry-eyed, he had kissed the casket before it was slipped into the family crypt. Her death had changed José—he carried himself with a man's gravity rather than with a child's gaiety. He no longer prattled on but spoke only rarely and thoughtfully. Sarmiento realized that the little boy who had alternately exasperated him and endeared himself with his dreamy vagueness had transformed himself into a serious-minded, self-contained young man. A stranger, one who looked more like Alicia with each passing day. Alicia's beauty, which the smallpox had destroyed in her, was ripening in her son, who was becoming luminously beautiful. It disturbed Sarmiento that another male should be so physically compelling. This was a gift surely intended for women, and he could not guess what purpose it could possibly serve his son.

The train was approaching the American border town of Douglas, Arizona, the place where he had parted from Alicia in what seemed another lifetime. As the dust of México churned beneath the wheels of the train, he wondered when, and whether, he and José would ever return to their country. His heart was so filled with conflicting emotions that they had cancelled each other out, leaving him numb. He stared out into the night, through the veil of his cigarette smoke, where there appeared in the desert darkness an archway lit up with electric lights. It spelled out a greeting so simple in its unintentional arrogance he did not know whether the tears that filled his eyes were tears of anger or gratitude, but he wept them all the same as he spoke the words aloud: "Welcome to America."

Acknowledgments

This is the first of a projected quartet of novels—*The Children of Eve*, a reference to the *Salve Regina*—that will follow the characters and the themes introduced here into the 1920s. I first began telling myself this story and undertaking the research required to bring it to life in the mid-1990s. The earliest draft material was written around 2000. This first book took three years to finish. I want to thank the two invaluable readers who helped me in that process, my cherished friend and fellow novelist, Katherine V. Forrest, and Michael Strickland, a more recent but equally treasured friend. I also want to thank my friend and guide in Ciudad de México, Jonas Vanruesel, for helping me find the remnants of Don Porfirio's city in that megalopolis. I enthusiastically recommend Jonas's services to any traveler to México.

Over the past seventeen years, I have consulted hundreds of books, maps, photographs, videos, and other materials. On my website (http://michaelnavawriter.com) is a detailed bibliography for the interested reader, but I would be amiss if I did not acknowledge two key sources of research and inspiration: Michael Johns's brief but excellent *The City of Mexico in the Age of Díaz* and Alan Knight's magisterial two-volume history, *The Mexican Revolution*.

Finally, I acknowledge my spouse, George Herzog, with whom I learned the secrets of a happy marriage that I then used in telling the story of the marriage of Miguel and Alicia.